Avail
from M

THE HEART OF BRODY McQUADE

"Why don't you just lock me in your bedroom so you'll have me right where you want me?"

His gaze snapped to hers and she realised what she'd said. It shouldn't have been a big deal. It should have just been a friendly joke, poking fun at his insistence on keeping such a close eye on her.

But that *thing* between them rose up like a dragon, assaulting them with the burning fire of lust. Victoria knew her cheeks were red with embarrassment.

Brody, on the other hand, was staring at her as if she'd just stripped naked in front of him or something.

She had no idea how long they stood there silently with her words between them.

She watched emotions chase each other across his face – surprise, lust, even curiosity. Was he wondering what it would be like to make love with her?

Because that's exactly what she couldn't get out of her mind.

"Do that again," she breathed joyfully.

He lifted her off her feet this time, his mouth hot and wet, moving across hers as if he were devouring a feast: "What have you done to me?" he murmured, an almost desperate note in his voice.

"I was about to ask you the same." She plunged her hands into his thick, dark hair and tugged. "Kiss me again. Please."

His hand slid down to her buttocks, lifting her tighter against his unmistakable reaction to her. She groaned, crawling even closer to him if possible, all but purring her pleasure. Her hands crept around his ribs to his back, kneading rigid muscles...and encountering something wet.

He hissed into her mouth and lurched upright, arching his back away from her.

"What did I do?" she asked quickly, in distress.

"It's my back. Some nutcase tried to stab you a few minutes ago and sliced me instead."

"Stab – me?" And then the rest of it hit her. "You've been *stabbed*?"

First published in Great Britain 2009
Harlequin Mills & Boon Limited,
Eton House, 18-24 Paradise Road, Richmond, Surrey TW9 1SR

The Heart of Brody McQuade © Rickey R Mallory 2008
Killer Affair © Cynthia M Dees 2008

ISBN: 978 0 263 87314 6

46-0809

Harlequin Mills & Boon policy is to use papers that are natural, renewable
and recyclable products and made from wood grown in sustainable
forests. The logging and manufacturing processes conform to the legal
environmental regulations of the country of origin.

Printed and bound in Spain
by Litografia Rosés S.A., Barcelona

THE HEART OF BRODY McQUADE

BY

MALLORY KANE

KILLER AFFAIR

BY

CINDY DEES

THE HEART OF BRODY McQUADE

BY
MALLORY KANE

Mallory Kane credits her love of books to her mother, a librarian, who taught her that books are a precious resource and should be treated with loving respect. Her father and grandfather were steeped in the southern tradition of oral history, and could hold an audience spellbound for hours with their storytelling skills. Mallory aspires to be as good a storyteller as her father.

She loves romantic suspense with dangerous heroes and dauntless heroines, and often uses her medical background to add an extra dose of intrigue to her books. Another fascination that she enjoys exploring in her reading and writing is the infinite capacity of the brain to adapt and develop higher skills.

Mallory lives in Mississippi with her computer-genius husband, their two fascinating cats, and, at current count, seven computers.

She loves to hear from readers. You can write to her at rickey_m@bellsouth.net

To Delores and Rita – here we go again.

Prologue

Christmas Eve

Lieutenant Brody McQuade, Texas Ranger, looked at the ornate casket for the first time since he'd walked into the quiet chapel. His heart twisted with pain so severe he couldn't breathe. That was his baby sister beneath that blanket of pink and white poinsettias. *Kimmie.*

Ever since he could remember, his mom had drilled into him that Kimberly was his responsibility.

If anything ever happens to us… Those words weren't just empty motherisms. His parents had been thrill-seekers, and wealthy enough to pursue their dangerous hobbies.

A pipe organ's dulcet tones swelled. Brody's throat closed and his shoulders bowed as if they could shield his heart from deeper pain. Out of habit he straightened them. He was a Texas Ranger and Rangers were always strong and straight— dependable and responsible.

Next to him, Sergeant Hayes Keller turned his head slightly. "You all right?" he whispered.

Brody lifted his chin. No way could he let Hayes or the third Ranger on the pew, Egan Caldwell, know the shape he was in. He was their superior officer. His responsibility to them and to the Rangers went beyond personal feelings.

Ah, dammit, Kimmie. What were you doing in that car without your seat belt on? He stared at his hands and pretended the blurriness in his eyes wasn't tears.

Hayes nudged him.

"The service is over, Brody. Let's go."

He raised his head. The music had stopped. In the silence he heard clothes rustle and a few quiet coughs. Everyone was waiting for him to make the first move.

He stood, bitter nausea clogging his throat. Why the hell hadn't he insisted on a private service? He felt the stares from the people in the chapel—most of whom could have prevented this tragedy if they'd paused in their partying and drinking for one second.

He approached the casket. He reached out a hand, but he couldn't bring himself to actually touch the polished surface.

"Bye, Kimmie," he whispered hoarsely. "I swear I'll put the bastard who did this away for the rest of his worthless life."

He felt a touch on his shoulder.

He looked up. It was Caroline Stallings, the socialite who'd let Kimmie die. What kind of woman drove with the top down three days before Christmas? And let a passenger ride with no seat belt?

"Lieutenant McQuade, please accept my condolences. I feel so bad about what happened."

He took in her pale face and bruised forehead. It was all he could do to rein in the anger that churned in his gut. He met her gaze, gleaning a grim satisfaction when her eyes widened with apprehension. "Thanks," was all he could manage.

With Egan and Hayes behind him, he navigated through the crush of attendees, most of whom he'd only met in the past three days as he'd interrogated them about Kimberly's death.

He'd had no idea that interning on the San Antonio City Board would throw Kimberly into the middle of the city's wealthiest inner circle. Caroline Stallings was on the board, and maybe that explained it. Kimberly had admired Caroline, had in fact raved about her.

But there was something fishy about the hit-and-run crash that had taken his sister's life, and before he got through with them, he planned to unearth all these Cantara Hills trust-fund babies' dirty little secrets.

Just as he reached the rear door he saw a familiar, squirrelly face. Gary Zelke, the SOB who had drunkenly slammed into Caroline Stallings's vintage Corvette.

Frustration, grief and anger roiled inside him like a toxic stew. He eased past a tall blonde who smelled like money and roses, and confronted the little twerp.

"What the hell are you doing here?"

Zelke turned white as a sheet. "Just paying my respects."

"Why aren't you in jail? You've got a lot of gall." Brody clenched his fists. His jaw ached. "I ought to—"

"Pardon me."

It was the blonde. Her tailored suit revealed legs that went all the way to the ground. In heels, she came close to his six foot two.

"I'm Victoria Kirkland. We met briefly at the police station the day after the accident."

He frowned, trying to place her. Suddenly the memory hit him. She was Zelke's ambulance-chasing lawyer and a potential witness. She'd driven through the intersection seconds before Caroline and Kimberly had.

"*You.* You bailed him out. After the dirt-wad left my sister lying in the street."

Victoria Kirkland flattened her lips and nodded. "Lieutenant, my deepest sympathy goes out to you and your family—"

Brody leveled his famous quelling gaze on her. "But...?"

Her green eyes sparked without faltering, and a tiny quirk of her lips surprised him. She gave him back look for look and her expression clearly said, *Don't even try.*

"*But* I'm Mr. Zelke's attorney. Anything you have to say, you say to me."

Brody ground his teeth. "He killed my sister."

Now her gaze faltered. "He didn't, but I won't argue the point here while you're in mourning."

Brody clenched his fists and his jaw. "Don't do me any favors, Counselor."

"You have my card. Call me and we can discuss the charges you're bringing against my client."

All of Brody's anger and pain transferred itself to the long, cool blonde. Sharp as a stiletto and twice as dangerous. If she were cut she'd probably bleed ice water. Why was she bothering with a two-bit drunk like Zelke?

She wasn't sleeping with him. Hell, she'd eat him alive.

Brody rubbed his eyes and turned away. One thing he knew for sure. When she tangled with *him,* she'd lose, because he had the advantage. Her heart wasn't in it. His was.

He was fighting for justice for his little sister.

Chapter One

"Hey, Caldwell, get up!" Brody McQuade pushed open the door to the second bedroom of the luxury conference suite at the Cantara Hills Country Club. His fellow Ranger was nothing more than an irregular lump under the fancy bedspread.

"Egan!"

The lump stirred. A rude, muffled comment reached Brody's ears. "Let's go. We've got another break-in."

The lump turned into a head with brown hair sticking out every which way. "Another...at the condos?" Egan cursed and sat up, kicking at the bedclothes. He yawned and rubbed his head.

"Yeah. Come on."

Egan squinted at him. "You're already dressed."

Brody didn't respond.

Egan sighed. "I'll catch up. What room?"

"Didn't get particulars. The police are there. Ask at the door." Brody left Egan sitting on the side of his bed with his head in his hands.

Grabbing his holster and hat, Brody stalked out to his Jeep Compass. The whine of police sirens echoed in his ears. He could see flashing blue lights in the near distance, over the Cantara Gardens Condominiums, south of the country club.

Adrenaline pumped through him and he had trouble reining in his impatience on the four-minute drive around the back nine holes of the golf course to the condos' gates. He'd have preferred to sprint across the manicured greens and straightaways. Probably wouldn't take forty seconds if he ran flat out.

But arriving at a crime scene sweaty and wrinkled wasn't the Ranger way. Nor was it Brody's style.

He'd been expecting this. There had been a break-in every month at the condos since January. Seven so far. Two fatalities. Trent Briggs in February, and Gary Zelke three months later, in May.

Deason hadn't mentioned the name of the latest victim. The San Antonio Police Department Detective Sergeant had sounded frantic.

Did that mean they'd had another fatality?

He pulled up to the gate where an SAPD officer waved him through. Normally the residents used a computerized access card to open the gate. He had a master in his pocket.

Pulling up beside a police car, he headed inside. He didn't recognize the officer at the front door, but the young man's eyes lit on the silver star pinned to his shirt pocket and nodded. "Sergeant Deason is waiting for you, sir. In the penthouse."

He raised his eyebrows. *The penthouse.* Victoria Kirkland's apartment. Naturally it had to be her. Anger bubbled up from his chest, hot and noxious as methane gas.

Suck it up, McQuade. Tonight she wasn't the shyster who'd

gotten Kimmie's killer off with nothing but a DUI. Tonight she was a victim. He didn't ask if she'd survived the break-in. If she hadn't, Deason would have told him.

He stepped into the elevator and eyed the button labeled "P." Beside it was a narrow horizontal slot. He inserted the master access card the condos' manager had given him into the slot and pressed the button.

The elevator car rumbled and started climbing, straight to the top. The doors opened into a foyer that could have been the lobby of a fancy hotel, complete with massive vases of flowers, illuminated artworks, and marble floors and columns.

Damn. Victoria Kirkland didn't make *this* kind of money practicing law. She was a trust-fund baby. He should have known.

He pointedly ignored the voice in his head that reminded him that he was, too. His situation was different. For one thing, he was never going to touch the money his careless, carefree parents had placed in trust for Kimmie and him.

As his boot heels clicked on the marble floor, he heard heavier boots on the dark mahogany staircase to his left. The tall, burly detective sergeant, Cal Deason, came down the stairs.

"McQuade," he said, holding out his hand.

Brody shook it briefly. He and Deason had worked together before. They both knew that the Rangers were in charge of this investigation, but Brody was careful to give Deason his full respect and consideration for his position. "What's going on? Have we got a fatality?"

Deason shook his head. "Nope. She was damn lucky."

Brody's gut clenched. Lucky? Yeah. Some people were born lucky. He concentrated on the slight weight of the unique silver badge pinned to his shirt and reminded himself that this wasn't personal.

Personally, he despised the leggy attorney for making good on her promise to get Gary Zelke acquitted of the charge of vehicular manslaughter. But as a Texas Ranger, he was bound to protect her and stop these break-ins and murders.

"Injuries?"

"Bruises on her neck. But other than that, just scared."

So the perp had gotten in. Tried to kill her. That fit the pattern. If he'd succeeded, this would have been the third killing in eight months—if he counted Kimmie's. One murder every three months.

"The guy got past the condo's security alarm system," Deason went on, "just like every other time. But Ms. Kirkland had her own system installed when she moved in." Deason nodded toward the ceiling.

Brody followed his gaze and spotted the security cameras trained on the doors. "You get the tapes?"

Deason nodded. "That's the only camera, and the guy didn't use the front door, but I'll have my guys go through them."

"No. I'll send them to Austin. Sergeant Caldwell will take them."

"I'll have 'em ready."

Deason's words were affable, but Brody detected a note of resentment in his tone. He couldn't blame the homicide sergeant. But Deason knew Brody had no choice. The request for the Rangers to take charge of the investigation had come from the mayor through the governor.

The residents of Cantara Hills had the clout to cover their butts. Once the Rangers had control of the investigation, there'd be no question of conflict of interest.

"I'd appreciate it. How'd the perp get inside?"

Deason shook his head. "My guys are checking. However he did it, he went out the same way. Ms. Kirkland's extra security may have saved her life, but it allowed the perp to get away clean."

"I assume your guys are going over that area with a fine-toothed comb. Give Sergeant Caldwell anything you find. As long as we've got the Rangers' crime lab, we might as well use it. Where is Ms. Kirkland?"

"In the kitchen. She wanted some hot tea."

His mental picture of her modified slightly to add a fragile expensive teacup to her perfectly manicured hand. He'd figured her as a fancy martini type.

"Sergeant Caldwell will be here in a minute to help you process the scene. I'm going to talk to her."

Deason nodded toward his right. "That-a-way. McQuade…"

He turned back.

"She hasn't been processed yet. I told her we could wait until she'd calmed down."

Wealth hath its privileges.

He knew that, too well. What he'd never been able to figure out was why great wealth didn't come packaged with wisdom and responsibility.

If his parents hadn't missed out on the responsibility gene, his and his sister's lives might have taken another path and Kimberly would be alive.

Quelling the urge to clutch at his chest where grief and loneliness still squeezed the life out of his heart, he stepped around a marble column, through a formal dining room and into the kitchen area.

The kitchen was as outrageously opulent as the foyer and

living room. It was more like a balcony than a kitchen, with paned windows running across one entire wall, Mexican quarry tile on the floors and teak lounging furniture taking the place of a table and chairs.

Victoria was sitting on a love seat holding a mug in both hands while a young police officer stood nearby looking bored and awestruck at the same time.

Brody caught his eye. "Crime-scene kit?"

The officer nodded. "Yes, sir. Right here." He toed a metal case at his feet.

"Help them upstairs." He gestured with his head. "Leave the case here."

Victoria looked up. Her mug jerked slightly, even though her pale face didn't change expression. "Lieutenant McQuade. I didn't expect to see you." Her voice was husky.

He bit back a retort. Did she actually think he'd send someone else just because she was the victim? This was his case, and he didn't let anything interfere with a case. "I was available."

She muttered something. It sounded like *Lucky me*.

"Tell me what happened."

She set the mug of tea down on the teak side table. "Can I make you some tea or coffee?"

"No. Tell me what happened."

Her lips compressed into a thin line and she sat back. For the first time he noticed what she was wearing. It was some kind of shiny satiny nightgown with a robe over it. Except that it wasn't exactly a robe. It was black and red and looked Oriental. A kimono? Whatever it was, it and the gown together hardly qualified as clothes. The material of both was so slinky and clingy that he could see the vague outline of her nipples and the V where her thighs met.

Lust speared through him. *Hell.* He swallowed and concentrated on her words.

"I went to bed fairly early, around eleven. I must have gone right to sleep because the next thing I knew something startled me." She lifted the mug and blew across its surface. The satiny fabric whispered and shimmered.

Brody's mouth went dry. Dragging his gaze away from her slender body, he focused on her feet. They were encased in delicate, ivory, open-toed slippers. Her toenails were unpainted—naked.

He shifted his gaze to the windows. "What startled you? A sound?"

"Maybe. I woke up and I knew someone was in my apartment. Sergeant Deason has already asked me all of this."

"Now I'm asking. And trust me, this won't be the last time."

"I'm aware of how investigations work, Lieutenant. I was merely pointing out that you might save yourself some time if you talked to him."

No. You're merely testing to see if you can intimidate me with your wealth and position. He crossed his arms. She was a victim here. As much as she irritated him, he couldn't forget that.

"I've got plenty of time. What happened next?"

Her fingers tightened on the mug. "I sat up and he—whoever it was—grabbed my throat." She closed her eyes. "He pushed me down and flipped me onto my stomach before I could react. Then the security alarm went off."

"It went off after he attacked you?"

"It's my personal security system, not the building's. It trips when a door or a window is breached. It automatically calls the police, then after fifteen seconds, the siren goes off."

"Fifteen seconds? You could be dead in fifteen seconds."

What little color she had in her face drained away. "Th-the theory is that the police get a head start."

"Brilliant theory," Brody muttered. "The condo's security system never went off, just like the other break-ins."

"What does that mean? Are you saying it's one of us?"

He bristled at her words. One of us. As opposed to whom? "Do you mean the residents of Cantara Hills, rather than the rest of San Antonio?"

She angled her head and assessed him. "I mean one of the residents of Cantara Gardens. Lieutenant, should I be talking to someone else? I'm afraid your personal grudge against me might jeopardize this investigation."

"There is absolutely nothing personal about my feelings for you."

"Are you sure? Because it certainly sounds personal."

Brody reined in his rising irritation. She was right. His question had been out of line. She was the victim of a potentially deadly crime. That was all that mattered. The fact that she was instrumental in freeing the drunken weasel who killed his sister had no bearing on this case. Nor did the unfortunate fact that despite himself, he was attracted to her.

"What about Gary and Trent? Do you think it means anything that they're the only two who've been killed?"

And there it was.

The one thing that kept gnawing at his brain and digging at his insides. He couldn't shake the feeling that their deaths had something to do with his sister's death eight months before. His notebook was filled with notes and charts and analyses of every detail of the break-ins and murders—their similarities and their differences.

Everything about the break-ins led back to one undeniable

fact. If he started with the night Kimberly was killed, the fatalities in Cantara Hills were three months apart. December, February, May and now August. The break-ins had started in January. There had been one a month since then. The theory was that the five people who weren't home when the break-ins occurred had been lucky. But Brody had a different theory.

Trent Briggs and Victoria Kirkland had left socialite Taylor Landis's party together that fateful night, just ahead of Caroline and Kimberly. Zelke had left a few minutes after Kimberly. Victoria had passed the intersection just seconds before Zelke plowed into Caroline's Vette and fled the scene of the crime.

Briggs and Zelke had been killed during *break-ins*. And now the last person who'd been near the scene at the critical time that night had been attacked.

And nearly killed.

But Brody didn't want to get into that with her. She'd denied seeing anything that night, and she'd gotten Zelke off with nothing more than leaving the scene of an accident and driving under the influence.

Brody hated her for that. Even though she'd proved that another vehicle had crashed into Caroline's car first. Even though the final coroner's report concluded that Kimberly had already been thrown from the car before Zelke hit it.

"Lieutenant? None of the other break-in victims were attacked, were they? Their apartments were broken into while they were gone." Her eyes glittered and the mug clattered as she set it down. "So why Gary? Why Trent? Why…me?"

Dammit. She was really spooked. Despite his resentment, the hint of tears in her eyes and the faint trembling of her lower lip tugged at his heart.

"The theory is that the others were lucky they weren't home," he said noncommittally.

"It's too much of a coincidence. Trent and I passed that intersection only seconds before Caroline and Kimberly, and then Gary."

"Let's get back to what happened tonight. Now, did you notice anything about your attacker? Was he big? Small? Fat? Skinny?"

"I don't know. His hands maybe. They were strong—big."

"Any scars? Any identifying marks?"

She shook her head without looking at him.

Dammit, he needed something to go on. She was the first—the only one who'd been attacked and lived to tell it. "What about his clothes? Long sleeves? What about smell? After-shave? Cologne? Bad breath?"

Her head still turned back and forth. "I can't tell you anything. I was asleep and then he was there." Her voice quavered.

Brody's frustration built. He planted his feet hip-width apart and crossed his arms over his chest. "So a man broke into your home, found his way to your bedroom and attacked you, and you can't tell me one thing about him? Are you even sure it was a man?"

Victoria opened her mouth, but the retort he expected didn't surface. Instead, she closed her eyes and the corners of her mouth grew white and pinched. "I'm sure it was a man."

"How?"

She glanced up at him. For an instant her green eyes flashed with fear. Then she dropped her gaze. "His breaths sawing in and out in my ear. He sounded—and felt—like a man." She wrapped her arms tightly around herself.

Then she shuddered, and her terror and revulsion reverberated inside him.

"All right. Good. Now stand up. I need to see your neck."

"It's fine."

"That's not your call to make. As an *attorney,* I'd think you'd know that. I need to examine the bruises and process you."

"Process me?"

He cleared his throat impatiently. "Look, Ms. Kirkland. I know you understand procedure. So it'd be helpful if you'd cooperate."

She stood, her green eyes glittering. "I apologize. I'm not trying to be difficult. I seem to be distracted." She lifted her chin, exposing the bruises on her neck.

Irritated because her distress was getting to him, Brody pulled out his cell phone and hit a prerecorded number. "Egan. You upstairs?"

"Yeah. I was going to let you know I was here, but it looked like you and the victim were butting heads, so I left you alone."

"Is there a female officer up there? I want to process Victoria."

"Yeah," Egan said slowly. "A very nice one."

"Send her down." He hung up and pocketed his phone, then retrieved the small green case labeled CSI. Inside he found a disposable digital camera and a small stack of fingerprint paper.

He stood in front of her. In bare feet she seemed a lot smaller than she had at Kimmie's funeral and Zelke's arraignment. Those high heels she always wore added a lot.

"Sir?"

"Yeah," he answered the female voice without turning around. "You're Officer…"

"Martin. Sheila."

"Good. Thanks for coming down." He got the camera ready, then spoke to Victoria.

"Can you lift your hair out of the way?"

She twisted her hair up, holding it with one hand, exposing her slender neck. Ugly black and purple ovals stood out against her creamy skin.

Rage against the bastard who'd attacked her clenched at Brody's insides. He had to quell the urge to touch her marred skin, to soothe it.

What the hell was going on in his head? He didn't soothe victims. His approach was to treat them with respect and detachment. The last thing they needed was to be treated like victims.

It was Kimmie's death. For the past eight months his emotions had been all upside down and backward. Things were getting to him that never had in the past.

In any case, Victoria Kirkland was the last person on earth he should be tempted to comfort. He ignored the supple curve of her neck and concentrated on the bruises.

Moving quickly and efficiently, he snapped several pictures from various angles, instructing her to turn this way and that.

There were obvious similarities between her injuries and those of Zelke and Briggs. The theory that he'd been forming clicked. Their deaths weren't random and neither were the break-ins of unoccupied apartments.

He needed to bounce this off his team. He'd known them both since childhood, but he'd never figured either one of them would amount to much. Egan had always been too bitter about his unfeeling father, and Hayes's home life had better prepared him to be on the other side of the law.

But they'd both grown up to be fine men and fine

Rangers. Egan's practical if surly outlook on life and Hayes's sense of irony had kept Brody grounded these past months. They'd tell him in a heartbeat if his suspicions were off base.

"Officer Martin, how long have you been on the force?" he asked.

"Seven months, sir."

"Ever seen a strangling victim?"

Victoria Kirkland turned her head at the question. What was Lieutenant McQuade doing? "I'd rather not be made a spectacle," she muttered.

"Just stay still. This won't take long."

Victoria closed her eyes and took a long breath. "I don't see the relevance."

He didn't answer her. "Get three or four small fingerprint sheets from the kit," he said to Officer Martin.

"Yes, sir."

"See these markings? They're the same as on the two previous victims. All three were strangled from behind." Brody's voice was detached, his attitude one hundred percent business. But Victoria could feel his finger hovering a millimeter above her skin as he traced the bruises on her neck.

"Yes, sir."

From her voice, Victoria could tell that the young officer was as awestruck as a teenager meeting her favorite rock star.

Not that Victoria blamed her. Brody McQuade was one big hunk of eye candy. All rugged and brooding and intense. The Texas Ranger badge and the in-charge attitude only upped his sex appeal.

At that very instant, his hand slid to her shoulder. His touch was warm and reassuring, until she realized all he was doing was turning her so that her back was to him.

"Hand me the sheets and pull back the neck of her robe please."

So that was why he'd called for the officer. Victoria should have known. He hadn't needed any help, and he wasn't going to let the female officer do the fingerprinting. He was insuring himself against any chance of a later accusation of impropriety. The thought made her ears burn. As if she'd stoop to lying.

"He turned her onto her stomach and wrapped both hands around her neck. Do I have that right, Ms. Kirkland?"

Victoria shuddered. His words brought back the terror, the helplessness, the dreadful certainty that she was going to die. Was he doing that on purpose? Taunting her? Forcing her to relive those awful seconds that she'd thought were her last?

She heard the sound of paper being peeled off its backing. She was expecting him to press the sticky film against her neck, but she still jumped when he did.

"Try to stand still," he said, his voice kinder than it had been so far, "and keep your hair out of the way."

He gently wrapped his fingers around the right side of her neck, pressing the paper firmly against her skin. Chills skittered down her spine. She stiffened. There was a vast difference between his firm hands and her attacker's thick, punishing fingers, yet the fear was still there.

He peeled the tape off, and after a couple of seconds he pressed a second strip onto the left side of her neck, against the worst bruise. She jerked away and bit off a gasp of pain.

The pressure eased immediately. "Sorry. It won't be much longer." He cradled the right side of her head in his right hand as he pressed the tape down with his left.

The warmth of his palm cradling her head sent a surprising tingle of awareness through her. She must be more rattled than she'd thought if she was reacting to this overbearing Texas Ranger who'd made it clear how much he detested her.

And she understood why. She'd believed in Gary Zelke's innocence or she wouldn't have given in to his plea to represent him. And although the expert she'd hired had found evidence the police had missed—evidence that proved another car had rammed Caroline's Corvette prior to Gary's— Brody McQuade still resented her.

He peeled the tape off her neck. "Okay. You can let your hair down."

She let go of her hair and massaged her cramped shoulder.

"Label those if you would," Brody said to Officer Martin. "Left side, right side. You know the drill. And take them upstairs to Sergeant Caldwell."

Victoria turned around and her kimono slipped down one arm. She grabbed it and pulled it back up, but not before Brody's dark, intense eyes zeroed in on her bare shoulder and nearly exposed breast.

She stared at him, daring him to look her in the eye.

He did.

"Why did you do that?" she asked.

His brows lowered and his gaze flickered briefly downward. "Do what?" he said harshly.

"Fingerprint my neck. Why didn't you have Officer Martin do it?" As antsy as she still was, she couldn't completely hide a smile at his reaction. Had he really thought she would ask why he'd looked at her nearly naked breast?

She did like the idea that he was enough of a guy to look. "Oh…"

Well, what do you know? He was cute when he was flustered. She'd seen him angry, cold, devastated by grief and disgusted. And she'd seen him calm, efficient and stiffly official. But although she'd noticed his even features, the cleft in his chin and his strong jaw, the word *cute* had never occurred to her in relation to him. She was pretty sure he wouldn't appreciate the description.

"I didn't want to depend on secondhand information. I wanted to see for myself."

Apprehension pooled at the base of her spine. "See what?"

He studied her for a moment, a small frown wrinkling his brow. He seemed to be trying to make up his mind about something.

Then he took a couple of steps backward, away from her, and looked at the floor. She was a good attorney, a good judge of people and an excellent reader of body language. He'd distanced himself from her because he was going to tell her something she didn't want to hear.

"There have been seven break-ins in the past eight months. Four occurred while the people weren't home." He walked over to the windows.

"Right. Everyone here has talked about how lucky they were."

"Were they?"

Brody was looking out over the Cantara Hills Golf Course. But she knew his eyes weren't on the spectacular view. He was turned inward, struggling with something.

"What are you saying?"

He didn't answer, nor did he move. He stood outlined by the darkness beyond the windows, his arms crossed and his feet planted shoulder-distance apart, his back at once strong-and vulnerable-looking in his white dress shirt.

She walked over and put herself between him and the window. "What are you saying?" she repeated.

He looked down at her. "Why do you think Zelke and Briggs and you were the only ones attacked?"

She shook her head. "That's what I asked you."

"Do you know what was stolen from each apartment?"

Victoria was having trouble following his logic. "Not much."

"That's right. *Not much.* The guy barely took enough to call it a burglary. And not one thing that can be traced. No custom jewelry, nothing large. Insignificant stuff."

"But he took an antique humidor from Byron Dalloway and about five thousand in cash from Mrs. Winger and a diamond-and-emerald bracelet from Jane Majorsky—"

"Insignificant."

She frowned. "But if burglary wasn't the motive, then…"

His intense gaze taunted her, dared her to say what she was thinking.

"You *do* think the break-ins were a cover. You think…"

"You three were the real targets. And if I'm right, he'll be back for you."

Chapter Two

Two hours later, back in the conference suite, their temporary headquarters at the Cantara Hills Country Club, Brody looked up from his laptop at the sound of plastic sliding against metal, and then the soft whirr of a computer-driven lock release. The hall door swung open. Egan came in, wiping a hand down his face.

"Where's the evidence?" Brody asked.

"It's in the car," Egan said on a yawn. "Could you give me time to get my tail in the door before you chew on it?"

Brody didn't bother to answer him. He finished typing in his impressions of the crime scene and Victoria Kirkland's condition.

Caucasian female, thirty years old, five foot nine inches— He stopped, picturing her standing in front of him with one shoulder of that black-and-red kimono sliding down her delicately muscled arm. She was slender but not skinny. He went back to typing—*130 pounds, blond hair, green eyes.*

"Hot and cool at the same time." Egan's voice came from behind him. "Like a hot fudge sundae."

Brody kicked his chair back and whirled in one motion.

"Whoa!" Egan backpedaled. Water flew in an arc across the tile floor as he fumbled with the plastic bottle he held.

"This is not a joke."

"Hey, I know that. But you've got to lighten up. I don't think you've slept a night through since…"

Since Kimberly's death. The unspoken words hung between them, echoing in Brody's head. His old life had ended and this new obsessed one had begun the night his sister died.

"I'm fine," he growled.

Egan took a step back. "No, you're not. Look, Brody. I respect what you're doing. God knows I've admired your abilities all my life, but you shouldn't be on this case. You're burning yourself out."

Brody sent him a glare and sat back down at the mahogany conference table. He stared at the laptop screen, but the words were a blur.

He heard the plastic water bottle hit the trash. "Do us both a favor and get your butt to bed. That report'll be there in the morning."

Brody wiped a hand across his face. When he did, the faint scent of roses drifted across his nostrils. He'd washed his hands. How did they still carry her scent? "Yeah, the report'll be here, but the perp will be back in his spider-hole. What have you got for evidence?"

"Damn little. Whoever did this is careful, but we already knew that from the other break-ins. There was nothing in the bedroom, but I've got the bedclothes."

"Nothing? No hairs? No fibers?"

Egan wiped his face. "Nope. Not that we saw. We picked up a few prints."

"What about how he got in?"

"It had to be the back door. We found prints on the back stairs."

"Back door? Back stairs?"

"Yeah. That is one big penthouse."

"I wish I'd known about the stairs."

Egan yawned. "I got it covered. I took fingerprints and got one good photo of a boot print in dust. Most of them were smudged."

"Good job." Brody closed the laptop and looked at his watch. "I want you up at seven. Get that evidence to Austin. We could have a partial print from Victoria's neck."

"Seven?" Egan checked his watch and groaned.

"You got a problem with that?"

Egan averted his gaze and shook his head. "Nope." He rubbed his eyes. "Two hours and forty-three minutes' worth of sleep. No problem."

"Where are the case files for Briggs and Zelke?"

"I haven't touched them. They're wherever you left them."

"I want the lab to compare fingerprints. I think I got a couple of good ones off Victoria's neck."

"*You?* You processed her?"

"The female cop was a rookie. I didn't want it messed up."

"I don't think they tried to take prints off Briggs's and Zelke's skin, and there were no usable prints in their apartments."

Brody cursed. "I don't guess it would do any good to exhume them."

"All right, Lieutenant. Now I'm sure you're losing it. They were washed and autopsied and embalmed. You've got to get some sleep."

"Yeah," Brody said on a sigh. "I guess I do."

Egan headed for his room.

Brody headed for his. At his door he turned back. "Caldwell."

Egan sighed and let his forehead fall against the door frame.

"Stay up there in Austin. I want to hear back on the lab's findings as soon as they happen."

"Let Hayes do it. He's already there. He can—"

"You were at the scene. I want you. Send Hayes back here. I've got a job for him, too."

"Yeah?"

Brody nodded. "I want him to chase down the items that were stolen from the apartments."

"I don't think Briggs or Zelke had anything stolen."

"I'm talking about the break-ins where nobody was home."

"What for? You said yourself nothing traceable was taken."

"The perp is smart. But what use has he got for an antique humidor or an emerald bracelet?"

Egan's mouth stretched in a yawn. "Maybe he smokes cigars. Maybe his girlfriend will get a real nice birthday present this year."

"I'm banking on him preferring money. If he pawned the stuff or sold it to an antique store, maybe we can trace it. And if we can trace it, we can trace him."

Egan rubbed his eyes. "Good point. What about you? What are you going to do?"

"I want every single entry card for Cantara Gardens accounted for. Victoria's penthouse card, the manager's master, the household staff. I especially want to know who's asked for a replacement card in the past eight months. And what they do with cards when tenants leave—or die."

"Makes sense. That's got to be how the perp gets in without setting off the alarm system."

"Somebody, either on purpose or accidentally, gave the murderer entry into Cantara Gardens, and I intend to find out who it is."

THE BRUISES WERE WORSE this morning. Victoria lifted her chin and touched the sore places with her fingers, watching her reflection in the downstairs-bathroom mirror.

Icy fear slid down her spine and nausea swirled in her gut as she recalled those hot, rough fingers cutting off her breath. She wrapped her arms protectively around her middle and rested her forehead against the cool mirror, waiting for the queasiness to pass.

She'd showered last night after the police and Brody had left, but this morning she still felt dirty—violated. And her pristine apartment had ceased to be a sanctuary. She'd slept on the sofa in the living room because she couldn't make herself get into the bed where the man had attacked her.

It didn't matter that Detective Sergeant Deason had stationed an officer in the elevator lobby. It wouldn't have mattered if the officer had been guarding her bedroom door. She didn't think she'd ever be able to sleep in that bed again.

The attacker would be back. Brody McQuade had said so last night, and she knew he was right.

A harsh jangling sent her heart into her throat.

Phone. It was just her phone. She took a deep breath and shook off the panic that had gripped her. Why hadn't she ever noticed how much the phone's ring sounded like her security alarm?

She picked up the handset on the third ring, glancing at the ornate clock perched on a shelf. Was it really only seventhirty?

"Victoria, sweetheart."

It was Tammy Sutton, the wife of the powerful chairman of the San Antonio City Board. Victoria grimaced. She could tell by the tone of Tammy's voice that she already knew what had happened.

"Hi, Tammy," she said, forcing a brightness into her voice.

Of course Tammy would know about the break-in. Not even uber-Ranger Brody McQuade could stop the police from reporting the incident to Kenneth Sutton.

"I do apologize for calling so early, but I heard about your attack and I just had to see if you're all right. What on earth happened?"

"I'm not sure I should be talking about it."

"Nonsense. I'm your friend. You need someone to lean on right now."

Friend? Hardly. She and Tammy were on a couple of charity committees together. Victoria's grandmother would not have approved of the cavalier way people threw around the word friend these days. She'd have called them speaking acquaintances.

"That's very nice of you to offer—"

"Sweetheart. It's what friends are for." Butter wouldn't melt in Tammy's mouth, she thought. The woman was up to something. Victoria almost laughed at that thought. When was Tammy Sutton not up to something? The woman could chew up and spit out anybody, then rinse her mouth with a Long Island Iced Tea.

"Tell me what happened. Could you identify the attacker? Did he say anything?"

"No. It all happened so fast. And he didn't say a word. He just tried to choke me."

"Oh, my God! And you didn't see anything?"

"Not a thing." Victoria wasn't about to give Tammy the

details of how she'd come awake just as the man grabbed her and flipped her onto her stomach. The horror of what could have happened still chilled her to the bone.

"Oh, Victoria. Are you sure you're all right? He didn't—"

"I'm fine. Just a little shaken. Now I really have to get ready for work."

"Work? Victoria, what is the matter with you? You're in no shape to work. My God, you could have been killed."

Victoria's mouth tasted like ash. She could happily have gone all day without hearing that. She licked her lips and sucked in a breath. "Working will help. In fact, it will help a lot, since I've got stacks of paperwork to finish. For once I'll welcome the boredom. I'm fine, really."

She was so *not* fine, but she wasn't going to let anyone know that. She'd built her reputation as an attorney—face it, she'd built her life—on her ability to stay cool no matter what the situation.

She'd had trouble hanging on to her signature cool last night in the presence of Brody McQuade, and that dismayed her.

She didn't like the sense of safety she'd felt from the moment he'd walked into the room. She didn't like the sexual attraction that had sparked between them in an arc of electricity that she'd have sworn was visible.

Most of all, she didn't like Brody's air of supreme confidence. He knew he was in charge and his confidence was palpable to anyone he came in contact with.

She'd dealt with guys like him, guys who used bullying to get their way. For some inexplicable reason, she was drawn to the caveman type, but at least she'd learned to recognize them and avoid them.

"Hello? Victoria?"

"Oh, sorry, Tammy. I…I thought I heard something."

"See? You're obviously too upset to work. Why don't you spend a few days at my lake house? It's got all the comforts—even the freezer's stocked."

"Thank you, but I can't leave in the middle of this investigation."

Tammy Sutton had always been gracious at dinners and teas, but she'd never made overtures to Victoria. Until today. Victoria couldn't help but wonder what Tammy's motive was.

A faint beep sounded in Victoria's ears. "Tammy, I have another call. It could be the police."

"Oh, of course. I'll let you go. We must get together for lunch soon."

"That would be lovely. Bye." *I won't hold my breath until I hear from you.*

She picked up the incoming call. "Hello?"

"Victoria, are you all right?" It was Caroline Stallings.

"What's going on, Caroline? How does everybody know about my attack?"

"It's on the early-morning news. They didn't say much about your condition, so I had to call. I'm so glad you're not in the hospital."

"How do they do it? The media, I mean. I didn't see a reporter anywhere."

"Tell me about it. I often get the idea that certain people would be happy to have every move they made played out on television. So they delight in talking to the press about anything."

"Well, I've had about enough of this latest media circus. I'm seriously considering moving."

"I know. This whole year has been so bizarre. Do you

realize that three people we know have died in the past eight months?"

"Three? Oh—you mean starting with Kimberly."

Caroline paused infinitesimally. "Yes, and all three were such tragedies."

An eerie chill spread through Victoria. "Sometimes I wonder—"

"If there's a connection? Me, too."

Victoria heard her sigh. "Caroline, Kimberly's death wasn't your fault."

"I was driving, and Kimberly didn't have her seat belt on. There are two people who are certain it was my fault. Lieutenant Brody McQuade and me."

"It was tragic, but it certainly wasn't your fault. The only person at fault was the driver who ran away from the scene."

"I'm the only one who can say what happened, and I have no idea," Caroline said. "Until I can remember what happened…"

"Still nothing?"

"Zero. Zilch. *Nada.* I'd always heard about amnesia, but I guess I never really believed someone could actually have zero memory of something that happened to them. And yet here I am, living proof."

Victoria heard the chimes of her intercom. "Now there's someone at the door. Looks like I'm the most popular person in Cantara Hills this morning." She'd tried to make her voice light, but knew she'd failed.

"Don't let them get you down. Are you going to work?"

"Planning to. I'm sure not staying here all day."

The chimes rang again. "I'd better go. It might be Lieutenant McQuade, wanting to harass me some more." Her words were sarcastic, but deep inside, Victoria felt a twinge of anticipation.

What the heck was wrong with her? Did she actually want to see Brody again? Want to experience that sense of safety and power again? Last night he'd filled her apartment with his comforting presence.

"Victoria, if you need to talk or if you just want to get a drink or have lunch or something, let me know."

Victoria thanked her and hung up. She looked down at herself. She was still in the ivory gown and black-and-red kimono. She started toward the intercom, reaching to turn on the security camera's monitor.

But before she got to it a *ping* announced the arrival of the elevators. She recoiled.

Who...? Nobody but the manager had a master access card capable of sending the elevator to the penthouse. She clutched her kimono together at the neck and waited, paralyzed with fear, as the doors slid open.

Chapter Three

It was him. Brody McQuade. He stepped into her foyer looking like a poster for the Texas Rangers in dress khakis, a crisp white shirt, shiny badge on his chest and the signature fawn-colored Stetson held in his left hand. The only thing missing was a tooled-leather holster.

She met his gaze and saw that he was eyeing her clothing just like she'd eyed his.

His brows rose. "Morning, Ms. Kirkland. I didn't mean to get you out of bed."

Victoria's hand tightened at her neck. "How…what…how did you get up here?"

He held up a plastic card. "Master. From the manager." Was that a twinkle in his eye? It couldn't have been. Brody's dark eyes weren't the twinkling kind.

"Mark Patterson is not supposed to give *anyone* access to the penthouse."

Brody didn't comment.

She narrowed her gaze suspiciously. "I wasn't in bed. I'm being deluged with phone calls. Apparently everyone in San Antonio knows about last night."

"Deluged?"

Dear heavens, it *was* a twinkle. Victoria felt her chest tighten in anger. He thought she was *funny?*

She propped her fists on her hips, then noticed what that did to her kimono. So she wrapped it around her again and crossed her arms tightly. "Two people have called already and now you're here."

"I see what you mean by deluged."

He nodded solemnly, but Victoria knew sarcasm when she heard it. She ignored it. "I thought the media had to have permission to use victims' names."

"You're the attorney. You ought to know."

"What can I do for you, Lieutenant?"

"I'm canvassing the tenants about their access cards. Whoever attacked you must have had a card, because there was no unauthorized access. No breach of the system, either."

"Well, that should be easy. Who used their cards last night?"

"I'm waiting for the manager to get me a printout."

"So you want to see my card?"

"Thought I'd start at the top."

"Could you give me a minute to dress?"

His gaze flickered. "Yes, ma'am. I'll go back down to the lobby and wait."

"Come inside, Lieutenant. There's no reason for you to wait downstairs." She excused herself and went upstairs for the first time since the police had left the night before. Her bedroom was still a wreck from the CSIs.

Victoria dressed quickly, averting her eyes from the stripped bed, the misarranged furniture and the fine film of fingerprint dust that covered every surface.

When she came back down, Brody wasn't in the foyer and the elevator doors were closed. Had he left? Gone down to the lobby to wait, after all?

"Lieutenant?" she called, suddenly nervous. The penthouse was huge, ridiculously large for one person. For the first time since she'd moved in she felt small and vulnerable. "Lieutenant? Brody?"

"In here."

The kitchen. She followed his voice across the quarry tile to the open door that led into her walk-in pantry, laundry room and trash bin. Brody was examining the door to the hallway.

"I wanted to see where the perp got in."

"That's the fire-escape door. The stairs are just to the left."

"And your penthouse card works in this door, too. My master does."

"Yes."

"Who comes in this way?"

"No one."

"How do you handle trash, recycling, laundry?"

"I set the trash and the recycling out this door and Maintenance picks it up. I do my own laundry."

"Where do the stairs go?"

"All the way down to the basement, I think. But Maintenance takes the elevator to the third floor, then walks up the fire stairs. They never come inside."

"Maintenance doesn't have a card for the penthouse?"

"No. That's why I put my trash out myself."

He gave her a hard look, then went back to studying the door. "There's no sign of forced entry. The perp had to have a master card or one that accesses the penthouse."

"I have never given anyone a card," she said sharply.

Brody took a pen-size flashlight out of his pocket and examined the door. "What about these dead bolts? They look like the original locks."

"They are. These condos were built in the late seventies. That's why there's a guardhouse. The guard would operate the gate to let the tenants in."

"Do you have a key to the dead bolt?"

"Yes, but I think I'm the only one."

"The only one. Why's that?"

"Well, other than the staff. I've never paid much attention. But it seems like I've heard the housekeepers rattling keys."

"So if the staff have a key, how can you be sure they don't come in?"

"They'd have to use the card and the key to get into the penthouse. This is the only apartment that requires an electronic card to get in."

"What about the other tenants? Zelke, Briggs?"

Victoria shook her head. "Their cards are for the gate and the lobby door. Oh, and their keys didn't fit each other's locks."

"How do you know that?"

"They told me. Because they were guys, they tried the keys."

Brody pushed his fingers through his hair in frustration. "Somebody dropped the ball on the keys. The manager should have told me about them, or the homeowners' association. *Some*body I've talked to had to have known about the keys. Either they're too dumb to know how important those keys are, or they're protecting someone."

As he spoke, Victoria remembered playing with a ring of keys on the floor of her grandfather's house.

I built you the biggest house in the world, Toto, and when you grow up, you'll live there like a princess in an ivory tower.

Thinking about her grandfather made her sad. Thinking about the *ivory tower* made her shiver.

She took a deep breath. "Well, the answer is 'too dumb to know how important they are.'"

"What are you talking about?"

"It's me. I know about the keys. Until you asked about them I hadn't thought about them in years."

"Years? What are you talking about?"

Victoria nodded. "My grandpa designed and built Cantara Gardens."

"Your grandfather?" Brody's tone dripped with exasperation. "Why didn't you tell me?"

"Because I didn't think about it. That was more than twenty-five years ago. I was in preschool, or grade school."

She knew she sounded defensive. She *was*. This…*Ranger,* with his hot intensity and unbending attitude, expected everyone to be as single-minded and passionate as he was. Not that she could blame him. His little sister, his only family, was dead, and the killer lived somewhere in Cantara Hills.

"So your grandfather owns the condos? I guess it's easy to see how you could forget that your grandfather is probably the one person who could tell us who has keys. Please tell me he's alive."

"Oh, don't worry. Lucky for you he's still around."

Brody winced. "I didn't mean it like that. It's just—"

"I know how you meant it." She angled her head and sent him a disgusted look. "No, Grandpa doesn't own the condos. He was a contractor. But his contract with the homeowners' association contained one caveat. That the penthouse at Cantara Gardens would always be available for use by the Kirklands."

Brody's expression deteriorated into disgust. "So you don't even pay for this massive waste of electricity and resources?"

Victoria stuck her chin in the air. "That's right, Lieutenant

McQuade. I don't even pay for it. I wonder how long it's going to take you to get over the money thing. I wouldn't have thought you were such a snob."

Brody gaped at her. "Snob?" He took a long breath. "I'm not a snob and I don't give a damn about whose money is whose. I just want to find out who killed Kimmie." He hadn't meant to say that. He'd meant to say *who was killing tenants in the condos.*

Her eyes, which had been sparking with anger, turned soft. "Oh, poor Kimberly. Brody, I am so sorry—I haven't even asked how you're doing."

He held up a hand. "Save it. You said enough at the time."

He looked at the keyhole in the back door, shining the little flashlight this way and that, trying to see if he could detect any metal flakes. He pulled out his cell phone and called Egan.

"Working hard, boss," Egan said as soon as he answered.

"Caldwell, did you check the dead bolt on the back door of Victoria's penthouse? Had a key been used?"

"I swabbed the keyhole. It looked like there might be some metal shavings. I've got the swab."

"Good. The shavings looked new?"

"I'll have to get them under the microscope, but I think so."

"Thanks." Brody pocketed his phone and turned to Victoria. "Where's your grandfather now?"

"He's in a nursing home near my parents' home."

Nursing home. His heart sank. "Is he lucid?"

Victoria's lips curled up in a little smile. "Oh, yes, indeed. He can still beat me at chess."

"So what's he doing in a nursing home?"

"He's diabetic, and he had a massive stroke several years ago. He's paralyzed on his right side. He needs constant care."

"Where are your parents?"

She cocked her head. "You mean you don't know?"

"I know where they live. I know they're retired and they spend a lot of time traveling. But no, I don't know exactly where they are."

"Let's see. This is August? Then they're on a photo-safari in Kenya."

"Can we talk to your grandfather? I'd like to be able to account for all of the old keys."

"I don't know. He's a proud man. I'm not sure he'd want a Lieutenant Texas Ranger to see him so helpless and weak."

Brody understood, but this wasn't about an old man's dignity or about respecting the elderly. This was about Kimmie.

It was a cinch, though, that Victoria was going to be protective of her grandfather. He'd ask the manager, but unless the manager could account for every single master key, he'd have to insist on seeing Victoria's grandfather.

"At least now I've got a pretty good idea how the perp got into the other apartments. Somehow, he has a card that lets him in through the front gate and the lobby door, and then he used a master key to let himself into the apartments."

He closed the back door. "But the penthouse is different. None of the other apartments have two levels. None have a set of back stairs. And none of the other apartments require the use of a master electronic card."

He looked around the small space. There was a second door between the clothes dryer and the wall. "I guess that's the door to the back stairwell?"

Brody opened the door, which meant he had to step backward. His arm pressed against her breast.

She pulled away and her back hit the wall.

Working hard at ignoring the feel of her breast against his arm, he shone his flashlight up the dark stairwell. "So the perp managed to get in the back door, and he came up the back stairs. That's how he got to you before your alarm sounded. He only had a fifteen-second window, right?"

She nodded.

"Caldwell processed the stairwell. He said he found a good bootprint in the dust. Do you not use these stairs?"

Victoria looked up at the narrow spiral staircase. "I don't like them. It's awfully cramped in there, and kind of spooky because it's so steep."

"What about your housekeeper?"

Her hackles rose. Why did everything he said make her defensive? "I don't have a housekeeper. So nobody uses it."

He looked up at her, his dark gaze mesmerizing. "Tell me exactly how long it's been since these stairs have been used."

"I moved in here two years ago last December. When I looked at the apartment the manager insisted on taking me all over, including up the stairs." She gave a small, dry chuckle. "I think he just wanted to watch me walk up the stairs in a straight skirt."

Brody's brain immediately conjured up an eight-by-ten glossy of the manager's view from the bottom of the stairs. He clenched his jaw. "So you've *never* used the stairs since?"

She looked him in the eye and lifted her chin. "Okay, in the interest of full disclosure—"

Ah, hell. She was about to spout lawyer crap for who knew how long, and when she was done he wouldn't know any more than he already did.

"The week I moved in, I had an open house. There were probably fifty people or more. Everyone was touring the place."

"So there could have been fifty people on these stairs? Fifty people who saw your back door with the dead bolt, and who know the back stairs lead right up to the hall outside your bedroom."

She hadn't thought about that. He could see it in her eyes. "It…it was just a party."

He sighed. "Tell me who was here, if you can remember."

"I have the list. I had a guest book, and afterward, I put the names into a database."

Brody stared. "A database?"

She shrugged and her cheeks turned pink. "For holiday cards."

"Okay. Who?"

"Gary Zelke, Miles Landis—he's Taylor Landis's brother—Tammy and Kenneth Sutton, actually the whole homeowners' association dropped by."

"Link Hathaway?"

"Yes, and his daughter, Margaret."

"What about Briggs?"

"He hadn't moved in yet."

"And I don't guess Carlson was there."

"No, thank goodness. But Jane Majorsky was."

"The woman whose bracelet was stolen? What about the others—Dalloway or Amanda Winger?"

"I don't remember. I'll get you the database."

"So that's it? One party two and a half years ago?" He wasn't sure he believed her. "No more parties?"

Clouds gathered in her green eyes. "I'm not much of a party person."

"Yeah? So if you've never had another party, what about your holiday-card list? They come around to visit you one at a time?"

"Are you saying that one of them did this?" Her words may have sounded indignant, but her voice didn't. She knew it was true. She just didn't want to know.

"It's likely that one of them hired someone—I'm sure most of the people on your list couldn't or wouldn't kill someone with their bare hands. But if I could narrow the suspect list to fifty people, I'd be happy."

She looked like she'd happily rip her tongue out if it meant she didn't want to answer any more questions. "There aren't fifty people anymore."

Now he was getting somewhere. He wasn't sure where. "Right. Zelke is dead."

Her gaze wavered. "Yes, and…"

"And?"

"Well, my ex."

Her ex? Ex-what? he wondered, and stopped his thoughts right there. It didn't matter. "He's not in the picture any longer?"

She paused, not looking at him. The tiny laundry room seemed to shrink as Brody tried to maintain his detachment. It shouldn't make a bit of difference to him whether she was in a relationship or not.

"No."

The word was curt.

Brody started to ask where the guy was, when suddenly Victoria stiffened and a hand flew to her mouth.

"Dear heavens, that's it!"

Brody's pulse jumped. "What's it?" He reached for her. "Are you okay?"

"Sorry, I'm fine. I just remembered something. He was wearing cologne. Expensive cologne." Her face was transformed. "I should have recognized it right away. It's called

Torture. It's a top brand in Europe. My ex used it. I think because he liked the name."

Brody frowned. "You're saying the perp smelled like this expensive cologne? So what kind of *expensive* are we talking about? Expensive as in *I'm worth it* or expensive as in *if you have to ask?*"

If Victoria Kirkland thought it was expensive, it must be made from unicorn blood or something.

Her mouth quirked up. "Expensive as in *nobody's* worth that. It's over two hundred dollars an ounce for the cologne. I bought my ex a bottle one Christmas."

"So I guess *he* was worth it."

"Like I said, nobody's worth that."

Brody took a small notebook out of his jacket pocket and jotted down the name of the cologne. Beside it he made a note to check with the other break-in victims to see if they remembered the scent. It was a long shot. The scent could easily have faded before the victims got home. The only two who could verify that the perp was wearing expensive cologne were dead.

"So what kind of ex was he? Husband?"

That question was totally irrelevant and Victoria's face told Brody she knew it. So he tried to make it relevant. "Could it have been your ex who attacked you? Maybe he still has a key?"

The storm clouds were back in her eyes. "What kind of question is that? There have been seven break-ins—eight now. Two of my friends have been killed. And you're trying to turn this into a lovers' spat? I can assure you it wasn't my ex-fiancé."

"What's his name?"

"It wasn't him." Her voice was harsh.

Brody met her gaze.

To her credit and his surprise she didn't flinch. She lifted her chin. "Rayburn Andrews."

Brody's eyebrows shot up. "The heir to the cosmetics fortune? I thought he died."

Victoria's eyes closed briefly. "He went down in his private plane on a trip to Cancun."

"Sorry," he said automatically. Her words conjured up unwelcome memories of his parents. Was her ex a jet-setting thrill-seeker like they were? Was *she?*

"So we've got a perp who can get past security alarms and into a secure penthouse, and who wears super-expensive cologne."

He thought about his long list of suspects. "Who else do you know who wears—" he glanced at his notepad "—Torture?"

"Unfortunately, I've noticed it a lot of places. It's become ridiculously popular, probably because it's so expensive."

Brody raised his brows.

"It's a distinctive scent, but it smells horrible if someone uses too much. I've noticed it, but I'm not sure I can say for sure on who. I really don't pay attention."

"Well, if you notice anybody, tell me." He glanced around the spacious penthouse. "You need to beef up your personal-security system, have them take that damn fifteen-second delay off the alarm."

"So you really think he'll try again?"

"He's extremely organized—one break-in a month, one fatality every third month. You threw a wrench into the works—upset his schedule. We have no idea what he's going to do next. But I want you prepared."

Her gaze met his. "You think you know who it is, don't you?"

Brody shook his head. "No. Not yet. But I think the man who killed Briggs and Zelke and who tried to kill you is one of your neighbors."

Chapter Four

The sound of a card triggering the door lock didn't surprise Brody. He'd been expecting Hayes Keller, the third Ranger working with him on the Cantara Gardens murders. He finished writing the last name on the whiteboard as the door opened.

"So where have you been?" he asked, glancing at his watch. It was after ten.

"Drinking beer and watching strippers."

Brody shot Hayes one of his patented silencer looks.

"Hey—" Hayes tossed his Stetson onto a chair and held up his hands, palms out "—I was finishing up a case. *Twenty-four/seven, we never sleep.* That's our motto, right?"

Brody allowed himself a tiny smile. It was an old joke. "Nope. The Ranger motto is *One riot, one Ranger.*"

"That, too." Hayes stepped over to the whiteboard. "What's all this?"

"The printout on the table lists every tenant of Cantara Gardens who used their access cards on the night of Victoria's attack." Brody pointed toward two thin manila folders. "Those are Briggs's and Zelke's case files with printouts of card use on the night each died. I'm comparing the lists."

Hayes looked at the board. "Lotta names." He pointed. "Do all these show up on all three nights? Damn busy place, those condos."

"Tell me about it. I spent all day today talking to the tenants. There are forty units. All are occupied. Fifty-two tenants total. The manager's records list seventy-eight active cards."

"Whoa! So I take it the manager isn't too careful about controlling card access. You got the breakdown of who's where?"

"Twenty-nine are singles. Eleven couples, and one couple has her mother living with them. Twenty-nine plus twenty-three accounts for the fifty-two official tenants. Who knows how many of the singles have live-in friends."

Hayes looked at the board. "He's got seventy-eight active cards for fifty-two tenants? That's twenty-six cards unaccounted for. You think there are that many freeloaders?"

Brody shook his head. "I'm hoping most of the cards are lost or destroyed, but there's no record. The manager apparently gave 'em out like Halloween candy. I don't think the man ever saw a request for a card he didn't grant."

"What are you going to do?"

"I'm calling a special meeting of the Cantara Hills Homeowners' Association to talk about changing out the condos' security system. If I had my way, I'd change out the manager, too. I've got an SAPD officer meeting with each tenant to round up duplicate cards. That'll narrow the field a little bit." Brody arched his neck and massaged the tight tendons of his shoulders.

Hayes yawned and headed for the kitchen. "Want a beer?"

"Nah. Just water." Brody stared at the grid he'd drawn on the whiteboard. He had three columns, headed *Briggs, Zelke* and *Victoria.* Under each he'd listed every card access recorded by the security-system computer from noon until 2:00 a.m. starting on the date of each attack.

He rubbed a hand over his face and sat down. All the numbers were beginning to run together.

Hayes tossed him a bottle of water and sat on the other side of the table. Brody turned up the bottle and drank half of it in one gulp.

"That's a lot of people coming and going," Hayes said, echoing the remark he'd made earlier.

"Look at the repeats." Some names had shown up on the entry log several times during one evening.

"Does the system show exits?"

"I wish. Just entries through the gate."

"So Jane Majorsky, for instance, who came in three times on the day Briggs was killed and once on Zelke's day, and twice the day Victoria was attacked, might have loaned her card to someone else."

Brody nodded again and then finished his water. "She could have loaned her card or she could have given somebody her original card and gotten a duplicate from the manager. There's nothing that indicates when the card was made."

"Pretty sloppy."

"And dangerous."

"So how many of those cards did you personally see?"

Brody dug his small notebook out of his pants pocket and flipped pages. He quickly counted the list of names he'd jotted down as he talked to tenants. "I've got thirty-four names. And there were twelve apartments where I got no answer."

"It's late and I never was good at the fox, geese and grain game. Figured out anything from all this?"

Brody leaned back in his chair, balancing it on the two back legs. He gestured with his empty water bottle. "Amanda Winger used her entry card three times on the night of Briggs's murder, once on Zelke's night and twice last night. And get this. Ms. Winger is seventy-eight."

"What's she doing in a ritzy swinging-singles' condo?"

"Actually, she's a special case. She's Tammy Sutton's mother, and of course Kenneth Sutton is head of the board."

"So Tammy Sutton probably has a card that reads Amanda Winger."

"Kenneth Sutton could, too. There's no telling."

"What about Miles Landis? His name is on there."

"Yep. His card was used twice each night. Between six-thirty and seven-thirty, then again later. Close to midnight."

Brody stood and checked off their names.

"There's no difference in the cards? Date issued? One says duplicate?"

Brody shook his head tiredly. "There's nothing on the card except the tenant's name and apartment number. And get this, the housekeeping and maintenance staff all use the same coded card. That one just says *staff.* The only place their cards don't work is on the penthouse. *And* if that's not enough, the staff also have master keys to the dead bolts, so they can get in to clean. Biggest mess I've ever seen. I'm recommending to the board that they find themselves a new manager."

"Security cameras?"

"I've already been through all that. There's no guard in the guardhouse to check ID and no camera on the gate.

"The only security camera in the whole place is the one in front of the elevators in Victoria Kirkland's suite. Egan has the disk, but Deason's right. We're not going to see anything. Whoever attacked her didn't come through the front entrance."

"So what about Victoria Kirkland? Egan said she wasn't injured. Did she see anything?"

Brody shook his head. "The perp attacked her from behind. She has bruises on her neck that are consistent with Zelke's and Briggs's injuries. I took fingerprints, but of course prints on skin are always a long shot."

"She's on all three lists."

Brody nodded. "She's obviously super-organized and efficient. She gets in within two minutes either side of six o'clock every day."

"Sounds more like super-anal. Any way she could have faked her injuries?"

Brody glowered at him.

"Hey—what? Did I step on toes?"

Brody ignored him. "Byron Dalloway has three entries last night, but none on the night of Zelke's murders and only one for the night of Briggs's murder."

Hayes stood and stretched. "So you're targeting the odd patterns, like the old lady going out three times in one night, and like Majorsky there. She's done a lot of coming and going."

"I'm working on the theory that whoever is doing this is using a duplicate card they got from one of the tenants. And has somehow obtained a master key to the dead bolts. The individual apartment keys are different."

Hayes started unbuttoning his shirt. "You don't think it's somebody who lives there?"

"I've got to start somewhere, and as flimsy as it is, the duplicate-card theory is the simplest. If it's someone who lives there…"

"We're screwed. Fifty-two suspects and no leads. I'm exhausted just thinking about it. I gotta take a shower and hit the hay."

VICTORIA SHIFTED POSITION on the sofa and tucked the afghan around her toes. She couldn't sleep—again. This was the second night she'd stayed downstairs. The idea of spending the night up in her bedroom with no way to escape if someone came after her sent fear skittering up and down her spine.

She stared up at the stars shining through the skylight. She'd get over it—eventually. But right now she was happy here, only twenty feet or so from her front door, with her cell phone tucked into the pocket of her silk pajamas. And a policeman was guarding the front lobby of the building again tonight.

She pulled the afghan up to her chin and closed her eyes, but her brain was wired and her muscles were cramped with tension. She tried to use relaxation techniques she'd learned in yoga to calm her mind and her body.

I relax my toes, my feet and my ankles. The relaxation spreads to my calves, my knees, and the muscles behind each knee. My feet and legs are completely relaxed.

The monotonous recitation began to loosen her tense muscles. *I relax my thighs, hips and tummy.* Maybe she could sleep, after all.

She took in a deep breath, using her breathing to help her relax.

A faint noise startled her. She froze. Had she really heard something, or was it her imagination? Holding her breath, her muscles tightening in the innate fight-or-flight response, she listened.

A creak sent her heart jumping into her throat. That was not her imagination. It was the door to the back stairs.

It was him. The killer. Her ears buzzed with panic. Her throat closed up. She couldn't swallow, couldn't speak.

Help me! She scissored her legs, kicking the afghan away.

The awful sensation of being overpowered and choked passed over her. Was it her imagination or could she hear his stealthy footsteps on the back stairs? Any second now he'd realize she wasn't in her bed.

She had to get out of here. Easing off the sofa, she moved quickly and silently to the entryway, sure she felt the killer's hot breath on the back of her neck.

She retrieved her cell phone from her pocket as she punched the call button for the elevator. Three stories below, she heard it rumble. Above her head, she heard a growled curse. He'd heard the elevator—or he'd found her bed empty.

A scream pushed against her tight throat. She pressed her knuckles against her mouth to stop it. Then she heard heavy footsteps headed toward the marble staircase.

He no longer cared about being quiet. He was stomping downstairs. He was coming after her!

She turned her back to the elevator and watched the stairs. What would she do if the elevator didn't come? She had absolutely nothing to use as a weapon.

She looked around the entryway. A large vase, a carved wooden box and a scented oil candle in a crystal bottle sat on an ornate table next to the elevator doors.

A vaudevillian image of a comic actor slipping on a banana peel flashed in her mind. She grabbed the bottle and threw it at the bottom stair. The musical crash of crystal shattering mingled with the *ping* of the bell as the elevator doors opened.

She heard his heavy steps on the marble. A shadow darkened the night-light that burned at the top of the stairs.

She hurled herself into the elevator and hit the button for the lobby. Then she jabbed at the close-door button until the doors slid shut. As the car began to move, she desperately tried to punch in the newest number in her phone—Brody McQuade's.

BRODY KNEW IT WAS Victoria before he completely woke up. He grabbed his phone.

"What's wrong?" He vaulted out of bed and reached for the nearest piece of clothing—his lightweight sweatpants.

"Help me! He's here." Her voice was raspy with panic.

"Get out. Not the back stairs! Not the elevator. Take the fire stairs!"

"I'm on the elevator," she panted.

"There's a cop in the lobby. Stay with him. I'll be right there." He pulled on the sweatpants and stuck his feet into running shoes and quickly tied them. Then he grabbed his gun and his phone.

He'd already decided that the four minutes it took to drive to the condos was three and a half minutes too long. So he pushed open the French doors that led from his sitting room out to the pool area. He hurdled the squat fence that surrounded the pool and broke into a run. Luckily there was a moon.

Arms pumping, chest heaving, legs pounding, he made it to the gates of Cantara Gardens in about forty seconds. He vaulted over the gate without breaking stride and took a quick glance around the grounds. Nothing seemed wrong. He grabbed his cell and dialed Hayes.

"Get up. Call Deason for backup. Here at the condos. Tell patrol cars in the area to get to the gate and not let any cars out."

"Wha—Brody?"

"Move it, Hayes. Do it! The killer's back."

"Gotcha." Hayes hung up.

Brody reached for the door to the lobby. Locked. He banged on the wood panels with the handle of his gun as he dug for the master access card. His fingers closed around it.

Before he got it inserted into the lock, the doorknob turned. He immediately went into weapon stance, holding the gun with two hands, but it was Victoria.

She dove straight into his arms. Her body shivered from head to toe. He wrapped her in his embrace for a few precious seconds. He wanted to hold her and tell her she was safe, but there was no time. And it would be a lie. Until he caught this guy, she'd never be safe.

He set her gently away and surveyed the lobby. The elevator she'd ridden in was standing open, as was the second car. The slick young MBA-type who managed the condos stood looking terror-stricken in silk pajamas with his spiked hair sticking out in all the wrong directions. "What's going on, Lieutenant? Do you think it's the same guy?"

"Where's the officer?"

"He, uh, he's checking the back stairs."

"Did you see him? Hear him?" he asked Victoria, ignoring the manager.

She shook her head, too fast. Too hard. "Heard him," she croaked.

"Take her inside," he instructed the manager. "I'm going to check on the officer."

"No!" Victoria cried. "Not alone."

"Go inside." He shot her a no-nonsense look as he pushed open the fire door.

The stairs were steep and the naked bulbs put out little more wattage than night-lights. Another thing to mention to the homeowners' association. He focused his full attention on the stairs above his head. He moved slowly, his weapon trained on the last two steps he could see before they curved. His running shoes made no noise.

Where was the officer? A heavy dread settled in his chest. He stopped, listening. *Nothing.* He calculated the amount of time it had taken him to get here. Probably forty or fifty seconds, once he was out the door. Maybe a minute and a half total. Time enough for the perp to get down the stairs and out? Almost certainly. Time enough for him to kill the officer? He sure as hell hoped not.

The door from the lobby opened. Brody swung around, aiming at the door. It was one of the officers who'd assisted the other night.

"How many with you?" he whispered.

The officer held up four fingers.

"Check the stairs. I haven't found the officer stationed here tonight. He may be up there. Don't let anyone leave. I'm going down."

"Yes, sir."

The fire stairs didn't end at the first floor. They went down to the basement. Brody descended carefully, checking each step with his flashlight. This set of stairs was darker than the ones above, but the flashlight's beam showed wet footprints. His pulse leaped.

Evidence.

As he stepped off the bottom stair, he tripped over something and almost hit the ground. Hanging on to his balance, he swept his weapon around him, listening for the slightest noise. Nothing.

In the distance he heard police sirens. *Good.* Maybe they'd caught the killer. He felt along the wall for a switch and flipped on the light. Two five-gallon gas cans had been left at the foot of the stairs. There was no way anyone could see the green plastic containers in the darkness—no way to miss stepping on them.

The bastard had some sense.

Brody crossed to the door, leading with his flashlight beam, avoiding the prints.

He pushed the panic bar on the door with his forearm and swung his weapon as the door opened. The rear of the condos was one floor level below the front. The perp had known this. Did the fact that he'd escaped through the basement rather than heading back to his own apartment prove that he wasn't one of the residents?

Fresh footprints crushed the clover. By the light of the moon he followed them around to the side of the building and up the small hill. He could tell the guy had slipped on the wet grass on the hill.

The blue lights of the police cars lit up the sky. Steering clear of the prints, Brody climbed up to the parking-lot level. If the footprints belonged to the attacker, the guy was gone.

After finding out that neither Deason nor his men saw a vehicle leaving Cantara Gardens, Brody asked Deason to put out an APB for the area for any vehicles, and to sweep the grounds of the condos. Then he walked back into the lobby. Hayes was there talking to the manager, and two officers were stopping tenants at the elevator doors and sending them back up to their apartments with a curt explanation.

"Where's Vic?"

The manager and Hayes both looked at him questioningly.

"Vic?" Hayes parroted.

"Where is Victoria?"

The manager nodded toward his door. "She's in my kitchen. I think she made herself some tea."

"Hayes, thanks for taking care of stopping the tenants. Get

a couple of officers to canvass them. I want to know what each and every one of them was doing at the time of the attack."

Hayes nodded.

"And he left through the basement. Process the stairs yourself. Photos, impressions, the works."

"I'll take care of it, Lieutenant."

Brody stalked through the manager's living room into the kitchen. Victoria had her back to him. She was wearing a man's purple silk robe with pale blue piping. It hung almost to the ground. She'd folded the sleeves back. She finished pouring hot water over a teabag and then turned around.

"Oh!" Her hand went to her chest as her wide eyes lit on his weapon. "I didn't hear you. Is he gone?"

He immediately saw why the manager had given her a robe. All she had on under it were slinky satin pajamas.

"He's gone—or back in his apartment."

Her throat worked as she swallowed. "Do you really think he lives here?"

"Right now, anything's possible." He loosened his grip on his weapon for the first time and holstered it.

She nodded, then ducked her head and turned her back to him. "Do you want some tea?"

"No!"

Victoria flinched at his tone and almost spilled hot tea on her hands. Apparently she was never going to be able to successfully drink a cup of tea around Brody McQuade.

"I want to know what happened. How did he get into your place past your fancy alarm system?"

She took a shaky breath. "You told me to get it upgraded and to—how did you put it?—*get rid of that damned fifteen-second delay.*"

His brows drew down. "Yeah?"

"So I called first thing this morning. They came out this afternoon, took the system down, then realized a part was missing."

"You've got to be… Why didn't you tell me?" he shouted.

"Because I didn't *know* until late."

"Then you should have notified me late." His voice was icy.

She was bewildered by the way he treated her. He barked at her, glowered at her, and in general acted like he couldn't stand her.

That part was no mystery. She'd blown his case against Gary Zelke, the man who had been accused of killing his sister.

The part she didn't get was the other side of him. Whenever he touched her, it was with such tenderness it made her want to cry.

Right now he was eyeing her with a mixture of pensiveness and skepticism, obviously trying to decide what to do with her.

"All right, then. That settles it. Get some clothes together. You're coming with me."

"Where?" she asked apprehensively.

His eyes were hooded. His determination was apparent in the tic of his jaw muscle.

"I'm going to put you in a suite at the country club. Close to me. And you're going to stay close until we catch this serial killer."

Close to him? Victoria shook her head. "No."

No, no, no. That couldn't happen. "You don't have to do that. I can go to a hotel. I'll be safe there."

Brody's black eyes snapped with irritation.

"Don't you get it yet? You're not safe anywhere."

Chapter Five

Damn Brody McQuade and his broad shoulders and black eyes and those biceps. Victoria stretched and turned over in the bed, but it was no use.

She gave up and opened her eyes. The sun shone in a narrow stripe around the heavy draperies in the suite where Brody had stuck her at two o'clock this morning. Throwing back the covers, she got up, uttering a small groan when her stiff muscles protested. The suites at the Cantara Hills Country Club were huge and opulent, but the king-size bed wasn't comfortable. It was much too soft.

She felt like she hadn't slept a wink all night. Of course the dreams hadn't helped. Last night she'd been too scared to notice anything except Brody's comforting embrace, and then his undisguised irritation at her.

But obviously her subconscious mind had noticed a whole lot more, because as soon as he'd deposited her in this suite and she'd showered and climbed into bed, she'd been flooded with very sharp, very specific memories.

Memories of her first glimpse of Brody before she'd thrown herself into his arms. His face had been creased with worry, his bare arms corded with tension. Sweat had dampened his brown hair. He must have run all the way from the country club.

Then he'd pulled her into his hot embrace and pressed his cheek against hers. *It's okay. It's okay. I'm here now.*

Now *that* was a dream. Because Brody McQuade didn't say things like that—at least not to her. Ever.

She pulled open the curtains and looked out at the pool area. More luxury. Sometimes she felt like she was going to choke on the claustrophobic crush of wealth surrounding her in Cantara Hills.

She'd been serious when she'd told Caroline that she was thinking of moving. Of course her grandfather would have a cow. Stanton Kirkland had designed the Cantara Gardens condominiums. And for whatever reason, he liked the fact that his only granddaughter was living there.

A chiming noise interrupted her thoughts. It was the room phone. She walked over to the delicate rolltop desk and picked up the receiver.

"Victoria?"

"Yes?"

"Brody McQuade. I hope I didn't wake you."

You don't hope any such thing. If he were concerned about her getting enough sleep, he'd have waited another two hours to call.

"Did you…sleep okay?"

She smiled. There was nothing about this situation that was funny, but the idea that the unflappable lawman had no idea how to talk to her amused her. She just wished she knew what it was about her that bothered him so much.

"Not really. It was difficult to shut my brain off after everything that happened."

"Yeah. I need to talk to you this morning. Do you eat breakfast?"

"Every chance I get."

"Is it too early for you?"

She glanced at the clock on the bedside table. Eight-fifteen. "No. I'm up. Can you give me thirty minutes?"

"If you need more time—"

"I don't. Thanks."

"I'll knock on your door."

He hung up. Victoria looked at herself in the mirror and decided all she could do in half an hour was put her hair in a ponytail and grab some clothes. It wasn't like she was trying to impress him. It wasn't like she could.

By the time she'd dressed and brushed her hair, her nerves were thrumming in anticipation. She told herself she just wanted to get this over with. The sooner she was able to answer all Brody's questions, the sooner he could catch the killer and she could get back to her ordinary life.

She looked up from brushing her teeth and met her own gaze in the mirror. *Ordinary life. It* was all she'd ever wanted. An ordinary life. A boring life. And in the two years since her playboy fiancé had gone and stupidly gotten himself killed, she'd gotten her wish.

She rinsed her mouth and gathered her hair in a stretchy band. No way would she impress Brody this morning. Last night he'd given her exactly *no time* to pack. So she'd grabbed the first things she could get her hands on. Her makeup case, a handful of lingerie and a few items of clothing. She hadn't even had a chance to think about a scarf to cover up the bruises on her neck.

By the time she pulled on a pair of white Capri pants and a blue-and-white-striped top, a brisk knock sounded at her door. Her heart skipped as she fastened her watch around her wrist. Exactly thirty minutes. Why was she not surprised?

She walked through the sitting room and opened the double doors. There he was, dressed in crisp khaki pants and a fresh white shirt. He didn't have his hat on, and his hair was slightly damp.

He looked her up and down and one brow shot up. "Are you ready?"

"I only had a chance to grab a couple of things..." she started.

He shook his head and met her gaze, his eyes darker and more probing than usual. "You're fine. Fine." His gaze traced the line of her jaw and neck before meeting hers again.

"Don't you have a scarf or something?"

She touched her neck as the quiver inside her that had begun when he'd gathered her into his arms last night returned. She felt as graceless and awestruck as a teenager.

"No."

He reached into his pocket. "Here's a fresh handkerchief. Will that do?"

She took the snowy-white square of cloth and shook it out. "It's perfect." She rolled it up by opposite corners and tied it around her neck. He stepped backward to give her room to pass him. When he reached for the doors his shoulder brushed hers and a clean, fresh scent wafted across her nostrils.

A flash from last night hit her. He'd smelled like rain and body heat and wet clothes. This morning he still smelled like rain, and freshly pressed cotton and a hint of soap. Her knees went weak.

Just a reaction to the man who'd saved her life, she was sure. But as long as she had his handkerchief around her neck, she was doomed to be surrounded by his scent.

Brody escorted her to the dining room. It was bathed in sunlight from multiple sliding glass doors that led out to the Olympic-size pool. All the doors were open and a breeze stirred the sheer white curtains that ran on rods across the entire wall.

There were a few other diners, mostly business types who were either reading the newspaper as they ate or talking with colleagues.

As the hostess led them to their table, Victoria spotted Tammy Sutton and Margaret Hathaway with their heads together. Neither woman glanced up.

Tammy looked frustrated and nervous. Margaret's face was pale and her eyes were red.

Victoria touched Brody's arm. "I should speak to Tammy."

"No. Don't."

She frowned at him, but he'd pressed his hand against the small of her back and led her toward a table near the wall.

"We'll sit here," he told the hostess.

The young woman opened her mouth, but then thought better of whatever she'd been about to say. "Certainly, sir."

He seated Victoria with her back to Tammy and Margaret, then sat across from her.

"Why didn't—?"

"Shh." He held up a hand without looking at her.

He was eavesdropping on Tammy and Margaret.

Darn it. She was dying to turn around and see what he found so interesting about them. She could hear their voices, but they were nothing more than a murmur.

She watched his face, but she couldn't tell anything from his expression. He looked slightly bored, slightly impatient, like a man waiting for his first cup of coffee.

Victoria's fingers tingled and she felt prickles on the back of her neck. Just when she thought she couldn't sit still another second, Brody met her gaze, his eyes dark with warning. Then he pushed his chair back and stood.

"Victoria! My dear, how are you?"

Victoria looked up. "Tammy. I didn't see you come in."

"We've already eaten. You were engrossed with your breakfast companion and walked right by us." Tammy pressed her cheek against Victoria's and then held out her hand to Brody.

"Lieutenant McQuade. You're the Texas Ranger who's come to clean up our town, aren't you?"

"This small section of it, anyhow," he answered glibly.

Victoria turned her attention to Margaret Hathaway, who stood behind Tammy. "Margaret, how are you?"

Margaret smiled, but the sadness didn't leave her eyes. "I'm fine. I heard about your attack. I'm so glad you weren't hurt."

"Thanks. Me, too."

"You must call me, Victoria," Tammy said. "We didn't finish our conversation yesterday. I want to hear about everything." She looked at Victoria and inclined her head in Brody's direction.

"It's good to see you, Tammy, Margaret."

"Come on, Margaret. I'm going to be late for my spa appointment."

Brody nodded at them and then sat down.

The waitress, a young woman who had been hovering nearby waiting for the women to leave, poured coffee for them and took their orders.

Brody stirred a lot of sugar into his. He tasted it, then stirred in some more. He looked decidedly uncomfortable as he checked his watch and glanced around them.

"I'd be happy to talk to Sergeant Caldwell."

"No. You'll talk to me, whether you want to or not."

"It's not that. You obviously don't want to talk to me."

He took another swallow of coffee and looked at her over the rim of the cup. "You don't trust me."

Her pulse skipped. It was true. Although not in the way he probably meant. She didn't trust him because he disliked her so intensely. She couldn't blame him. She'd defended Gary Zelke, and it appeared that Brody would never get over that.

He set the coffee cup down and rested his hands on the table. He was one of the few people she'd ever seen who could sit with their hands still and relaxed. She hadn't taken a good look at his hands before. They were like the rest of him— large, spare, beautiful. Looking at them, she remembered their gentle touch on her neck.

She realized his comment about her not trusting him still hovered, unanswered, in the air.

She shrugged. "I know how you feel about me."

"I told you before, my personal feelings don't enter into this. You're my only witness—my only link to this guy. And I'm not about to let him get to you."

"Thank you for that," she said wryly, just as the waitress brought their food.

Brody dug right into his eggs and hash browns.

Victoria broke apart her cranberry muffin and buttered it, but she wasn't hungry. "Well?" she said.

Brody looked up, one brow raised. "Well what?"

"What were Tammy and Margaret saying?"

"What makes you think I know?"

"Don't give me that." She waved the buttered piece of muffin. "You were listening—eavesdropping. It was killing me that I couldn't turn around. What did you hear?"

"How are they connected?"

"How come you answer every single question with a question?"

"Do I do that?"

There was that twinkle again. She bit her lip to keep from laughing. "You know you do."

"So...Tammy and Margaret?" he asked.

"Well, I guess they're about the same age, so maybe they went to school together. Margaret is Link Hathaway's daughter, and Link is on the city planning board with Kenneth."

"Yeah. They're both members of the Cantara Hills Homeowners' Association, too. I'm meeting with them this afternoon about buying a new security system for the condos."

He took a swig of coffee. "Whose baby would Tammy and Margaret be talking about?"

"Baby?" Victoria dusted muffin crumbs off her fingers. "I have no idea. Neither Tammy nor Margaret have ever had a child. Margaret's never been married." She leaned forward. "What did they say?"

"I didn't catch much of it. Tammy was doing most of the talking and Margaret was upset."

"Who said something about a baby?"

"Tammy. She said, 'Get the baby,' or 'It's the baby.' I couldn't tell exactly. But she was ticked off, and Margaret looked miserable."

"There's a couple who live near Taylor Landis, I think, who're pregnant. Maybe Tammy and Margaret are planning a baby shower. You want me to see what I can find out?"

"No." Brody scowled. "You're not going to do anything except stay put. I need you alive and well. You're my only witness."

"I won't be well if you keep me locked in that room. I'll be out of my mind."

"You'll manage. Now I've got a few more questions for

you. What do you know about the bottle of oil that was smashed at the bottom of your stairs?"

"I threw it. I was hoping it would slow him down."

Brody nodded. "It not only slowed him down, it gave us some good footprints."

Victoria felt a small triumph. "I'm glad. I felt so helpless, so much like a victim. I'm glad something I did helped."

He picked up his mug and drank. "You did good. We can get an idea of his size and weight from the print."

The wave of pride and pleasure that swept through her at his words warmed her cheeks. She took a drink of ice water, hoping he hadn't noticed her blush.

He was filling his fork with hash browns. "What do you know about Amanda Winger?" he asked.

"She's Tammy Sutton's mother."

"I got that much. Do you know her?"

Victoria speared a pineapple wedge from her plate of fresh fruit. "Not really. We speak. I don't think she's comfortable in her condo. She had money stolen, didn't she?"

He nodded and didn't say anything else until he'd finished eating. Then he picked up the coffeepot from the nearby stand and poured himself and her another cup of coffee. He loaded his up with sugar again.

"You always use that much sugar?"

"Yeah, why?"

"I'm surprised you're not climbing the walls."

He shrugged. "Do you know anything about her comings and goings?"

"Who? Mrs. Winger? Not really. Why?"

"On the night you were attacked she used her access card twice. Three times on the night Briggs was killed and once when Zelke was killed."

"I don't understand. She's a victim, too. Had five thousand dollars stolen."

"Right. So she says. She can't prove she had the money, and she can't prove anyone was in her apartment. There was no physical evidence found in any of the apartments of victims who were gone at the time of the break-ins."

"Are you suggesting *she* killed Gary or Trent? That's ridiculous. I can guarantee you a small woman in her seventies did not attack me."

His eyes snapped. "I'm not suggesting she did. I think she loaned somebody her card."

"Tammy?"

"Didn't you tell me it was a man who attacked you? It would help a lot if I could eliminate the females, but since anyone could have given the killer their card, I can't rule out even a small, seventy-eight-year-old woman. Trouble is, when I tried to talk to her, she told me her daughter made her promise not to answer any questions."

"I've visited her a couple of times," Victoria said. "I took her some flowers once when she was sick. She'll talk to me."

"I told you, you're not talking to anyone. No." Brody tossed down his napkin. "You want more coffee?"

Victoria shook her head. He topped off his cup again, then reached for the sugar bowl. He checked his hand in midair, glanced at her and left the bowl sitting there. He drank his coffee black.

She hid a smile. "Come on, Brody, it makes sense. I could go talk to her, she'll ask me if I'm okay and I can mention how the man got in. I'll bet you I can get her to tell me about her comings and goings."

He shook his head, but before he could speak, she went

on, "You have to let me help. I can't just sit in that sterile suite and do nothing."

"You don't have any briefs you can work on?"

"In my job I spend most of my time meeting with clients and advising them on their businesses or investments. I do most of my work face-to-face."

"Then I guess you'd better get used to doing nothing."

Victoria leaned forward and put her hand on Brody's where it rested next to his cup. "Please let me help. I can talk to her."

Brody pinned her with his dark gaze. Then he looked down at her hand on his.

Her face heated again. She pulled her hand back.

"I still have about twenty or so people to talk to at the condos," he said. "You come with me. You see Mrs. Winger, and then you call my cell phone and I'll bring you back here. You don't go anywhere else. You don't talk to anyone else. Got it?"

Victoria breathed a sigh of relief. Talking to Mrs. Winger wasn't the most exciting way to spend a morning, but at least she wouldn't be stuck in the country club where her choices were to watch daytime television or sit out in the sun. "Yes, sir."

"Well, well."

Brody winced and quelled an urge to groan. He'd know that whiny voice anywhere. He tore his gaze away from Victoria's sparkling gaze to meet the beady brown eyes of Carlson Woodward, tennis pro.

What a joke. Whiny, spoiled Carlson being a pro at *any*thing was worthy of a belly laugh. Brody cut his eyes over to Carlson's too-tanned legs sticking out from under a pair of white shorts. He could see the streaks of self-tanning stuff that had rubbed off on the hem of the shorts.

He'd known Carlson was working at the country club, but until now he hadn't run into him. He'd been thankful for that. He wasn't pleased that Carlson had found him with Victoria.

"If it's not the big bad Texas Ranger, Mr. Brody McQuade." Carlson's too-full, too-pouty lips curved into a sinister smile. "My dear foster brother. I heard you were investigating the rampant terror engulfing Cantara Gardens. And now here you are, caught in an early-morning assignation with the lovely Victoria Kirkland."

Carlson stepped over and held out his hand to Victoria. After a swift glance at Brody, she reluctantly offered her hand. Carlson grasped it and bowed over it. Brody nearly laughed at the moue of distaste that marred her features as his lips touched her skin.

For himself, Brody wanted nothing more than to knock the smirking Lothario across the room. He had to unclench his fist.

He had no idea how Carlson got women to fall for him and he didn't want to know. But he was glad Victoria had better sense than to be charmed by him.

Victoria took her hand back as quickly as she could. Carlson turned his smug smile toward Brody, missing Victoria's swipe of her napkin across the back of her hand.

"I heard about the near tragedy. Lucky you were there to save our damsel in distress." He picked an invisible speck of lint off his white polo shirt. "I know everyone in the condos of course, so if you need anything—anything at all, Brody— please just call on me."

He adjusted a terry cloth wristband and hiked the strap of his tennis-racket bag higher on his shoulder. "Meanwhile, toodles."

Brody wrapped his hand around his cup, ignoring the

handle, and drank a big swallow, hoping it would wash away the bad taste Carlson left in his mouth.

"Foster brother?" Victoria was still scrubbing at her hand. "What's that about?"

Brody clenched his jaw. He was just about to tell her it was none of her business, not because it wasn't, but because he was thoroughly PO'd from just seeing Carlson. He needed her cooperation, however. It would complicate his life a *lot* to have her angry with him.

Not his life—his *job,* he corrected himself.

"Carlson's the natural son of my foster parents." He heard the bite in his voice.

"Foster parents? Oh, I'm so sorry. Your parents died?"

"It's a long, sad story. Come on. I'll take you to your penthouse to get some more clothes, then we can arrange for you to talk to Mrs. Winger." Brody stood and held her chair.

At the door to her suite, she thought of something and turned, catching Brody too close for comfort. "I just remembered, I see Carlson at the condos all the time."

"His name isn't on my list of tenants."

She shook her head with a little smile. "No. A tennis pro's salary, even here, wouldn't be enough to rent an apartment in Cantara Gardens."

Despite his long-standing animosity toward Carlson, Brody bristled at the implication of the class differences between those who lived in Cantara Hills and those who just worked there.

"So what's his business at the condos?" he asked, a hard edge he hadn't intended darkening his tone.

Her eyes widened and she moistened her lips. "It's just that I thought you might find this important. I wasn't trying to insult your foster brother."

"Trust me, insulting Carlson is one of my favorite pastimes. What about him in the condos?"

Victoria glanced up and down the hall. Then she leaned in and lifted her chin so she was speaking close to his ear. "I think he gives *private* lessons to some of the women. I've seen him use an access card to get through the gate."

Brody lifted his head. "Private lessons? To whom?"

"Well, Jane Majorsky, for one. She's the only one I've actually seen with him. I could talk to her, too, while I'm there talking with Mrs. Winger."

"Don't even think about it. You won't have time. So you said you've seen him teaching tennis lessons to *some* of the women."

"That's not what I said."

Brody clenched his jaw. *Lawyers.* "All right, Madame Attorney. What exactly did you say?"

"I said I think he's giving *private* lessons. I meant it as a euphemism. You know, a—"

"I know. So you're saying Carlson has access to the condos. You're saying he could be the killer."

IT WAS ALMOST DARK by the time Brody left the Cantara Hills home of Kenneth Sutton, where he'd met with the homeowners' association. And he was steaming.

He'd presented a bulletproof case for upgrading Cantara Gardens' security system, including a better tracking system for access cards, recording of duplicate cards, an alert for more than one entry in a three-hour period, plus a number of other measures to ensure the safety of the tenants.

But to a man, the board had balked at more expensive and intrusive precautions. Kenneth Sutton had been the loudest.

Cantara Hills was a peaceful community made up of responsible pillars of business and society in San Antonio, Sutton had argued. He didn't want the people who lived there to be treated like prisoners.

Brody had hammered back with the obvious—eight break-ins resulting in two murders, as well as two attempts on Victoria Kirkland's life, all taking place in Cantara Gardens Condos. And all within the past eight months.

It had taken three hours to wrangle an agreement to replace all security cards and institute a no-duplicate-card policy in Cantara Gardens.

That wasn't his only frustration of the day, either. He'd gotten Victoria back to the Country Club after she'd talked with Mrs. Winger, and had told Egan to keep an eye on her.

Once he'd realized how long the meeting with the home-owners' association was going to take, he'd called Egan to let him know, but the sergeant had bad news for him. He'd been called back to Austin to be deposed in a pending case and was already on his way.

Victoria had been there at the country club for two hours alone. Brody was antsy to get back and make sure she was okay.

As he walked across the massive paved driveway, a breeze kicked up and he smelled rain in the air. He surveyed the dozen or so luxury vehicles in Sutton's driveway. They ranged from a vintage Town Car to a sparkling new Mercedes Cabriolet convertible.

Six drivers were there, waiting for their bosses. They leaned against the cars shooting the breeze, or inspecting the polished surface with a snowy white rag in hand, or just staring into space.

Brody knew the first driver. It was Walt Caldwell, Egan's father. He'd worked as a chauffeur for Link Hathaway for as long as Brody could remember. And Egan had always resented him.

Walt looked up as Brody approached. Then he looked down at his feet and folded his arms. He wasn't sure whether he was supposed to acknowledge that he knew Brody.

"Mr. Caldwell," Brody said, stepping up to him and holding out his hand. "How've you been?"

Walt straightened and shook Brody's hand, still without looking him straight in the eye. "Not too bad. I hear you're investigating those killings over at the condos."

"That's right. Egan's here, too."

"That boy. I haven't seen him in…well, in a long time. He doing okay?"

"Yeah," Brody answered. "He's doing good." He chatted with Walt for a few minutes about the break-ins. Walt knew most of the people involved.

"The night of the party, you drove Hathaway to Taylor Landis's house?"

Walt nodded and looked down at his feet again. "Listen, Brody—Lieutenant—I'm really sorry about your sister."

Brody winced internally. "Thanks. I appreciate that. See anything unusual that night?"

"Not really." Walt kept his eyes on his shoes. "All I know is a bunch of people left really fast, around eleven."

"Like who?"

"The blond lawyer and her lawyer friend in her new Lexus. Ms. Stallings in that Corvette with…you know, with Kimberly, and a couple more people."

"When did Hathaway leave?"

"Not till later. Around 1:00 a.m. or so."

"Who else was here? Any of these guys?" Brody nodded toward the other vehicles.

Walt shifted and crossed his arms. "Can't say."

"Can't or won't?"

"Don't remember."

"Come on, Mr. Caldwell. You know I can have the police bring you in and question you. Maybe that'll jog your memory."

Walt shrugged. "Whatever you got to do."

"We'll see. If your memory comes back, give me a call." Brody flipped Walt a business card, turned on his heel and walked down the row of cars.

He recognized the city-owned license plate of the mayor's car, and the vanity plates on Devon Goldenrod's vintage Town Car. But he wasn't interested in either of them. At least not yet.

As the driver of a new Mercedes Cabriolet raised its convertible top in preparation for the coming rain, Brody headed toward the four-car garage on the west side of the house. A man dressed in dark-blue livery was putting the last polish on a black Jaguar. Brody strolled over.

"Looks good." He crossed his arms and leaned against the driver's side door. It wasn't much of a stretch to figure that the Jag was Kenneth Sutton's. The chauffeur looked very much at home compared to the other drivers.

"Thanks," the man muttered, rubbing at an invisible smudge on the hood. "Mind not leaning?"

Brody didn't move. He assessed the driver. At first glance he seemed fairly typical of the usual driver for a wealthy businessman. He was relatively young, maybe late thirties, and Hispanic, with the high cheekbones that hinted at some Native American in his ancestry.

Most of the other drivers were dressed in business suits or jackets and slacks, but this man, like Walt Caldwell, wore full livery. And unlike the others' bored expressions, this man's sharp black eyes missed nothing.

He reached to flick away a speck of dust from the hood, and Brody saw a telltale bulge at the small of his back. He was carrying.

Not just a driver. A bodyguard.

Just as the chauffeur took a step toward him, a warning look in his eye, Brody casually straightened and stepped away from the car. He didn't want to antagonize the man. He wanted information.

"I'm Brody McQuade. I'm looking into the break-ins at Cantara Gardens."

The man nodded and buffed the door where Brody had leaned. "Texas Ranger." His tone was noncommittal.

"And you are…?"

No answer. More buffing.

Brody adjusted his stance and rested his palm on the handle of his holstered gun.

"Montoya. Vincent." Montoya tossed the buffing rag onto the hood of the car, where it slid across the immaculate surface, and crossed his arms. He stood balanced on both feet and looking out across Sutton's manicured lawn.

Brody recrossed his arms and looked in the same direction. "How long have you been driving for Mr. Sutton?"

"A year."

"So you drove him to the Christmas party at Taylor Landis's estate?"

No answer.

"And you waited there for him?"

"That's what he pays me for."

"You're not just a driver, are you?"

"You have a good eye."

"It pays, in my business."

"Yes. I understand. It pays in mine, too."

Brody pushed the brim of his hat up slightly. "Mr. Sutton have a lot of enemies?"

"I drive, and when I drive, I am responsible for Mr. Sutton's safety."

Brody smiled inwardly. Montoya was a cagey one. "Do you drive Mrs. Sutton, too?"

"Mrs. Sutton enjoys her Jaguar."

"So you have a lot of downtime."

Montoya retrieved his buffing rag and went back to polishing the immaculate surface of the Jaguar. "I'm involved in many things."

I'll bet. "Any of them take you to Cantara Gardens Condos?"

Montoya shrugged and tugged his cap down over his eyes. "Mr. Sutton has a lot of business interests in this area. Now I need to check the oil, and gas up the car. Mr. and Mrs. Sutton are going out to dinner."

Brody pulled the brim of his hat down. He removed a card from his breast pocket. "If you think of anything you've noticed that could present a danger to your boss or any of the residents, give me a call."

"No problem."

Brody walked on down the driveway, got into his Jeep and glanced in the rearview mirror. He'd given Montoya a perfect opportunity to mention Tammy Sutton's mother, but he hadn't. Maybe Montoya did have some business, legitimate or otherwise, at the condos.

He started the engine and pulled out. Most of the drivers were unconcerned with him. Only two, Walt Caldwell and Vincent Montoya, watched him leave. Did they have reason to keep up with his movements? Brody filed that information away as he pulled out onto the highway and dug into his pocket for his cell phone.

He called Victoria. "Where are you?"

"In the suite. I just got out of the shower and am about to watch a rerun of *Friends*."

She sounded totally disgusted and bored. It almost made him smile. "Good. I assume you had a good talk with Amanda Winger?"

"Yes. And Byron Dalloway. Jane Majorsky wasn't home."

"You weren't supposed to talk to anyone else."

"I had plenty of time while I was waiting for you."

"Yeah, sorry. I got held up. I've got some more questions for you, and I want to hear about Winger—" he took an irritated breath "—and Dalloway. Have you eaten?"

"Not since breakfast."

"I've got to shower, then I'll come get you. Is pizza okay?"

"Sausage and mushroom?"

"Pepperoni and extra cheese." For some reason he got a kick out of baiting her. He couldn't care less what kind of pizza he ate. Pizza was pizza. His favorite part about it was that it appeared at the door and the packaging was disposable.

He heard her sigh. "Okay. Pepperoni and extra cheese."

"Good. Stay in your suite with the doors locked until I get there."

"We're going out?" she asked hopefully.

"Just down the hall to my suite. Come as you are."

There was a pause on the other end of his phone. Then, "Probably not a good idea."

His mouth went dry. He'd seen her in a slinky nightgown and slinky satin pajamas. What could she possibly have on that was more revealing?

Just got out of the shower, she'd said. Now his brain answered *Nothing* as it zeroed in on the memory of the faint shadow between her breasts and the subtle outline of nipples beneath the pale ivory gown she'd had on.

Whoa! He reined in his escalating libido. "Uh, okay. Something comfortable, then. I'm ordering in."

He heard a muffled noise. Was she laughing at him?

"I'll see you in forty-five minutes," he snapped, and shut off his phone.

VICTORIA PACED HER bedroom floor. It had been forty-six minutes since Brody had hung up. He was late. She'd had him figured for a guy who was never late.

The phone had rung just as she was getting out of the shower. When he'd said *Come as you are,* she'd been dripping wet with a towel wrapped around her. The thought of him seeing her like that sent ripples of desire down to the deepest part of her.

She glanced at the table where a foil-covered tray sat. Feeling silly and a little embarrassed, she picked it up and sat it on the floor on the far side of the bed, near the French doors. Brody didn't need to know she'd ordered a cold lobster salad from the kitchen that had come just before she'd jumped into the shower. She told herself pizza sounded much better.

Just as she debated covering the tray with the curtains, a knock sounded.

Relief tingled through her, irritating her. She didn't like how much she'd come to depend on Brody being there for her. Shaking her head and pressing her lips together, she opened the door—and stifled a gasp.

"Hello, Victoria." Carlson Woodward took a step forward. He smiled, parting his too-full lips and baring his too-white teeth.

Victoria tried to push the door closed, but Carlson didn't move. The look he gave her sent nauseating chills down her spine and made her shudder. Apprehension sped up her heartbeat. She looked beyond him.

Where was Brody?

Carlson leered at her. "I assume you were expecting someone else?"

Chapter Six

"What do you want?" Victoria gripped the door handle, but Carlson's weight kept her from pushing it closed. He gave the door a little shove and stepped into her room. She had to back up or find herself mere inches away from his dissipated face.

"Now, Victoria, be nice. Here I am taking the time to check on you. I've been worried about you, and you treat me like this."

She gritted her teeth. She'd never spoken more than a few words to Carlson, mainly *hi* and *how are you*. But she could see why Brody didn't like his foster brother. He was creepy, and he practically oozed slime.

"I'm expecting company." She looked at her watch. "Any second now."

Carlson had changed from his tennis whites to a pair of white dress slacks, a red polo shirt and a blue-and-white-striped sweater that he'd flung over his shoulders and tied in front by the sleeves. The outfit was impeccable and obviously expensive, but on him it looked like a costume.

Still, it didn't decrease the air of menace that emanated from him.

"Now that definitely is disappointing. I was going to ask

you to have dinner with me. We've never had the chance to get to know each other, and that's a shame." His intense gaze never left hers. And he never blinked. "I'd love to hear about your attack."

He took another step forward. Victoria backed up a step. Her apprehension was climbing like a cartoon thermometer about to explode out the top. When the top blew off, she wasn't sure what she would do. All she knew was that she was trapped in her room by a very scary man.

Carlson leaned toward her and she got a whiff of his cologne. *Torture*. Terror streaked through her. The same scent as the killer. "You…" she started, but her throat seized. She swallowed. "You need to leave."

Carlson's smile widened and he reached behind him to push the door closed, but just as he touched it, it flew wide open and slammed against the wall.

Brody.

Thank God. Victoria almost cried with relief. Her shaky legs barely held her up as the tension drained away and her head stopped pounding. She'd been so scared.

"What the hell's going on here?"

The color drained from Carlson's face, making him look like a kabuki dancer with those pink lips and black eyes.

"B-Brody," he stammered. "I thought Victoria might want to get out for a while. I was offering to take her to dinner."

Brody's eyes met hers and a jaw muscle twitched. "She's having dinner with me."

Carlson pasted on a smile and held out his hand toward Victoria. This time she didn't offer hers.

A dangerous glint sparked in his eyes as he turned the gesture into a little affected bow. "Another time, then. Now if you'll excuse me…"

Brody stood his ground, forcing Carlson to go around him. Just before Carlson rounded the corner, he shot Brody a look that sent fear skittering down Victoria's spine. If looks could kill, Brody McQuade would be dead.

"Dear heavens," she whispered, putting her hand over her mouth.

Brody crossed to her side. "Are you okay? He didn't do anything, did he?"

She shook her head. "He's so…the look he just gave you…" She was bordering on a meltdown. She swallowed and tried again. "He looked like he wanted to kill you."

Brody just shrugged. "He always has."

She couldn't suppress a shudder. "He has the creepiest eyes I've ever seen."

Brody squeezed her shoulder reassuringly. The warmth of his hand banished the chill that had collected inside her in the presence of Carlson Woodward. "Come on. Let's go eat some pizza."

Victoria blew out a long breath and took her first good look at Brody. He had on jeans. And a white T-shirt that hinted at the planed abs she'd felt when she'd vaulted into his arms the night before. His hair was damp and bore the furrows of his comb.

He'd just showered, too. Her pulse jumped and her heart leaped. She swallowed.

When he lifted his head, she was struck, just like every other time, by the intensity in his dark eyes. For a couple of seconds he took in her appearance. The feel of his gaze on her breasts and waist and below sent a thrill sliding along her nerve endings. She suppressed a shiver.

What was he looking at? Of all the clothes she'd brought with her from her penthouse, she'd chosen the least sexy. A pair of baggy madras shorts and an oversize T-shirt that read Take a Walk on the Riverwalk. She'd twisted her hair up and caught it with a clip, and she hadn't put on any makeup.

"Ready?"

"Yes. I wore loose shorts so I can eat a lot of pizza." She smiled, but his attention was on closing her door and checking to make sure it was locked.

"Pizza's not here yet. It should be coming in a few minutes." He put his hand on the small of her back as they walked the few doors down to his suite.

She took a deep breath, trying to stop the tingling inside her. His fresh-rain scent mingled with the rose-scented body wash she'd used. The mixture was heady and titillating. An image of them in the shower with water streaming down their faces and suds sliding over their slick skin assaulted her inner vision.

"What?" he said.

Oh no. Had she said something? Made a noise? "What?" she countered.

He shrugged. "I don't know. I thought you said something."

"No. No. I was just…" She had no idea how to finish the sentence.

Then she remembered Carlson's cologne. "Oh, Brody." She grabbed his arm.

"It's okay. You're fine."

"No. I mean, I know. It's Carlson. He had on the same cologne as the attacker—the same as my ex-fiancé."

Brody stopped in the middle of the hall and looked both ways. "Are you sure?"

She nodded, but immediately questioned herself. "It was pretty strong. But there was something a little off about the smell."

"Off? You mean it smelled different on Carlson? That doesn't surprise me, since he's a skunk."

"It had more to do with the undertone. It seemed a little stale or old or something. Not like…my attacker and not like my ex."

"Humph. Probably fake, knowing Carlson."

"An impostor fragrance," she said. "That's probably it. I'll have to get some of both and compare them."

"Here we go." He unlocked the door and stood back. She stepped into a large conference room with three doors spaced equally on the far wall.

A huge mahogany table filled most of one side of the room, and a wet bar and refrigerator plus a sofa and chairs occupied the other side.

Behind the mahogany table stood a whiteboard with bold black writing all over it. She saw several names she recognized, including her own. "What's this?" she asked.

Brody closed the door and gestured for her to sit at the table. "What do you want to drink?"

Irritation pricked at her chest. He wasn't going to answer her. She wanted to jump up and yell at him, but she didn't. "What have you got?"

He opened the refrigerator. "The club keeps us stocked. Just about anything you want, from water to beer to juices." He reached in and pulled out a beer and held it up.

"I never really developed a taste for beer," she said. "Is there any wine?"

He sent her a look that telegraphed what he thought about a woman who didn't like beer, then pulled out a six-pack of single-serving wine bottles. "White zinfandel?"

"Perfect." She didn't like the way he made her feel like a prima donna. "You know, not liking beer is just a personal thing. It has nothing to do with money."

He popped the top on his beer and took a long swallow. "I didn't say it did."

No, but his tone did.

He brought a bottle of the wine and a glass to the table. "There you go. White zinfandel for the lady."

Victoria seethed, knowing he was baiting her. But before she could say anything, he spoke.

"So could Carlson be your attacker?"

She wrapped her arms protectively around her middle. "I don't think so. He's…he doesn't look like he weighs enough. The man was—" she shrugged "—bulkier. Plus, that cologne wasn't right."

"I'm going to have him pulled in, anyway. He could use being brought down a peg or two."

"How did your meeting go with the homeowners' association? I should have warned you, they probably don't like beer, either. You know how we trust-fund babies can be."

Brody turned back to the refrigerator. Hearing her use the term he'd thought of the first time he'd seen her made his cheeks burn. Was it that obvious how he felt about the idle rich?

Goodness knew his parents fit that category. Even at eleven he'd understood how selfish they'd been, flying off to obscure and dangerous places, leaving their two small children with nannies. When their private plane crashed into the side of a mountain in Nepal, he'd decided then and there that money did nothing but break hearts.

But by the time he was twenty-five and able to draw from the trust, Kimmie was getting ready for college, so he'd altered his oath never to touch their inheritance, and used some of the money to give her the best education it could buy.

"People who have always been rich don't understand the

world the way ordinary people do. They don't know what it's like to know they've earned their place rather than having it handed to them. They think they can do anything and not be touched. They think they're immortal."

He grabbed a second beer and brought it to the table.

Victoria was studying him with her head slightly cocked to one side. "Who are you talking about?"

He took another long swallow of beer as he replayed what he'd just said. *Crap.* He hadn't meant to go on like that. "Nobody. Just something I heard someone say once."

Victoria frowned and opened her mouth, but a pounding on the door saved him from whatever she'd been about to say.

"Pizza," he said unnecessarily. When he got to the door, he put his right hand behind his back.

Victoria noticed the bulge of a gun under his T-shirt.

"Yeah?" he called out.

"Pizza delivery."

He opened the door, dug cash out of his pocket, handed it to the pimply kid and took the box from him.

He kicked the door closed and set the box on the table in front of Victoria. Then he took the paddle holster and gun and laid them on a side table.

She opened the top. "Mushroom and sausage!"

His eyes twinkled at her surprise. "I'm not a complete ogre."

She grabbed a slice and took a big bite.

"No, I can see that you're not complete," she mumbled as she chewed. "You still need some work." She could swear she saw him clamp his jaw to keep from smiling. As she took a second bite, she made herself a promise. Before this was all over, she *would* make Brody McQuade laugh.

Victoria was fascinated by the way he ate. She'd noticed

it in men before. He concentrated on eating until he was finished. Assessing his body, she wondered where he put it. His lean physique didn't appear to have any room for four slices of pizza. Her grandmother would have said he had a hollow leg.

He put down the last piece of crust and finished his beer. "So what did Amanda Winger say?"

Typical. No small talk, certainly nothing personal. "At first she didn't want to let me in. She didn't recognize me. But I told her my apartment was broken into, also, and that I knew Tammy."

Brody picked up the pizza box and tossed it into the trash. "You want to sit on the couch?"

Victoria frowned at him. What was he trying to do? This was a business meeting. In her world, and she suspected in his, business was carried on at polished wood conference tables. "Why?"

He gave her a puzzled look. "Because it's more comfortable."

"Oh, of course. Sure." She picked up her wineglass and walked across the room to the sofa. She settled in and sipped at her wine.

Brody sat on the other end. "What did she say about her access card?"

"It took a while to get her around to talking about that. I spent quite some time telling her about my attack and listening to her complain about Tammy wanting to buy her a better security system. Finally that led to talking about how the attacker got in."

Brody shifted impatiently. "Yeah? And *then* did you ask about her card?"

"It was what we expected. She finally admitted she'd given Tammy a card and told the manager she'd misplaced hers."

"That explains all those comings and goings. What about Kenneth Sutton?"

"I asked her, but she said no. Just Tammy. I guess Kenneth could use Tammy's card."

"I guess. Or she was lying."

"Why would she lie about that? Or about anything. She seems so sweet."

Brody sent her a sidelong glance. "Everybody lies."

"Wow. That's pretty cynical."

He shook his head. Was she really that trusting? He was going to have to watch her closely. "It's not cynical. It's the way the world is."

"Still, what about a master access card? Maybe the manager gave Kenneth a master."

"Nope. The masters show up as 'master' on the computer."

"And there's not enough use of the master to account for the times of the break-ins?"

Brody shoved himself up off the couch. "Not nearly enough. Take a look." He walked over to the whiteboard where he and Hayes had tracked the movements of the residents.

"What *is* all this?" she asked, stepping up beside him.

"A grid showing all the Cantara Gardens residents who used their access cards on the nights of the attacks."

"You just have the three nights on here. What about the other break-ins, where nobody was home?"

Brody assessed her. He liked her logical mind. She was a lot like him, fitting the pieces together carefully and methodically. He'd bet she was a whiz with a jigsaw puzzle. "I've got them on paper. The pattern is the same."

She studied the board for a few seconds. "I see what you mean about Mrs. Winger's comings and goings."

"Did you ask her about the cologne?"

She nodded. "She didn't remember anything, but she said she uses an inhaler, and it's damaged her sense of smell."

"What about Dalloway? Since you managed to find the time to talk to him, too."

"Have you never met him?"

Brody shook his head. "He wasn't in. I tried four or five times in the past couple of days, but he's always out."

"Well, he was in today. You should see his apartment. You literally could eat off the floors, and the entire place is spotless—dustless. He's got scented candles and air fresheners everywhere."

"So he didn't notice the cologne, either. What else did he say?"

"According to Byron, the humidor is extremely valuable. He claims it's from the seventeenth century. He showed me where he kept it on his mantel. He nearly cried."

"The police report stated that he valued the thing at several thousand dollars, but he couldn't provide proof he had it."

"Apparently his mother had it appraised years ago, and the total was something in the neighborhood of ten thousand dollars. But the certified appraisal was destroyed when his mother's house burned. He told me he polished it every day."

Brody looked at her. "Every day?"

"Yes. With lemon oil." She took a deep breath. "Brody, I think you should let me go back and talk to Jane Majorsky."

Brody sent her a glare. "Not a chance. So whoever stole the humidor probably has his fingerprints all over it." In spite of his determination to stay focused and not get his hopes up, Brody's heart leaped. "If Hayes can find that humidor, we could have our killer."

Chapter Seven

Victoria shivered at the notion of the brute who'd tried to strangle her holding the polished humidor in his murderous hands. "How can Hayes find it?"

"I'm betting that the guy's only motive for stealing the items was to create a red herring to throw us off. If he's a burglar who killed in desperation because he got caught, that's one thing."

"But you think the burglaries were committed to cover up the murders." She shivered again. "I still don't understand how that's going to help Hayes find the humidor."

"This guy doesn't have any use for those items. But everybody wants more money."

There was that tone again. What was it with Brody and money?

"I'm counting on them showing up in a pawnshop or an antiques store sooner or later—hopefully sooner," he continued. "I've got Hayes out scouring the city. If that humidor is out there, he'll find it."

His dark eyes gave her the once-over, stopping at her face. "Come on, I'll take you back to your room. You look like you could use some sleep."

"Thanks," she said wryly.

Brody scowled. "All I meant was you look tired—"

"Please." She held up her hands. "Stop now. You're killing me with compliments. Thanks for the pizza. I think I can make it ten steps up the hall to my door."

"No. I'll walk you back there and wait until you lock the dead bolt."

"Fine, then. Are you sure you can stand having me two whole rooms away? Why don't you just lock me in your bedroom so you'll have me right where you want me?"

His gaze snapped to hers and she realized what she'd said. It shouldn't have been a big deal. It should have been just a friendly joke, poking fun at his insistence on keeping such a close eye on her.

But that *thing* between them rose up like a dragon, assaulting them with the burning fire of lust. Victoria's face felt as if the dragon's breath had touched it. She knew her cheeks were red with embarrassment.

Brody, on the other hand, was staring at her as if she'd just stripped naked in front of him. In a metaphorical sense she had. Her reaction to her own words was all too revealing. She knew it. And worse, he knew she knew it.

She had no idea how long they stood there silently with her words between them.

She watched emotions chase each other across his face—surprise, lust, embarrassment, even curiosity. Dear heavens, was he wondering what it would be like to make love with her? Because that was exactly what she couldn't get out of her mind.

He cleared his throat and took a step backward—his way of distancing himself. She knew it well already.

"Let's go," he said.

"Right. Let's."

Brody opened the door and held it for her. When she passed him she breathed in his rain-fresh scent. Oh man, she was going to have to stop doing that. She wished she could ask him to stop bathing, or at least stop using that soap or shampoo—whatever it was—because it acted on her like an aphrodisiac.

Once she stepped out into the hall, she was glad he was walking with her. The guest wing of the country club had only faint night-lights over each door. Shadows lurked in alcoves and the side halls that led out to the pool area.

She'd never been afraid of the dark, but the attack on her had changed all that. She felt Brody's hand on the small of her back and her knees went weak.

Gratitude, she told herself. She was grateful that his intense, conscientious nature made him obsessive about her safety.

At her door she pulled her card out of her shorts pocket. He reached around and took it from her hand. For a brief instant his heat surrounded her. Not just his hand on hers but his bare arm against her shoulder, his body so close she could feel his life force through the two layers of cotton that was all that separated them.

A sweet ache traveled from her hand up her arm and all the way through her. She let him take her card. Then she did something she never thought she would do. If anyone had suggested it two days ago when she'd first met him, she'd have scoffed.

She turned toward him. When her breasts brushed his chest, she didn't pull away. Even more amazing, neither did he. Then she stood on tiptoe and pressed her cheek against his—torturing herself with his scent.

"Thank you," she whispered.

He stiffened, and she knew in the next instant he'd be at least two feet from her. But to her surprise he didn't move. Instead, he looked down at her, his eyes the color of rich, dark chocolate.

"Vic," he whispered. "Don't get the wrong idea."

Her cheeks heated again. What an idiot she was. She moved to step back, but his arm circled her, stopping her.

"I'm sorry, Brody. I didn't mean—"

He stopped her from talking by kissing her—sort of. He lowered his head enough that she could imagine she felt his lips on hers. His warm breath slid across her mouth like a butterfly's wing. She shivered and closed her eyes. At that moment she couldn't make herself care that she was throwing herself at him. She'd never in her life felt as safe, as protected, as turned on, as she did right then.

Then his lips did touch hers and she knew what had gone before *was* imagination because this—this was the real thing.

His mouth was firm, demanding, yet in its own way gentle. He didn't force the kiss, but he didn't hesitate, either. It was perfect—a perfect instant that held her in an erotic world between earth and heaven.

She had no concept of time passing, although she was aware of his arm tightening, pulling her closer. When he ended the kiss, it was all she could do to keep from moaning in frustration.

He pressed his forehead against hers. "I can't do this. I need all my senses, all my energy, to track down the killer. I don't want you to think…"

"Don't worry," she said quickly. "I don't think anything. I'm a big girl."

"Look, Vic, it's not—"

A noise cut off his words, like metal against metal. Brody froze, listening.

Victoria moved but he stayed her with a hand.

Crap! He didn't have his gun. "Stand back," he whispered. "If anything happens, run for the office and call 9-1-1."

"What are you—"

He silenced her with a gesture. Then he rammed the card into the slot and shoved the door open, his pulse pounding.

Nothing. There was nobody in the room. But the French doors were open and the gauzy curtains ruffled slightly in the breeze.

"Son of a—" he muttered. Someone had broken into her room.

He stepped over the spilled room-service tray and through the doors, then looked around, but as he expected, the pool area was deserted. Whoever had broken in was gone.

"Brody?"

He turned. Victoria was standing in the doorway.

"I told you to stay back. Did you leave the French doors unlocked?" He knew the answer. She wasn't the kind of person to forget to lock up.

"Of course not," she said.

He pulled his cell phone out of his pocket and hit a number. "Sergeant Deason, McQuade. Just had a break-in here at the Country Club. Get your closest units over here. Stop all vehicles leaving the area. And send some officers to question the guests and the staff."

Victoria's eyes were wide and shocked. "Is he gone?"

He nodded and kicked at the spilled tray. "This is what made the noise." He didn't ask her why she had an untouched lobster salad sitting on the floor of her suite, but he wondered. Had she ordered it from room service before he'd called her about the pizza?

He dialed another number. "Lieutenant McQuade here.

You're the night guard? Check the area around the pool and grounds. We've had an intruder. Police are on their way." He pocketed his phone and turned to Victoria.

"You…come with me." He took her arm and guided her out the door and back down the hall to his suite, a little surprised that she wasn't peppering him with questions. Thankful, but surprised.

"Sit there." He pointed to the conference table as he turned the dead bolt on the door to the hall.

"Why? What are you going to do?"

And there she went with her questions. He didn't answer her. He just shot her a look. She got it because she sat down and clamped her mouth shut.

He headed into his sitting room, grabbed his hip holster and buckled it on. It was time to let people see his weapon. He sure as hell wasn't going to get caught without it again.

He grabbed his Stetson and returned to the conference room. Naturally Victoria wasn't sitting where he'd left her. She'd gone over to the sink and was washing her hands. She pressed wet fingers to her temples and under her eyes.

"I told you to stay put."

She jerked slightly and reached for a paper towel. "I felt grimy."

Right. He knew tears when he saw them. She was probably scared to death, and with good reason. He'd promised to protect her and he hadn't lived up to that promise. That was something else that was going to change. Right now.

She patted her cheeks and temples with the paper towel, her eyes on his weapon. "What are we going to do now?"

"What you're going to do is wait here until I get back."

"Wait? Alone? Oh, no, you don't. I'm not sitting in this room all by myself. I'm going with you."

"This is not negotiable, Vic. I'm in charge. I'm responsible. You do as I say."

"I don't see why—"

"Because there's a man out there who wants you dead!" he yelled.

Dammit, he never raised his voice. What was it about her that brought out the worst in him? "If I have to lock you in the bathroom I will."

Green sparks flashed in her eyes. "How can it be a good idea for me to stay here alone? Look what happened in my suite. I assume your bedroom has French doors, too."

"You'll stay here in the conference room. I don't have time to argue."

"And yet you are."

Brody clamped his jaw to stop an angry retort. "Just stay here and don't open the door to *anybody* but me. I'm locking you in." He turned on his heel, then turned back. "Do you know how to use a gun?"

She shook her head. "I've never even held one, but I'm sure I can point and shoot."

"Could you kill someone if your life was threatened?"

She looked at her hands. "Yes." She raised her head. "Yes."

She could. He had no doubt.

Propping a boot on the coffee table, he retrieved the small semiautomatic from an ankle holster. "Will you promise me you won't shoot yourself?"

"Will the bullet go in the direction I point the barrel?"

He did his best not to smile as he flipped the gun and handed it to her handle first. "That lever is the safety. The gun won't fire with it on. Flip it with your thumb and squeeze the trigger and you'll blow a hole in whatever you're aiming at— even your foot."

He wondered if he was an idiot to give her a gun. But he only had two choices—take her with him or give her a means to protect herself.

"I've watched TV shows and movies. I don't rattle easily."

"It's not as easy as you think, shooting someone."

"Have you?"

Brody pushed his pants leg back down over his boot and reached for the doorknob. "I've got to get out of here. Who do you open the door for?"

"Nobody—except you." She set the gun down on the table, its barrel pointed toward the far wall. Her face was pale, but her fingers didn't shake and she had that determined tilt to her chin that he'd learned to believe.

"Good. I'm locking the dead bolt. I'll be back soon."

"Brody?"

He stopped on his way out the door.

"Be careful."

He stuck his hat on his head and touched the brim in a small salute. "Always am."

Victoria heard the steel bolt snick into place. She hadn't noticed that the rooms had double dead bolts operated by keys. She'd assumed the magnetic card was the only lock. While she looked at the keyhole on the inside of the door, it occurred to her that she couldn't get out through that door if she wanted to.

But what about the other doors—the French doors? She studied the layout of the conference room. She'd already noticed the three doors in the back wall. Those were the suites—like hers except that these were obviously designed for several people working together. She was certain that two of the doors led to the rooms of Brody's team.

She walked over and examined the doors. They all had

dead bolts, too. She tried each knob in turn, just to be sure they were locked.

Then she looked around. What if she had to go to the bathroom?

Oh, please, Victoria. "As if going to the bathroom is your biggest problem," she muttered. She sat with the gun on the table in front of her.

If someone else had a key, or if someone broke down the door, could she shoot them? She'd told Brody she could.

She took a long, shaky breath. Well, she'd better be ready to put a bullet into someone if she wanted to stay alive.

THE UNMISTAKABLE SOUND OF an electronic lock whirring woke Victoria. Her head snapped up and her hand closed around the gun before she even took a breath.

Calm down. It's Brody. It had to be. She was in the Rangers' conference suite at the country club. Who else would have a key?

Nobody—except the man who'd gotten into her apartment *twice* and into her suite at the country club. Nobody except the man who was trying to kill her.

She held the gun with both hands. With her right thumb she flicked the safety off. What had Brody said? *Squeeze the trigger and—*

The whirring stopped and started, stopped and started. She heard a muttered curse word. Then a key turning in the dead bolt sent her heart bouncing into her throat. She swallowed, wondering if she should say anything— even if she could.

Raising the gun a fraction of an inch, she slid her finger into the trigger guard. She hoped she didn't look as scared to death as she felt.

Could you kill someone if your life was threatened?

Brody's words echoed in her ears. If someone lunged at her, *could* she pull the trigger? She was about to find out.

The doorknob turned with excruciating slowness, like a scene in a grade B movie. Victoria straightened her arms.

A long arm in a white dress shirt with the sleeves rolled up pushed open the door. When the rest of him appeared around the door, Victoria knew she'd never seen him before.

"Why the hell is the dead bolt—"

"Stop right there!" she commanded.

"Holy crap!" The intruder froze. "Don't shoot, lady." His dark-lashed eyes were wide with shock as he slowly raised his hands. "You got me."

"Don't move a muscle," she said.

"Not moving a muscle. Get to the next part—who *are* you? I'm Hayes Keller, Texas Ranger. I'd show you my badge, but I left it in the car." He raised one hand toward his hat.

Victoria gripped the gun so tightly the barrel shook. "I said don't move."

"Whoa, lady. I don't like how you're holding that gun. Now, I'm not going to hurt you. I live here, at least temporarily. And judging by that gun you're holding, which belongs to Brody, I'd say you're either his guest or you've taken him captive. And since he's not sitting here hog-tied, I'm guessing it's the former. Mind telling me why my usually levelheaded lieutenant let you have a loaded weapon?"

Victoria shook her head to try to clear the haze from her mind. The guy was talking fast and her sleepy brain was listening slow. "Who did you say you are?"

"Name's Hayes Keller. Can I put my hands down? They're getting tired."

"No! I asked you a question."

"Yeah." His gaze narrowed for an instant, then he lowered

his hands and took a step inside. "I don't think you're going to shoot me. At least not on purpose. So why don't you lay the gun on the table and let's talk."

"Brody told me not to let anyone in except him."

"Right. Good plan. Except he didn't know I was coming in tonight." Hayes jerked a thumb toward the east. "Just drove in from Austin."

He sounded sincere. His ironic tone and devil-may-care attitude was too easy to be forced. She knew Brody had two men on his team. And he'd talked about Hayes. Maybe she *could* set the gun down.

"That's right, Annie Oakley. Just set it down."

She flipped the safety back on and put the gun down, but she didn't take her eyes off him.

"What the hell?"

"Damn!" Hayes jumped a foot in the air.

Victoria saw Brody behind him, and the breath she hadn't known she was holding whooshed out.

"You didn't tell me—" she started.

"You're not supposed to be here, Keller—"

"Crap, Brody. She could have shot my head clean off."

Everybody was talking at once, but Victoria managed to sort it all out. She clasped her hands and pushed her knuckles against her teeth.

Hayes gave Brody the five-second explanation for why he'd come in tonight. Brody gave Hayes the five-minute explanation of the break-in at Victoria's suite and why she was here with his spare gun.

She listened intently and never took her eyes off Brody. He was restless, pacing back and forth, grabbing a bottle of water from the refrigerator and downing it in one gulp, fiddling with his holster.

"Deason's got a roadblock set up, but so far the only person he's caught is Miles Landis. Landis had just parked here and was on his way to the bar for a nightcap before heading to the condos. At least that's his story. He doesn't look coolheaded enough to break and enter and then act like he's just out for a drink. I'm sure the perp hightailed it out before the police got here."

Brody sent a look Victoria's way. "You okay?" he asked belatedly.

She was tired and scared and a little intimidated by all the testosterone in the room. "Sure. I'm fine. I don't know if you had fun tonight, but I sure did. Everything from the pizza to the break-in to meeting..." She nodded toward Hayes, who took off his hat.

"Hayes," he said, affecting a little bow.

She glared at him, then turned her gaze back to Brody. "...to meeting *Hayes* when he just waltzed in using a key you told me nobody had."

"I didn't tell you that."

"Well, you implied it."

"Look, Vic. You're exhausted. You can sleep in my room and I'll sleep on the couch in the sitting room. That way you'll be safe and I'll know where you are."

"Here? You want me to stay here?" She looked from him to Hayes and back to him. "With the two of you? There's another one, too, isn't there? Three of you? No."

"Vic—"

"No, no, no." She shook her head. "Find me another suite. Isn't there one that doesn't open to the outside—or isn't full of men?"

"I'll show you to my room and Hayes will go get your clothes."

"Hey, leave me out of it. I'm on her side. Can't she stay somewhere else?"

Brody quelled him with a glance.

Hayes held up his hands. "Fine. Fine. Going to get the clothes." Brody handed him her card and he left the room.

Victoria crossed her arms and tried to cut Brody in half with a look. It didn't work. He didn't even wince.

"What did I tell you?" he said evenly. "I'm in charge. You listen to me. You're in my—in the Rangers' protective custody, and if I tell you you're sleeping in the same *bed* as me, that's what you'll do. Understood?"

Despite his words, which conjured up an image in Victoria's brain that melted her anger and heated her insides, she saw that he was really angry.

Black fire raged in his dark eyes. Something else did, too, or she thought it did. But it was probably a trick of the light. Either that or Brody McQuade took his job much more seriously than anyone she'd ever known. Because she saw a steely determination in him that could bring a professional wrestler to his knees.

She ought to be cringing. But for some weird reason, all his fierceness made her feel safe. "I apparently don't have any choice," she said grudgingly.

"That's right. You don't."

"Here you go." Hayes shouldered the door open. He was hauling a sheet that he'd obviously dumped everything into. "I think I got everything. Want this in your bedroom, Brody?"

Victoria looked at the makeshift sack. "Please tell me you didn't dump the food tray in there."

"I didn't dump the food tray in there."

"Put it in my bedroom." Brody nodded toward the middle door, then turned to her. "You can sort it out in the morning. Right now you need to get some sleep."

Hayes threw the sheet over his shoulder like a duffel bag, and Victoria winced at the sound of glass and plastic clanking together. He unlocked the door in the middle of the far wall.

"He has a key to your room?"

"They're all the same key. You can trust Hayes and Egan, just like you trust me."

"That much, eh?"

Brody frowned at her.

"Sorry. I'm getting loopy. I must be tired."

"Come on, then, I'll get you settled in."

Hayes came out minus the sheet, pointing with his thumb over his shoulder. "Your bedroom's kind of messy for a *girl*, Brody."

Brody shot him a look, then placed his hand on the small of her back and led her through the door into a small sitting room with French doors leading out to the pool.

"See. My room has the French doors out here. So you won't have to worry about someone breaking into the bedroom." He went into the bedroom ahead of her and grabbed up a towel and an undershirt and a pair of boxers from the floor.

"Sorry."

She looked around. The room wasn't luxurious—it was obviously designed for businessmen—but it was large enough for a king-size bed and a dresser. The bathroom door was open and she saw a spa tub and a walk-in shower. Dear heavens, a bath sounded good.

"Is this the only bathroom?" she asked.

"Yeah. There's one off the conference room, which I can use. No shower, though."

She stared at him helplessly.

"I'll use Egan's—or Hayes's." He looked at the floor. "Well, good night."

"Brody? Aren't you going to tell me what happened to the man who broke into my room?"

"You heard most of it. Basically he got away."

"Nothing? No fingerprints? No tire tracks?"

He shook his head. "We'll go over the area again in the morning, but I'm afraid he got away clean."

"So he's still out there and still wants me dead."

"Yeah, but you're here." He lifted a hand, then checked it before he touched her. "Safe."

Her heart skipped a beat. Probably because of the excitement and the danger and her exhaustion. "I hope you're right."

"I'll be just outside this door, on the sofa. You call out if you need me."

Victoria nodded.

Brody turned on his heel and walked through the sitting room and out into the conference room. She watched him—his strong, broad shoulders, his lean hips and sexy butt, the slight wave in the hair at his nape that made his otherwise straight back and neck look vulnerable.

Just as she was about to close the door to the bedroom, she heard Hayes.

"What the heck are you doing?" he asked. "What's the point of putting her in here? You don't think that's going to stop him, do you?"

"I think it'll draw him out. And when he tries to get to her, he'll fall right into our trap."

"Damn, Brody. You're using her as bait?"

"Keep your voice down."

Chapter Eight

Victoria couldn't breathe. Invisible hands closed around her throat and a soundless voice rasped in her ear. "He used you as bait, but I caught you." The hands squeezed tighter.

Victoria gasped. She flailed her arms, trying to fend off the faceless attacker. Her chest burned. Her throat hurt. She couldn't breathe.

Then she woke up.

It took her a couple of seconds to ground herself in reality. She was in Brody's bedroom. She was safe.

But her face was bathed in sweat, her mouth was dry and her body radiated heat. The tiny bedroom was closing in on her. She needed to get out of there.

To do that she'd have to go past Brody, who was asleep on the couch in his sitting room.

She tried to swallow, but her throat was too dry. Her heart fluttered in rising panic. Throwing on her kimono, she quietly opened the bedroom door.

The solar lights from the pool area seeped in around the lined curtains and bathed the sitting room in soft golden light. The *empty* sitting room. Her heart skipped a beat.

Brody wasn't there.

Settle down, she admonished herself. He was probably in the bathroom or had gotten up to get some water.

Victoria opened the suite door and stepped into the conference room. Cool air swirled around her. She took a long breath—and coughed.

"Vic?"

She jumped. *Brody.*

"You okay?"

He was standing at the sink, dressed in those truly sexy jeans and no shirt. Shadows planed his long, sleek muscles and the strong bones of his face.

Looking at him, she couldn't help but remember hearing him earlier, when he'd come into the sitting room. He'd tried to be quiet, but she'd woken up when the door closed.

She'd heard the rustle of clothes and the sound of boots hitting the floor, one at a time.

Finally he'd sunk onto the couch with a soft groan. It had taken her a long time to stop thinking about him lying there not thirty feet away in—what? Those jeans? Boxers? Nothing?

So now she knew the answer to that question.

"I just—" her hand flew to her throat "—just needed some water."

He opened the under-counter refrigerator, retrieved a bottle and loosened the cap. When he handed it to her his hand brushed hers and her heart fluttered again.

"Couldn't sleep?" His sleepy voice rumbled through her.

She shook her head. "I had a bad dream."

"About your attack?"

"And then the room started closing in." She walked over to the sitting area where she plopped down with her feet tucked under her.

She turned up the bottle and let the cool water slide over her aching throat. "What about you?"

He shrugged and gestured with the bottle in his hand. "Thirsty."

"I'm sure that couch is uncomfortable. I'm sorry for kicking you out of your bedroom."

"You're not kicking me out. I can sleep anywhere." He propped a hip on the high, overstuffed arm of the leather couch opposite her. "Now, tell me about your dream."

Victoria touched her throat. "It was nothing. I guess my throat was hurting, so I dreamed that he was choking me."

"Any specifics? Anything you haven't already remembered?"

"No." She took a long swallow of water. "He did tell me I was bait."

Brody winced. "Hayes shouldn't have said that."

Victoria's mouth curved up in a rueful smile. "It's true, though."

"I would never risk your life."

"I know that, but he's going to come after me, no matter what. I'm just glad I'm here with you."

Brody didn't answer. He finished his water and stood.

"Are you going back to bed?" Her eyes caught the light and sparkled like jade.

"I was. Do you need something?"

Her gaze faltered. "No, that's okay."

"Vic? Are you still spooked?"

"Could you just sit with me for a little while? Just a few minutes?"

Brody sat back down and rested his elbows on his knees. He didn't really want to sit here dressed in nothing but jeans while she sat across from him in that clingy kimono, but as much as he wanted to get away from her enticing presence, he couldn't refuse.

She sat there looking at her half-empty water bottle.

He studied her. Her hair was twisted up into a messy little knot at the back of her head, and strands of it had fallen around her face. It was soft and honey-colored, the kind of hair that made a man want to pull out whatever was holding it up and let it fall.

"Tell me about your parents."

"What?" She'd caught him totally off guard.

"You said Carlson was your foster brother."

"Right." Brody suddenly felt like his skin had been flayed off. "I also said it was a long, sad story. Too long. You need to go to sleep."

She looked at him, a small wrinkle between her brows. "I'd like to know."

He opened his mouth to refuse, but that would just make her more curious. And he had the definite feeling she wouldn't stop asking until she got her answer.

"Okay, here's the short version. My parents died when I was eleven. My sister was six. There were no close relatives, so we went into foster care. That's how I ended up with Carlson as a foster brother."

"Oh, Brody. Both your parents at the same time? What happened?"

And there he was. In the middle of a conversation he didn't want to have. He was not going to talk about his parents. He was not going to tell Victoria Kirkland anything else about his life. No useful purpose could be served.

He stood. "They died in a plane crash. Now—we both need to get some sleep."

"I HAVE TO GO IN to the office today. There's a partners' meeting, plus I have a brief due on Monday, and as I've already told you, my files are there." Victoria stood in the doorway of Brody's suite and glared at him.

He blew across the surface of his mug, then took a sip of coffee. He was in those ridiculously sexy jeans, but at least this morning he wore a T-shirt. It was faded green and read Habitat for Humanity. His hair was tousled, as if he'd tossed and turned all night.

She'd slept badly, too, after their brief midnight encounter. She hadn't had another nightmare, but it had taken her a long time to calm her mind enough to sleep. His matter-of-fact recitation of how he and his sister had ended up in foster care hadn't fooled her. His ironclad control telegraphed how much the deaths of his parents had hurt him. And now he'd lost his only sister. She'd cried for him.

"You should've brought your stuff home with you. Want some coffee?"

So much for feeling sorry for him. The annoyingly single-minded Texas Ranger was back.

She sighed in exasperation. "Brought my stuff? And why would I do that? Because I was *planning* to be attacked?"

He ignored her sarcasm. He turned his back and poured a mug of coffee. "You like sugar, right?"

His toned body made her mouth go dry.

She closed her eyes so she couldn't see his butt. "Not as much as you do."

The smell of coffee made her eyes fly open. He was holding the mug out toward her. "That's what I thought."

"Thank you. I need to go to the office." She flattened her mouth.

"Why didn't you tell me earlier?"

"Because I've been a little distracted. I'd forgotten about it until my PDA alarm rang this morning."

He nodded. "Okay. I have an appointment in Austin at ten o'clock. We'll swing by your office when we get back."

"Wait a minute. *You* have an appointment? What were you planning to do with me?"

"Take you with me."

"And when were you going to tell me that?"

Typically he didn't answer. He sipped his coffee and added another half-teaspoon of sugar to it.

"Well, I can't go with you. My meeting is at ten, too."

"Cancel it."

"Absolutely not. I can't do that. This is a twice-yearly international video-conference call. There are dozens of people involved. You change *your* appointment."

Brody blinked and she'd have sworn he winced. But before she could consider what had bothered him, he glared at her. She could practically see the wheels turning in his head. He was about to order her not to go.

"Look, Lieutenant. This is important. In fact, it's in my contract that I attend."

"Okay."

"You can't just— What?" Had he said okay? She looked at him suspiciously. "You did not just agree to let me go to my office alone. What's the catch?"

"No catch." Brody drained his mug, letting the undissolved sugar in the bottom slide into his mouth. Then he set it down and crossed his arms.

"I can't hold you prisoner. I know you have things you have to do. But you need to remember that there's someone out there who wants you dead. And I need to know where you are every minute. When I can, I'll send someone with you. When I can't, I want you in touch by phone."

He'd prefer to keep her glued to his side every minute. But today he had to sign some legal papers involving Kimmie's estate. He'd already put it off twice. He couldn't cancel again.

Egan was still in Austin, and Hayes had left before seven to get an early start scouring pawnshops all over the city for the humidor and the other missing items from the condos.

She searched his face for a few seconds, then hers turned pale. "I know you think whoever's doing this is the person who killed your sister. And that he's targeting me because he thinks I saw something. But I didn't. If I had, I'd have told the police long before now."

"We've been over this. We don't know what's in his head. And we can't afford to let down our guard for even a second. He could be a neighbor of yours, an employee either here or at the condos."

"Or a stranger."

"Or a stranger." He nodded and poured himself another mug of coffee.

"You really need to use less sugar."

Her voice was close. How quietly had she moved that he hadn't heard her approach? He looked down at her bare feet showing below her pale-green nightgown. She'd slung on the kimono, but as usual it was hanging open. All he had to do was raise his gaze to see the material clinging to her hipbones and that hint of a V that drove him nuts. A little farther up and he'd encounter her perfect breasts. He knew if he let his eyes linger there long enough for her to notice, he'd see their tips tighten with awareness.

And he wanted to see that more than anything in the world. But speaking of tightening, he had to get control of himself or she was going to know exactly what he was thinking. He grimaced as he stirred his coffee, but his brain wasn't ready to let go of the erotic image of her in her seemingly unending supply of slinky lingerie.

This was what hell must be like—or heaven. Doomed to an eternity of Victoria Kirkland parading around in lace and satin, torturing him with what he couldn't have.

"Brody?"

He tapped the spoon on the edge of the mug for a second or two until he decided it was safe to turn around without embarrassing himself.

"You said the attacker could be an employee at the condos or here at the country club."

"Yeah?"

"What if it's both?"

He stopped stirring. "Both? What do you mean, both?"

"I'm pretty sure there are a few employees I've seen working here and at the condos."

Both! Of course. "I'll be damned. Vic, you're a genius!" It made perfect sense! He'd talked to the employees about what they'd seen. But she was right. He needed to question the ones who worked both at Cantara Gardens and at the country club. Whoever was after Victoria had access to both.

He needed to get a list of every employee who used a key, instead of an access card, anyhow.

Even if the employees weren't involved, they could have noticed something he'd missed, since he was unfamiliar with the area.

"You don't have to sound so surprised. I do occasionally have a good idea."

He looked at his watch. "I've got to shower. I need to leave by eight-thirty. When are you leaving?"

"About the same time. I shouldn't be gone more than two or three hours. Four at the most. I was going to shop for some clothes, since my apartment is still off-limits, but I can do without that. I'll just wear my black pants every day."

Brody tried unsuccessfully to hide a smile. "I'm sure you can manage for a couple of days without a new outfit."

Her chin lifted a fraction. "I don't need a new outfit. I just need something to wear besides pajamas or shorts."

At least her pajamas covered more than those slinky night-gowns she'd worn the first two nights. "Here's what you're going to do. You go to your office and come straight back here, and you call me—" he counted off on his fingers as he spoke "—when you park the car, when you get to your office, when you're ready to leave, when you get into your car, and when you get back here. In fact, I want you to call if you change lanes on the interstate. Got it?"

"Sure. Call you every five minutes. Got it."

"It's not a joke, Vic."

"I know. But what about your appointment? I hate to call—"

"You call! There's nothing—" He stopped, thinking of his meeting with his lawyer about the disposition of Kimmie's estate, which brought out all the grief and anger of the past eight months. "There's nothing more important than your safety. If you call, I'll be there."

She nodded, and he saw the terror gathering like storm clouds in her eyes. "You're starting to scare me," she said.

"Good. Use that fear to sharpen your senses. You've got to be aware of everything that goes on around you. Don't let anyone surprise you or sneak up on you. Don't ignore anything that's even slightly out of the ordinary."

She wrapped her arms around herself. "Could you stop, please? I get it."

"I hope so, because it's the only thing that's going to keep you alive."

THAT CAR WAS STILL riding her tail. "Come on, pass me already."

Victoria turned her attention back to the Anderson Loop that wound above the city of San Antonio. Her hands tightened on the steering wheel. She didn't like this road. Didn't like knowing that a flimsy metal guardrail was all that stood between her car and a plunge down the side of a limestone bluff. Particularly didn't like that it was nearly dark.

She slowed down a little more. There was a relatively straight stretch of road ahead. "Okay, you're in such a darn hurry. Pass." She glanced in the mirror again, wishing the impatient driver would put on his headlights. It was that awful time between daylight and dark, when everything faded to a colorless gray and it was almost impossible to distinguish shadows.

Frustrated, she lowered her window and gestured for the car to go around her.

This was all Brody's fault. When she'd called to say she'd be leaving her office and heading back to the country club within an hour, he'd berated her about staying all day and commanded her to leave right away. He wanted her home before dark. If she'd waited like she'd wanted to, maybe the traffic pileup on the interstate wouldn't have forced her to take this detour.

A low-slung red Ferrari roared past, startling her. Maybe that was the problem. The Ferrari had been crowding the car behind her, forcing him to speed up.

Now the guy would pass.

Sure enough, he crept closer and closer. It took all her willpower not to speed up. She didn't like being tailgated. She set her jaw and waited for him to pull out and around, but he seemed content to ride her tail. Was he too chicken to pass?

Her cell phone rang. *Great.* She wasn't going to answer it at first—she didn't want to take a hand off the wheel. But if it was Brody and she didn't answer, he'd likely mobilize the entire Texas Ranger force.

She dug in her purse and finally came up with the phone. It was Brody.

"Where are you?"

"I'm on the way home, on the Anderson Loop. I told you…"

"What's the matter?"

The car had dropped back a few feet so she slowed down a little more. "Nothing. There was a massive accident on the interstate so I took the Anderson. I do *not* like driving up here."

"You should have called me. How long before you get here?"

"Maybe half an hour. Sooner if this car won't pass me. I'm going to have to speed up. I can't stand to have a car tailgating me."

"Tailgating? What kind of car is it?" Brody's voice rose.

"I don't know. Maybe a GM? Midsize, kind of medium or dark blue. It's hard to say in this light."

"Listen to me, Vic. Drive as fast as you dare. That road's not as dangerous as it looks. But be careful. Don't let him rattle you."

"No worries. I have you to do that."

"Vic, I told you, this is not a joke. Where are you? What was the last exit you saw?"

"I've passed Hollywood Park." She didn't like the urgent tone in Brody's voice. He was beginning to scare her.

"Okay. Take 1535 and drive straight to the police station. It's on Shavano Park on your right. Don't stop anywhere. If the guy follows you off that exit, call me. I'm heading over there now."

"Brody, you don't think it's the killer..." But Brody had hung up.

Victoria's apprehension rose exponentially. She looked in the rearview mirror. She couldn't see anything except the glare from the car's tinted windows.

Victoria set her phone in the passenger seat. Talking to Brody, hearing the innate assurance and confidence in his voice always made her feel better. But this time, he hadn't disguised his concern about the car following her. He'd sounded anxious, and that scared her to death.

A bump threw her head back.

Ouch. What was that? A rock? She glanced in the rearview mirror just in time to see the dark sedan speeding toward her. Instinctively she braced herself.

It happened again. Her head hit the headrest—hard.

Dear heavens, he was ramming her. Her cramped fingers gripped the steering wheel more tightly. She sped up, following Brody's instructions.

The car fell behind. Victoria blew out a shaky breath. She sat stiffly, holding on to the steering wheel for dear life. She drove as fast as she dared, looking for the turn onto 1535. She didn't drive this road enough to know how far she was from it, but she suspected it was almost to the end of the road. How much farther did she have to drive up here, suspended above the world?

A movement in her mirror caught her attention. The car was speeding toward her again. She floored the accelerator, her heart slamming against her chest, her sweat-slick palms slipping on the wheel. For some reason she was hyperaware of everything—the darkening sky, the guardrail, the sound of the car behind her.

She couldn't keep up this speed. She'd crash. Sweat broke out on her forehead and slithered down her back. She set her jaw and kept her tight grip on the wheel, afraid to let go even long enough to wipe her clammy hands on her pants.

The dark blue car loomed in her rearview mirror.

Objects are closer than they appear. Was that even possible? She didn't think the car could get any closer.

Then she heard the crunch of metal. Her head slammed backward. Hot panic ripped through her like an electric shock and stars danced in front of her eyes. She stomped on the accelerator again.

Brody!

Another crunch. Another jarring blow. This time the metallic shriek went on and on, echoing in her ears from behind her, in front of her—from everywhere.

And then all sound was gone and the world was spinning. Somewhere in the back of her rational brain, she knew it wasn't the world, it was her. But her eyes and her senses were feeding her brain mixed messages.

She gripped the steering wheel like a lifeline and fought for control, but nothing stopped the endless silent spinning. There was nothing to steer—her wheels weren't touching the ground.

The front of her car sideswiped the guardrail, throwing all her weight forward into the seat and shoulder belts. Metallic screeching filled her ears as the car slid sideways along the rail.

She saw nothing except streaks—the world flying by. It looked like a time-lapse shot of a car race—red and black and blue blurry stripes. She closed her eyes. Soon she'd be weightless—flying—falling—dying.

Another bump, another earsplitting screech, then nothing.

Vaguely, distantly, Victoria heard the sound of sirens. She forced her eyes open and tried to make sense of what she saw.

Her brain fought the truth. Dizziness and nausea engulfed her. She blinked again and again, but the reality didn't change. Relentlessly, cruelly, it taunted her with the truth laid out in front of her. She was looking down at the bottom of a cliff. The seat belt bit into her flesh. Her neck hurt. Echoes of screeching metal still filled her ears.

What she saw couldn't be real, could it?

She cut her eyes to the side, trying not to move, and saw a curled piece of galvanized metal. It looked like a used sardine-can lid. It was the guardrail.

Suddenly, whatever part of her brain controlled her balance rebelled at what her eyes saw. Her world began to spin again, and nausea burned in her throat. She closed her eyes, but it didn't help.

Her car was tipped precariously over the edge of a precipice and every few seconds it creaked and teetered.

Her throat ached with the need to scream. Her stomach clenched with panic. She dared not move, hardly dared to breathe. One deep breath, one tiny shift in position could upset the tenuous balance and send her crashing dozens of feet to the ground.

Somewhere behind her a car's engine roared and a muffled yell rang out. It was him! The man who'd forced her off the road. He was coming to finish her off.

She gasped, and pain sliced through her chest. Dear heavens, that hurt! She carefully tested her arms and legs by moving them slightly.

More pain.

She held her breath as she did a mental inventory. Head—pounding. Chest—shrieking pain with each breath. Arms and legs—tingling.

She tentatively peeked down at herself. She didn't see any blood. That was good. Wasn't it?

Or was it? No blood didn't mean no injuries. Her tummy and chest ached. Her head pounded, and all she could think about was that if her car tilted another inch, she'd plunge to her death without seeing Brody again.

She became aware of more noise. Suddenly the dark world around her was awash with light. She squinted. The light hurt her eyes.

More shouts and a loud roar that sounded bigger than a car engine.

Victoria tried to turn her head and look behind her, but when she did metal screeched in protest and she felt her world tilt a little more off center.

Brody! "Get Brody," she screamed, but her brain knew that the sound coming out of her mouth was nothing more than a whisper.

"Hang on, lady! Don't move!"

She lifted her head. Had someone said something to her? A trickle of warmth tickled her cheek. She peeled her fingers off the wheel and touched the itchy place.

Blood. It was blood. She *was* injured. Fear sliced through her. Was it better to plunge down a mountain or bleed to death? Either way, she wasn't going to make it.

Her chin dropped to her chest. She was so tired. Maybe she'd just close her eyes and rest for a few moments.

"Ma'am? Miss Kirkland? Can you hear me? Don't move, just speak."

"I can hear you," she whispered. "Who are you? Are you here to kill me?"

"No, ma'am."

Her head ached and it hurt her chest to talk. If he wasn't going to kill her, what was he doing here?

"Go away." If she took a nap, surely Brody would be there when she woke up. "I'm waiting for Brody."

"Ma'am, can you tell me who you are?"

"Of course I can."

"Ma'am?"

Why was he bothering her? "Call Brody," she said drowsily.

"First tell me your name." His voice was young, very young.

She lifted her head and frowned. Her name. "Vic. It's Victoria."

"That's good. Victoria what?"

"Um…Kirkland. Who are you?"

"I'm one of the EMTs, Ms. Kirkland. Are you hurt anywhere? Bleeding?"

"Just my head."

"Nothing else? Your legs? Can you feel them? Can you wiggle your toes?"

"Yes, I already checked. But my chest hurts. Can you help me out of here?"

"Hold on, ma'am. Don't move just yet. We need you to wait just a little while. We need to make sure the car is steady before we extract you. So can you sit still for me? Help me keep the car steady?"

"Steady. Slow and steady wins the race."

"That's right. Now we're going to attach a chain to the frame of your car. The car will probably move, but don't worry. We'll have you. You'll be okay. And stay still!"

The end of his sentence was drowned out by the sudden, discordant sound of metal against metal.

"No!" she screamed. "No!" The ground below her and the darkening sky above dipped and soared. She braced herself. Any second the car would tilt forward and plunge down the cliff.

"Ms. Kirkland?" a different voice said. "Are you awake?"

"Yes," she mumbled. "The car's going over, isn't it?"

"Not right now. I'm Pete Chaney, Ms. Kirkland. I'm the fire chief. We've got the chain around your rear axle, and I need you to help me with something."

"All you guys need my help, don't you?"

Victoria heard Pete Chaney chuckle, and she wondered what was so funny.

"Yes, ma'am. We can't do it without you. Now, I've got a fireman here who needs to put a belt around you."

Victoria tried to open her eyes, but the lights were bright and she was getting really tired. "I've got a belt around me. I always wear my seat belt."

The voice got closer. It was a deep voice, strong. Not as deep or strong as Brody's, but close. "Here's the fireman. His name's Dave."

"Hi, Victoria. People call you Vicky?"

"No. People call me Victoria." She smiled. "Brody calls me Vic."

"Okay then, Victoria. I need to cut your seat belt so it doesn't get in our way."

"I need my seat belt."

"I'm going to give you a better one, okay? It slips under your arms and over your shoulders."

"Like yours?"

"Exactly like mine. We want to make sure we hang on to you. I promise it will only take a minute."

Victoria felt his warm hands on her. "Are you getting into the car?"

"No." His voice sounded a little strained. "I've got to do this without touching the car, and you need to stay perfectly still. Let me move your arms, okay? You just go limp."

He touched her left arm. "Don't stiffen up, Victoria. We're almost done."

The next thing Victoria knew, the man was gone and the fire chief was talking to her again.

"Hi, Ms. Kirkland. You're all harnessed up. Now comes the scary part. We're going to haul the car up. It's going to be loud and really scary, so I need you to be very brave. Can you do that?"

"Where's Brody? Did somebody call him?"

"Lieutenant McQuade called us. He's on his way." Chaney turned.

"Where are you going? You're not leaving me here, are you?"

"No, ma'am. I'm just going to wait over there while my guys do their job. It'll just be a couple of minutes. Remember, we've got a big chain around your car and a harness around you. If everything goes perfectly, you and the car will be back on solid ground in no time, safe and sound."

Victoria nodded, praying he was right, praying that her car wouldn't break apart, praying Brody would hurry up and get there.

She heard a monstrous engine roar. Less than a second later, the bottom fell out of her world.

The car plunged forward, throwing her back against the seat and slamming her head against the headrest.

The fireman had lied to her. She was going to die.

Chapter Nine

The first thing Brody saw was Victoria's car slipping over the precipice. The noise was deafening as the chain attached to her rear axle creaked and strained. The rescue vehicle's engine roared as it worked to pull the Lexus backward, away from the cliff.

Sick horror closed Brody's throat. Was she still in there?

He leaped out of his Jeep and barreled through the circle of police and fire vehicles.

Dear God, hold on to her, he prayed.

At that instant a metallic clang echoed through the air. The massive chain snapped like a rubber band. It catapulted backward, missing one of the firemen by inches.

The Lexus teetered on the edge of the precipice, grating against the shredded guardrail.

"Vic! No!" His voice broke. He hurtled toward the car as panic and desperation burned through him. *You can't die. Not you, too.*

Brody slammed into a rock—that's what it felt like. Pete Chaney grabbed him just as the shriek of metal against metal split the air and Victoria's Lexus tipped forward and slid over the edge of the limestone bluff.

Brody froze, unspeakable pain searing every cell of his body. A raw, wordless cry ripped past his throat. Then he shoved Chaney, doubling his fists. "Let go of me! Bastard!"

"McQuade, she's not in there!"

The fire chief's voice echoed in his brain but the words made no sense. He broke Chaney's grip and stumbled.

"She's safe!" Chaney shouted.

Safe? Safe. It took a second for the word to make sense. He whirled around, his stomach churning with adrenaline. "What? Where?"

"Over there. They're putting her in the ambulance now. We extracted her through the driver's window."

Brody's tense muscles shivered in relief. His eyes stung. His throat spasmed. He covered the distance to the ambulance in two long strides.

"Hold it!" he croaked.

They stopped.

He saw a small shape under a sheet. "Vic?"

One of the EMTs looked up. "Are you Lieutenant McQuade?"

"Yes," he snapped, as he swiped a hand over his damp face, a hand that shook. "Texas Ranger. Victoria Kirkland is in our protective custody. I need to see her."

"We're taking her to County General. You can ride with her if you like."

Brody glanced over at his vehicle.

Chaney walked up beside him. "I can have someone take your car in for you."

Brody nodded, and climbed into the ambulance beside Vic's gurney. He met Chaney's eye. "Chief, I'm—"

Chaney touched the brim of his hat. "Don't mention it, Lieutenant. Just doing our job." As Chaney pushed the ambulance door closed, Brody nodded his head in thanks, then turned his attention back to Victoria.

Her eyes were closed and her mouth and nose were covered by an oxygen mask.

His heart leaped into his throat and lodged there. She looked so small and vulnerable. So breakable. He wanted to cradle her in his arms and promise her that nothing bad would ever happen to her again. But that would be a lie and Rangers didn't lie.

As the ambulance started up, Brody dug his cell phone out of his pants pocket, dismayed to notice that his fingers still shook. He pressed a familiar number.

"I need you back here."

"Dammit, Brody. Can't you take care of anything yourself?"

Brody knew Egan was just being his usual cranky self. He also knew he was joking, but Brody didn't have time for it. "Egan, listen to me."

His friend stopped grousing. "What's the matter?"

"Vic's car was forced off the road. She almost went over. I'm going to the hospital with her. I want you to process her car. If there's one speck of paint on it that doesn't belong, I want it."

"Crap! She okay?"

Brody looked at her. The delicate skin around her eyes looked bruised. Her skin seemed stretched too tightly across her cheekbones. And her hands were clenched into fists.

"Brody?"

"I don't know. I hope so."

Egan was silent for a fraction of a second. "What about you?"

"What about me?" He heard the edge to his voice.

"Yeah, well…nothing. I'll be there in a couple of hours."

"Make it one, Caldwell."

"You got it."

Brody pocketed his phone. The EMT sitting beside the gurney gently removed the oxygen mask from Victoria's face. When he did her eyes fluttered open.

Brody took her hand in his. He tenderly opened her fist, then ran his thumb across the half-circle imprints of fingernails on her palm.

"Br-Brody?"

"Hey, Vic. You had an adventure, but you're okay." He had a sudden, overwhelming urge to clear his throat.

"Where am I?"

"In an ambulance. We're taking you to the hospital, to get you checked out. How're you feeling?"

Her green eyes flashed with panic. "He ran me off…off the road. I couldn't get away. I couldn't make the car go fast enough."

"It's okay, Vic." Brody squeezed her hand. "You're safe now."

Her fingers squeezed his weakly. "I thought I was going to die. I was afraid you wouldn't come."

He lifted her hand and kissed her knuckles. "I swear on everything that's holy, Vic, I will always be there for you." Even as he said it, he knew he was lying.

It was a promise he couldn't make good on. He was a Texas Ranger and she was…she was Victoria Kirkland. After this case was over, he had no reason to ever see her again.

But Vic's pale face lit up and a little smile curled her lips. "Always," she whispered.

Brody put her hand down on top of the sheet that covered her. He patted it awkwardly. "You're safe. And I promise we'll find whoever did this. Could you see anything?"

Her gaze never left his. She shook her head. "The car was dark, maybe blue. The windows were tinted."

She closed her eyes and tried to moisten her dry lips. The EMT took her blood pressure and checked her pulse.

Then her fingers tightened convulsively around the sheet. "Brody?"

"Yeah?"

She opened her eyes and he saw that they glittered with dampness. "I'm so sorry. I swore I was going to be brave."

"You were. You are." He took a deep breath. "I'm the one who should apologize. I never should have let you out of my sight."

BACK AT THE COUNTRY club, Brody stopped the car and ran around to the passenger side. Victoria already had the door open.

"Hang on," he said. "I'll help you."

"Brody, I can walk. I'm not hurt." She wasn't sure she liked him like this—hovering, worried, acting as if he thought she'd break.

"Yeah? Those stitches above your right eye say otherwise."

She swung her legs out and started to stand, but pain from the massive bruise that ran from her left shoulder to her right hip surprised her. She gasped and tumbled back into the seat.

"See? There was a reason they brought you out to the car in a wheelchair."

"Right. The usual reason. They don't want a patient to fall on their way out of a hospital. Big lawsuit. Big money." She tried the standing-up thing again. But before she even managed to get upright, Brody was there, his arm around her waist.

"Spoken like an attorney," he murmured close to her ear.

A thrill slashed through her, weakening her knees. She was still spooked by her brush with death, but apparently Brody had the power to wipe the terror from her mind and replace it with lust. No, not lust.

It wasn't lust. It was probably gratitude and relief at being rescued.

"You don't have to help me."

"Indulge me," he said, his low voice rumbling through her. He held on to her and guided her up the steps and into the main reception room of the country club.

"I can walk by myself."

"You're groggy. The doctor gave you a tranquilizer."

"I don't remember taking anything."

"It was while you were in the ambulance."

Brody unlocked the door to the conference complex and guided her inside. He took her straight back to his suite and into his bedroom. "Can you change clothes by yourself?"

"Of course I can. You're acting as if I'd broken something."

"Vic, you almost plunged over a cliff. That drop would have killed you. You have a right to be scared and hurt. You have a right to depend on someone else. The doctor told me that between your seat belt and the rescue harness you've got a bruise the size of Oklahoma from your shoulder to your hip."

His gaze slid down her torso like healing fingers, leaving her skin sensitized and hot. Then his eyes snapped to her face.

Could he feel her response to him? She blinked and looked down at her hands, which were clasped in front of her.

All she wanted was to strip off her sweaty, wrinkled clothes and climb into bed. To feel the cool sheets against her burning body. To fall asleep feeling safe and protected.

She closed her eyes and took a deep breath. Brody's rain-fresh scent floated past her nostrils, weakening her knees.

"Whoa," Brody said, and suddenly she was enveloped in his strong arms, shielded against his broad chest. She felt the strong, steady beat of his heart against her palm.

"Vic, you're asleep on your feet. Let me get you into bed."

As he said it, she realized that was exactly what she wanted—for Brody to take her to bed. It had been over a year since her fiancé had died. She'd hardly dated—she certainly hadn't slept with anyone.

But Brody was all wrong for her. No, she was all wrong for him. She was too tired to think, but she knew somebody was all wrong for somebody.

"I think I need a bath," she murmured. "I'm filthy."

She felt a soft rumbling in his chest. It almost pushed aside the sleepy haze that enveloped her. Was Brody McQuade laughing?

"Yeah, you're all stinky," he muttered.

"Just point me to the bathroom and I'll be fine."

"There's no way I'm letting you get into that tub by yourself."

Victoria smiled at his choice of words. "You're going to get in with me?"

He turned red.

The sight of his cheeks blazing with color wiped a lot of the drowsiness from Victoria's brain.

"No," he snapped. "I'm going to sit you down on the side of the tub and give you what my foster mother used to call a spit bath."

He wrapped an arm around her waist and guided her into

the bathroom and sat her down on the wide edge of the spa tub. Then he started unbuttoning her blouse. His fingers, so much larger than hers, fumbled with the tiny pearl buttons.

"I'll do it," she said. "Just run some hot water. There are washcloths on the back of the toilet."

"I know. This is my room, remember?"

Brody set the stopper and ran hot water into the lavatory. He immersed a soft, white washcloth and squeezed it out, then lathered it with a miniature bar of glycerin soap. When he turned around, Vic had shed her blouse and pants. She sat on the edge of the tub in nothing but her bra and panties, and not much of them.

An ugly red-and-purple bruise ran from her left shoulder down across her midsection to her right hip. There were smaller matching blotches on her shoulders and upper arms.

His imagination fed him a horrifying image—Victoria, jerked like a rag doll through the window of her Lexus as the vehicle balanced crazily on the edge of the limestone cliff.

He cursed, lengthily and inventively.

Victoria's eyes widened and she spread a hand across her chest.

He pushed her hands aside and brushed the tips of his fingers over her damaged skin. "Dammit. This is my fault. I am so sorry, Vic. I didn't protect you."

She put a finger against his lips, and it was all he could do not to pull her to him and kiss every bruised millimeter of her body.

"Don't, Brody," she said. "You can't be everywhere. You warned me to be careful, and you told me to come straight home. It was my fault. I stayed and signed papers."

Would she have been safe if she'd followed his instructions? He'd like to believe she would have, but he had a sick feeling that whoever was after her was becoming bolder—or more desperate. Obviously the driver of the dark car had followed her. Had he waited all day for her to leave?

But tonight wasn't the time to remind her of how close she'd come to death.

Brody squeezed out the washcloth. Carefully, doing his best to avoid touching any intimate area, he washed her. From her dust- and tear-streaked face, down her delicately curved neck, across her bruised shoulders and down her arms, back to the tops of her breasts and her tummy, and the length of her thighs, the curve of her calves and the turn of her ankles and feet.

By the time he'd finished, he'd broken every last promise he'd made to himself. He'd touched the tops of her breasts and seen them tighten under the flimsy fabric of her bra. He'd seen—hell, he'd *lingered* on—the V formed by her pale, lacy panties. He'd run his hand, covered only by the square of terry cloth, up her inner thighs and nearly lost it when he saw her thigh muscles contract in response to his touch.

He'd ended up sporting a painful, throbbing hard-on there was no way in hell he could disguise. But to be fair, he'd been doomed from the start. When it came to Victoria, there wasn't a millimeter of skin that wasn't sexy.

"Okay," he croaked, tossing the cloth into the lavatory and standing. "I hope you feel better…" He left the rest of the sentence unsaid. There was no doubt in his mind that she knew the state he was in. But if she didn't say anything, he could escape with at least a smidgen of his dignity still intact.

He headed for the door. "I'll let you change clothes, and then you can go to bed."

Victoria had never been treated so gently, so reverently, in her life. It was that unbearable tenderness that Brody only exhibited when they were alone.

He'd made love to her body with that washcloth, and all her aches and fears had melted away in a sensual awareness of the thing between them. The thing that breathed dragon's fire through her down to the center of her sexuality.

She reached out and caught his arm.

He turned.

"Brody, don't leave."

He opened his mouth to protest, but she stopped him. She stood on tiptoe and kissed the side of his neck.

He ducked his head for an instant, then put his hand around the nape of her neck and kissed her forehead—not a quick good-night-sleep-well kiss.

His lips lingered on her skin like a lover's, and their touch swept through her like a whirlwind. She couldn't suppress a tiny moan. She lifted her hand and slid her fingers through his collar-length hair.

He raised his head, meeting her gaze with a questioning look. Then he lowered his mouth to hers. His lips and tongue explored hers thoroughly, intimately, in an imitation of love-making that stoked the fire he'd ignited.

Feeling Brody's arms enveloping her, his chest rising and falling with his rapid, steady breaths, energized her and tit-illated her.

For a few seconds he stood there, his nose pressed into her hair, one hand cradling the back of her head. She felt his erection pressing insistently, declaring his need for her.

She doubled her fists, catching and wrinkling his shirt. "Brody?" she whispered.

He lifted his head. "Vic…"

"Do *not* tell me not to get the wrong idea," she said. "I don't have the wrong idea. I have the *right* idea, and I *know* you do too." She ground her pelvis against his erection in case he had any doubt whatsoever about just exactly what she meant.

He tensed. "This is impossible. I can't do it."

"I'm pretty sure it's not impossible." She smiled at him.

He grabbed her upper arms and set her away from him. "I can't hide how much you turn me on, but I can't give in to it. You're in my protective custody. I can't take advantage of that."

"You've never once told anyone I was in *your* custody. You've always said the *Rangers'* protective custody."

"It's no different."

Victoria nodded. "You must have thought something would happen. Otherwise why make the distinction?"

He shrugged and looked away. "I needed everyone to understand that Egan and Hayes were just as responsible for you as I am."

"Brody…" She lifted her head and stood on tiptoe again. For an instant he strained away, trying to resist. But finally he bent his head so her mouth was near his ear. "Why do you call me *Vic?* Another attempt to distance yourself from me?"

His head snapped up. "Distance? No." He sounded genuinely bewildered.

"Then why?"

"I don't know. It fits."

She reached up to put her arms around his neck, and her sore muscles screamed in protest. She bit her lip.

"What's wrong?" Brody's brows drew down. "It's your shoulder, isn't it? See, you're too sore. I need to put you to bed."

She touched his mouth. "No. Don't put me to bed. *Take* me to bed."

"This is a big mistake," he muttered.

"I promise it isn't," she whispered back.

"You can't promise that. You don't understand all the ramifications."

"Of course I do. Want me to draw up a disclaimer?"

Irritation and something else flashed in his eyes and he took a step backward.

Victoria's stomach sank to the floor. She'd lost him with that last remark. It was probably for the best. He was right.

He'd be violating the code of any lawman, especially a Texas Ranger. Even though she'd only known him for three days, she knew upholding that honor was the cornerstone of his life.

"I'm sorry, Brody. I appreciate everything you've done. I didn't mean to make light of it—or of you." To her chagrin her voice broke on those last words. Her throat suddenly felt clogged with tears. She was going to cry.

Damn. Not in front of him. She turned away.

"Hey." He caught her arm. "Are you okay?"

She nodded, swallowing hard and blinking.

He stepped in front of her. "You're crying."

"No, I'm not." She wouldn't look at him. She wasn't one of those delicate, lovely, movie-star criers. When she cried her eyes got red immediately, her nose ran, and her cheeks grew blotchy. It wasn't a pretty sight. She took a deep breath.

"But I am tired." Good. Her voice was steady—sort of.

"Vic, it's okay to cry. You've been through a lot these past few days. Especially today."

"I don't cry." There went her nose. She sniffled and looked around for a tissue, but her eyes were growing blurry.

Brody stuck a handkerchief in her hand. She took it gratefully and blew her nose and wiped her eyes. "I'm sorry," she said with a short laugh. "I must have been more shaken by the accident than I thought I was."

Without speaking, Brody pulled her into his arms and cradled the back of her head. "Sure you were. And it was no accident."

Victoria's shoulders tightened at his words. She nodded against his shirt. "I know. Do you think you can find him?"

"I've already got Egan on it. He's processing your car. If the other car even grazed it, we'll get a paint sample that we can compare to the one on Caroline's car."

Victoria looked up at him and caught an odd expression on his face. His velvety black eyes searched hers. She just stood there, mesmerized, as he slowly lowered his head and pressed a kiss to her forehead.

It was a comforting kiss. A polite kiss. Certainly not the kiss of a lover—not this time. And yet it sent a sexual thrill through her. She slipped her arms around his waist and moved closer. The feel of him growing harder against her gave her courage to throw aside her inhibitions and take what she wanted.

She ought to respect his position, ought to accept that he didn't want to be distracted by sex. She ought to consider how angry he was going to be later if she succeeded in urging him to give in. But her body was alive with need—not just sexual. She needed his strength and craved the comfort of being surrounded by him, filled by him.

She kissed the side of his neck again and slid her palms up his back, feeling his hard planed muscles. Her pulse raced. She didn't know if it was from fear or excitement.

He pulled away.

"Brody, don't."

"Don't what?" he muttered. "Don't listen to my conscience? Don't remind myself that I'm a Texas Ranger and you're under my protection? Don't stop this before it goes too far?"

She put her fingers over his mouth. "Shh." Then she rose on tiptoe to kiss his mouth.

He lifted his head and put his hands on her shoulders. She braced herself, expecting him to push her away.

He thought about it—she could tell from the tensing of his forearms and the determination in his face. But instead of setting her aside and walking out, he held on to her shoulders and lowered his mouth to hers.

Victoria's insides went liquid and hot as he deepened the kiss and urged her mouth open with his tongue. She'd never experienced anything like his kiss. Unlike the last time he'd kissed her, he didn't stop and turn away. He kept going.

He stole her breath away with his firm, demanding mouth, his hot, delectable tongue, and the unmistakable promise of his erection pressing urgently against her as he pulled her into his arms.

"God help me," he whispered, his breath warming her lips. "Because obviously you're not going to."

Chapter Ten

Victoria could tell by the hardening of Brody's jaw that he was struggling with his conscience, his sense of duty and honor.

Part of her wanted his Ranger side to win. At least then she wouldn't be saddled with the guilt of compromising his principles. If he didn't stop himself, she knew she wasn't going to stop him. She couldn't. She wanted him too badly.

He flipped off the light and quickly shed his clothes.

When she saw his naked body backlit by the bathroom light, she had to suppress a gasp. He was less bulky than he looked in clothes, lean and toned and sexier than she'd imagined.

His long, sleek body was as perfectly toned as a swimmer's. The muscles of his arms and legs were smooth and well-defined, covered by golden skin that was paler on his torso and thighs.

He didn't waste time. He slid into bed beside her and pulled her close. She ran her fingers up his arms, touching his rock-hard biceps. "You're so beautiful," she whispered.

"Hey." He chuckled. "That's my line."

She shifted so her thighs rubbed against his. His erection pulsed against her belly and she gasped.

He froze. "Are you okay?"

"Yes." She sighed. "I just can't believe how wonderful, how beautiful you feel." She touched him.

He groaned quietly and pushed her hand away. "Don't. You don't know how close I am…"

She caught his hand and pressed it against her belly. "I know how close I am."

He kissed her and spread his fingers on her rounded belly, then slid his palm up her waist to her breasts. He undid the front clasp of her bra, tossing it aside, then he touched each breast, tracing its shape with his fingers, then dipping his head and drawing the puckered nipple into his mouth. He suckled on it until it stood taut and fiery red with sensation.

Victoria felt the gentleness of his touch as he skimmed her bruised flesh. He was so sweet, his fingers so tender and gentle—too gentle.

"I'm not made of porcelain, Brody. I won't break."

"But look at you," he growled. "Look at your skin. I don't want to hurt you."

"Listen to me, Lieutenant." Victoria put her lips on his and spoke against his mouth. "I'll be ten times as sore tomorrow morning, so please don't make me wake up frustrated, too."

He raised his head, his eyes as dark and bottomless as a pot of bitter chocolate. "You need to stop me."

In answer, Victoria wrapped her fingers around him and squeezed, until he groaned with pleasure.

"Vic!" His buttocks tightened and he strained toward her. "Be careful!"

Victoria bent her head and touched the tip of her tongue to his flat nipple, feeling it pebble under her mouth. She teased it with her teeth, then bent farther and ran her tongue along the hard ridges of his abdomen, then she moved lower.

"Ah, Vic, don't. If you keep that up, it'll be all over."

He grabbed her arms and pulled her to him, taking her mouth in a deep, erotic kiss. Then he set her back against the stack of pillows at the headboard and moved in front of her on his knees.

"What are you doing?" she panted.

"I don't intend to cause you any pain, just pleasure."

"Thank you," she whispered as he peeled her bikini panties down and off, then spread her legs and settled her so that her legs draped over his thighs.

Then he touched her, caressing and massaging the nub at the center of her being until she was moaning with pleasure and need. She felt liquid flow, felt her own slickness as he probed with his fingers, searching for the center of all her sensation.

And when he found it, she arched and curled as he gave her release. Then he wrapped his arms around her and kissed her.

Just when she thought she was drained of all sensation, he pushed into her, opening her more fully than she'd ever been opened, pushing more deeply than she thought possible, touching a point of ecstasy that no one had ever uncovered before.

He flattened his palm on her belly and slowly slid his hand downward until it pressed on her mound. She was boneless, completely at his mercy. He continued to move inside her as his fingers brought her to another, higher pinnacle of pleasure.

She moaned as her body strained toward the two equally erotic sensations—his erection pulsing inside her and his fingers driving her crazy. "Brody, please…"

But he didn't stop. He caressed and probed until her climax took her.

He threw his head back and growled as he thrust deeply into her. She caught his rhythm and met each stroke, taking all that he gave her until he hit yet another magical point.

She lost control as he found his own release. He pushed into her hard, again and again, intensifying her ecstasy.

Finally, when Victoria didn't think she had the energy to breathe, much less move, Brody pulled her into his arms and cradled her head against his shoulder. He ran his fingers up and down her curved spine and pressed his cheek against her hair.

"Vic, you okay?"

She nodded against the silk-over-steel smoothness of his skin. It took her a minute to find her voice.

"I'm fine." There was no way she could tell him just how fine she was. Brody McQuade had taken her further than she'd ever been before. He was strong and forceful, yet somehow gentler than any man she'd ever been with. The combination was a huge turn-on.

He eased off her and turned to lean back against the pillows. She laid her head on his shoulder again.

"You call me Vic," she murmured. "I've never had a nickname before. Nobody ever called me Vicky or Tory or anything like that. Not even my mother. Well, my grandpa called me Toto when I was little."

A soft chuckle rumbled in his chest, and he kissed her on the nose. "Go to sleep," he whispered. "You're half there already."

He slid his arm out from under her head, sat up and threw the covers aside.

"Where are you going?"

"I've got a few things I need to recheck, and I need to make arrangements to interview all our major suspects, see if they have an alibi for this—that is, yesterday—evening."

By the time he finished the sentence, his voice had turned harsh, and he didn't look at her.

"Brody? Are we okay?"

He didn't move for a moment, then finally he raised his gaze to hers. His dark eyes were still soft, but as she watched, they turned stone cold.

She sat up, pulling the sheet with her to cover her breasts. "Brody?"

"I don't know, Vic," he said, shaking his head. "I just don't know."

BRODY PULLED ON PANTS and left the bedroom. He pushed his fingers through his hair, grimacing. What the hell was he going to do now?

His pulse was still racing and his body was still tingling with the adrenaline rush of climax. The thought of Vic, languid and supple in his arms, her green eyes shining, sent a current of renewed lust rippling through him.

Calling himself some very rude names, he stalked across the small sitting room. He needed a bottle of cold water— maybe to drink, maybe to douse his head with.

He jerked open the door to the conference room and nearly ran smack into Egan.

"Whoa, Brody."

Great. He could hope Egan wouldn't pick up on what he'd been doing, but in his gut he knew his fellow Ranger was too sharp to miss it. He pushed past him with an aggressiveness that wasn't warranted.

"Hey!"

Egan grabbed his arm, but Brody shrugged him off and kept going. When he straightened from grabbing a bottle of water out of the refrigerator, the surly Ranger sergeant was right there.

"What's going on? You're throwing your weight around like a pissed-off bear."

Brody glared at him and pushed past him again. He took a big swig of water and wiped his face. The water cooled him down—a little. But dammit, the last thing he needed right now was Egan crawling his butt.

He turned and did what he did best. Turned a poor defense into a good offense. "What the hell are you doing here?"

Egan frowned. "You called and ordered me back here just a few hours ago. What the hell's wrong with…" Then his face changed.

His brows shot up and his mouth dropped open in shock. After a couple of grueling seconds of stunned silence, Egan glanced back at the door to Brody's suite.

Brody took another gulp of water and steeled himself for the explosion. It didn't take long.

"Son of a— Is Victoria in there? What the hell have you done?" Egan got in his face. "Are you out of your ever-loving mind?"

"Take a step back, Caldwell."

"Yeah. You should've taken that advice yourself." Egan threw up his hands. "I can't believe…I'd never have thought…damn!"

Egan was speechless. If Brody had been in the mood, his friend's reaction might have been funny. But Brody was *not* in the mood.

"What are you going to do now?"

Brody shrugged and then finished his water. He stalked across the room and threw the empty bottle into the trash can. Hell if he knew.

He'd screwed up royally.

"Where was your head?" Egan slapped the mahogany table with his palm. "Don't answer that. I know where it was."

Brody took a deep breath and hoped what he was about to do wasn't insane. If it was, he was sure Egan would let him know. "Nothing's going to change. Tonight was a…an aberration. She could have died. She was scared."

"So you thought you'd give her the *cure?*"

Anger set sparks exploding in front of Brody's eyes. He made a fist and took a step forward, but Egan just lifted his chin.

"Really?" Egan growled. "You're actually going to try that?"

Brody flexed his fingers and cursed. "It won't happen again. She's still in my protective custody. And, Caldwell, if you even *think* about this when you see her…well, just don't."

"Don't worry. I won't embarrass *her.*"

Egan met his gaze and Brody saw a look of disdain on his face. He felt like the world's biggest heel. He crossed his arms and waited to hear what else Egan had to say.

"Wow, Brody." The younger man looked stunned. He shook his head. "You're the last man on earth I'd have believed would get involved with a victim. Ever since we were kids, I thought you were a damned *saint*. But you're just as horny and lowdown as the rest of us."

Brody winced internally. He didn't need Egan to tell him what a jerk he was. If Egan was shocked by his actions, Brody himself was staggered—and outraged. This case was the most important one he'd ever worked. It was for Kimmie.

Ah, hell. That must be the problem. His feelings were too close to the surface. The case was too personal. Well, he'd just have to work that much harder to keep his feelings out of it. Personal agendas had no place in a criminal investigation.

"Brody? What now?"

Brody sucked in renewed determination with a long breath. "What now? What now is nothing's changed. What'd you find on Vic's car?"

"Not much. Impound was anxious to take it away. I'm going down there first thing in the morning."

Brody scowled. "You do that. There's got to be paint from the other vehicle on it somewhere. I want that paint ID'd."

"And you? What are you going to do?"

"I'm going to carry on as if nothing's changed." Brody cleared his throat. "Nothing *has* changed."

Egan shook his head and turned on his heel. "I'm going to bed."

BRODY WOKE UP IN A cold sweat. He'd dreamed that Victoria was teetering on the edge of a cliff as a dark shadow slithered around her. She was screaming his name, but he couldn't get to her. The shadow was blocking him. Then it curled around her and she fell.

He sat up and wiped his face. Damn, he almost never remembered his dreams. But this one involved Victoria. Pushing himself up off the couch, he snagged his cell phone on the way out of his sitting room. He pounded on Egan's door, but the empty cup on the counter and the hollow sound of his knuckles on the metal door told him the Ranger sergeant was already gone.

Brody speed-dialed Hayes with his left hand as he reached into the fridge and grabbed an orange juice with his right. He downed the juice, and still Hayes's phone rang.

Growling in frustration, he slammed open the door to his sitting room just in time to see his bedroom door open.

Victoria came out, dressed in black pants, white top and a black-and-white-print sweater. Since it was summer and the temperature outside was well over ninety, he figured the sweater was to hide the bruises on her shoulder.

When she looked at him, her expression was carefully

neutral, but bright spots in her cheeks told him she wasn't as comfortable with what had happened the night before as she was pretending to be.

He blinked, trying to rid his brain of the image of her falling wrapped in shadow. "I thought you didn't have but one pair of black pants," he said.

"I picked up a few things when I was at the condos talking to Amanda Winger. Tammy Sutton called and invited me out for brunch." She lifted her chin a fraction.

"Is Kenneth Sutton going, too?"

"Yes. Do I have permission?"

Tammy and Kenneth Sutton. He'd already sized them up as single-mindedly ambitious, both of them. But were they murderers? He thought about Kimmie's phone call on the night she was killed. The call that could have saved her life, if he'd answered it.

Her voice on his voice mail had been choked with tears. *Brody? Why aren't you answering your cell phone? Call me. I'm at Taylor Landis's party. I need to talk to you. Mr. Sutton is probably going to fire me. I'm afraid he's really mad. Call me.*

He wished like hell he could refuse to let Victoria go, but she was probably almost as safe with the chairman of the city board and his wife as with Brody. Even if Sutton were behind the murders, he wouldn't dare risk his position by allowing something to happen to Victoria while she was out in public with him.

"I didn't realize you were such good friends with them."

"I'm not, but Tammy has been nice since all this happened. She's called me several times to do something with her, and I've turned her down every time. I'd prefer not to turn her down again. She offered to pick me up."

"Don't talk about what happened."

Her green eyes snapped to his, and he knew what she was thinking.

"About the hit-and-run," he said.

"Are you kidding? Kenneth and Tammy probably knew about it yesterday evening."

"How?"

Victoria gave a little laugh and shook her head. "The mayor...the police chief...who knows? But nothing, and I mean *nothing,* goes on around here that Tammy doesn't know about."

"Tell them you have to be back here by two, because this afternoon I want to drive the Anderson Loop with you. I want you to talk me through everything that happened."

"Yes, *sir.*" She walked across the sitting room to the door.

He couldn't blame her for her aloof, sarcastic response. He deserved it. In a way her attitude was a relief. She obviously regretted their...aberration as much as he did.

Still, she was pale and he could tell by the way she was moving that she was sore from her bruises.

"Vic, are you okay?"

She shot him an ironic glance. "Sure. I'm fine."

"If anything happens, *anything,* call me right away."

"With Tammy and Kenneth?" She laughed.

He caught her arm. "Kenneth Sutton said something to my sister on the night she was killed, something that upset her. Don't underestimate him."

"I knew she was upset. Everyone was talking about it. Are you saying Kenneth had something to do with the hit-and-run? He and Tammy were still at the party."

"I'm not dismissing *anybody,* not even if they have an ironclad alibi."

"I'll be careful."

"Keep your eyes and ears open, too." He let go of her arm before she could pull away.

BRODY SPENT THE MORNING reinterviewing the employees who worked both at Cantara Gardens and at the country club. The club manager, Michael DeCalley, arranged for the employees to come to the conference suite one at a time. There were seven workers who divided their time between the condos and the country club. Most of them were less than helpful. Either they knew nothing or they were excellent actors. But one young Hispanic woman, obviously several months pregnant, was visibly nervous.

"Your name is Eleana?"

She nodded, rubbing her tummy. "Yes. Eleana Mondavi. I work in the kitchen. I make the desserts."

"What about the condos? What do you do over there?"

"I don't work at the condos."

Brody assessed her. She was frightened of something. He made himself relax in his chair. If he was stiff and uptight, she'd be less likely to open up to him. "Mr. DeCalley sent you to talk to me because you have duties both at the condos and here."

Eleana looked down at her tummy and rubbed it more vigorously. "The baby kicks a lot," she said apologetically.

"When is your baby due?"

"In November." She smiled at him. "Not long, and yet very long."

Brody nodded. "Why did Mr. DeCalley send you here to talk to me?"

"Oh. I deliver the correspondence between here and the condos. It's only in the afternoon, before I leave work. I usually take it on my way home."

"What time is that?"

"I leave here before six o'clock."

"And where do you take the correspondence?" Brody asked.

"I place it in a box next to the manager's—Mr. Patterson's—apartment door." Eleana ducked her head and clasped her hands.

"And that's the only place you go inside the condos?"

"Yes, sir."

"Have you ever let anybody in? Or let anybody use your card or key?"

"No, sir."

Her answer was too quick, and she looked away.

"Eleana, are you sure?"

She glanced up at him. "Well…"

Brody clenched his jaw, forcing himself to remain relaxed. "Yes?"

"A week ago, on Wednesday, Mr. Woodward, the tennis man, followed me in. I told him I couldn't let him in, that he should call Mr. Patterson, but he just pushed against me and walked in when I did. He said he was visiting his friend."

Wednesday, the night Victoria was attacked.

"Friend? Who did he say his friend was?"

"Miles, I think. I don't remember his last name."

Miles Landis. Taylor Landis's freeloading brother. Brody shuddered at the idea of Carlson and Miles putting their heads together. He made a note on the pad in front of him.

"Has Carlson Woodward done that before? Or has anyone else?"

Eleana's face closed down. She wasn't going to tell him more. She shook her head. "No. No one else. Please, sir, I must go."

Brody stood and held out a hand to help Eleana rise. "Thanks, Eleana. You've been very helpful."

He talked with a couple of others, but Eleana's revelation was the most information he got.

As soon as he was done with the employees, he called Detective Sergeant Deason. "Pull in Miles Landis and Carlson Woodward. I have a witness who puts Woodward in the condos on Wednesday, the evening Victoria was attacked. According to what he told her, he was there to visit Landis. See what you can scare out of them."

"Will do. Woodward doesn't have access to the condos, does he?"

"Not according to the manager. And there's no card in his name. I'd like to find out how often he's there and how he gets in. This time he followed an employee in."

Just as Brody hung up from talking to Deason, his cell phone rang. It was Hayes.

"Where the hell have you been?" he said without preamble as soon as he picked up the phone. "I need you back here right—"

"Brody!" Hayes's voice was sharp with excitement. "I found the humidor. I'm leaving the pawnshop now."

"Great! Good going, Hayes. Are you sure it's Byron Dalloway's?"

"Dalloway mentioned a nick in the back left corner. It's the same one."

Brody closed his eyes as relief washed over him like a cool shower. Maybe this was the break he needed. "I don't suppose the owner could tell you who brought it in?"

"The owner wasn't there. I talked to a kid. He didn't know diddly except that he wanted two hundred dollars for the dang thing. The owner's supposed to open up the shop tomorrow morning. I'm going back to talk to him."

"Okay. What kind of shape is it in? Please tell me it hasn't been polished."

"I don't know, it looks pretty shiny, but I bagged it and I'm on the way to the lab this afternoon. We'll get the lab guys on it first thing in the morning."

"I want to hear as soon as you talk to the shop owner. We need everything he's got on whoever brought it in. Are there surveillance tapes?"

"I've got 'em. What'd you need me back there for? Isn't Egan there?"

"Yeah. He's processing Vic's car."

"Her car? What for?"

Brody quickly filled Hayes in on Victoria's brush with death.

"Damn. What the hell's going on there?"

"I don't know, but I'm going to find out. Stay there until you have something from the lab. I want prints, and I want them to match the partials we got off Vic's neck. I'm ready to stop this guy, whoever he is."

"Me, too, Brody. Me, too."

Brody heard Hayes take a long breath. "Brody? Can I talk to you about something?"

"Is it urgent?"

"No."

"Then let it wait. That humidor is priority. Got it?"

For a second, Hayes didn't say anything. "Got it," he said finally.

Brody hung up. He rubbed his eyes, thinking about Kimmie's death and the two men who had died since. He looked at the whiteboard, scanning the list of people who had used their access cards on the night of Victoria's attack.

He walked over and picked up the marker and wrote Carlson Woodward underneath Victoria's list. Then he wrote Eleana Mondavi.

How many times had Carlson bullied his way into the condos—or charmed his way in? He remembered Vic talking about him and his private lessons.

Brody's gut clenched in disgust. He'd always considered Carlson the worst kind of slimeball. There was nothing he wouldn't put past the man. Not even murder.

The hall door opened and Victoria walked in.

"Have fun?" Brody growled. He hadn't intended to growl—it just came out that way because of his dark thoughts.

"Not really."

"I guess brunch turned into lunch and cocktail hour."

"Well, it wasn't a total waste of time. I did enjoy eavesdropping on Kenneth Sutton."

Brody sent her a glance. Her eyes sparkled and her cheeks glowed, and his double-crossing body leaped into action. He clenched his jaw and turned back to the board. "Yeah?"

"After lunch, while we were finishing our coffee, Link Hathaway came up."

Hathaway. "That must have been a powerhouse meeting." Between them, Hathaway and Sutton controlled much of the business in San Antonio.

"Tammy kept talking, but luckily I was facing Kenneth, so I took a page from your playbook."

"My playbook?"

She nodded. "I looked bored and impatient, nodded at Tammy, and did my best to read their lips."

"Well?"

"Link said something about bids, and Kenneth nearly bit his head off."

"Bids?" Brody's brain zeroed in on the voice mail he'd received from Kimberly the night of the party. Sutton had been upset with her about something. Could it have been bids? Kimmie had mentioned irregularities with bids before.

"I didn't hear much, but my guess is that they were talking about the sealed bids put in by contractors for the new city library."

"Just how important are these bids?"

Victoria shrugged. "Every large project the city takes on has to be opened for bids from private contractors. The city planning board handles them. For a project like the library, for instance, the revenue could be in the tens of millions."

"So if somebody tampered with the bids, that would be a big deal."

"We're talking fraud involving local and federal funds. So yes, a very big deal. Anyone caught tampering with sealed bids would be staring at years in prison."

"People have murdered for less."

Victoria met his gaze. "You're saying that Kenneth or Link could be behind Gary's and Trent's murders? And Kimberly's?"

"Sutton and Kimmie had an argument the night of Taylor Landis's party. She called me, really upset." He dropped his gaze and turned back to the whiteboard.

Victoria watched his back and shoulders curl inward. *Pain.* He looked as if he'd been punched in the stomach. She wanted to reach out, to touch his shoulder and offer him comfort, but she didn't dare. Brody didn't invite comfort. When he hurt, he bore it alone.

She tried to keep the conversation as businesslike as possible. "I know. I remember that from the questioning that night, and from Gary's trial. When you talked to Kimberly, did she mention bids?"

He shook his head. "I didn't talk to…"

He swiped a hand down his face and then stalked over to the refrigerator and grabbed a bottle of water.

Victoria watched his throat move as he downed the water. When the bottle was nearly empty, he poured the last of it into his hand and splashed it on his face.

Her heart twisted in sympathy. He couldn't talk about his sister. His grief was still too new, too raw, even after eight months. She understood. It had taken her months to get over the razor-sharp pain that cut through her heart when her fiancé died. And she'd had her granddad to talk to. He'd taught her a lot about dealing with grief and heartache.

It was a cinch Brody hadn't talked to anybody. She went to his side and placed a hand on his back. "Brody, if you want to talk, I'll listen."

He turned his head and looked at her. His black, stabbing eyes cut her in two. But what almost knocked her to her knees was the dampness—she knew it wasn't water. Brody McQuade had tears in his eyes.

It was a good start.

Victoria rubbed his back and didn't say anything else. He'd talk when he was ready. Meanwhile, she could be there for him.

He straightened and stepped away. His demeanor transformed. The sadness and vulnerability were gone and he was one hundred percent Texas Ranger. He stalked back over to the whiteboard.

"Kimmie told me weeks before that something was going on with bids. She didn't say what. But the night of the Christmas party, Sutton apparently got very upset with her." His voice was as cold as his eyes.

Victoria sat down at the conference table. She didn't know what to say.

"Did you see the argument?" he asked her. "See them talking? Anything?"

She shook her head. "I told the police—and you—everything I saw. I didn't know Kimberly that well. We'd spoken a few times. All I know is that Caroline and Kimberly left suddenly, everyone was whispering, and Trent came up to me and said it was probably time to leave."

"So you left *after* Caroline Stallings and Kimmie? But you got to the intersection before them."

"Right. I had to maneuver around Caroline's Vette to get out of Tyler's driveway. She and Kimberly were sitting in it, talking. By the time I got my car clear so we could leave, Trent came out. He'd been trying to talk Gary into going with us."

"Zelke." Disdain dripped from Brody's lips.

Victoria knew he blamed Zelke for Kimberly's death, and her for defending him. But the paint chips her forensic analyst had found proved that another car had hit the Vette before Zelke's did.

"Can you remember who was still at the party when you left?"

Victoria frowned. "You know, all this is in the police reports."

Brody nodded impatiently. "I know. But there's a whole lot of difference in reading it in a typed report and talking to an eyewitness. I'd like to hear your description of the evening."

That she understood. It was the same reason she liked to have two adversaries in her office at the same time. People often said more than they meant to. And everybody noticed more than they realized. Once someone felt comfortable enough to talk easily, it was possible to find out all sorts of things.

"There were so many people there," she said. "It was hot and muggy, so people were drifting in and out. I know Kenneth and Tammy were still there by the time we left. And Link Hathaway. Obviously Taylor, since it was her house, and her brother Miles, who managed to hang around the buffet table all night."

"You're sure about Sutton?"

"Yes, I am. When Trent told me that he'd yelled at one of his interns, I succumbed to curiosity and looked around. He was talking on the phone. Oh…"

Brody shot her a glance. "What?"

"Like I said, Kenneth was standing in a reading alcove, talking on the phone. He looked up so I turned away. That's when I saw Tammy. She was on the other side of the room, and she was talking on her cell phone, too. I remember wondering if they were talking to each other."

"Could they have been?"

Victoria shrugged. "I suppose so. But get this. Trent almost ran into Link Hathaway on his way to get me to leave. Link was also on his cell phone. Something had definitely happened."

Brody's black eyes snapped. "Or was about to."

Chapter Eleven

It was after eight by the time Victoria and Brody got back from driving the Anderson Loop. Brody had insisted that she recount every minute of her harrowing experience.

The sight of the peeled-back guardrail and scarred pavement rekindled the terror of teetering on the edge of the world, trapped inside a hot metal car that at any second could become a coffin.

She'd wanted to see her car, but Brody had refused. It was being processed, he'd said. It would serve no purpose for her to see it.

He'd made her stand at the edge of the guardrail while she described everything she remembered about the car that had forced her off the road. He'd grilled her with an aggressiveness that more befitted a crack trial lawyer. At least he'd held on to her and kept her from getting too close to the edge.

By the time he was done with her, Victoria was amazed at how much her subconscious mind recalled, even during the terrifying moments when she'd thought she was going to plunge to her death.

Brody had latched on to her memory of the one vehicle that had roared past her on the winding road. A red Ferrari. Now as he unlocked the door to the conference suite and stood back to let her precede him inside, he talked to Egan on the phone.

"So how many have you talked to?"

Victoria took off her shoes and gestured toward the bedroom, indicating she was going to take a shower.

Brody didn't even acknowledge her. "I know," he said into the phone. "Nineteen. How hard can it be to locate nineteen people in this city who own red Ferraris?"

She went into the bedroom and closed the door, then plopped down on the bed with a sigh. The day had been oppressively hot, one of those scorching days when even the sun going down hadn't helped. And Brody had stopped the car at least a hundred times—well, ten, anyhow—and forced her to walk with him up and down the searing pavement, looking for any small sign, a skid mark, a scrape, that might yield a clue to the vehicle that had run her off the road.

She'd pointed out the obvious—that the SAPD crime-scene unit had combed the area—but in typical Brody fashion, he double-checked every inch himself. And it paid off. He'd found a tiny fleck of blue paint wedged between two bits of concrete paving. He'd knelt down and fished out the minuscule chip with his pocket knife and put it into an evidence bag.

Victoria had watched in fascination as he'd straightened and stood, his long thigh muscles straining the material of his tan dress pants. A wave of heat that had nothing to do with the weather washed through her. She took a deep breath and groaned quietly.

She'd known a lot of powerful men in her position as a partner in one of the most prestigious law firms in the city. Men whose strength took many forms, not just physical, but monetary, influence, control. But none of them compared to Brody McQuade. His power was physical, yes, but it was also built of integrity and leadership. When he was in the room, there was no doubt who was in charge.

She'd have loved to see him deal with the Cantara Hills Homeowners' Association. Men like Kenneth Sutton and Link Hathaway would have chafed at Brody telling them how to run their association.

Through the closed door, she heard Brody raise his voice, although she couldn't make out what he was saying. She knew he was talking to his sergeant, Egan Caldwell. The couple of times she'd met Egan, she'd gotten the impression he had a will of iron, too. It would be interesting to see those two butt heads.

She rubbed her eyes and forced herself to sit up. She had to have a shower. Right now she was so hot and tired her brain kept drifting. If she wasn't careful, within moments she'd be asleep.

Maybe a shower would help her shake off her torpor, and she could process everything she'd recalled today more rationally, without the heavy weight of fear squeezing her chest.

She opened the shower door, but after a second's hesitation, she filled the spa tub and relaxed in the swirling warm water for half an hour. Then she washed her hair under the jets and reluctantly climbed out. Her limbs felt steadier, and she felt clean and refreshed.

Now she was hungry.

She wrapped her kimono around her damp body and opened the bathroom door, anxious to dress and raid the little refrigerator in the conference room.

She ran smack into Brody's nearly naked body. "Oh!"

"Sorry."

Victoria clutched her kimono closed with both hands. "What are you…?"

The only thing covering him was a towel knotted at his lean

waist. His shoulders, arms and chest were slick with water, and droplets rained from his hair onto his forehead and neck.

"I needed some…boxers." Brody's words sounded apologetic, but he didn't seem to be able to take his eyes off the neckline of her kimono. "I thought I could get in and out before you finished in there."

Victoria swallowed. "I'll go back in." She gestured vaguely toward the bathroom. "I forgot…um…"

"Vic…"

She closed her eyes and felt herself surrendering to the low, sexy way his voice wrapped around the nickname he'd given her. Her insides quivered, her breasts tightened. How could a single syllable promise erotic delights beyond her wildest dreams?

His hot breath fanned her temple. His energy radiated toward her like body heat. She lifted her head slightly, longing for more than his breath to touch her.

But the brush of air turned cool. When she opened her eyes, he had his back to her and was reaching for the dresser drawers. "I'll get the rest of my clothes. I didn't mean to walk in on you."

"Brody—"

"When you're dressed, come on out. I'll order room service. Cold lobster salad for you, right? Should I order champagne?"

She heard the censure in his words. He would never let himself forget her status as a trust-fund baby.

"I'll make do with the white zinfandel, thanks," she said coolly.

Whirling, she stomped into the bathroom and slammed the door. She sat on the edge of the tub until she heard the bedroom door close.

BRODY PACED THE FLOOR. He wasn't good at waiting. Never had been. The day had started out badly. It was miserably hot, and Victoria obviously hadn't wanted to relive the most harrowing experience of her life, hanging by a thread on the side of a limestone cliff.

Brody had forced her to relive every agonizing, terror-filled second. He'd hardened his heart and treated her like any other witness in a murder investigation.

She'd taken it, too, without a complaint. But the later it had gotten, the more pinched her expression had become, until by the time they got back here, she was pale as a ghost and about to collapse from the heat and the stress.

So in his stubborn way, after putting her through hell, he'd reacted defensively when she'd caught him in his bedroom—the room he'd given her, the room where he'd promised her she'd be safe. And to top it all off, he'd made a rude dig with that remark about the lobster salad and the champagne.

He was so frustrated in so many ways. He'd expected to hear back from Egan by now with the name of the owner of the red Ferrari, it had been over an hour since he'd ordered room service, and it was beginning to look like Victoria might not feel like socializing this evening.

A knock sounded on the door and at the same time, Brody's cell phone rang. He waved the room-service guy in and signed the ticket.

"Egan? What have you got?"

"We're in luck. I found the guy. Sometimes your bulldoggish ways pay off. He's on his way out of town for two weeks. If we hadn't caught up to him today—"

"What'd he say? Did he remember the car?"

"Yeah. I've got his statement. He said it was an older-model Chevrolet. Said it looked like it had new paint."

"Could he ID the driver? Did he get a partial plate?"

"Listen to this, Brody. He thinks the plates started with

666. Obviously, he remembered that. And he thinks it might have been a Lumina or a Caprice. But that was all he saw."

"Have you talked to Deason?"

"Nope. Not yet."

"Call him now. Get him the Ferrari guy's statement and let the police track down that vehicle. I need you back in Austin."

"Again?"

"Right. You and Hayes are working in the lab tomorrow. Hayes found the humidor."

"No way! That's great! Fingerprints?"

"That's what he's going to be doing tomorrow. I want you there, Caldwell. I need one hundred percent infallibility on the chain of evidence. With you and Keller, I can be assured that nobody can question our findings."

"What about tracking down this Chevy?"

"The cops can handle that. As soon as they locate the vehicle, I want a paint sample compared to the sample I picked up at the scene and the fleck we retrieved from Caroline Stallings's car."

"I'll get with Deason and then I'll head on up to Austin. Maybe we'll catch a break."

Brody massaged his neck. "I sure as hell hope so. Nobody will be happier than me to get this case over and done with. I've about had it with Cantara Hills."

Victoria eased the bedroom door closed. Her ears burned with irritation and, if she was truthful, humiliation. Her grandmother had always told her that eavesdroppers never heard anything good about themselves, and she'd just proved it.

She'd pouted for a few minutes after Brody's champagne remark, but the idea of lobster salad and a glass of wine had lured her out. Of course she would have been equally happy with a taco and iced tea, but Brody hadn't given her the chance to tell him.

Just as she'd eased the bedroom door open, she'd heard Brody talking to one of his fellow Rangers. He'd sounded tired but upbeat, as if something had broken in the case. Her heart had leaped—maybe finally there was some good news, but then he'd thrown out that comment about Cantara Hills.

She shouldn't have taken it personally, but how could she not? He was talking about where she lived—her neighbors, her home…*her.* In a way she understood. Sometimes she felt like she'd had it with the snobbery and the posturing and the whole sense of entitlement that permeated this exclusive area of San Antonio.

And to be fair, Brody had made it clear from the beginning how he felt about her and her *trust-fund*-baby neighbors.

Still—maybe she was overly sensitive—his words hurt.

A brisk knock sounded on the door, and Victoria realized she was sitting on the edge of the bed with her arms wrapped around herself.

"Victoria, dinner's here."

His voice through the door grated on her nerves. It was so…neutral, so just-the-facts-ma'am. He didn't even call her Vic. How had he ever turned her on with just the sound of his voice?

"I'm not hungry," she yelled back. "I'm going to bed."

"You've got to eat," he said evenly, spouting that maddeningly even tone that drove her nuts. "Besides, I need to talk to you."

"About what? Some break in the case that will get you out of Cantara Hills that much faster? Congratulations."

He knocked again. "Victoria, come out here or I'll come in and get you."

She looked down at herself. She'd put on red-silk lounging

pajamas with long, flowing sleeves. How ridiculous! What had she been thinking? She jumped up and ran over to the closet where the floor was littered with her dirty clothes. She rooted around until she found the baggy T-shirt and madras shorts. Both were wrinkled, and the T-shirt had a small stain of pizza sauce on the front, but she didn't care. She threw them on and twisted her damp hair up into a messy ponytail. She stomped over and threw the door open.

"I heard your cell…" she started, but there was nobody there. She stomped across the sitting room and opened the door to the conference room, but all the stomping and slamming lost much of its punch when she had to do it twice.

Brody was sitting at the conference table, shoveling lobster salad into his mouth and washing it down with beer. He barely looked up. "Your salad's wilting."

"I heard your cell ring—any news?" She folded her arms and glared at him. But he kept on eating, and try as she might, she couldn't keep her gaze from drifting to the beautifully presented salad with the big pink chunks of lobster artfully arranged on top. French-toast rounds garnished the plate, and next to the salad was a tiny lemon tart with raspberry syrup drizzled over it. Her stomach growled loudly.

Brody's mouth quirked up.

"Well, it's a shame to let it go to waste," she muttered. She stalked over to the table and sat. As she dug in, Brody finished. He sat back and up-ended his beer.

"So?" she said around a mouthful of lobster.

"Hayes found the humidor."

"Byron's humidor? Where?"

"In a pawnshop just outside of Austin. He's taking it to the lab to lift fingerprints. We're hoping one of the prints will match the partial I got off your neck."

Victoria's hand flew to her neck. She shuddered. "Oh, I'd almost forgotten about that." She still saw the bruises when she looked in the mirror, but they had faded to a pale, ugly green that didn't compare with the discoloration that ran from her shoulder to her hip.

Brody sat up and peered at her neck. He ran his thumb along the still-tender skin. "They're almost gone," he said.

She did her best to ignore the erotic sensation of his warm fingers brushing her skin. "So you were right about the things that were taken from the apartments? The killer had no use for them? He got rid of them for money?"

"Looks that way. The guy at the pawnshop where Hayes found the humidor didn't remember a diamond-and-emerald bracelet. Maybe our perp pawned it somewhere else, or maybe he kept it for his girlfriend."

Victoria finished the lobster and was picking at bits of lettuce and celery. "What about the print from my neck? No matches?"

Brody shook his head. "In the first place, you're an attorney. You know it's never a sure thing to match a print."

"I'm a corporate lawyer. I've never tried a criminal case. The closest I ever came was representing Gary in the hit-and-run."

Brody frowned.

"Anyway, they always seem to match them on television."

"Trust me, it's not that easy."

Brody picked up the room-service tray and reached for her plate. She put a hand over his.

"Wait. Leave me the lemon tart."

He shook his head and left both tarts on the table, then quickly cleared away the dishes and set them on the floor near the door.

"It all depends," he said, "on whether the perp has a record or has been printed for some other reason. Then the partial has to have enough clarity to match. Sometimes the print is too smudged or faint to get a computer match. Yours, for instance, was right on the edge of unreadable. In that case, it has to be matched by a human eye, and that's definitely a long shot. And hard to prove in court."

"The print on my neck was too faint?"

"We were lucky to get anything at all."

The memory of her attacker's hands on her neck, his weight on top of her, sent chills down Victoria's spine.

She wrapped her hand around the cold glass and sipped at her champagne. "What are we doing tomorrow?"

He straightened. "You're not doing anything. I'm meeting with Detective Sergeant Deason about the evidence they've gathered, and then I've got another meeting with the homeowners' association to coordinate the installation of the new security system. There'll be a couple of hours when the condos won't have security. I plan to be there, along with several officers and some private security guards hired by the homeowners' association. And depending on what Egan and Hayes find, I may need to go to Austin."

"Isn't there anything I can do?"

"You can stay here—safe—so I don't have to worry about you."

"I could go with you. As long as I'm with you, we both know I'm safe."

Brody's dark gaze met hers and for an instant she felt as if she were swimming in a pool of bittersweet chocolate. The thing between them rose to life. Sometimes it roared like a dragon, but other times, like now, it felt like a spider's silk, winding around her, pulling her toward him. No matter whether she wanted to be or not, she was bound to him by silvery, invisible threads.

"Brody?" She had no idea why she said his name. No idea what she was asking for. Not just sex, although that was a part of it. She craved him, now that she'd had him. His hot, powerful body wrapped around hers, his pulsing heat inside her in that most intimate joining, his whole attention focused on her. That was safety.

He stepped closer. His palms slid up her arms, warm and possessive. He bent his head and she closed her eyes, but the deep erotic kiss didn't come.

Instead, he kissed her temple, a heartbreakingly sweet kiss, but not a lover's.

Her eyes flew open.

"Get some sleep, Vic. Your job is to stay safe. I've got an employee of a private security agency to guard you tomorrow." He dug in the pocket of his jeans. "Here's a photo of him. His name is Lou Riviera. Do not open the door to anyone else. If he doesn't show up, call me immediately, or call Detective Sergeant Deason. You have the gun I gave you."

Victoria nodded, swallowing nervously.

"When do you use the gun?" he asked.

"Only if someone threatens my life."

"Remember, Vic, if you pull that trigger, you can never take it back. Riviera will be armed. Maybe it would be better if you didn't carry the gun, because if you freeze up, your attacker can take it from you and use it on you."

Victoria lifted her chin. "If you're not with me, I want to be armed. That man was on top of me, choking me. I couldn't do anything to stop him. I don't ever want to be that helpless again."

"I swear, Vic, I'll get him if it's the last thing I do."

Chapter Twelve

By the time Victoria got up the next morning, Brody was gone. A brief inspection told her the suites were empty. She opened the curtains in the sitting room, which looked out over the pool. A good-looking Hispanic guy stood near the pool. She recognized him from the photo Brody had given her.

His biceps strained the material of a white short-sleeved shirt that sported a badgelike logo on the breast pocket. The black leather holster belted around his waist and his toned body made him look very official and very competent.

He smiled and mouthed, "Good morning." Then he took a step backward and planted his feet and clasped his hands behind him in the classic military at-ease posture.

She was impressed. He understood body language. He appeared capable, even formidable, and at the same time un-threatening toward her. Leave it to Brody to find the best bodyguard in San Antonio.

She unlocked the doors.

"Ms. Kirkland, I'm Lou Riviera. I work for San Antonio Security Systems. I'll be here all day, guarding you, while Lieutenant McQuade is out. Is there anything I can do for you?"

"Good morning, Mr. Riviera. Bro—the lieutenant told me about you."

"Call me Lou."

"Thank you. You can call me Victoria. I can't think of a thing you can do for me except keep the bad guys away." She smiled and he smiled back. He really was a nice-looking guy.

"I was just about to order breakfast," she said. "May I order you something?"

Riviera shook his head. "I ate earlier, but it looks like it's going to be a scorcher today. Orange juice and water would be great."

"We've got all the water you could need in here. There's a small refrigerator in the main conference room. I'll order a tall glass of orange juice with breakfast. Do you think it would be all right if I sat out by the pool to eat?"

Riviera grinned, showing even, white teeth. "I think you can do whatever you want, as long as I'm right beside you."

As she closed the doors and picked up the phone to order breakfast, she felt a shiver of fear along her spine. Lou Riviera was charming and handsome and completely at ease around her, but the fact remained that he was there because someone wanted her dead.

BRODY MADE IT THROUGH the changeover of the security system at the Cantara Gardens Condominiums without a hitch. Once again, he saw proof of the old adage that wealth had its privileges.

Apparently a phone call from Kenneth Sutton was all it took to get a custom-designed security system ready and delivered in four days. The company's tech guys were at the condos by seven o'clock in the morning and finished by just after nine. Brody had seized the opportunity to talk with Sutton again.

He'd questioned the businessman back in December about the argument he'd had with Kimberly on the night of her death. At the time, Sutton had sidestepped the question by claiming it was a work disagreement. He'd had a couple of drinks and was short-tempered.

He'd apologized sincerely for upsetting Kimmie. Although Brody pegged Sutton as a prime suspect, he had to admit that no one could have faked the clammy pallor and the shock on Sutton's face that night.

Today, with eight months' healing time since the death of his sister, and without much more proof than he'd had back then, Brody still didn't have a better suspect than Sutton. And he wanted him to know it.

"Phone call?" Sutton repeated the gist of Brody's question. "I don't remember making a phone call." He looked genuinely bewildered. "Hell, it was probably Tammy calling me from across the room to tell me she was ready to leave." Sutton chuckled. "She does that all the time."

"I'm sure when we check your phone records and your wife's, they'll back that up."

Sutton's brows drew down. "I'm sure they will. What's going on here? I know you're dead set on proving that the murders in Cantara Gardens are connected with your sister's death. But you can't think I had anything to do with it."

"Kimmie called me on the night she was killed. She was upset about something you'd said to her. What was that about? Something about missing sealed bids, maybe?"

"Look, McQuade, I went over all that with the police at the time. We had some irregularities involving bids, but it had nothing to do with Kimberly or me. She was a great kid. Everybody loved her."

Sutton shook his head impatiently. "But face it, she was a

kid. I don't remember what upset her so much that night, but I can tell you, every intern I've ever had has been moonstruck over the amount of money the city planning board deals with. And the sealed-bid process is complicated."

Sutton stopped walking and turned to Brody. "Like I said, I'd had a couple of drinks, and I wasn't interested in talking business. I might have said something mean, and I regret that I upset her, but I never threatened to fire her."

Brody stepped out through the front doors of the condos with Sutton right behind him. He didn't contradict Sutton, but he had Kimmie's message on his phone, if it came to that.

"I can guarantee you one thing, Sutton," he said. "Kimmie wasn't moonstruck about money. Power maybe, but not money."

Sutton turned to him and held out his hand. Brody was oddly reluctant to accept the hand the smooth businessman offered. Or maybe not so oddly, considering that it was Sutton who'd upset Kimmie and precipitated the events that led to her death. He hesitated, but finally took Sutton's hand. "I'll be in touch about your phone records," Brody said. "I'm sure it will clear everything up."

"I want to thank you for kicking our butts about the security system," Sutton said. "I feel better already. Maybe the break-ins and attacks will stop now."

"I don't think so. Victoria's life has been threatened more than once."

Sutton sent Brody a thoughtful glance. "Are you sure what's happening to Victoria is connected to the break-ins? She dated a train wreck of a playboy, name of Rayburn Andrews, for a long time. If that's her taste in men, her problem may be with an ex."

Brody's knuckles itched to feel Sutton's capped teeth

crunch against them, but he kept his cool. "My evidence suggests otherwise," he said evenly, gratified when Sutton's eyes widened in sudden apprehension.

Sutton paused for a few seconds, but Brody held his tongue. He wasn't giving out any information to anybody. Especially his certainty that Sutton was in this up to his eyeballs.

"Well, here's my car," Sutton said unnecessarily. "I'd better get going." As he walked toward his car, Vincent Montoya got out and opened the back door. He was the consummate chauffeur. He didn't even glance at Brody.

Brody watched the car drive away before he got into his Jeep.

Had Sutton's phone call been to someone who'd lain in wait and hit Caroline Stallings's car on purpose? Montoya maybe? Was Kenneth Sutton guilty of murder, or just guilty of being a slimeball?

As Brody cranked his Jeep and prepared to leave, his cell phone rang. It was Deason.

"McQuade, we got a probable match on the license plate of the car that rammed Victoria."

"What? Who is it? Have you picked him up?"

"Whoa, hold your horses. Like I said, it's a *probable,* not an exact match. Its first three digits are 666. But there are several thousand plates with 666 as the first three letters. Frankly I'm surprised they even print plates with that number on them."

"So how are you narrowing it down?"

"Both Victoria and the driver of the Ferrari described it as an older, dark-blue Chevrolet sedan. That cuts the field down to ninety-seven vehicles."

"Ninety-seven." Brody sighed. Then he remembered the paint chip from Caroline Stallings's car. "Dark blue isn't the original color, remember? The paint chip Vic's forensic specialist analyzed had dark blue over dark green paint, plus two types of primer."

Deason snorted. "Way ahead of you there, Lieutenant. I've got three vehicles with that partial plate that are registered as dark green and are now dark blue."

Brody's heart leaped in his chest. "Three?"

"Right. One is a teenage boy who painted his car in his high-school shop class. The second is an older lady, and the third is a guy named Harold Young. Thing is, Young's been dead for two years. Someone's been sending in his registration."

Brody didn't want to get his hopes up, but they were already soaring. "This could be it!"

"I've got a couple of officers checking out Young's LKA. We'll see what turns up."

"If the guy's dead, his last-known address is probably meaningless by now."

"I'll let you know what I find out."

"Thanks, Deason."

So they'd identified the car. It wasn't much, but it was more than he'd been able to put together up until now. Essentially a bunch of names on a whiteboard and a bunch of incidents that only he seemed able to connect.

The most frustrating thing for Brody was that while he'd kept everybody busy running down leads and searching for clues, he felt like he'd done nothing except babysit Victoria—not that it was a chore.

It occurred to him that at some point his focus had changed. This was no longer just about avenging his sister's death and nabbing the SOB who'd killed her. Somewhere along the way he'd found another purpose, another life that meant as much to him as Kimmie's had. Victoria's.

As much as Kimmie's? He rubbed his temples. When had that happened? For as long as he could remember, his baby sister had been the one person he loved more than anything. His parents had been there—sort of, between their great adventures. But Kimmie had always been his family, his responsibility. When she'd died, he'd been sure his heart could never open up enough to love anyone that much again.

As if to mock him, Victoria's beautiful face rose in his mind and his chest squeezed with a sweet, painful ache.

Doing his best to ignore it, he checked his watch and saw nothing but bare wrist. *Damn.* He'd left it on the side table in his suite.

His gaze slid to the clock on the dashboard. At least he didn't have to worry about Victoria today. He'd hired Lou Riviera to guard her, which left him free to do some investigating on his own. He'd told Lou not to leave her side until he got back. He'd used Lou before. He was a topnotch bodyguard and investigator, employed by the most highly-thought-of security agency in the area. He could feel assured that she was safe.

He pushed the call-back button on his cell phone. "Deason, I want to go with the officers to check out Young."

"Sure. Tell you what. I'll meet you there." Deason gave him the address.

A visceral thrill ran through Brody's gut. He'd always loved fieldwork the most. Being a lieutenant had its good points. It satisfied his natural leadership instincts. But sitting behind a desk analyzing data and filling out reports could be boring as hell.

Today, though, he was a Ranger. And before the day was out, he would be at least one step closer to finding the man who'd killed his sister.

VICTORIA PRESSED THE channel-up button on the remote control for the seventy-seventh time. And each click had upped her irritation and escalated her boredom. She paused on a weather channel. The day was destined to be a real scorcher, as Lou had said. San Antonio was in the middle of a heat wave that wasn't going anywhere anytime soon.

She tossed the remote down and stepped over to the French doors. There was nobody sitting out by the pool. They were probably all either in the dining room drinking a cold drink or on the other side in the air-conditioned indoor pool.

Even Lou had knocked on the door about twenty minutes earlier and told her he'd move inside to the hall outside the conference suite for a while, if it was all right with her. She'd tried to get him to come inside and have a cold drink, but he'd declined.

"If Lieutenant McQuade found me sitting with my feet propped up and drinking a bottle of water like a card-carrying member of the country club," he'd said, "he'd have my job."

Victoria had protested, but Lou had stood firm. She thought Brody would like the idea of Lou being glued to her side, but she didn't want to get him in trouble.

She put her palm against the glass of one of the French doors. It was hot to the touch. Behind her the morning weather girl was ecstatic that temperatures were expected to exceed 103.

Bored and restless, Victoria let her gaze wander around Brody's sitting room. There wasn't much of *him* there, but that wasn't surprising. These were temporary quarters. He'd been here a week, and probably in less than another week he'd be gone.

He lived and worked in Austin. And while in reality the

state's capital was only a little over an hour away, it might as well be on the other side of the earth.

The thought saddened her, which was ridiculous. Brody McQuade meant nothing to her—or at least he shouldn't. He was a lawman with a job to do. When this job was done, he'd move on to the next job.

And once her life was no longer threatened, she'd go back to her ordinary life.

But whether it made sense or not, the idea of Brody no longer being in her life, no longer worrying about her, no longer close enough that she could breathe in his warm fresh scent, broke her heart.

Her gaze lit on the side table. He'd left his watch. It was sitting on top of a small stack of papers. She'd never paid any attention to his watch, except to note that he always wore it. She stepped over to the table and picked it up. *Heavy.*

As soon as she looked at it she knew what it was. It was a Tag Heuer Carrera. At least three grand retail. She was surprised.

In the first place, Brody didn't seem the kind of guy who cared about affecting an expensive, trendy watch. And in the second place, who knew Texas Rangers made that kind of money?

She slipped it onto her wrist, feeling like a little girl playing dress-up. The watch face more than spanned the width of her wrist. As she fingered the stainless-steel case, she felt something on its back.

Slipping the watch off, she turned it over. It was engraved. She switched on the lamp and held the back of the watch close to the light.

For my big bro Brody. HB, love, Kimmie. And then the date. *HB.* Happy birthday? So Brody was a Scorpio. It shouldn't have surprised Victoria. He certainly had the sting. But he also had an unexpectedly gentle side.

Victoria started to lay the watch back down where she'd found it when the oddity of the year hit her. The date was six years earlier. Kimberly would have been no more than nineteen. Where would a nineteen-year-old get that kind of money?

A scant memory tugged at the edge of her brain. A word that had flashed across her vision from one of the papers under the watch. She sent a slightly furtive glance toward the conference room—a reflex, because she knew she was alone. Then she let her gaze fall to the stack of papers.

There, sticking out from underneath a bill. It was a manila folder from an estate attorney, with the words "Kimberly Noelle McQuade Estate" scrawled across the front and a pink sticky note attached. The sticky note read, "B.McQ. Just sign where indicated and return. The estate will revert to you. Thanks."

Estate? Brody had an estate? The more she stared, the more her surprise morphed into anger. She felt like screaming in frustration, jumping up and down like a spoiled brat— a trust-fund spoiled brat.

The one thing she'd counted on with Brody was his integrity, his truthfulness. Okay, she'd counted on a lot more than that, but she'd believed in his innate honesty.

He'd lied to her. He'd been so contemptuous of her wealth. He'd called her a trust-fund baby, as if the name was a vile curse. He'd curled his lip at her dislike of beer. He'd made fun of her lobster salad.

Victoria was so angry her ears were burning. He was the worst kind of snob—a snob and a liar. A vague, sick feeling wrapped around her heart. She couldn't think of any reason he'd hide his wealth from her.

But then, she couldn't think of any reason he owed her an explanation, either.

Still, if he couldn't bother to be truthful with her, then why should she bother being such a good little victim?

He'd told her he was hiring a bodyguard to keep her safe, but he hadn't said anything about where they could or couldn't go. At least not overtly.

She stomped into the bedroom to dress. She didn't deserve to be punished for being a *victim*. Obviously there was no reason for her to have to stay there in that cramped, claustrophobic bedroom, except that Brody McQuade wanted it that way.

"Well, that's just tough, Lieutenant," she muttered, tossing her kimono on the bed. As long as she kept Lou with her, she could go anywhere she wanted and be just as safe as she would be here. And she had a couple of places she wanted to go.

BRODY MET DETECTIVE Sergeant Deason on St. Mary's Street. It was a run-down barrio on the south side of San Antonio. When he pulled to the curb behind the police car, his heart sank. The tiny rowhouses had a gap in them, like a missing tooth. Where Young had lived was a burned-out shell.

Deason was standing with a uniformed officer in front of the burned-out building, rubbing the top of his balding head as the officer talked and gestured.

Brody walked up in time to hear the officer say something about the neighbors.

"Anyone remember Young or the car?" he asked without preamble.

Deason wiped a trickle of sweat from his forehead and slung it away. "Officer Barnes, this is Lieutenant McQuade of the Rangers. I think you may have met him the night of the attack on Ms. Kirkland at Cantara Gardens."

"Yes sir." The officer nodded at Brody.

"Tell the lieutenant what you've found out."

Barnes pulled a small notepad from his shirt pocket and flipped a few pages. "The family living in the next house up just moved in a year ago, after the fire. The folks on the other side—the Guzmans—knew Young. Said he was a drunk, a loud one. Fell asleep with a cigarette one night." The officer flipped another page. "Mrs. Guzman said he would have killed them all if his daughter hadn't woken up."

"Daughter?" Brody turned from surveying the blackened mess that was once someone's home. "She didn't die in the fire, did she?"

"No, sir. She called the fire department. Too late for her dad, but she got out and alerted the neighbors." Barnes pointed at the Guzmans' house. "You can see some fire damage, but no one else was hurt."

Brody nodded and walked over to the burned-out building. He slid his hands into his pockets and kicked at a charred board with the toe of his boot. "Where's the daughter now?"

"Mrs. Guzman told me she'd seen her a few months ago. She was asking about the company that rents the houses."

"Maybe thinking about suing for wrongful death," Deason added.

He turned to Barnes. "Did you find out anything about her?"

"No, sir. But Mrs. Guzman is home."

Brody turned on his heel and headed for the Guzman house. As he stepped onto the minuscule porch stoop, the front door opened.

"*Hola, Señora Guzman,*" he said, removing his hat. "*¿Cómo esta usted? Me llamo Lieutenant McQuade. Soy un Texas Ranger.*"

"Good morning, Lieutenant. You are very charming, and your Spanish is passable, but I think my English is better." She stepped out onto the stoop, wiping her hands on a dish towel. "You have more questions about Harold?" She glanced toward the burned house.

"Yes, ma'am. Actually about his daughter. Did you know her?"

"Of course. She would come over here when he got drunk. She and my son were friends in school."

"Do you know where she is now?"

Mrs. Guzman shook her head. "Working for some rich people somewhere. When I saw her a few months ago, she was *embarazada.*" Mrs. Guzman clicked her tongue.

"Pregnant?" Brody's heart slammed against his chest. He gulped in air, telling himself it was a coincidence. Warning himself not to get his hopes up. "What's her name?"

"Eleana. Pretty girl. I didn't see no wedding ring."

"Eleana Young?" His pulse hammered in his ears.

"No, no. Harold was not her real father." Mrs. Guzman slung her towel over her shoulder and shook her head. "Her mother's name was Mondavi. Eleana Mondavi. Lieutenant, are you all right?"

Brody's mouth was so dry he could hardly swallow. *Eleana Mondavi.* "Yes, ma'am. Thank you."

"You see Eleana, you tell her my Carlos is in Iraq. You tell her she should have married him when he asked her."

Brody stalked back to Deason's side. "Young's stepdaughter works at the country club. Eleana Mondavi. She's in this up to her eyeballs. I want her picked up, *now!*"

BRODY HAD JUST PULLED onto the interstate when his cell phone rang. He pulled it out. It was Egan. "McQuade. What's up, Caldwell?"

"Brody!" Egan's voice was sharp with excitement. "I hope you're sitting down. We got hits on the prints."

Brody's fingers spasmed around the phone. He fought to keep his voice steady. This was the break he'd been afraid would never come. The identity of the person who'd killed his sister.

"Hits? Whose?"

"Three sets. Dalloway of course. And Carlson Woodard."

"Carlson? Damn. Are you sure?"

"Absolutely. His prints are on file from a couple of DUIs."

The heat of fury surged through Brody's veins. "That weasel. Could he have done this?"

"Brody, the third set match a Vincent Montoya. He's got a sheet for grand theft auto."

"Montoya? That's Sutton's chauffeur."

Egan was silent for a second. "So the chauffeur did it? That's rich."

Brody ignored Egan's bitter words. "What about the print from Victoria's neck? Any match?"

"The print from her neck is consistent with Montoya's right forefinger. Can't say it's a slam dunk, but the two prints have about a fifty-percent match."

"Caldwell, get back here right now. Call Deason to get a warrant to search everything Montoya ever even thought about owning—house, car, storage facilities, safe-deposit boxes, garbage cans. Don't leave out anything. Soon as you've got the warrant, pick him up. I'm on my way to question an employee of the country club. Her father is the owner of the car that hit Kimmie and ran Vic off the road."

"Got it. What about Carlson?"

"Get Hayes down here to help. Tell Deason to have Carlson picked up and interrogated within an inch of his disgusting life. I don't think he killed anybody, but nothing else would surprise me."

"I'm with you on that."

"Once you've got evidence from the search, Hayes can hand-carry it back to the lab. With any luck we'll have Montoya's prints to process, paint chips to compare, and who knows what else once we get our hands on that car. This is the break we've been waiting for."

His phone beeped. "I've got another call. I'll talk to you later."

"I'm on my way."

The other caller was Deason. Brody answered. "Caldwell just let me know we got a match on prints," he said.

"Lieutenant—"

Brody stopped. "Yeah?" He didn't like the tone of Deason's voice. "What is it?"

"Eleana Mondavi left work early."

"Early? How early?"

"About an hour ago."

"Mrs. Guzman must have called her. Have you checked her house? Called her cell phone?"

"Yes. We're taking every possible step to find her. I've talked to DeCalley at the country club, as well as Patterson at the condos, and I've dispatched two officers to her house, just in case there's been foul play."

"What about the hospitals? She's pregnant. Something could have happened with the baby."

"That, too. I've even got a BOLO out to airports, rental-car agencies and bus stations."

Brody wiped his face. A *be on the lookout for* was a great

tool for stopping fleeing criminals or even searching out victims in hiding. "Great. Thanks, Deason. I appreciate it." He took a deep breath. "Now listen. The prints we lifted off the humidor and off Vic's neck belong to Vincent Montoya. He's Kenneth Sutton's driver. He and Eleana must be connected. Sergeant Caldwell is probably calling you right now about getting a warrant to search everything Montoya ever touched."

"You want us to pick him up?"

"Let Caldwell go with you, if you don't mind. And as soon as you've got him in custody, let me know. I want to question that lowlife myself."

Chapter Thirteen

Brody headed to Kenneth Sutton's house, hoping to catch Montoya there. He could bring him in for questioning and hold him until Deason secured the warrant.

He got out of his jeep and strode to the front door. Before he had a chance to ring the bell, the door swung open. It was Tammy Sutton, in a slinky silk robe that looked kind of like Vic's kimono, except that while Vic looked exotic and sexy in hers, Tammy looked as if she'd been interrupted in the middle of sex. Her hair was mussed and the robe gaped open in front, revealing a little bralike thing underneath.

"Lieutenant…?"

"McQuade. Brody."

"Right, Brody." Tammy smiled and raised a perfect brow. "Is there something I can *do* for you this morning, Brody?"

Brody clamped his jaw and reminded himself why he was here. "Is your husband here?"

"Why no, he's at the office. Now why would you think he'd be here at this time of day?" Her smile turned catlike.

She was baiting him. If he made a move on her, he had a feeling she wouldn't turn him down. Not that he was even tempted, but he'd seen her type. She was definitely a cougar.

"Actually I wanted to talk with Vincent Montoya."

Tammy's soft gaze turned hard and curious. "Montoya? Whatever for?"

"Just some routine questions."

"I see. He drove Kenneth in to work this morning as usual."

Brody clenched his jaw. She wasn't going to make this easy. And in about ten seconds she was going to ask him to come in.

"What does Montoya do after he drives Sutton to work?"

Tammy chuckled and pressed a hand against her exposed cleavage. "Goodness, Lieutenant. You do have a lot of questions. Why don't you come in? I can offer you something."

He ignored her implication. "No. That won't be necessary. Montoya?"

"What does he do? Oh, I don't know. I think he's free until Kenneth needs him. Possibly for a lunch meeting, possibly not until he leaves for the day."

"He never comes back here?"

"Not usually. I drive myself."

Brody's cell phone rang. He pulled it out. It was Egan. Maybe they'd found something at Montoya's house. He touched the brim of his hat.

"Thank you, Mrs. Sutton. I appreciate your help."

"Anytime, Lieutenant. Come back when you can stay longer."

Brody answered his phone as he headed back to his car. "McQuade."

"Brody, we got our warrant and we're at Montoya's house. He's an interesting guy."

"Get to it, Caldwell."

"It looks to me like he's got what you might call a *used-car* business going."

"You mean a chop shop? So he's got car-painting equipment?"

"He's got a full-service body shop in a building behind his house."

"The warrant covers that, right?"

"You bet. We're collecting paint samples now. I've got a feeling we're going to find the same paint we took off Victoria's car—and from the Stallings woman's car."

"Well, hurry it up. Montoya apparently has his mornings free after he drives Sutton into work, so he may show up."

"Great. We'll be ready for him."

VICTORIA LOOKED AT HERSELF in the mirror. She looked cool and confident in a slim skirt and a crisp white blouse. On her feet were white, high-heeled, backless sandals, and on her face was a look of fierce determination.

She consciously relaxed her jaw. She knew it was going to take some persuading to convince Lou Riviera that he could guard her just as efficiently at the Cantara Gardens Condominiums as he could here.

She'd wanted Brody to question Jane Majorsky, the boutique owner whose emerald bracelet had been stolen, but as far as she knew, he hadn't. And the one time she'd had the chance, Jane hadn't answered her door.

She knew Jane had let Carlson Woodward use her access card at least once to get into the condos. She'd seen him coming in. Jane was one of his *private* tennis students. She felt sure that with a little shared gossip, she could find out a lot about Carlson.

She pasted a smile on her face. Then she patted her hair. "Okay, Victoria," she murmured. "If you can't charm a good-looking guy into taking you where you want to go, then you deserve to stay cooped up in this suffocating room."

She raised an eyebrow at her reflection. A niggle of doubt tickled the edge of her brain. Lou had refused to sit down because he'd thought Brody wouldn't approve. How much more would Brody object to Lou's allowing her out of the country club, even if he was right beside her?

She took a long breath. "You're just lucky it's not Brody out there."

She smoothed the front of her blouse, and her fingernail snagged the material. "Dammit." She ran the tip of a finger over the chipped nail of her ring finger.

She glanced at her watch as she searched in her makeup kit for a fingernail file.

Clutching the metal file and worrying the chipped nail with her thumb, she walked through the sitting room and out into the conference room.

She opened the hall door with a smile, only to find the hall empty. A frisson of fear slid down her spine. Where was Lou?

Come on, Victoria. He probably went to the bathroom, or walked back around to the pool side.

She closed the door and went back into the sitting room. The curtains were open and the sun was glaring on the glass of the French doors.

Victoria peered out at the pool. The place was empty, except for one lone kid out in the triple-digit heat. It was a teenage boy who looked like he'd already gotten too much sun. As she watched, he turned over onto his stomach and emptied the last of a bottle of water over his head.

Victoria paced the sitting room.

Should she call Brody? Should she go out and look for Lou? *No!*

She almost jumped. She'd have sworn that was Brody's voice barking at her.

Okay, okay. She'd be a good girl and wait. It was less than twenty minutes until Lou's regular hourly check-in.

Just as she started to file her chipped nail, a brisk knock sounded on the hall door.

Lou. Thank goodness. She hurried over to the door and grabbed the knob. But that feeling of fear was still tingling at the base of her spine. Where had he been?

"Lou?" she called out. It was silly, but better safe than sorry.

No answer.

"Lou?" she called a little louder. "Is that you?" She looked through the peephole in the door, and saw Lou's white shirt filling her vision.

Thank goodness. She unlocked the dead bolt.

The door slammed into her and knocked her backward. Burning shock paralyzed her.

"What—" she started.

"Shut up!"

It wasn't Lou. This man was shorter, bulkier. And he smelled like Torture cologne.

Shock gave way to panic. It was the man who'd strangled her. She stared at him, too frozen with fear to move, too shocked to make sense out of the thoughts that flew through her head.

Then something inside her broke loose, and her instincts took over. She turned and ran for Brody's sitting room.

The man lunged at her. He grabbed at her arm and caught a handful of her blouse.

Fabric tore as he jerked her off her feet. She fell back against him, nearly gagging on the hideous smell of his cologne.

"Stop it! Help!" she screamed. "Help! Police!"

A blinding pain slammed into the side of her head.

Her cheek hit the carpet. Dazed, she tried to push herself up and forward, but before she could move, he'd flopped down on top of her and wrapped his big rough hands around her neck.

Déjà vu ripped through her in an adrenaline rush. She bucked and kicked, trying to get him off her, but he was too big, too heavy, too strong.

His fingers squeezed, gagging her. She couldn't breathe. She scratched at him impotently. Still, she tried.

"Why—?" she rasped.

"*¡Usted es el último, puta!*"

"Last?" she whispered. She was the last what? Victoria had a vague notion that whatever he was saying was important.

As her lungs burned for air and pain blinded her, she threw the last of her strength into pulling herself forward, trying to get away from him.

Something stabbed the underside of her breast.

At first her cloudy brain didn't catch the significance of the stinging pain. His fingers were crushing her throat. No air was getting through. Her lungs were spasming, her heart was racing out of control.

Her breast still stung. With a strangely bright flash of insight she remembered.

The fingernail file! She'd dropped it when she'd fallen. If she could get her hand under her...

Her heart was pounding desperately. Her whole body was screaming for air. Her vision grew black. With what she knew was the last burst of adrenaline in her body, she bowed her back, pushing with more strength than she thought she had against her attacker's bulk.

Her fingers closed around the file.

But her throat hurt, and her head was swimming. She needed to stop, just for a minute, and catch her breath.

Someone was talking but she didn't care.

She couldn't think right now. Her body was collapsing. She'd been without breath for too long. His hands were squeezing too tightly. Any second now her neck was going to snap.

No! She clenched her fists and felt the fingernail file. She was supposed to do something with it.

"Die, *puta!*"

Stars exploded in her eyes, her ears rang. With her last conscious thought, she jabbed the metal file into the hands that were killing her.

Something changed.

He let go, spitting a string of vile curses.

Victoria's chest and throat spasmed, but it was too late. She couldn't get any air. *None.*

She stretched her neck, tried to push herself upright, but she couldn't. She gasped, and felt a tiny whisper of air on the back of her throat, but it wasn't enough.

She collapsed. He'd killed her.

As soon as Brody rounded the corner of the conference wing of the country club, he saw something wrong. The conference-suite door had a thin stripe of light showing around its edge.

It wasn't locked. He sprinted down the hall and shouldered the door open, drawing his weapon.

The sight in front of him nearly drove him to his knees.

Victoria was crumpled on the floor with Vincent Montoya standing over her, a gun pointed at her head. Montoya's head jerked in Brody's direction, but his gun hand didn't waver.

Every fiber of Brody's being wanted to dive for Vic, to cover her body with his, to protect her from Montoya.

But that would be suicide. And if he died, she surely would, too.

"Montoya! Drop the gun, now!"

Montoya looked up at Brody and shrugged. "It don't matter, Mr. Texas Ranger. She's already dead. I found her like this."

Dead. *No!* "You're a liar," Brody croaked.

"Hey, I'm just trying to help. I think someone choked her. The gun was lying right there."

"Drop it or I'll shoot you right now."

"Now what you want to do that for, Mr. Texas Ranger? I was just trying to help."

"Drop it!"

Montoya's face changed and he swung the gun toward Brody and took a step backward.

In one motion, Brody aimed and shot.

Glass shattered, Montoya screeched and the gun went flying. The chauffeur fell to his knees, clutching his bleeding right hand.

Brody started forward, but Montoya recovered and dove for the gun, which had slid over to the French doors.

In two strides, Brody ground his boot heel into Montoya's wounded hand and put the barrel of his gun against the back of his neck.

"Move and I'll blow your stinking head off," he growled, and racked a bullet into the chamber.

Montoya flattened himself against the floor. "Don't shoot, man. I didn't do nothing!"

Brody's gun barrel shook. His gaze flickered toward Victoria. She still hadn't moved. Dark red streaks stained the side of her neck.

Blood. The sight ratcheted his anger at Montoya up into rage. He put more weight on the man's hand.

Montoya screeched again.

"Move! Make a move!" he growled. "Because I'm dying to watch your brains splatter all over this room."

"Hey, I didn't do nothing—"

"Brody!"

Shock sizzled through him like lightning. His index finger tightened reflexively, and he felt the trigger give.

"Brody, I got him." It was Egan.

Carefully, slowly, Brody relaxed his hand. Egan put a hand on his shoulder for a split second. Then he took Brody's place and wrenched Montoya's hands behind his back, paying no attention to his squeals about brutality.

Egan jerked Montoya to his feet and shoved him toward two uniformed officers. "Get him out of here."

Brody looked down at his gun, ejected the chambered bullet, and then slid it back into its holster.

Victoria! He fell to his knees by her side and gently turned her over. Her eyelids fluttered.

His heart twisted in relief. *She was alive.*

His fingers hovered over her face and neck, where angry red marks were already turning purple.

"Vic, can you hear me? Can you talk?"

She stiffened. Her eyes opened. They were dilated with fear. Then she focused on his face.

"Brody." It was nothing more than a movement of her lips. No sound came out.

"Shh. It's okay. You're going to be okay. Get the paramedics!" he yelled. "Vic, where are you hurt? Just your throat?"

"They're on their way, sir," someone said.

His hand hovered over the streaks of blood on her neck. "Vic, is this your blood?"

She closed her eyes.

"Vic, look at me. Where are you hurt? Can you breathe okay? Vic?"

But she didn't move. He leaned down and listened. Her breaths sounded hoarse, labored, but it sounded like enough air was getting through.

He brushed her hair away from her face and touched the dried blood on her neck. It wasn't hers.

Montoya was still yelling about brutality and assault when the officers hauled him out of the room.

"He'll live to stand trial," Egan said. "Riviera's going to need stitches where Montoya brained him. They're taking both of them to the hospital in the police car. How's Vic?"

Brody let his index finger brush her cheek.

"Brody?" Egan again.

"Where are the damn paramedics?" Just as Brody said it two emergency medical technicians burst in.

"What have we got here?" one of them said as the other brushed Brody aside and knelt beside Victoria.

"She—"

"It's her throat. She was strangled," Egan said.

Brody felt a hand on his arm, pulling him out of the way so the EMTs could examine Victoria.

"She's got blood on her neck," one EMT said to the other. "I don't see a wound."

"Look at her hand," Brody said. "I think she—" He had to stop. His voice wouldn't work anymore. He'd been too late. He'd promised her he'd keep her safe and he'd failed.

"She stabbed him." The EMT pointed. "Look at what she's holding. It's a metal fingernail file with a sharp point."

Dear God, he prayed silently, *thank you for making her so brave.*

If she hadn't managed to stab Montoya with that little fingernail file, the scumbag would have killed her.

The EMTs fixed an oxygen mask over her face and lifted her onto the gurney.

She moaned.

"Be careful, dammit."

The EMTs ignored him. They left, pushing the gurney.

"Brody, go with her." Egan laid his hand on Brody's shoulder.

He shrugged it off. "No. This is my crime scene. I've got to process it."

"Hayes is on his way right now. Believe it or not, we can handle this."

"I said *no.*"

Hayes walked in just in front of the crime-scene investigators. "Everything okay here?"

Brody acknowledged him with a nod. "Start here," he said to the lead CSI. "All the blood should be Montoya's. This is where he strangled Vic—" His throat spasmed.

Dammit, what was the matter with him? Had he lost his nerve?

"Lieutenant McQuade," Egan said, "go to the hospital with Victoria. Sergeant Keller and I can handle it here."

Brody looked at Egan, then at Hayes. He itched to hit something or someone, but they'd taken Montoya away.

"Whoa, Brody," Hayes said, holding up his hands, palms out. "We're the good guys, remember?"

Egan clapped Brody on the shoulder. "They're taking Montoya to the same hospital. You're going to want to escort him to lockup, anyhow."

Yeah. He was. He nodded and headed for the door.

Behind him, he heard Hayes. "Damn. What's the matter with him?"

"I'm afraid Brody McQuade is in love."

Chapter Fourteen

Victoria's throat hurt really badly. She tried to touch her neck, but her hand wouldn't move. She opened her eyes, and gasped.

She was in a hospital room. The realization was instinctive. She'd never been a patient in the hospital before, but the low lights, the nearly silent beeping that reverberated in her head, and the smell of disinfectant and alcohol was unmistakable.

She wasn't dead. The quiet beeping sped up.

The last thing she remembered was stabbing at the man's hand with the fingernail file. She'd stopped him from choking her, but it was too late. Even with his hands gone, she still couldn't breathe.

The last thing she remembered was giving in to death.

No. Her pulse leaped and the beeping surged for an instant. That wasn't the last thing.

The last thing she remembered was Brody's voice.

She took a deep breath and whimpered a little when the harsh air hit her throat. Something tickled her nostrils. It was an oxygen tube. She felt the plastic tube running across her cheeks and the two little nipplelike bits of rubber stuck up her nose. The dry cold air made her want to cough.

She closed her eyes, but just as she did, she heard a quiet rustle of fabric. Someone was in the room. A nurse?

She turned her head slightly, wincing at the pain in her throat.

It was Brody, sitting beside her in a hard-backed chair. His arms were crossed and his head was bowed. He was asleep. His jaw was dark with stubble, and his eyelashes cast fuzzy shadows on his cheeks. He looked haggard and achingly vulnerable.

Victoria's eyes filled with tears.

He'd saved her. He'd gotten there in time. Somehow she'd known he would never totally trust her safety to someone else.

Then the memory hit her.

Dear heavens. It was Montoya. Fear and nausea swept through her. That sickening cologne. Those beefy, punishing hands. She'd been sure he'd killed her. The beeping sped up again.

She tried to move her arm again, to wipe away the tear that rolled down her cheek, but there was tubing and tape attached to it. An IV.

She laid her head back on the pillow and just watched Brody sleep. From the first time she'd seen him, wild with shock and grief over the death of his sister, she'd known she would never forget him. He was honorable, determined, larger than life.

Another tear fell. So what came after never? Because now that she'd had a glimpse into his heart, seen, if only for a moment, his tender side, his fierce passion, his undying love for his sister, forgetting him was going to be even harder.

She knew what came after never—*ever.* She would never forget him—even until forever.

A sob erupted from her chest before she could stop it. She

pressed her lips together and lifted her free hand to cover her mouth. She didn't want to wake him. He looked so tired.

She discovered her heart ached more than her throat did.

Brody stirred. His head shot up and his black eyes zeroed in on her face. "Vic? You okay?"

Stupidly his words brought more tears. She nodded.

He shot up, nearly knocking the chair backward, his face drawn and etched with worry. "I'll get the nurse."

"No," she managed. Her voice was gone. The only sound she could make was a feeble whisper.

"What's the matter? Are you hurting? The nurse is right out there—"

"Brody, stop." She held up her hand and tried to smile.

His gaze roamed over her face and neck.

After a few seconds he relaxed. "You're sure? No, don't talk."

She nodded. "What happened?" she mouthed, her hand touching her bruised throat. "It was Vincent Montoya?" Every word was painful, but she had to know.

"Please, Vic, stop talking. I'll tell you." He grabbed the chair and pulled it closer to the bed. He sat and took her hand in his.

"It *was* Montoya, Kenneth Sutton's driver. We've tracked down the owner of the car that rammed you. The driver of the Ferrari saw part of the license plate. He remembered it because it was 666. It was Montoya's girlfriend's car that killed Kimmie."

Victoria squeezed his hand.

"Best we can figure, he rammed Caroline Stallings's car on purpose. Montoya won't say, Stallings apparently has total amnesia regarding the event, so she can't tell us anything."

Unbearable sadness clouded Brody's face and bowed his

shoulders. Victoria wanted to take him into her arms, but she had to settle for holding on to his hand.

"The break-ins at the condos were a cover-up. He admitted that he went after Zelke and Briggs and you because he thought you'd seen him that night."

Seen him? She hadn't seen anything. She'd been concentrating on her driving. She shook her head.

"I know you didn't. But Montoya couldn't take that chance. The Ranger lab already examined the angle of impact on Caroline Stallings's vehicle and determined that the car came out of a side street. We've got the paint samples. As soon as we turn up the car, we can prove it's the one that killed Kimmie."

"Why?"

"That's what we can't figure out. Everything else is falling into place. My sergeant got a hit on the print they lifted off the humidor. The partial from your neck matched Montoya. But he's decided to lawyer up." Brody shook his head. "I figure someone tipped him off that we were on to him, and that's when he decided he had to get to you. He couldn't take the chance that you'd seen him that night."

Victoria closed her eyes.

"Vic. Get some sleep. You're safe now. We've got him. He's having surgery on his hand this morning, and then he goes straight to lockup. He's got three deaths on his hands, plus an eyewitness—you. He'll never see this side of a cell again."

A quiet knock sounded on the door. Before Brody could slip his hand from Victoria's, Egan stuck his head in.

"Hey, how's she doing?"

Brody had no trouble reading the look in his sergeant's eyes. "She's okay. Any news?"

"Deason's men tracked down the girlfriend, Eleana. She's apparently on a plane to San Diego. Deason called me to let me know she used a credit card at the airport."

"Did they find her car?"

"Yep. We've impounded it, and CSI techs will compare the paint with the samples we've got."

"Get Hayes to work with them."

"He's already there. With the paint samples we got from Montoya's body shop, and the scrapings from Victoria's and Caroline Stallings's cars, I think we can prove it was used in both attacks." Egan stepped into the room and took a look at Victoria. Then he eyed Brody again, a frown on his face.

"Man, you look worse than she does."

"Thanks," Brody said wryly, glancing at her. He couldn't stop a small smile from curving his lips. "Vic's tough. A lot tougher than she looks."

"Right, I see."

He met Egan's gaze and frowned. Why was Egan looking at him like that? "What the hell's wrong with you?" he asked.

"Me? Nothing's wrong with me. We've been wondering what's wrong with *you*. But I think we've figured it out."

Brody remembered what he'd heard as he'd sprinted to catch up with the EMTs. He wasn't going there, not even in his own head, certainly not with Egan.

"Where'd you say Eleana went? San Diego?"

Egan nodded.

"Dammit. We're going to need her to testify that Montoya had access to her car. And that she was the one who gave him access to the condos and the country club."

"We'll get her." Egan ran his hand over his short dark hair. "I think Montoya's going into surgery in about an hour or so."

Brody looked at his watch. "It's almost 6:00 a.m."

"Yep. It's been a long night. I'm headed over to pay a visit to Kenneth Sutton. I'm pulling him in for questioning."

"Good. What about Carlson?"

"That weasel? He's still cooling his heels in an interrogation room." Egan laughed. "He practically peed his pants when we brought him in."

"Has he got an explanation for how his prints got on that humidor? According to Vic, Dalloway polished it every damn day."

"He claims Dalloway wanted to sell it. That's all he'll say."

"Lean on him. He'll crack. He came very close to threatening Vic one night. Besides, he seems to gravitate toward lowlifes. He's driving a fairly new BMW—"

"And Montoya's got that chop shop. I'll make sure to check on his registration and the vehicle ID number."

"Good deal, thanks."

Victoria stirred and Brody stepped over and took her hand.

"Brody…" Egan said.

Brody leveled a glare at the sergeant. "Yeah?"

"She's a prize."

He frowned at his friend, about to throw out a flippant remark. But at that instant Victoria made a small sound, as if she was hurting, and his heart squeezed in his chest, making it impossible to speak.

He swallowed and nodded.

"See you later, Lieutenant."

Brody took a deep breath and sat back down beside Victoria. Her neck was blotchy with dark purple and angry yellow ovals, where Montoya had bruised her with his fingers.

Brody's trigger finger twitched, and he recalled just how close he'd been to pulling that trigger. He'd never consciously thought about killing anyone before, but in that moment, when he'd seen Montoya standing over her with his gun aimed at her head, Brody could have killed him.

BRODY'S CELL PHONE VIBRATED. He realized he'd been watching Victoria sleep. He glanced at the clock opposite her bed. After seven. Then he looked at his phone. It was Deason.

He walked out into the hall before he answered.

"Lieutenant, Montoya's gone."

"What? What the hell?" Brody sprinted toward the elevator, dodging a nurse with a medication cart and a maintenance woman mopping up a spill. "When? Why didn't they call me?"

"The nurse's aid left him on a gurney in the hall, waiting to go into surgery. When he came back to roll him in, Montoya was gone. He was medicated."

"How long's he been gone?"

"At least half an hour. I've got officers rounding up the hospital's security guards. They're watching all the exits and mounting a search."

"It's too late for that."

"I know but—"

"We've got to do it," Brody said. "I'm heading over to his house."

"I've got a plainclothes officer already there. The second Montoya shows up, we'll know it."

TWO HOURS LATER Brody stood in a rented warehouse near downtown San Antonio, staring down at Montoya's body slumped over a scratched wooden desk. A small black hole marred the side of the man's face. His other cheek lay in a pool of blood that dripped off the edge of the desk.

"Get a close-up of that," Brody said, pointing to the entrance wound.

The CSI technician aimed the digital camera and snapped a shot, then a second one. "Powder burns," the tech said.

Brody nodded. "Whoever did this, Montoya knew them, and was comfortable enough to turn his back to them." He looked around for Deason. The Detective Sergeant was talking with an officer over by the side door.

When Brody walked up, Deason was examining the door's lock.

"The door wasn't forced," the officer was saying. "And it appears it wasn't even locked."

"Is someone looking at the tire tracks outside?" Brody asked. "Whoever killed him came here for that purpose. This was an execution. Somebody was afraid Montoya was going to talk."

"Brody! Come take a look at this," Egan called. He was on the far side of the building, standing at a counter that appeared to serve as a snack area.

Brody strode across the width of the building, marveling at how clean it was. There didn't seem to be a speck of dust anywhere, and certainly not on either of the three cars that were lined up in front of the massive rolling door.

"We found two beer bottles in the trash. We're bagging them, but look at this." Egan pointed to the various cups and mugs and glasses lined up beside the sink. "All of them are bone dry, except for this one," he said, indicating a serviceable green ceramic mug. It was sitting facedown, just like the others. But there was a small wet circle on the counter where it sat.

"Is that beer?"

Egan shook his head. "Water."

"Whoever drank that second beer used a glass." Brody commented thoughtfully. "And cleaned up after they shot Montoya. A woman?"

"Well, it's not the girlfriend."

"Nope. We've verified that she's on that plane to San Diego. Besides, I think it's more likely to be a man."

"Yeah." Egan's mouth curled in distaste. "Some rich arrogant prick like Link Hathaway or Kenneth Sutton. I mean, can you see a man who keeps a *chauffeur* drinking beer out of a bottle?"

Brody frowned at him and shook his head. "So we're looking at every person, male or female, Montoya ever came in contact with, especially in Cantara Hills. But considering the circles Sutton and Hathaway ran in, conceivably all over the city."

"At least that narrows it down from everybody in the known universe."

Deason walked up in time to hear Brody's comment. "What about his ties to car theft and chopping?"

"It's possible, but the way this looks, and the fact that it happened right now, makes me think it's got to be connected with his murder spree."

"Somebody was afraid he'd try to cut a deal—that he'd talk." Egan glanced over at the body. "Guess he won't tell us anything now."

"Whoever killed him is going to be worried about the same thing he was—that Vic saw something. She could still be in danger. I need you to take over the case, Egan. I want to get Vic out of here. I'm thinking Eleana knows something about Montoya's contacts. She might even know who killed him. I'm going to find her and question her. And I'm taking Vic with me. Then I'll set her up in protective custody until we solve this thing."

"You're leaving me with a murderer's fresh corpse and a city full of suspects?"

Brody clapped his sergeant on the back. "If there's one thing I'm sure of, Caldwell, it's that you can handle it."

"Right," Egan said wryly. "Thanks for the vote of confidence."

Epilogue

That afternoon Brody was able to take Victoria home. Her voice was still hoarse, and angry fresh bruises stood out against the older ones on her neck, but she was thrilled to be out of the hospital, and Brody was glad to have her out.

He gave her one of the tablets the doctor had prescribed and put her to bed. He sat down beside her. There was no way she'd be out of his sight ever again—not until he could be sure she was safe. He took her hand in his.

If he was right, and he was certain he was, whoever had killed Montoya was connected with his sister's death eight months before. If Montoya had been afraid Vic had seen him, then whoever killed him was probably worried about the same thing. She wouldn't be completely safe until the person who'd murdered Montoya to keep him from talking was caught.

"Mmm." Victoria moaned and opened her eyes.

Damn. He'd squeezed her hand too hard. "Sorry," he whispered. "Go back to sleep."

She looked at him and smiled. It was a tiny little smile, but it sent an arrow of something really painful straight to his heart.

"I'm tired of sleeping," she whispered. Her voice was a little bit stronger. "Besides, people keep waking me up."

"Sorry."

"Stop saying that, Brody." She pushed herself up in the bed. "Can I have some water?"

"Sure." He let go of her hand and reached for a bottle he'd set beside the bed earlier. He tried to hold it for her, but she took it from his fingers.

"Thank you." She closed her eyes. "Brody? Why are you here?"

"I…uh…"

She opened her eyes to narrow slits. "Lieutenant McQuade speechless?"

Brody clenched his jaw. What was he going to say to her? That he couldn't bear to let her out of his sight? That he feared that if he left her side for one second something could happen?

While he was thinking that, her eyes drifted closed again and her breathing evened out. She'd gone to sleep.

He took the bottle of water and set it on the bedside table and took her hand in his again. Something he'd never felt before made him lean over and press his lips to her fingers. Then he pressed her hand to his cheek.

"Brody?"

He jumped and let go of her hand.

"Why didn't you tell me about your inheritance? I assume from your parents."

Her words sliced through him. He swallowed. How did she…? Suddenly he remembered the envelope he'd left sitting on the side table.

"I never wanted that money. It's blood money. Having too much money killed my parents."

She nodded. "I know. It killed my fiancé, too."

Brody stared at her. She *did* know. "Vic, I'm sorry. I should have come clean."

Her hand went to her throat and her green eyes looked at him steadily. "Yes, you should have. You know it's not money that's the root of evil. It's the *love* of money."

"Yeah."

"What are you going to do with it?"

He wiped a hand over his face. "What do you mean?"

"I saw the note. You'd given it all to Kimberly, hadn't you?"

"Put it in trust. She actually was the trust-fund baby." He smiled ruefully. "As to what I'm going to do with it, I'll probably start a scholarship to let people who can't afford it go to law school."

Vic nodded sadly. She rested her hand on his knee and patted it comfortingly.

She was so good, so trusting. *What will I do when you're gone?*

"Good question," she said.

"What?" His head shot up.

She squeezed his knee. "I've been wondering the same thing," she whispered.

"Wondering?"

She raised her brows. "What I'm going to do when you're gone. So I decided that it doesn't bear thinking about. So..."

Brody realized he was holding his breath. And that his heart was pounding like mad. "So..."

"This is really hard for me—not because of my throat." She sent him a tentative grin. "I don't suppose you could help me out here?"

Brody didn't think he could talk, but he knew he had to try. "Vic, do you...would you..."

Her grin grew wider.

"...want to, that is...?"

Her green eyes sparkled.

He took a deep breath. "M-marry me?"

She reached out and touched his cheek. "It would be my great honor and pleasure."

"Vic, I...I'm...really bad at this. I've never done it before." He felt his face heat up. "But...I love you."

"That was very brave of you," she said.

"It was a lot harder than chasing bad guys."

She laughed.

He couldn't help it. Her laughter swirled through him like a summer breeze, lifting his spirits and making him want to laugh, too, for the first time in eight months.

Victoria's eyes lit up and she placed her hand on his chest.

"What now?" he asked, covering her hand with his.

"Feel that rumbling?"

"That's me laughing." He chuckled.

"That's your heart, Brody McQuade."

* * * * *

THE SILVER STAR OF TEXAS:
CANTARA HILLS INVESTIGATION
continues next month!
Don't miss Delores Fossen's Questioning the Heiress
only in Mills & Boon® Intrigue.

KILLER AFFAIR

BY
CINDY DEES

MILLS & BOON

Cindy Dees started flying aeroplanes while sitting in her dad's lap at the age of three, and got a pilot's licence before she got a driver's licence. At the age of fifteen, she dropped out of school and left the horse farm in Michigan where she grew up to attend the University of Michigan. After earning a degree in Russian and East European Studies, she joined the US Air Force and became the youngest female pilot in the history of the Air Force. She flew supersonic jets, VIP airlift and the C-5 Galaxy, the world's largest aeroplane. She also worked part-time gathering intelligence. During her military career, she travelled to forty countries on five continents, was detained by the KGB and East German secret police, got shot at, flew in the first Gulf War, met her husband and amassed a lifetime's worth of war stories.

Her hobbies include professional Middle Eastern dancing, Japanese gardening and medieval re-enacting. She started writing on a one-dollar bet with her mother and was thrilled to win that bet with the publication of her first book in 2001. She loves to hear from readers and can be contacted at www.cindydees.com

This one wouldn't have been possible without
Nina, Sheree and Tashya. Thanks, ladies, for the
inspiration, laughter and sand between
my toes when I needed them.

Chapter 1

Another gust flung the tiny airplane sideways like a storm-tossed cork. Tom Laruso's formidable muscles strained as he fought the controls, leveling out the Cessna floatplane's wings and easing it down toward a lower and hopefully smoother altitude.

"Are we going to die?" the woman beside him quavered.

"Nah. This is just a little turbulence. No big deal. Think of it as a giant roller coaster. Take my advice, little lady, just sit back and enjoy the ride."

She subsided, white-knuckled, beside him. Didn't look as if she was buying the roller-coaster line. She'd been insane to insist on this trip, and he'd told her as much before they left the big island. But the client, who'd called herself only Madeline C., had been adamant. She had to get to Vanua Taru *tonight*. Hey, if she had a death wish, who was he to stand in her way? It wasn't like staying alive held any great appeal to him. He was game to dance with death if she was.

But now that they were out here flirting with the leading edge of a Category Three hurricane—cyclones, they were called out here in the South Pacific—he wasn't so sure this was the way he wanted to go. He'd much rather lose himself in the bottom of a whiskey bottle and just drift away, numb and painless.

The plane lurched, its left wing jerking up suddenly and half flinging him into Ms. Madeline's elegant lap. His right hand gripped her thigh, which went as rock hard beneath his palm as any self-respecting stair-climber queen's. He murmured an apology and pushed himself upright. His biceps strained as he wrestled with the yoke and finally bullied the plane back into more or less level flight.

She *would* have to look just like Arielle. Tom glanced over briefly at his passenger in the waning dusk. Hell, she even smelled like Arielle, all light and floral like some damned butterfly. It was uncanny, actually. The fine bones, silver-blond halo of hair, the dreamy, mint-green eyes. How many women anywhere looked like that? And to have two so similar come into his life one right after another… Yup. Weird. If Arielle was haunting him, he'd kill her…oh, wait. She was already dead. Searing guilt twisted in his gut. God, he needed a drink.

Something flashed at the edge of his vision, a streak of light, falling from above and slashing through the arc of the propeller. The plane bucked. The engine hitched and coughed. Not good. Instinctively, he pushed the yoke forward, putting the plane into a descent. When in doubt, get out of the sky and land. Or in this case, float. Miles and miles of ocean stretched away in every direction. All the landing zone a guy could ever ask for. Even if it was heaving into massive mountains and valleys of salt water as the cyclone approached.

He started to glance down at the engine gauges to see if any caution lights had illuminated on the master warning panel, when another flash of white light streaked past his peripheral vision. Crap. Another lightning strike.

He had no more time to think on the possible implications of the strike as flames erupted from the engine cowling directly in front of him. His passenger screamed. Immediately he shoved the nose over as hard as it would go. They had to get down!

The steep dive blew out some of the fire, but it was coming out the other side of the engine, if the woman's continued screams were any indication. No time to reassure her, though. Not as if he had any comforting words for her, anyway. They were in a world of hurt. He fought the jerking plane grimly. The wild aluminum bronco was winning. This wasn't turbulence. Something was terribly wrong. The propeller wobbled, horribly unbalanced, all but shaking the little plane apart.

The ocean loomed near. He literally stood on the rudder pedals and hauled back on the yoke for all he was worth. The Cessna groaned its protest, metal creaking and wing spars shuddering under the strain of the g-forces he was violently overloading them with.

C'mon, baby, hang together just a few more seconds. Every muscle in his body strained, pushed to the limit to maintain control of the aircraft. Were he not as strong a man as he was, they'd already be spiraling out of control into the sea.

Something tore off the nose of the plane and flew back, slamming into the windshield directly in front of him. The Plexiglas cracked into a crazed spiderweb that completely blocked his vision of the angry mountains of water just below.

He shouted at his passenger, "We've got to bail out! Open your door and jump! It's not far to the water!"

He glanced over only to see her face contorted into a soundless scream of terror. She'd frozen on him. He let go of his own door handle to reach across her and push her door open. He shoved her toward the yawning void.

And then the plane exploded.

The burst of light and heat was blinding, like being consumed by the sun. He registered a vague sensation of the Cessna evaporating around him, flying outward until nothing remained but fire and the deafening roar of it. He floated weightless for a millisecond, then the explosion slammed into him in all its fury.

The world went black.

Madeline hit the water feetfirst, stunned by how much the impact hurt and how *cold* the ocean was. It shocked her horrified mind into a moment of utter, frozen panic, but then the icy chill penetrated and jolted her back to full awareness.

The great pressure of water all around her was terrifying. She opened her eyes, squinting against the violent sting of salt. But there was faint light above. She swam for it, her lungs burning. Her arms and legs were unbearably heavy, and she fought for all she was worth toward that flickering beacon of life.

It must have been only a few seconds, but each arm stroke, each desperate kick, each sluggish lurch toward the surface seemed to take an eternity. Her lungs were ready to explode and her eyes screamed their pain, but she fought on grimly.

And then she burst through to the surface, her head and shoulders erupting from the sea's deathly embrace, breaking free to air and a deep, blessed gasp. *She was alive.*

She treaded water, turning in a slow circle to observe the debris littering the surface around her. Huge ocean swells bobbed her up and down in twilight's last light. Now what the heck was she supposed to do? Her arms and legs were tiring fast. She paddled toward the nearest floating object, a large panel of metal lined with some sort of foam. Upon closer inspection, she saw it was the backseat of the airplane, a double-wide bench affair.

Whaddiya know. Those airplane seat cushions did float after all. She grabbed it and dragged her tired body across it. And as she glanced beyond the cushion, she spied something that tore a scream out of her hoarse throat.

A man's face. Floating just below the surface of the water, pale and ghostlike, slipping away slowly into the abyss.

The pilot. Tom Something. Alicia had recommended him.

She lunged across the cushion, kicking wildly, and grabbed for him. She got a handful of his shirt. She pulled with all her might and managed to bring his face up to the surface. Lord, he was heavy. She rolled off the long cushion and wrestled awkwardly to shove it underneath the man's back. She swallowed what seemed like gallons of salt water as she flailed frantically, trying to keep herself afloat, support the pilot's dead weight and get the damned cushion under the guy. Finally, she got him draped awkwardly on his back across the cushion and situated herself in the water beside him with one arm thrown across his chest to keep him from rolling off.

Ahead, she saw a faint line of twinkling lights on the horizon. Was it land? Or was it no more than a hallucination born of her desperate desire to be safe?

She did a slow three-hundred-sixty degree turn timed with when the swells lifted her up high and saw nothing else in the descending vacuum of night. Just a long, uninterrupted line where the gray-black of the sea met the blue-black of the sky to the north and south. Far to the east, she made out flickers of distant lightning. Tropical Cyclone Kato was roaring toward them.

She'd been a fool to try to race the storm to Vanua Taru, but she'd really wanted to just get the job done and go home to safe, boring Chicago before this awful trip got any worse. One of her Secret Traveler colleagues, Zoë Conrad, had gotten involved with a resort owner accused of murder and they'd nearly died before the police figured out another man had done it. Her second colleague and good friend, Alicia Greco, had been kidnapped and nearly killed by the same murderer, a serial killer who was still at large. The way their luck had been going, she was next in line for some disaster to befall her. Apparently, trying to run away from that bad luck had led her straight into it. A plane crash of all things!

For lack of anything else to do or anywhere else to go, she aimed the pilot's limp body at the lights and started kicking. She didn't even know if he was alive or dead. But if their positions had been reversed, she'd have wanted him to take her body ashore and not leave it for the sharks and whatever else lurked beneath the sea.

How long she swam, up and down the enormous waves, on and on in a morass of fatigue and pain that clenched her entire body in its vise, she had no idea. She threw up a few times. Probably a combination of swallowed seawater and shock. She stopped to rest a couple of times, too, but each time the flashes of lightning behind her seemed closer. She had no idea how far the electrical charge of a lightning strike could travel underwater, but she bloody well didn't want to find out the hard way. She dug deep and forced herself to get moving again.

True night fell quickly, the last vestiges of daylight wiped out by the encroaching storm bands of Kato. It was unbelievably dark out here. She could barely see her own hand in front of her face. Literally. Whenever she and Tom swooped down into the bottom of a trough and the line of shore lights was blocked, it seemed as if she'd been swallowed up by the depths of hell. But then the ocean would fling them dizzyingly, frighteningly high and she'd get a quick fix on her goal before being sucked down into the belly of the beast once more.

At some point, the pilot groaned and moved a bit. He was alive, then. Her exhaustion was such that she barely had time to register exultation that she wasn't entirely alone out here in the vast ocean. She didn't even particularly like water. She'd grown up on a farm in central Illinois, about as far from oceans as it got.

But in a flash, the Pacific Ocean had become her entire world, her entire existence. Just her and the cold, seductive embrace of the sea, slowly, inexorably sucking the life out of her. Well, the unconscious pilot was here, too. But at the moment, he was still little more than deadweight.

With dogged determination, fighting for both of their lives, she plowed on, pitting her tiny will against the massive expanse of ocean all around her.

That line of lights might possibly be drawing a little closer, but it could also totally be her imagination. And then, all of a sudden, she became aware of a black silhouette on the horizon. A jagged hump above the line of lights. *Land.*

Relief coursed through her, making her limbs warm and weak. Not far, now. She became aware that she was sobbing, breathing in ineffective gasps, but she didn't care. *Almost there. Almost safe.* With renewed strength, she swam on, using her free arm to paddle while she kicked the fiery spaghetti that was her legs.

Finally, she heard waves breaking nearby and smelled the

green, living scent of land. She was close to shore now. Something banged into her foot, startling her. It was rough. Oh, God. Was that a shark? To be this close to land and be attacked now....

She kicked furiously. Again, something banged into her feet, hard.

Then enlightenment broke across her mind. That was *sand* dragging against her toes! She tried to stand up, but the bottom past the sandbar was still a bit too deep. She paddled on a few more yards and was able to stand up between waves this time, her chin barely out of the water. She pushed off the bottom and swam a little more. In a few seconds, she was able to walk between sets of waves. When the breakers weren't rolling in, the water was no more than chest-deep. But when the angry surf caught them up and flung them forward, she guessed the water was ten-feet deep beneath them.

The good news was the waves pushed the pilot's makeshift raft shoreward in front of her. The even better news was a sandy beach stretched before them. They wouldn't be dashed to death against rocks tonight. A violent undertow of waves rushing back out to sea sucked at her legs and lower torso. It was all she could do to hang on to Tom's raft and ride the surface waves to shore.

But then she could stand up, no more than thigh-deep. Even when a big wave came in, she was able to jump into it and land mostly back on her feet. She dragged Tom the last few feet to shore on his floating pallet. Without the sea's buoyancy to hold him, he abruptly was unbelievably heavy. But she had to get him far enough out of the water so he wouldn't drown.

Using the piece of metal backing still attached to the cushion as a sort of sled, she dug in her heels and leaned back, pulling on his inert form with all her strength. By inches, she managed to wrestle him up the beach to what seemed a safe distance from the water.

They'd made it.

Relief making her even shakier than she already was, she knelt down on her hands and knees to check him for injuries. Not that there was a whole lot she could do about it even if she had found something wrong with him, but it seemed like the thing to do. She ran her hands over his bare legs…they were muscular and hard. Under the tattered remnants of his short-sleeved shirt, the guy had an impressive set of shoulders. She didn't find any obvious broken bones or cuts.

The guy sure was in great shape—and shaped great. Were she not so exhausted, hardly able to keep her eyes open, she'd have enjoyed drinking her fill of the sight of him. As it was, a thrill of…something…tingled through her palms and throughout her body at touching him like this. It was terribly personal. So…intimate.

Despite getting felt up by her, he remained unconscious. A head injury, maybe? She pressed her ear to his chest to listen to his heart, and its beat was a slow, steady thump beneath her ear. Stymied as to what to do for him, her own exhaustion finally overcame her. Shivering, she stretched out on the warm sand beside him, pressing the length of her body against his solid, reassuring heat. Mmm. Nice. She laid her head on his shoulder. Whether she passed out or merely fell asleep she couldn't say as the darkness closed in around her, sucking her down, down, into nothingness.

Tom roused slowly. His first sensation was of a splitting headache. And then pain. Grinding slowly through his entire body. He must've gone on a hell of a bender to feel this bad. He was wet. And lying in sand. He struggled to sort through the fog enveloping him. Something heavy was sprawled across him.

And that something was soft. Curvy. Intensely feminine. *Hello*. He made a habit of never picking up women when he went on a binge. He hated not remembering anything about them the morning after, not their name, nor where he'd met them or even what they'd done together. But apparently he'd broken his rule.

He lifted his impossibly heavy arm and looped it around the woman's tiny waist. Her toes tickled his shins, and her head rested on his shoulder. She felt small against him. Fragile. That was odd. He never went for the petite, delicate ones. They usually made him feel big and awkward and clumsy.

He cracked one eye open. The sky overhead was black. Turbulent. Looked like bad weather brewing. Groggy recollection swam through his head, half-understood. Something about a storm coming.

His brain might not be working, but his ears were. A sound not of the night registered. The ocean was rumbling like a ticked-off Rottweiler to his left. But this noise came from his right. From the shoreside. A rhythmic whoosh of sand, too slow for someone walking at normal speed. But if that person were creeping cautiously toward a threat of some kind, the measured noises were about right.

Instinct roared through him. *Danger!*

The man crouched in the shadows, stunned. He couldn't believe what he was seeing! After all the publicity, all the news coverage, this pair in front of him had the temerity to roll around like a couple of savages on a beach?

For the past few weeks—ever since the last cleansing of souls he'd undertaken—the beaches he prowled had been satisfyingly deserted. Pure. This part of the world was unbelievably sinful. Tucked far away from most of the world, the South Pacific attracted people who wanted to hide their dirty affairs.

The woman in front of him moved, draping herself even more blatantly across her lover. Rage exploded behind his eyes, sending ice picks of unbearable agony through his skull. He grabbed his head with both hands to keep it from splitting in two.

Must. Stop. The. Pain.

He fumbled at his waist blindly, feeling for God's instrument of punishment. His palm caressed the form-fitted rubber grip, his loyal and trusty friend. His vision cleared, and the sinners—all but naked—writhed before him.

Usually, he waited until they were lost in the throes of their sin, but these two were taking too long, and the pain in his head…ah, God, the pain…he couldn't take it anymore….

He moved farther out of the shadow of the trees, one cautious step at a time.

Tom struggled to rip away the gauze obscuring his brain, to bring himself to full battle alert. But his head wouldn't cooperate. And his body responded even more sluggishly. He flailed against the awful feeling of paralysis gripping him.

Threat! He didn't question the intuition. It had saved his neck and his clients' more times than he could count. If only his body and mind would obey him…he silently cursed himself.

With effort, he managed to slit his right eye open enough to make out a pale ankle protruding from a khaki pant leg. It was hairy. Male, then. Caucasian. Easing forward, rolling from heel to toe with each careful step, like a hunter stalking his prey.

The screaming voice of caution in Tom's head was deafening. *Trouble! Warning! Wake up!* But still, his mind and body steadfastly refused to answer the call. He felt drugged, unable to swim free of the haze of it.

The feet stopped maybe six feet away.

Below the crashing noise of the sea, a male voice muttered something just beyond the edge of Tom's hearing, syllables that didn't quite form meaning in his sluggish mind. But the tone of voice was unmistakably hostile, dripping in vitriol.

Tom forcibly readied himself for action, ordering his muscles into a state of relaxed readiness. He was probably deluding himself that they would react with any semblance of speed or accuracy to his commands. But his threat-response training had been drilled into him so deeply over the years that even now, barely conscious, mind and body went through the motions.

The woman, perhaps because of his arm tightening about her waist, moved against him, a sinuous, sexy stretch across his sprawled body that would have riveted him had it not been for those feet paused in the sand so close.

"Whore," the voice gritted out. "Sinners."

Blank incomprehension was all Tom's mind could muster to the unexpected words. But as he regained his senses bit by bit, he became aware of evil radiating from the stranger. Malice rolled off the man in waves as every bit as powerful as the ocean's fury beside them.

The guy leaped.

In sheer reflex, Tom exploded into motion, rolling away from the pouncing attack, carrying the girl with him, covering her protectively with his body, presenting his back to the attacker. Something slashed past him, burying itself in the sand where they'd been lying, not a second before. Agonizing pain sliced across his back. His skin melted like butter before a hot knife. *A knife.* The bastard had just cut him!

Tom surged up onto his hands and knees, driven by the pain, some primitive part of his brain taking over completely. On pure instinct, he leaped to his feet and whirled, dropping low into a fighting crouch, his hands outstretched before him. Killing rage roared through his brain. This wasn't fight or flight. This was kill or be killed. Fury erupted from his throat in a feral snarl.

The attacker was already running, a dark shadow fleeing up the beach and melting into the jungle beyond. Tom lunged forward, intent on catching his prey and crushing him, when a mewl of distress from behind drew him up short.

The woman.

Reluctantly, he turned away from the trees and dropped to his knees beside her. Had the bastard hurt her with that deflected knife slash?

Quick concern sent his hands skimming over her baby-soft skin. No dark welling of blood marred her body anywhere. He squatted on his heels and pushed her wet, stringy hair away from her face.

His mind stumbled. Arielle? No, not Arielle. Not even asleep had *she* ever looked this sweet. This angelic. Who was this woman he'd apparently picked up and made love to on the beach, if her mostly unclothed state was any indication?

He plucked at the scrap of cloth clinging to her slender shoulder. The edge of it was black. Almost charred-looking. No accounting for fashion among the jet-set party girls who came to the South Pacific to play, far from the prying eyes of the paparazzi.

A remembered flash of something black blinked past his mind's eye. Sprinkled with round shapes. He frowned. Reached for the vision again. Dials of some kind.

An airplane instrument panel. What did that have to do with anything?

The woman at his feet groaned. He ran his fingers across her forehead and down her cheek to the graceful, elegant line of her neck. She reminded him of an expensive Persian kitten. Even soaking wet and passed out cold, she was stylish. How in the hell had he landed a classy act like her? She was way out of his league these days. He had to give himself credit; he'd sure picked himself a looker. Man, the two of them must have painted the town red. He wished he remembered it.

He shrugged, and the movement sent glass-sharp daggers streaking across his back. The pain accomplished more to clear the cobwebs from his mind than anything else, so far. Tom glanced up at the jungle and then back down at the unconscious woman at his feet. They had to get out of here before that sicko came back to finish them off.

Who was that bastard, anyway? And why in the hell had he tried to stab this woman? Or maybe the guy'd been after him. Lord knew, he had plenty of enemies of his own who could account for the attack.

He reached down and scooped her up in his arms, startled at how light she was. What were the odds he could stretch their one-night stand into two? And this time he would stay stone-cold sober. He'd give his right arm to remember making love to a woman like this.

Chapter 2

A blinding flash of light, followed in a moment by a giant crack of thunder, finally roused Maddie to full consciousness. Groggily, she reminded herself that she was no longer Maddie Crummby, farm kid from central Illinois. She was Madeline C., world traveler and hotel connoisseur. At the moment, it didn't seem to really matter, though. She felt...floppy. And the universe was moving rather oddly around her.

She blinked her gritty eyes open and was startled to see a solid wall of darkly tanned skin. And muscle. Acres of it. *What the—* She jerked upright, or at least tried to. Strong arms gripped her tightly, preventing her from actually moving more than her pinkie fingers.

"Easy, kitten. I've got you."

She looked up at the deep, raspy voice. The hunky pilot who'd been flying her to Vanua Taru, who yelled at her to bail out of the airplane just before it blew up, whose life she'd saved in that interminable swim, on whose chest she'd collapsed when they finally reached shore. His name came back to her. Tom.

What a chest. Muscles rippled beautifully over it, not so thick as to be ungainly, but manly in no uncertain terms. She snuggled closer until it dawned on her what she was doing. She stiffened abruptly.

"You can put me down. I'm fine," she said quickly.

He let her feet slide slowly to the ground, which had the startling effect of pressing her body against his from her neck to her toes for an unforgettable instant. Heat built between them like chain lightning, flashing back and forth, faster and faster until it painted a dizzying chaos of light and heat in her eyes.

She clung to his strength, steadying herself as his hot skin scalded her palms. His dark eyes glowed down at her, the only steady reference point in her spinning world.

"Maybe I should carry you," he murmured. His arm tightened around her preparatory to picking her up once more, pulling her close against that magnificently naked chest of his again. She couldn't help it. She melted into him like warm butter soaking into fresh bread. An urge to lick his chest, to see if it was as rich and delicious as she imagined, overcame her.

She drew her tongue delicately across his skin. Salty. Warm. Smooth. Mmm. She liked that. He jolted away from her mouth, swearing.

She'd just *licked* a total stranger. What was *wrong* with her?

But then he was back, one arm around her shoulders, the other hand splayed against her lower back, pulling her against him, sending her whirling thoughts tumbling once more. Up and down, left and right, they tangled together, the same way her limbs did with his. Where he stopped and she began, she had no idea.

His mouth closed on hers, sucking the life out of her and breathing his back into her all in one devouring, devastating kiss. *Ho. Lee. Cow.* Never, ever, had she been kissed like that. She hadn't even known a kiss like that was *possible.* Stars exploded behind her eyes and unadulterated lust tore through her. She gasped at the sudden throbbing in places she'd never throbbed before. It wasn't that she didn't enjoy sex. It was just that she was…focused…when it came to sex. It was something she studied, even when she participated in it. She wanted to be good at it so when she landed the perfect husband she'd be able to please him. But this…this tore anything but wanting *more* clean out of her mind. She stretched up on her tiptoes hungrily.

"Do that again," she breathed joyfully.

He lifted her clear off her feet this time, his mouth hot and wet, moving across hers as if he was devouring a feast. "What have you done to me?" he muttered, an almost desperate note in his voice.

"I was about to ask you the same." She plunged her hands into his thick, dark hair and tugged. "Kiss me again. Please."

His hand slid down to her buttocks, lifting her tighter against his unmistakable reaction to her. She groaned, crawling even closer to him if it was possible, all but purring her pleasure. Her hands crept around his ribs to his back, kneading his ridged muscles…and encountered something wet.

He hissed into her mouth and lurched upright, arching his back away from her touch.

"What did I do?" she asked quickly in distress.

"My back. I got cut," he gritted out between clenched teeth. "How?"

To her dismay, he released her and stepped back, frowning down at her. She felt terribly cold and alone without his arms around her.

He answered reluctantly, "Some nutcase tried to stab you a few minutes ago and sliced me instead."

"Stab—me?" And then the rest of it hit her. "You've been stabbed?" she cried. Fear ran cold in her blood, chilling her all the way through. "Let me see."

He turned to face her when she would've darted around behind him to see how badly he was hurt.

"It's just a scratch," he bit out, his gaze skimming down her body and back up again. A flash of something hot and forbidden glinted in his gaze. "Damn, you're beautiful," he murmured. "As much as I'd like to tear off the rest of your clothes and make love to you right here, we've got to get off this beach."

She glanced down at the remnants of her clothes and gasped. Scraps of sodden cloth clung to her chest enough to provide a minimum of modesty, but not much more than that. Her silk Chanel blouse, no less. It had cost her a week's pay and the neckline draped exactly perfectly. Drat. She'd loved that blouse.

The man in front of her shifted impatiently, peering suspiciously over her shoulder as if he expected the attacker to come back any second. Abruptly, the pieces fell together in her head. They'd been lying on a beach…it was nighttime… and he said that out of nowhere a stranger had tried to attack them…

She exclaimed, "I bet that was the Sex on the Beach Killer!"

"The who?" Tom responded blankly.

This guy hadn't heard about the psychopath roaming the South Pacific killing pairs of lovers on beaches? He'd have to be a complete hermit to have missed that news flash. The killer had last struck on Fiji's big island a couple of weeks back. He was due to strike again, according to Agent Griffin Malone, the FBI profiler who'd saved Alicia's life.

"The Sex on the Beach Killer," Maddie repeated. Cold chills that had nothing to do with being wet and nearly naked snaked down her spine. A psychopath had tried to kill them? A fine trembling erupted throughout her entire body.

"How—" Her voice broke. She tried again. "How did you scare him off?"

He shrugged.

"Did you get a good look at him? Police have been chasing him all over the place. No one knows what he looks like. Well, besides the fact that he's Caucasian and around six feet tall. I know that because my friend found a pair of his victims, and she got involved in the investigation and met the FBI profiler and she told me a little about the case, you know, what to look out for and…" And she was babbling. She did that when she got really nervous.

He stared down at her as if she was jabbering a foreign language at him.

She huffed, "You have heard of him, right? The guy who's been running around the South Pacific stabbing lovers on beaches while they…do the deed."

His eyebrows lifted at that, but he made no comment. Not real talkative, her handsome pilot. But, hey, the guy kissed like a god. She swayed toward him once more.

"C'mon," Tom growled. He took off striding down the beach, his long legs outdistancing her quickly.

"Wait up!" she called after him. She ran through the heavy sand, feeling as clumsy as a drunken chicken. Ugh. *Style note to self: never run on beaches.*

He stalked onward without slowing down to wait for her. Not exactly the most social guy on the planet when he didn't have his arms around her and his mouth on hers. Exasperated, she tagged along, wishing he'd slow down, but too unaccountably annoyed at her uncontrollable attraction to him to ask it of him.

Eventually, they came to a stretch of beach bordered by tall, rocky cliffs. Before long, he veered away from the water and headed for a pale shape zigzagging up the face of the black, wet rocks. Her gaze followed the jagged line upward. She spied a dark, rectangular hulk at the top of it, perched not far from the edge of the cliff.

They drew a little closer and she saw that the pale line was a set of stairs. It led to a *bure,* a traditional Fijian dwelling made of stucco, logs and thatch. The house nestled within a grove of banyans and palm trees.

"Who lives there?" she asked cautiously. The last thing they need to do was walk into the Sex on the Beach Killer's hideout.

Tom tossed over his shoulder, "The weather's about to get nasty. We need to seek shelter now."

"But—"

"Ladies first," he interrupted gently.

With a sigh, she set her feet to the long staircase. Something inside her was disappointed that they'd found civilization. For a minute there, she could've really enjoyed being stranded in a deserted paradise with a hunky pilot who made her knees weak when he kissed her.

Not that the fantasy *ought* to do a blessed thing for her, of course. Madeline C. didn't go for sand, drinking out of coconuts and building palm-frond shelters. She was a city girl all the way. She liked her plug-in creature comforts and was never caught without a makeup kit or the perfect shoes. Of course, she had neither at the moment. Her hair was a sodden mess, and her clothes were destroyed. She'd have to extract a promise out of the pilot never to reveal to anyone that he'd seen Madeline C. without her chic armor polished and firmly in place. And no cameras! If he took a picture of her looking like this, the Sex on the Beach Killer wouldn't be the worst of his worries!

The Plan. She had to stick with the Plan. Build a new life for herself firmly anchored in the bright lights and big city. Find herself the richest—and nicest, of course—guy she could find and marry him with all due haste. No way was she spending the rest of her life working her fingers to the bone through drought and freezing cold and searing heat to scrape a living out of the ground. She was absolutely not repeating her mother's mistake. No, sir. She was Madeline C.

She took a deep breath and peered upward, trying to catch a glimpse of the dwelling above her. Even if Tom did kiss better than ought to be legal, there was no room in her life for heavy panting with some beach bum bush pilot. Focus. It was all about focus. It was how she'd dragged herself out of the ocean, and it was how she would drag herself off the farm and into a new life.

She tromped up the stairs, her already exhausted legs burning fiercely. Her personal trainer back at the gym would be appalled that a simple set of stairs was doing her in like this. But hey! She'd spent a couple hours fighting the Pacific Ocean in all its fury. That had to count for something.

Man. What a day. This trip had been jinxed from the moment she and her fellow Secret Traveler reviewers left Chicago. She just wanted to get home, go to her favorite spa, get a mani-pedi, a full body wrap and a facial and forget she'd ever been to this miserable corner of the world with its cyclones and serial killers and tempting strangers.

She glanced at the ocean pounding behind her. The waves were getting bigger by the minute, swallowing a few more inches of the beach with every crash of surf upon the shore. She didn't know a whole lot about the South Seas, but common sense told her that spending the night down on the beach might not be the smartest thing in the world to try with a storm rolling in. Reluctantly, she continued up the long line of steps.

Finally, several stories above the ocean, she set foot on level ground once more. Tom took her elbow and escorted her firmly to the house's front door. He fiddled with the doorknob for a few seconds, and then the door opened under his hand. Good grief, the guy'd just broken into the place! She stared, appalled.

"Are you coming or not?" he tossed at her.

"I don't think we should just walk in there like this."

"Why the hell not?"

"Well, the owner might be scared if we barge in. What if he's got a gun?"

Tom snorted. "The owner has several guns."

Her eyebrows shot up in alarm. "How do you know that?"

He bit out, "I'm the owner."

She stared. "What?"

He glanced over at her and didn't bother to repeat himself. A girl could get tired of listening to herself talk, trying to have a conversation with this taciturn guy. She followed him inside. If she thought it was dark outside, it was inky black in here. She banged into something about knee-high and yelped.

"Stand still," he ordered.

She was more than happy to oblige. A light flared on the far side of the room as he lit a match. He held it to the wick of an old-fashioned oil lamp and put a glass globe down over the flame. A dim, but warm, glow suffused the open space.

The hard thing that had attacked her knees turned out to be a beautifully carved wooden end table.

The *bure*'s interior was bigger than she'd expected. A vaulted ceiling high overhead added to the impression, giant logs forming an inverted V of cantilevered support beams. If she wasn't mistaken, that was a thatched roof on top of the log frame. Lovely. Grass for shelter from an approaching hurricane.

Bamboo and mahogany furniture blended seamlessly with the white gauze curtains and crisp, ice-blue linen upholstery. A kitchen occupied one corner of the space, separated by a gorgeously carved mahogany breakfast bar with a pair of elegantly curved stools before it. It was a shockingly stylish room. And *he* lived here? Clearly, he'd bought the place furnished.

She glanced over and saw him standing in front of a mirror, peering over his shoulder at his reflection. Checking out his deltoids? She knew guys were vain, but sheesh!

And then she saw the dark slash across his back, about two inches below his shoulder blades. The Sex on the Beach Killer. He'd said the guy had scratched him, but the cut extended almost all the way across his back!

"Good Lord!" she exclaimed. "You call that gash a scratch? I'd hate to see your idea of a serious wound. Let me see that." She rushed over to examine the cut, which still oozed blood. "You need to see a doctor. That thing needs stitches."

"No doctor," he replied sharply.

"Why not?"

"Only medic on Vanua Taru is also the sheriff."

She didn't know which question to ask first. Why he wanted to avoid the law, or if they really were on Vanua Taru, which had been her destination this evening in the first place. Caution won out and she asked the second question, for fear of the answer to the first. "We're really on Vanua Taru?"

He nodded, his lips pressed together in a tight line.

"Are you in pain?"

He shrugged, a tense move of a single shoulder.

She knew that look. Her brothers and father used to get it when they'd been hurt but didn't want to act like sissies in front of one another. Tom was having a bout of macho maleness.

She rolled her eyes. "Well, at least let me clean that cut out. It has sand in it."

"I'll take care of it."

"You can barely see it, let alone reach it. Where's your first-aid kit?"

He scowled at her for a moment, then moved through a doorway into what looked from a glimpse like a bathroom. He came back in a moment with a big backpack crammed with a shockingly well-stocked first-aid kit. A person could practically perform surgery out of it. Growing up on a farm far from any immediate help, she and her siblings had all learned basic first aid early. It was surprising how much veterinary medicine applied to human beings in a pinch, too. She rummaged through the supplies until she found what she needed.

"Let's go into the bathroom. When I flush out that wound, it's going to make a mess."

He sighed, but did as she suggested. In the end, they both stepped into the big, Roman-tiled shower, clothes and all. He stood under the water until the sand and blood were gone, then she soaped up his back gently but thoroughly and finally he rinsed off again.

He turned to her, his hair slicked back from his strong, tanned features. He looked like a freaking cover model, even if he was white around the mouth at the moment. An errant urge to kiss away his pain washed over her. *Focus, girlfriend. The Plan.*

"Thanks," he murmured.

Butterflies leaped in her stomach and she took a step backward, her back coming up against the cool, tiled wall. He braced his left hand beside her head and smiled down at her a slow, lazy, sexy smile that promised hours and hours of mind-blowing lovemaking.

"Have you got any scratches I can clean out for you?" he drawled.

"I…I don't know."

"We'd better check. Cuts infect fast in this climate."

He plucked at the scrap of cloth clinging to her shoulder and she glanced down. Then stared down in shock. In the dim light of the oil lamp flickering on the counter outside the shower, the remnants of her silk shirt and her lace bra clung to her breasts transparently, leaving absolutely nothing to the imagination. She watched, mesmerized as his brown fingers trailed over the pale fabric, around the outside curve of her breast, then lightly along the sensitive underside of the mound. Her nipples puckered hard, standing up proudly, begging for his touch. She closed her eyes in mortification— and longing. Something warm and firm touched her temple.

His mouth. He was kissing her again. Her toes started to curl. Ohboyohboyohboy. *The… What was it that she was supposed to remember?* He straightened and she tipped her mouth up to his. In the midst of the warm spray of water, he captured her lips with his, sucking her lower lip into his mouth and laving it with his tongue.

Her hands crept up to his shoulders. Urged him closer. His arm swept around her waist, pulling her away from the wall and against his big, hard body. The shower pounded down, raining heat and steam all around them.

He sucked in a hard breath as the spray hit his back and

she lurched. *His injury.* And here she was, crawling all over a wounded man. She sagged against him in frustration, pressing her forehead against his chest for a moment before pushing herself away from him.

"Let's get you out of here and get that cut dressed and covered," she sighed.

He matched her sigh with one of his own. "But I didn't finish scrubbing your back yet."

"Next time."

"Promise there'll be a next time?"

Whoa, baby. There'd be a next time if she had anything to say about it! Belatedly, she recalled herself. Madeline C. The Plan. This man was trouble with a capital T.

They stepped out of the shower and dried themselves quickly, and Maddie—*Madeline*—then used paper towels to blot his wound dry. She couldn't bring herself to ruin one of the fluffy, snow-white Turkish towels from his linen closet. She had to give the guy credit. She would never have guessed he even *had* a linen closet, let alone one neatly stocked with high-end bath and bed linens.

She carried the oil lamp back into the kitchen and set it down on the counter beside the first-aid kit. "So do you not have electricity at all, or is this a temporary power outage?"

"I haven't tried the lights. It's usually pretty reliable, though."

"Then why in the world am I trying to patch you up in the dark?"

"I prefer to live simply."

Simply? The very word made her shudder. Give her every electrical convenience modern technology could summon up, thank you very much. She liked her zoned air-conditioning, and her blow dryer, and towel warmer and wireless-Internet-capable cell phone/camera/television.

"Oh, for heaven's sake. Where's a light switch? I need to see what I'm doing."

He sighed and pressed a rocker switch on the wall beside him. Bright halogen lights imbedded in the beams overhead suddenly shone down, making her squint for several moments. Tom's wound came into focus.

"This definitely needs stitches. It's pretty deep."

"Just slap some butterflies on it and call it good," he growled.

She sighed. "All right, but you're going to have to be careful. I don't know if butterflies will hold or not."

He threw her a look so hot it made her bare toes bend into hard little knots of anticipation. "I can be careful," he murmured. "Very careful."

Her hands inexplicably shaky, she tore open a half-dozen sterile wrappings and laid the butterflies out on the counter as he turned his back to her.

"Are you always this cussedly independent?" she asked as she gently drew the edges of the wound together and commenced taping them in place.

"Nope. I'm usually worse."

"Great." She finished with the butterflies and laid a strip of rayon over the wound, covered it with gauze pads and secured it all with long strips of adhesive tape. She studied the bandage, pondering its chances of staying in place. Not good. She rummaged in the first-aid kit and found an elastic bandage. Perfect.

She held one end of the long, beige wrap against his left side and passed the three-inch-wide strip under his right arm. Her palms skimmed across his ribs, and her own stomach couldn't help but contract at the way the slabbed muscles of his abdomen tensed into impressive ridges under her touch. To reach all the way around him to pass the bandage from her right hand to her left, she had to lay her cheek against his chest and all but hug him. His big body radiated enough heat to scald her.

Her hands wanted to stray lower, to test his desire for her. Sheesh! The poor guy was hurt, for goodness' sake, and here she was, pawing him like some sex-starved desperado. Except, at the moment, she felt *exactly* like a sex-starved desperado.

She jerked back, startled by the thought. She did *not* chase after guys. She didn't even particularly crave sex! Yet here she was, her palms itching to run all over his naked body. Must be some weird hormonal reaction to almost dying.

Forcing herself to pay attention to the job at hand, she moved around behind him, passing the bandage carefully across the cut and leaning forward to reach around him again, this time from the back. And again, a visceral need, electric and disturbing, ripped through her as she hugged his athletic form. Wouldn't you know it—the end of the bandage ran out smack dab on top of his stomach. She ducked under his raised arm to pin the end of the bandage in place.

And made the mistake of looking up at him. His eyes blazed, black as night, consumed by a fire that incinerated her to her very fingertips. *Yowza.* She jerked her hands away from him, and actually glanced down at her palms to see if the skin burned from touching him. Her every nerve felt raw and exposed.

She stumbled backward, staring at his back hungrily as he carried the first-aid kit into the bathroom. She looked away hastily as he came out. He offered her the bathroom for a solo shower and she didn't hesitate to take him up on the offer. Did cold showers work on women, too?

She chickened out on testing the theory and opted instead for the relaxation of a nice, hot shower. However, when she finally turned the water off and stepped out into the bathroom, she was appalled to see a neatly folded man's T-shirt lying on the counter beside the sink.

He'd come into the bathroom while she was bathing? Her gaze whipped around to the shower door, and she was relieved—and disappointed—to see it was milky glass with wavy patterns through it.

"Hungry?" he asked as she slid onto one of the bar stools.

"I don't know. I suppose so." She'd been so wrapped up in staying alive and then her inexplicable reaction to him that she hadn't stopped to think about anything as mundane as food. But now that he mentioned it, she realized she was ravenous. And *thirsty.*

He set a beautiful double old-fashioned glass on the counter in front of her. The elegantly carved crystal caught the light from overhead and cast prisms all over the mahogany kitchen cabinets. She recognized the crystal pattern. Her brows lifted slightly. Waterford crystal? Who *was* this solitary pilot for hire? Silently, he poured water from a pitcher he took from the brushed stainless-steel refrigerator for her. She drank down the whole glass in a few gulps. He filled it again, seeming to know that she'd be desperately thirsty.

He went to the refrigerator and emerged with a green and yellow fruit about the size of his fist. He pulled a knife out of a drawer and peeled and sliced it efficiently. He stabbed a piece of the fruit and held it out to her on the end of the knife.

"Mango," he announced.

She nodded and took the juicy fruit. It was sweet, a cross between a peach and an orange. Odd, but tasty.

"Are you sure this place belongs to you?" she asked dubiously.

He frowned at her. "Yeah. Why?"

"It doesn't seem to…fit you."

He glanced around. "What's wrong with it? You don't like my decorating taste?"

He'd decorated this place? "Nothing's wrong with it." That was the point. It was too perfect. Too elegant, too…classy. This was the sort of place she'd pick for herself. But he…he was rough around the edges. Primal. She'd picture him in a beach shack with empty beer bottles and old pizza boxes overflowing the trash can. She opened her mouth. Closed it again.

He glanced at her wryly as if he knew what she was thinking. He turned away and fiddled with putting his water glass in the sink. "You can sleep on the couch."

"Where are you sleeping?" she blurted.

He cocked an eyebrow at her. "Why? Are you offering to share my bed?"

Just how tempted she was at the idea shocked her into silence. It was all well and good to be turned on by this guy but to sleep with him? That was a big step.

To get naked with him…to experience all that masculine power unleashed…to completely let go of her inhibitions with him…

Man, it was tempting. And totally out of character for her. Obviously, she was suffering some sort of strange aftereffect of the accident and her brush with death. She'd regret it tomorrow if she took him up on his offer tonight. Reluctantly, she shook her head. "Thanks for the offer, but I'd better not."

He frowned, almost as if confused. Opened his mouth to say something, but then closed it again. He turned off the overhead lights and left the room without speaking. At least he left her the oil lamp. In its soft glow, she turned to face the couch, which was underneath a wide picture window that framed a magnificent view of the ocean below. Even in the darkness, she could make out the rolling and crashing white of the breakers rushing in toward the beach. Drawn to the view, she moved over to the window. A light rain whipped around the *bure,* driven by a sharp breeze. Cyclone Kato was beginning to breathe upon them.

She started when something heavy thunked down behind her. Jumpy, she whipped her head around. Tom had just dropped a blanket, pillow and sheets on the coffee table.

He shrugged apologetically. "I'd sleep on the couch, but it's too short for me, and with my back, I'll need to lie on my stomach."

She smiled understandingly at him, grateful that he was being a gentleman about the sleeping arrangement. Truth be told, she felt like a heel for climbing all over him, but then turning him down when he took her up on her unspoken offer. "I don't mind sleeping out here. The couch will fit me just fine."

He nodded once, turned and disappeared on silent, bare feet into the bedroom. Suddenly, she was so exhausted she could hardly see straight. Mechanically, she made up the couch into a bed. She left the oil lamp burning. For some reason, she wasn't quite ready to face the dark and her suddenly overactive imagination. She stretched out on the couch.

As exhausted as she was, her brain wouldn't unwind enough for her to immediately contemplate going to sleep. She lay there for a long time. Eventually, she forced herself to extinguish the lamp and still, sleep eluded her.

Without warning, it all hit her. The terrifying plane crash, the desperate swim for her life, the shock of finding out about the attack on the beach. She started to shiver, and then to shake. And then the tears came. At first they were no more than hot streaks down her cheeks, but before long they'd blossomed into racking sobs. She turned her face into the pillow to muffle the sound, but for the life of her she couldn't stop the sobs from coming.

She started violently when a male voice rumbled from above her, "Oh, for crying out loud."

Reluctantly, she looked up at his dark form within the larger darkness of the room. Even as exasperated as he sounded, his presence was insanely comforting.

He rumbled, "I suppose you want me to hug you and tell you everything will be all right, don't you?"

Miffed at the humor lacing his voice, she snapped, "Far be it from me to force you into such an onerous task."

He made a noise that could have been laughter bitten off sharply. But she wasn't sure. He sighed and sat down on the couch beside her. "Fine. Come here."

She sniffed, "No, that's all right."

He ignored her and gathered her up in his arms, drawing her easily into his lap, surrounding her in his big, comfortable embrace. As hard as she tried to stop it, the floodgates opened up again. She sobbed into his shoulder for several minutes before it dawned on her that his shoulder was naked. And warm. And sexy.

And in an instant, the nature of their hug changed completely. She felt it in the way his arms suddenly tightened around her, in the electric energy zinging between them, in the sudden pounding of his heart underneath her ear. Despite herself, her own pulse accelerated, her breathing growing shallow and fast. She was *not* going to randomly crawl all over him, darn it! Her lust for him was just a reaction to her near death experience. Nothing more. She wasn't actually attracted to him in the least.

Liar.

When his finger tipped her chin up to him, she didn't fight it. When she gazed up into the dark planes and shadows of his face, she didn't say anything to forestall what was coming. And when his head started down toward hers, her lips parted in breathless anticipation. Nope, not attracted to him in the least.

Chapter 3

Tom inhaled the scent of her, female and faintly sweet beneath an overlay of deodorant soap, unable to stop himself from wanting to inhale the rest of her. Sex poured off her in powerful waves that belied her feeble attempt at maintaining her distance from him.

When her sobs first woke him, he'd been asleep in his bed, dreaming disturbing images of fire and water and spiderwebs. He'd have to talk to Joe, the local bartender, about the quality of the whiskey the guy was stocking these days. He really wished he could remember how he'd ended up on that beach with that woman draped all over him.

Maybe Joe could shed some light on that, too. When he didn't just stay home and drink himself into a stupor alone, the other place he went to drown his sorrows was Joe's place, the Paradise Lost Bar & Grill. That would undoubtedly be where he'd picked up Maddie.

Her name rocketed through him. As clear as a bell, the moment came back to him, a bolt out of the blue. He'd stared, shocked, into her light green eyes as she introduced herself. None of the context of the moment came with the memory, though. Not the setting nor any conversation before or after. Just that one disembodied moment. "Hi. I'm Madeline-and-I-prefer-not-to-be-called-Maddie."

She'd looked just like Arielle. *Just* like Arielle. The same willfulness gleamed in her striking green eyes, the same determination was apparent in her firm handshake. They were two women who knew what they wanted and both went after it full bore.

Maybe Arielle was a little more exotic in her features. But Maddie—how could he *not* call her that after she'd made such a point of it? He loved the fire in her eyes when she got hot and bothered—definitely looked less dissipated. Arielle had been an exceptionally hard-partying girl, and at age twenty-four, her lifestyle was beginning to take its toll on her looks. Although he'd place Maddie in her mid-to-late-twenties, she seemed worlds more…grown up. Heh. Not hard to achieve in comparison to Arielle, who had been a pampered and extremely spoiled pop star since her early teens.

Maddie snuggled closer as if she was cold, and he pulled the blanket across both of them. Nope, definitely not Madeline material. Maddie just seemed to fit her better.

Why had an obviously classy lady like her condescended to spend time with a guy like him, anyway? What did she want from him? Unfortunately, suspicion of everyone and everything came with his line of work. Well, his former line of work. He used to be a bodyguard. A damned good one. Fought over by a who's who of international celebrities. Until Arielle. Or rather, until she died. On his watch.

Damn, he needed a drink.

He'd noticed several new bottles of whiskey in the cabinet in his room earlier. He shook off the memory of Arielle's dead, green eyes staring up vacantly, her back arched in death spasms, her blond hair matted black with dried blood. He swore silently to himself. How rude would it be to dump Maddie off his lap and make a beeline for the liquor cabinet?

Probably unforgivably rude. And he really liked the warm, soft, cuddly feel of her in his lap like this. She fit just right against his chest, her forehead tucked against his neck, her arms wrapped lightly around his ribs. Holding her, like he was now, was…comforting. Made him feel not so alone. He wasn't lonely, of course, he told himself hastily. But a hug felt nice now and again. Even to a bastard like him.

Maddie's sobs renewed themselves, although quieter this time. She swiped at her eyes, dashing away tears, then tucked her fist under her chin, childlike. He recognized the body language. She was crying out some sort of trauma that had transformed itself into a desperate need for comfort. Any kind of comfort. A cuddle, or sex or whatever. And he happened to be the nearest able-bodied male able to fill her need. And Lord knew, he was willing.

No guy in his right mind would care about being used for comfort sex by a woman this hot. Not that he'd been in his right mind for the past six months or so. But still. He was totally okay with being this woman's shoulder sponge and sex toy.

Alarm jolted him. Jeez. What if *he* was the cause of her being this upset? He racked his brain. What boneheaded thing had he said or done to her within the massive black gap yawning tauntingly in his memory?

He worked through the logic quickly. She wouldn't have come home with him if he'd hurt her or been rude to her, would she? Was she on the rebound from some other jerk, maybe?

He swore under his breath. He really had to cut back on the booze. He couldn't recall a damned thing about the past day or so.

Thing was, Tom sighed, he knew better than to be some socialite's casual beach fling like this. He'd watched Arielle blast through men like a demolition derby driver, leaving a messy trail of wrecked lives in her wake. The sour taste of it in his mouth washed away the lingering traces of Maddie's impossibly sexy scent.

He probably ought to do something to draw her out of her crying jag. She'd been at it for a while now. He sighed. Ever the good guy, he was. It was probably why he never got the girl. He'd vowed to hang up his good guy white hat once and for all when he came here to the end of the world. But apparently, a few vestiges of it lingered, dammit.

Instead of kissing her like he'd originally intended, he halted, his mouth inches from hers. "Can you feel it?" he murmured.

"Feel what?"

"Blood flowing through your veins. Air moving in and out of your lungs. Heat on your skin."

She blinked a couple of times as if she was having trouble registering the meaning of his words. Lost in a sexual haze, was she? An instant of male triumph surged in his gut. So, sue him. Yeah, he got a rush out of turning on a good-looking woman.

He half whispered, "We made it to shelter before the storm. We're safe. Doesn't it feel great just to be alive?"

Her eyes were big and wide as she gazed up at him in the dim lamplight. Sudden, intense awareness of their bodies rushed over her face as plain as day. He didn't have to see her blush to feel its sudden heat radiating off her. She swayed closer to him, her fingers toying with his chest hair in unconscious flirtation.

He could *so* have her right now. And she'd *so* hate him for it in the morning. He sighed and drew back slightly. He wasn't the kind of jerk who took advantage of a woman when her emotional defenses were down. He might want to be that kind of unfeeling ass, but it just wasn't in him to take advantage of any female like that. Not to mention he had no intention of dragging anyone else into the train wreck of his life. Despite the occasional one-night stand, at the end of the day he wanted to be alone. End of discussion.

Except, a small voice whispered at the back of his head, *Maddie feels damned good in your arms.*

He ought to invite her into his bed, not for wild bunny sex, but just to hold her and make her feel safe so she could sleep. But panic flitted through him at the idea. No one was allowed into his bedroom. Ever. It was his last retreat, his most private, personal sanctuary.

Instead he offered, "Do you want me to sit with you until you fall asleep?"

One perfectly plucked eyebrow curved up at him. "Do I look like a five-year-old?"

He tilted his head and studied her. "Nah. I'd put you at nine or ten at least."

Her mouth pursed in disapproval, but her anxious eyes told a different tale altogether. And he noticed she wasn't making any aggressive move to remove herself from the circle of his arms.

He let her off the hook and announced in a tone that brooked no argument, "You're lying back down here on the couch, and I'm moving over to that armchair and not budging until I hear you snoring."

She laughed. "I don't snore!"

"I bet you do."

"Do not," she retorted indignantly.

He grinned down at her. *Better.* "I'll let you know." He let go of her and went to stand. But he hadn't counted on the lady having other ideas.

"Don't move," she whispered, looping her arms around his neck.

"But—"

She cut him off. "I want to listen to your heart beat. It lets me know you're really alive. When I was swimming to shore—I didn't know if we would live or die—I was so scared—and it was so dark…"

She'd had some sort of drowning scare? When was that? She was talking as if he already knew about it. Dammit. She'd no doubt confessed all the gory details while he was drunk off his ass. Unfortunately, he wasn't one of those men who got loud and obnoxious when he was wasted. People often mistook him for being much more sober than he was.

Maybe her big scare was how he'd gotten her into the sack with him in the first place. He'd played the "I can keep you safe, little lady" card. And at one point, that might have been true. Before Arielle got killed—stabbed to death by a stalker fan—when he'd been in charge of her security detail.

Careful not to promise to protect her, he thought and gathered Maddie close. "You're safe now. Everything's fine."

Except apparently, everything was not fine. She wriggled in his arms until he turned her loose. He expected her to climb out of his lap, but noooo…she threw her left leg across his hips and straddled him. Right there on the couch. Groin to groin. Pressing down on him just like she would if they were making love. Only a few pieces of flimsy cloth kept him from plunging up into her wet, tight heat, of sliding her up and down his length until he forgot everything and exploded…

Jeez! What the hell was wrong with him tonight?

She laid her right ear against his heart and stilled, listening intently. And for some reason, it was one of the sexiest things a woman had ever done to him. Maybe because it was real. A reaching out for human connection at the most fundamental level of existence. Confirmation of a simple heartbeat. And it all but pushed him over the edge.

"We're alive," she murmured in awe. "Both of us."

Ohh-kay. Poor kid had definitely had some sort of major fright recently. "Uh, yeah," he mumbled. "Alive. Miraculous, isn't it?" More like a nightmare from where he sat, but he wasn't going to quibble with her about the relative benefits of being alive or dead while she was straddling him like a cowgirl about to ride him until his knees buckled.

"It's a wild thing inside me, this feeling of having cheated death."

Oh, Lord. He knew exactly the sensation she was talking about. It tore through a person like chain lightning, making every inch a soul tingle, every nerve jangle on edge, every breath a triumph. Blood pounded through him, hot and thick, and abruptly he could count his pulse in the throbbing of his male flesh, so hard and needy he couldn't stand it.

Gritting his teeth against an urge to throw her down and drive himself into her until they both screamed, he managed to force out, "Honey, you're going to have to climb off me or be prepared to do something about where you're sitting because I'm about to have some serious self-control issues."

She laughed. She *laughed!*

A noise escaped the back of his throat. Whether a growl

or a groan, he couldn't exactly say. But it made her jerk her head up off his chest and stare at him, startled, her eyes big and wide and…have mercy…*aware.*

He actually saw her breath hitch. Her chest started to lift, then hesitated, then finished the breath. He closed his eyes in pain. Must. Not. Do. This.

She made a little sound, a soft, "Oh," that shot through him like a fifty-thousand-volt taser. And then she leaned forward as if to kiss him. Except the movement also had the effect of rocking her gently against parts of him that didn't need any more rocking at the moment. She froze, her pupils black in the subtle, and suddenly unbearably sensual, light suffusing the room.

He muttered, "Yeah. That."

She melted on top of him, flowing over him like warm honey, her body softening and relaxing against his. Her hands slid over his shoulders to toy with the short hairs at the back of his neck. Her breasts came to rest against him, hard nipples cushioned in the gently resilient softness of her breasts. Her thighs opened wider, pressing her even more firmly against him.

He closed his eyes. Threw his head back against the sofa cushions in an agony of need so great he barely noticed his back protesting. And damned if she didn't lick his throat. She really had to quit that licking bit unless she planned to lick all of him. Soon. Hands tugged at his head, drawing it forward once more. And then she was kissing him, her mouth open and wet and inviting. How could a guy say no to being eaten alive like this?

His own adrenaline rush answered hers. He had no idea where it came from, but it tore through him like a tornado. With her body surfing his, sliding across him with her mouth—with her whole self—he rose up to meet her helplessly.

Her hands fumbled at his waist, untying the drawstring of his shorts. She lifted up enough to slide them down his hips, and then he was spilling into her hands, hard and hot and jumping beneath her touch.

"Oh, my," she sighed.

She had to quit that sighing thing, too. It was driving him out of his mind. He reached forward, lifting the hem of her— his—shirt off her. She rose out of his lap, a naked nymph called forth from the heart of nature, perfect. Ethereal. Beautiful. Her breasts were high and firm, not large, but beautifully shaped. With a chest like that, she ought to walk around topless all the time. He restrained the urge to reach for the pale mounds and just looked at them, savoring the way they rose and fell with her rapid, shallow breathing. His gaze traced the slim inward curve of her waist, the gentle flare of her hips, the shadowed place where their bodies met.

"Well, touch me, already!" she demanded.

He glanced up at her, startled. And grinned. "Sorry. I was enjoying the view."

She leaned down and kissed him voraciously, biting his lower lip hard enough to draw his undivided attention to her mouth. *Vixen.* He slid a hand up to the back of her head under her silky hair, anchoring her in place as he took control of the kiss, plunging his tongue inside her mouth. It tasted of the ocean, salty and primeval. It called him home. He sucked at her, drinking in her sighs, devouring the taste of her, the smooth slide of her tongue against his, the way she surged against him.

He skimmed his fingertips down her body, and she stretched sinuously under the light caress, inflaming the inferno already raging inside him. "Yup, you're definitely alive," he murmured.

She arched her back, rocking her hips against his provocatively. Except now there was nothing between them, just hot, slick flesh on hot, slick flesh.

He leaned forward, wrapped his arms around her and lifted her up and away from him. "Are you sure about this?" he murmured.

"I'm not sure about anything except that by some miracle we made it. We're here. We're *alive.*"

He could wait no longer. He plunged into all that vibrant exuberance and groaned when she cried out in joy. His buttocks clenched until they nearly cramped, driving him up and into all that heat and energy, hot and tight upon him and around him. He touched her very core, and it pulsed against him once. Twice. He surged beneath her, drawn into her as if she was a force of nature. Her internal muscles milked him powerfully, sucking life from the very dregs of his soul. And he gave it all to her. He pumped into her with abandon, holding her hips down to push into her more and more deeply.

The sea roared outside and he shouted his release inside. She threw her head back and let out a keening, shuddering cry of pleasure that broke something loose within his soul. Something he'd not even known was bottled up within him. He collapsed as new awareness of it, of her, of himself, flooded over him.

Wonder suffused his consciousness. Indeed, she was right about one thing. He was *alive.* For the first time in a long time. Since before Arielle. Before…

Inexplicably, the end of the thought slipped away from him. Before what? How long had it been since he'd felt like this? His short-term memory might be shot to hell, but his long-term memory was just fine, thank you very much. And he couldn't remember the last time he'd felt this good.

"Mmm." She curled up in his arms, his wild, elemental force of nature back to being a kitten once more, limp and sleepy.

"You need to rest," he murmured.

"You, too," she murmured back drowsily. "Big night. Almost dying and all."

He had no idea what she was talking about. The cut on his back? It was no big deal. Annoying, yes. But life-threatening? No. The only threat some guy with a knife posed to them was catching him drunk enough not to defend them. The bastard had come close to that tonight. But it wouldn't happen again, Tom vowed silently to himself. As long as Maddie was with him, he would not get so drunk that he blacked out or that he couldn't fend off some asshole with a blade.

Tightening his arms around her, he leaned forward. She made a sound of protest as he stood up with her in his arms, but she settled quickly against his chest. He laid her down gently on the couch, tucking the blankets in around her chin.

"Sleep," he murmured, smoothing her hair away from her creamy brow. There was something eminently satisfying about making love to a woman until she lost consciousness. He watched her eyelashes flutter down. She was out like a light in a matter of seconds.

His arms felt unaccountably empty and he frowned at the sensation. True to his word though, he sat down gingerly in the armchair opposite her. After their athletics, his back stung like hell. But it was worth it. And how.

He propped his feet up on the end table he'd carved last month in a failed attempt to climb out of the bottle. His sharp eyes picked out her profile against the larger blackness of the storm outside. The seas were worse than he'd ever seen them. Vague memory of a storm approaching tickled his consciousness.

He and Maddie had stirred up quite a storm of their own in here, tonight. Fascinating woman. A study in contrasts. Calculating the odds of turning their now two-night stand into a three-peat, he locked his fingers across his stomach and settled in to watch over her.

An uncomfortable sensation of déjà vu crept over him. He used to watch over Arielle like this wherever she happened to pass out after one of her wild escapades. She used to tell him to quit hovering over her like a nervous mother hen, to go get some sleep in a real bed. She actually thought she could out-stubborn him. It had never worked. But she'd never given up trying.

Right up till that last night. He'd been ready to strangle her for insisting on going out on an evening when he was not only off duty but had other plans. But he'd never broken the implacable calm that was part and parcel of his job. Bodyguards weren't supposed to show emotion, and they certainly weren't supposed to throttle their impulsive, immature, spoiled, self-destructive clients. Even if the client richly deserved it. Not even if the client snuck out when her chief of security was out and her other guards were sleeping, and the client went and got themselves carved up by a nutcase. But it didn't stop him from wanting to wrap his hands around Arielle's neck and squeeze some sense into her.

Nor were bodyguards supposed to seduce females in their living rooms and make love to them until they screamed, even if *they* richly deserved it, too. Particularly when the poor woman was clearly upset and exhausted. What Maddie had needed was a decent night's sleep.

But in spite of what he should have done, he couldn't stop relishing what had happened. Images of Maddie in the throes of screaming pleasure danced across his mind. As he sat there in the dark, listening to her quiet breathing, fantasies of her crawling all over his willing body again and again in as many different ways as his imagination could conjure stole his breath away. Who'd have guessed he had such a vivid imagination?

Desperate to distract himself, he listened to the storm gathering steam outside. *Kato.* The name popped into his head. A moment later, its meaning came back to him as well. That was the name of the cyclone spinning in toward Vanua Taru. He hated it how these random snippets of memory kept dropping into his mind like capricious gifts from a prankster deity.

The ocean sounded furious below. Like a woman whose lover, almost in her grasp, had been stolen out from under her nose. What an odd thought that was. But then, this had been an odd night all around.

If these rain bands got much worse, the island would be completely shut down by morning, cyclone or no. That could be a problem since he had food and drink in the house for one. He hadn't expected to ride out the cyclone with company. He had some shopping to do, assuming he could convince her to stay with him until Kato passed. Three or four days marooned in his villa with nothing to do but listen to the storm and try out a couple dozen of his fantasies sounded like a little slice of paradise.

Looked like a trip to town was in order first thing tomorrow—or rather, later today. Given the searing pain in his back, he'd probably have to give in and get some stitches in his back, too. Which would also give him a chance to tell the sheriff about the attack on the beach.

He frowned, considering the chances of the attacker escaping the island before Kato hit. He bloody well wouldn't fly in this weather, and neither would any of the other island-taxi pilots. People wishing to leave Vanua Taru would be down to ferry service or private boats. Joe the bartender, also the local ferry pilot, was extremely stingy about sailing his precious ferryboat in heavy seas. The Merry Widow was probably already tucked safely in her boathouse and not likely to emerge until after the storm. Unless the attacker had his own boat and a death wish, he wasn't going anywhere until Kato passed. Nope, the Sex on the Beach Killer was stuck on Vanua Taru for at least the next several days. If that was, in fact, who'd attacked them.

Without any great heat, the thought that he could use a drink passed through his mind. But it was overridden by a much more pressing concern. He seriously didn't need to be trapped on this tiny piece of real estate with some crazy bastard looking to slice folks into bits. Truth be told, the thought made his blood run cold. Six months ago, he'd have laughed at the prospect. Back then he was still invincible. Had still never lost a client. He'd still been the baddest badass bodyguard in the biz. Nothing had gotten past him. But all that had been before.

And besides, Maddie was with him now. He had her safety to think about.

A flash of Arielle's bloody corpse flashed through his mind's eye. By some trick of his imagination, or maybe his subconscious, the face in his memory morphed from Arielle's into Maddie's. And suddenly he felt sick to his stomach.

Shaken to his core, he unfolded quietly from the chair and made his unsteady way into his bedroom. *Go away!* he screamed at the image of Maddie's dead face stuck in his mind. Oh, God. Please go away. No. No. Not another one dead on his watch.

His hands shaking so badly he could hardly hold the door knob, he managed to lock the door. Clumsily, he tested the knob to be sure it was secure. Safely barricaded in his private hell, he headed for the tall cabinet in the corner. Gut churning, he opened the door and stared at his wide selection of poisons. Tonight, he needed something fast and brutal—180 proof grain alcohol. Guaranteed to wipe the brain clean of unbearable memories in ten minutes flat.

Come to papa.

Too rattled to bother with a glass—not that he usually bothered with one anymore—he picked up the bottle. A pair of green, laughing eyes swam before him. The flash of a knife. Green eyes wide with fear. He lowered the bottle without taking a drink. Turned to head for his bathroom. *Green eyes, shining with pleasure after mind-blowing sex.*

He tipped the bottle…and poured the contents down the sink. The amber liquid swirled into oblivion just as green eyes swirled around him. Madeline's eyes…Arielle's eyes…accusing eyes he'd failed to protect…a green-eyed girl who'd died because of him…would die again…

Chapter 4

Maddie blinked awake in a gray gloom that was half morning and half something else indeterminate. Rain lashed against the window above her head, and she lay there, listening to it groggily while she assessed the pain shooting through her literally from her head to her feet. It was the sharp discomfort of overexertion so violent as to be abuse to her body. Not since she'd reinvented herself from curvaceous farm girl to rail-thin high-society girl had she hurt like this.

How in the world had she gotten so sore—

Oh. Yeah.

The plane crash. The swim for her life. Dragging Tom ashore.

Of course that didn't account for all her aches and pains. A few of them in places that had nothing to do with swimming and everything to do with throwing herself wildly at a complete stranger and humping his brains out. Heat sprang to her cheeks as memory of her wanton assault on her host last night came back to her.

What in the world had gotten into her? She didn't do things like that. Ever. Heck, she didn't even particularly *like* sex. Not even after a few too many drinks. Of course, she didn't much like alcohol, either. But she'd been worse than drunk last night. She'd been…horny. It was a complete anomaly for her. No doubt some sort of survival reflex. Nothing more than that. She'd been overwrought. Burning off adrenaline. Blown away to be alive. She probably ought to be grateful the guy didn't look and smell like a troll. As it was, her morning-after regrets weren't so bad. The guy was a hunk, after all. Even if he was basically a beach bum. Really. It was nothing personal between her and Tom.

Yeah. That was it. Nothing personal. He would understand that. Heck, he'd been as edgy as she'd been, as revved up on an adrenaline surge of his own. Survival sex. That was all it had been.

Of course, she had no idea if such a thing actually even existed. It sounded good, though. Besides, if it didn't exist, it should. She groaned and rolled carefully onto her back, daggers of pain shooting through her. She was one giant cramp from head to toe. She subsided on the sofa cushions. Whatever kind of sex they'd engaged in last night, she had to admit, it had been unbelievably good.

She lifted her arm just enough to see her watch, which was probably toast after last night's wild events. Wow. It still appeared to be working. Gotta love those Swiss watchmakers. Hers was apparently going strong after surviving an explosion and spending hours dunked in salt water. Then the actual time caught her attention. Almost noon? Her jaw dropped. She rarely slept past seven o'clock and *never* past nine. A lifetime of getting up to do her morning farm chores at five o'clock had seen to that.

Using the back of the sofa to lever herself upright by slow, painful degrees, she eventually managed to look out the window at the ocean below. The raging surf had all but swallowed the beach. Only a narrow strip of sand was left and the largest of the waves rolled into the base of the rocks below, sending up plumes of spray. The water was a dull, metallic gray, partially obscured by the lighter gray curtain of rain, blowing across it in sheets. So much for Paradise Cove, the sunny island resort she'd come to evaluate for her travel agency employer.

She glanced around the spacious room. Where was Tom? No sign of him yet. Of course, his night had been every bit as rough as hers had been. She climbed to her feet, her joints all but creaking aloud, and shuffled to the bathroom like an arthritic patient.

At least her underwear, which she'd washed and rinsed out last night, was dry this morning. It wasn't much, but it was one small, intact piece of her from before the plane crash. She shimmied into the lacy black-satin bra and panty set and felt worlds better.

Then she spied herself in the mirror. And stared, appalled. No makeup, no hairdo and nothing but a baggy T-shirt swathing her in what seemed like acres of olive-green cotton. If anyone she knew in Chicago saw her now, they wouldn't recognize her! Madeline C. had been taken over by a disheveled stranger. At least, a stranger to them…she recognized the alien, and it made her shudder. Maddie Crummby was back.

Panic clawed the inside of her rib cage, seeking release. No! Not after all her hard work! Two painstaking years of creating an image, building a new persona of herself from the ground up…she wouldn't let a single, disastrous night ruin it all!

Using the lone pocket comb sitting on the bathroom counter, she painstakingly put her hair back into order. Thank God she had a great cut. Even unstyled and left to air-dry, or pillow-dry as the case might be, it fell in bouncy layers around her shoulders.

If only she had some makeup. She felt positively naked like this. Not only her regular kit, but also her emergency back-up bag of makeup, were at the bottom of the South Pacific. Some lucky mermaid was going to have a great time with her top-of-the-line designer collection of cosmetics. Maddie hated to think what it was going to cost to replace all of it.

Frantic for something, anything, that might work to restore Madeline C. to the mirror in front of her, she hunted through Tom's drawers. She pounced with a cry of joy when she spotted a probable-looking tube wedged in the back of one of the drawers. Some former "guest" must have left the mascara here. Bless her, whoever she was. More searching in the dark recesses at the back of the drawer yielded a little pot of maroon lip gloss even a hooker would think twice about wearing.

The cosmetics were drugstore brands Madeline C. would never *dream* of using except in this, the direst of emergencies. But sometimes a girl just couldn't be picky. She opened the mascara tube and pulled out the applicator brush. Dried out and gloppy. Hyperventilation threatened. She could handle this. She could make it work. Think, *think!* What would a chic, in-charge sort of woman do now?

She rummaged again, this time through Tom's medicine cabinet, which she dimly noted in the midst of her panic was an orderly affair sporting some rather snazzy brands of men's grooming products.

Aha! Baby oil. Perfect. She added a dab of it to the tube and worked it in vigorously with the applicator until it regained a credible consistency. She brushed some on her lashes. She went easy with it because it turned out to be a true-black mascara instead of the more understated black-brown she preferred. But it would do. A tiny dab of the lurid maroon lip gloss diluted in the palm of her hand with some talcum powder and she had a crude, pale pink blush. She massaged it into her cheeks carefully. Wouldn't want to look like a clown, now would she? She shuddered to recall her first efforts at makeup application after her move to Chicago.

A tiny bit of the full-strength gloss on her lips—just enough to give them a little extra color—and she was starting to look halfway presentable again. She surveyed her emergency makeover critically in the mirror. Blotted off a little of the gloss. There. Better. Not half bad, given what she had to work with. Visceral relief flowed through her gut at having her Madeline C. armor back in place. Odd. She never used to wear makeup at all. Ahh, if she'd only known in high school what she knew now about grooming and self-presentation. She'd have knocked the boys dead and made cheerleader for sure.

Not that she'd regretted going through high school largely invisible. That, too, had had its advantages. Still, it was strange how dependent she'd apparently become on her makeup. Equally strange was her desperate need for some of it before she faced Tom Laruso this morning after…well, after.

Was her transformation all part and parcel of some deep-seated identity crisis or something? She frowned, considering it, until she remembered that frowning prematurely aged a person's facial skin and caused wrinkles. She carefully went through the breathing exercises to relax and smooth out all of her facial muscles. Supposedly, if she mastered keeping her face perfectly relaxed all the time, she would never need Botox to stave off wrinkles.

She opened her eyes once more. Nah, this was nothing as deeply psychological as an identity crisis. She simply wanted to catch a good man and marry well. There was nothing wrong with taking good care of herself. Okay, obsessively perfect care of herself. Maybe she was a teensy bit whacked. She'd calm down after she had a three-carat diamond on her finger and the I dos had been traded.

She could really use some of her own clothes. This hideous T-shirt was barely better than a burlap sack by way of style and appeal. She spied a leather belt hanging on a hook on the back of the bathroom door and appropriated it. Cinched in around her waist and carefully folded into wide pleats, the T-shirt didn't make a half-bad minidress. Thankfully, she'd just had her legs waxed, and the past two weeks spent evaluating other swanky Fijian resorts had given her a great tan. She looked pretty good in the shirt now, if she said so herself.

And with that thought, Madeline C. was finally back in charge. Calmer, cooler and already feeling worlds more sophisticated.

Thus restored, she stepped out of the bathroom. Still no sign of Tom. She puttered around the main room for nearly an hour, and even read a months-old woodworking magazine out of sheer desperation. How did he survive with no TV, no Internet, heck, not even a radio that she could find?

Finally, in grave danger of losing her marbles completely from boredom, she moved over to his bedroom door and stared at it. Should she wake him up? He really ought to be up by now. Maybe he had some sort of concussion and was in trouble. After all, he'd been unconscious a long time after the crash. Yup, she'd better wake him up.

Her boredom thus armed with a semblance of logic, she knocked on the door, butterflies jumping in her stomach. No answer. She knocked harder. Still no answer. Alarm blossomed for real in her throat. Had something happened to him? She reached for the doorknob, hesitated and then turned it. Or tried to. It was locked.

Oh, God. What if he'd gone into shock in there? Slipped into a coma? Died?

"Tom!" she called. "Wake up!" Slapping her palms painfully against the heavy wood panel, she pounded frantically on the door.

It flew open beneath her fists and he burst out into the main room. His hair stood up in every direction and his shorts and T-shirt were rumpled. But his eyes were fully alert, roving the room quickly. Danger poured off him, and—*good Lord, that was a gun in his right fist.*

"What's wrong?" he bit out. Death vibrated in his voice. He hooked her with his left arm, pulling her behind him as he scanned the *bure,* ready and obviously willing to kill. He all but shoved her through the doorway into his bedroom.

"Uh, nothing's wrong, Tom. I was just worried about you. You were sleeping so late and I thought you might have a concussion or something…"

Tom's tall frame sagged. He turned slowly. Glared at her blearily. "Good God, woman, you'd wake the dead with the racket you're making. Pipe down before you rupture my skull with that shrieking."

"I'm not shrieking," she retorted indignantly.

His gaze narrowed into a distinctly menacing expression. "You're still shrieking."

She frowned. "Headache?"

"Splitting."

She recalled seeing a bottle of aspirin in the bathroom. She stepped around him gingerly, made her way as quietly as she could to the medicine cabinet and pulled out four pills. After all, he looked as if he had the mother of all headaches. When she stepped back out into the main room, he was seated at the breakfast bar, his elbows propped on the granite surface and his head cradled in his hands. She poured him a big glass of water and set the pills in front of him.

"Can I make you breakfast?" she offered.

He scowled at her over the rim of the glass. Not in the mood for food, then. Well, she was hungry. She opened the refrigerator. Typical bachelor stash. A few beers, some steak sauce and a crusty bottle of mustard. A jar of olives, a few other random condiments and a couple of pieces of local fruit. She did find a half-dozen eggs, some bacon and a can of Cheez Whiz, though. Mmm. Tasty. Hardening-of-the-arteries in a can. The freezer yielded a loaf of bread, but that was about it for useful food.

"I thought there was a hurricane coming this way," she remarked as she laid the frozen bread on a cookie sheet to broil in the oven for toast and pulled out a skillet to fry the bacon.

"There is."

"You don't have a whole lot of supplies laid in that I can see. Shouldn't you have a week or two supply of food and drinking water? Some candles or something?"

"I've got everything stored elsewhere. The power will go out and refrigerated food will spoil."

Ah. That made sense. Still, he should eat. In her limited experience with bad headaches—all two of the real hangovers she'd ever had—she'd felt better after she'd eaten. Keeping her voice low and smooth in deference to his pain, she commented, "I hear Kato's a big storm."

No answer. Still feeling like crap, apparently.

He nibbled gingerly at the toast she set before him, gradually gaining enthusiasm for food. Before it was all said and done, he devoured all four of the slices. She toasted another batch of bread and grabbed a couple of pieces for herself before the human eating machine consumed the rest. The bacon finished cooking and she snagged a strip of it, setting the rest of it on the counter.

Mmm. Bacon. She couldn't remember the last time she'd indulged in its salty goodness. She nibbled at the slice, drawing out the experience for as long as she could. The kitchen was starting to smell like home. For a moment, she allowed herself to relish the memory of the big, warm kitchen back at the farm, redolent with the smells of bacon and biscuits and fresh milk.

She was surprised when Tom stood up and made his way around the breakfast bar. Bemused, she allowed him to shoo her away from the stove and even took the bar stool he indicated with the spatula he'd appropriated from her. In a combination of fond nostalgia and horror, she watched as Tom commenced scrambling eggs in the bacon grease. But when he pulled out the Cheez Whiz and sprayed a generous pile of it into the pan with the eggs, Madeline C. revolted entirely.

"You're actually going to eat those eggs?" she asked in distaste.

"Yup. So are you. They taste great this way."

"Have you got a defibrillator packed away in your pantry, then? Eat like that and you'll need it."

He shrugged. "If you get plenty of exercise and eat lots of

fresh fruits and vegetables, food like this won't hurt you. It's all about balancing the good with the bad."

Hmmppff. Might work for him, but no way could she eat like that. It had taken her endless grueling workouts and nibbling like a rabbit to get the figure she had now. No way was she blowing it on bacon grease and Cheez Whiz!

She watched Tom enthusiastically chow down his breakfast while she daintily consumed a piece of dry toast. At least, as the food filled his stomach, his face gradually took on a more pleasant expression. In fact, by the end of the meal, a definite glint was coming back into his eye. Uh-oh. She recognized that from last night. It might have been pitch-dark, but she'd still been able to make out that entirely male expression.

And darned if an answering flutter didn't leap to life in her stomach. No. No, no, no! Madeline C. was back in charge and she didn't jump into the sack with the Tom Larusos of the world. Period. End of discussion. She was holding out for a man who could give her security. Comfort. No worries. *Not* bacon and Cheez Whiz, darn it.

"So what's on the agenda for today besides getting you some stitches?" she asked, hoping to steer the conversation— and her errant urges to jump his bones—into safer waters.

He shrugged. "Delivering you to wherever you're staying, I suppose. Unless you'd rather wait out the storm here…"

And spend days on end stranded with him, alone, with nothing better to do than repeat last night's insanity over and over? Her breath actually caught for a moment at the idea. Oh, come on Maddie. Wake up and smell the Cheez Whiz. Belatedly, practical reality set in. Without the rush of having just escaped death, sex between them would be plain old, run-of-the-mill sex. And that she could definitely do without.

She mumbled, "Uh, my job…have to get back before the storm…"

Her company's A-list travel clients were always on the hunt for exclusive and private getaways in new and different places. And it was her job to scout out such retreats and review them. Paradise Cove had come highly recommended to her firm, so here she was, to check it out. Although, with a cyclone bearing down on Vanua Taru, she wasn't sure how good a look she was really going to get at the place.

If nothing else, she'd take a quick peek at the facilities. And, hey. She'd get a great firsthand look at the resort's evacuation procedures and customer service under duress. It wasn't ideal, but she would cut the place some slack in her write-up.

"C'mon," Tom said abruptly, startling her. "Let's go."

"Where are we going?" she blurted, stunned by her reluctance to end this relatively normal and companionable moment between them. After all, she'd never see him again after this. He'd crawl back into his bumlike existence and she'd return to the glitz and glamour of her real life, back in Chicago. Frigid, windy, gray Chicago, caught in the grip of winter's last arctic hurrah. For just an instant, she envied him for this carefree tropical existence. Even as she had the thought, the rain stopped outside and sun broke through, streaming through the big picture window and into the *bure,* filling it with cheerful light.

"We're going to town," Tom announced grimly.

Her pretravel research had shown there was a village on the island called Taru. It supposedly boasted local crafts, fresh, locally grown foods and a few high-end boutiques for the discriminating shopper…read, bored tourist with money burning a hole in his or her pocket. It sounded nice. Why, then, did Tom sound as if he'd rather have a root canal than go to Taru?

Perplexed, she followed him out onto the porch and looked around for some sort of conveyance. "How are we getting there?"

He glanced over at her in surprise. "Walking. It's only about a mile."

"A mile?" she exclaimed.

"Aww, c'mon. You do more than that on the treadmill every day."

Her gaze narrowed. "I prefer an elliptical machine."

He rolled his eyes.

She tried again. "I'm barefoot."

He glanced down at her toes, which suddenly developed a tendency to curl. "And?"

"I can't walk that far barefoot!"

He frowned. "Where are your shoes?"

"I lost them last night, of course."

He gave her a confused look, which, in turn, confused her. What was up with that? He was acting like the plane crash and their nearly dying had never happened.

"You can walk to town. I do it all the time. It is how Mother Nature designed us to get around."

"But I'll destroy my pedicure and…and…get blisters!"

"Heaven forbid," he retorted in mock horror.

It was her turn to glare at him. She'd forgotten just how taciturn and antisocial he could be. On the plane ride over here he'd hardly spoken two words to her—not until the crash and he'd yelled at her to bail out, and then, of course, pushed her out the door and scared a decade off her life. Jerk. Never mind that he'd saved her life. He was still a jerk.

Finally, she grumbled, "There had better be a decent boutique in Taru where I can stock up on makeup and clothes and shoes."

He didn't deign to reply, but merely took off walking down a one-person-wide sand path through the lush growth behind his villa. Thoroughly annoyed, she stalked after him. She'd worked for *months* after she moved to the city to soften her feet into their current cute, sexy condition. And all of that work was going to be destroyed in one half-hour hike.

After the rain, the strong noon sun heated the jungle into a steam bath that no doubt made her hair frizz up as if she'd stuck her finger in a light socket. She had undoubtedly sweated off all her makeup, too.

And after she'd worked so hard to improvise with a pot of gloss and some old mascara! It was a bloody miracle she'd managed to make herself look half-decent. But did he care? Noooo. Wasn't that just like a man, to totally not appreciate all the trouble she'd gone to in order to look good for him? She stomped along, taking out her frustration on the feckless sand beneath her feet.

Whoa. Rewind. Why was she fuming because she didn't look her best for Tom? She seriously didn't care what he thought of her looks. In fact, she hoped he thought she looked terrible. The more terrible the better, darn him! Making her traipse through the jungle like this, melting with heat and her clothes all sticky. Lord help her if her T-shirt was clinging to her as revealingly as Tom's was clinging to his bulging, sculpted, impressive back muscles....

Stop that.

The walk might be a mile, but through the soft sand, it felt like three. She was exhausted and drenched when the single row of traditional *bures* finally came into view. *This* was "town"? Great.

"This way," Tom directed.

"But I see a store over there."

He retorted shortly, "Shop later. Business first."

She scowled at his back. Did he have any idea how close to dying he was, coming between a desperate woman and her shopping like that?

"C'mon, slowpoke," he groused.

She'd liked him a *lot* better last night when they were crawling all over each other in their shock-induced sexual haze. She probably ought to be thankful he was showing his true colors like this. At least she would shed no crocodile tears when the two of them parted ways today. The sooner the better, in fact.

Roundly irritated, she minced across the hot asphalt of the village's lone street, cursing Tom with every blistering step. She cooled her heels in the strip of grass beside the road, then she marched after him to an unmarked building beyond the last shop. She stepped inside behind Tom's big, forbidding silhouette.

Oh, thank God. Cool air-conditioning wafted across her overheated skin. Civilization. At last. She closed her eyes and gave thanks to the electricity gods for their generous bounty.

When her head quit feeling like a hard-boiled egg about to explode and her face no longer felt tomato-red, she opened her eyes and took a look around. This place was built nearly identically to Tom's house, except the interior was outfitted as an office. The back half of the building was partitioned off by cubicle-style, partial walls.

The man seated at the desk just inside the door leaned back in his chair, with a not particularly pleased expression on his face as he gazed up at Tom. "What brings you in here, Laruso? Turning yourself in?"

"I'm here to report a crime," Tom replied evenly.

A glint of silver on the pocket of the man's tropical print shirt caught her attention as he tucked his thumbs in his belt and rocked his chair back on its hind legs. This must be the sheriff-cum-medic Tom hadn't wanted to see for his gash last night. Despite his casual pose, the guy's laconic expression suddenly wasn't nearly so laconic.

Tom spoke grimly. "Madeline, this is Herman Marquez, sheriff, mayor and resident EMT of Vanua Taru island. Herman, meet Madeline."

She smiled pleasantly at the sheriff. He had a competent air about him. Looked to be in his middle forties and had a nice smile.

"Tom forgot to mention that I'm also the public utilities commissioner, road maintenance man, pseudoveterinarian and volunteer fireman."

Her smile widened. "Do you fix toilets, too?"

"Yup. I'm a regular jack-of-all-trades."

"You must really have your hands full getting ready for this storm to hit, then."

Marquez's dark gaze clouded over with the myriad details obviously still in need of doing before Kato arrived. "Actually, I am rather busy. You're lucky you caught me at my desk. I was just on my way out."

Tom interrupted their exchange with a clearing of his throat. He sounded a tiny bit surly. Her eyebrow lifted faintly. Could it be? Was the strong, silent pilot jealous of the attention she was paying to sweet Herman? Would wonders never cease?

"Maddie—Madeline—and I were…taking in the view of the ocean last night…when we were attacked by a guy with a knife."

The sheriff's gaze swiveled to her in alarm, then back to Tom. His chair thumped to the floor. Abruptly, his eyes were grim and not the slightest bit laconic. "Tell me about it. Everything."

Tom complied emotionlessly. "We fell asleep on the beach. I don't know for how long. I woke up to the sound of someone approaching us. I wasn't…entirely alert…at the time."

Herman interrupted. "Drunk off your ass again, eh?"

Tom appeared unaffected by the jab. He continued as if the sheriff hadn't spoken. "The person attacked us with a knife. I rolled away from the initial strike and covered up Madeline, but I got scratched in the process. The guy ran away."

She interrupted with a snort. "Tom's got a big old slice across his back that needs stitches."

Marquez bolted to his feet at that, the EMT apparently subsuming the sheriff for the moment. "Lemme see," he ordered Tom.

Scowling at her, Tom shrugged out of his T-shirt. Maddie hovered protectively as the sheriff unwrapped her makeshift bandage and whistled. "Nice gash, buddy. The lady's right. That needs stitches. Lemme go get my suture kit."

Tom sighed in resignation and sat down on the edge of the guy's desk. Marquez was back in a moment. He spoke quietly to Tom. "I'd offer most patients a painkiller, but I think not for you."

She frowned. Huh? Tom just shrugged and didn't protest. She moved around in front of him so she didn't have to watch needles pierce his flesh.

"What can you tell me about the attacker?" Marquez asked as he commenced sewing up Tom's back.

Tom replied from between gritted teeth. "Male. Caucasian. Six feet tall. Athletic build. Maybe two hundred pounds, but no more. Light hair. It was too dark to see if it was blond or light brown."

The sheriff's mouth went nearly as tight as Tom's. "Sounds like the Sex on the Beach Killer."

"That's what Maddie said, too."

Given the way his lips were pressed together until they turned white and the way his fingers were digging into the side of the desk, Maddie refrained from correcting him aloud about her name. But she thought it in her head. She was Madeline C., darn it!

Herman's gaze swiveled to her apologetically over Tom's shoulder. "Then you two were…"

Tom answered quickly, "No. We were just lying there together in the sand."

Maddie winced. The way she vaguely recalled it, she'd been sprawled mostly on top of him and beginning to get some rather frisky ideas as she regained consciousness. It was sweet of Tom to edit the facts and protect her reputation like this.

"Anything else you can tell me about this attacker of yours?" Marquez asked intently.

Tom frowned. "He said something before he jumped us. I don't remember exactly what it was, but I remember being surprised by it. I think he called Madeline some sort of name. Something ugly."

Marquez nodded slowly. "An American FBI team is tracking this guy. They worked up a profile that suggests he's a woman hater. Has big hang-ups about sex. Were you two…uh…without clothes?"

Maddie's eyebrows shot up and her cheeks abruptly felt hot again. Tom replied dryly, "All but."

The sheriff nodded. "You said you were asleep. Perhaps in a position suggestive of…intimacy?"

Tom answered from between pain-gritted teeth, "When I woke up, Madeline was…uh…" he cast her an apologetic glance "…stretched out kind of, uh, across me. To a stranger, it would have looked more than a little suggestive."

Marquez swore under his breath and stepped back from Tom's back, surveying his work. "I gotta make some phone calls. Let the FBI boys know their killer may be here on Vanua Taru."

They waited while he placed a call and had a monotone, monosyllable conversation with the person at the other end. Marquez hung up the phone and looked over at both of them. "I'd appreciate it if you not spread it about that this guy may be on the island."

"Why not?" Maddie burst out, shocked. "People need to be warned!"

"Ma'am, we're about to be hit by a cyclone. Nobody's going to be down on the beaches messing around anyway. And I don't want to cause a panic when nobody can do anything to get away from this guy."

Tom moved his shoulders experimentally, then grimaced. "When he missed me with his knife, I jumped up with the intent to rip his head off. He took off and disappeared into the jungle. I think I scared him good. Maybe he'll go into hiding and not bug anyone for a while."

Marquez shook his head. "The profile says he's likely to be obsessive about secrecy. If he thinks you two have seen him and might be able to identify him, he'll need to take you both out."

Maddie stared in disbelief. She didn't even want to know what the sheriff meant by that. *Take them out?* As in permanently? She restrained an urge to squeak in dismay.

Tom said casually, "For all we know, he's already fled the island."

Marquez shook his head in the negative. "Nobody's gotten

on or off the island since sunset yesterday. Seas are too dangerous and flying conditions are too lousy." He threw Tom a withering look with that last phrase.

"We got onto the island after sunset," she piped up. "Of course we had to swim the last mile or two."

Both men turned to stare at her.

"What? When?" the sheriff and Tom asked simultaneously and incredulously.

Startled, she replied, "Our plane blew up just after sunset. I found Tom unconscious in the water and pulled him onto a piece of the debris that floated. Then I had to swim with Tom for what seemed like forever to get to shore. I'd guess it was a couple hours."

Both men talked over each other at once. *Blew up? How? Why? Where?*

She stared at Tom in disbelief. "Don't you remember it? We were hit by lightning and the engine caught on fire. You put the plane in a dive and it about shook us to pieces. At the last minute you leveled it off and told me to—"

"—bail out," he finished, partial comprehension lighting his dark eyes.

"So you do remember!" she exclaimed, relieved.

"Not entirely. But it explains a couple of images I had in a dream last night."

The sheriff swore under his breath as he reached for the phone. "And here I was already up to my elbows in crocodiles getting ready for a cyclone to strike and you had to go and drop this in my lap. What the hell were you doing flying in this lousy weather anyway?"

Tom glanced over at her, then back at Marquez. "She insisted. I told her it was suicide to try it, but she wouldn't listen."

She would've protested being painted as a bossy female

with a death wish, except he was mostly right. She'd just wanted to be done with this stupid trip to Fiji.

She, Alicia and Zoë had all leaped at the chance to review several world-class resorts in Fiji when their coworkers— known back at the office as the A-Team—had all contracted serious food poisoning at a sushi bar in Tokyo. The Secret Traveler Agency was due to put out a set of reviews of new and exclusive travel destinations for its wealthy and celebrity clients so they had called in Maddie, Alicia and Zoë to pinch-hit at the last second.

It was a great opportunity for the three of them to move up to the next level as travel reviewers, and they'd all been excited as they'd set out on this trip together. Of course, that had been before both Zoë and Alicia had crossed paths with this Sex on the Beach Killer. And they'd both had the good sense to get the hell out of Dodge already.

But she'd been determined to get the job done at all costs. It was a chance to prove herself to her employer, to demonstrate what a can-do girl she was. And to be honest, she'd also seen it as an opportunity to get a little ahead of Zoë and Alicia at the office. She liked both women well enough. In fact, she considered both of them good friends. But her under-riding sense of being a giant phony also gave her a bit of an inferiority complex at work. Zoë and Alicia were both beautiful, intelligent, sophisticated women, just like she wanted to be. She felt as if she had to work a little bit harder than they did to keep up. Hence, pressing a little too hard to get to Vanua Taru last night.

A disturbing thought occurred to her. If no one had gotten off the island since last night, how was she going to get out of there tonight like she'd planned? After all, she didn't want to get caught by the cyclone.

She asked the two men, "I'm going to be able to catch a ride of some kind out of here today, aren't I?"

Marquez replied without hesitation. "Not a chance. Everything's shut down until Kato passes through."

She stared at him in dismay. "But there's a killer loose on this island!"

He stared back at her grimly. "Let's sincerely hope not."

But they both knew darn good and well that she was right. They were trapped, all of them, on Vanua Taru with a vicious killer and a major cyclone blowing in.

Chapter 5

Tom had enough experience with both the FBI and crazies to fully believe the profiler if he said the killer would try to take out anyone who could identify him. He swore under his breath. Just what he needed. A killer gunning for him and Madeline. Frankly, this nutcase sounded out of Marquez's league altogether.

A year ago, he'd have been all over tracking this guy down on his own. But now…no way. Especially not with someone else's neck on the line, too. He glanced over at Maddie who, by the way, was as pretty today as she had been in the dark last night…although he liked her better completely without makeup. After their hike to town, only a little still clung to her skin, but it was enough to remind him of the rather unappealing plastic doll of a woman he'd picked up on the big island of Fiji yesterday afternoon.

Hey! Another memory! He remembered walking up to her

in an airport lounge and introducing himself. He also re-membered the thinly veiled disdain with which she'd perused his sloppy khaki Bermudas and casual polo shirt. It had chapped him a little, and the fact that he'd been bugged had bugged him even more. He was happy wallowing in his sorrows and his booze, and he didn't need the likes of her passing judgment on him.

He still didn't need her passing judgment on him. Although, he had to admit she hadn't been too judgmental last night in the dark when it was just the two of them. It was a novel sensation to be a comfort-sex guy that a woman would bed in private but wanted nothing to do with in public.

Tom forcibly unhunched his shoulders. The stitches knitted across his back hurt like hell. He could've used the painkiller the sheriff had withheld, but he understood the guy's decision. Tom was already well down the road to being a heavy substance abuser. No need to play with fire and expose him to narcotics.

And there was no need to expose Maddie to any further danger. Problem was, it would be a bitch to keep it away from her. Especially if Marquez was right and the killer was likely to try to murder the two of them.

A sinking feeling took hold of his gut.

Even if the sheriff and his men went after this Sex on the Beach Killer, Marquez only had a couple of part-time deputies at his disposal. The sheriff was a reasonably sharp guy, but neither he nor his compatriots had the training to handle a full-out serial killer. Add to that the fact that Marquez would have his hands full with crises related to the cyclone for the next week or two, and Tom saw the handwriting on the wall. He didn't even have to look at the sheriff to know what was coming next.

"I need you to do me a favor, Tom."

Nope. Didn't even need to hear the words. He *so* didn't want to go there. "No. No, no and...no!"

"Buddy, the statute of limitations has not run out for you on about twenty drunk and disorderlies, an assault charge or two and a couple more charges related to busting up Joe's bar. Stonewall me on this and I'm sure I can cook up a few dozen more to throw at you."

"Aww, c'mon, Herman. You know why I can't do this."

"Laruso, there's a cyclone coming. I've got a million and one things to do. And after the storm hits, me and the boys will have our hands full helping take care of folks and cleaning up. I need you to do this."

Maddie looked back and forth between them as if they were Martians speaking an alien tongue. Which was just as well. What she didn't know about how he'd spent the past six months was just as well.

The hell of it was that Herman was right. Reluctantly, he made eye contact with the sheriff. And did something he never did. Silently begged the man not to do this to him.

Marquez was implacable. "I need you to keep an eye on Miss Crummby."

Crummby? Her last name was Crummby? *Secret Traveler.* The name of the firm she worked for popped into his head all of a sudden. With the name came a few more details. She'd hired him to fly her to Vanua Taru and deliver her to Paradise Cove so she could stay there for a few days and write it up for the company's clients. He'd been sworn to secrecy over her identity and job. Whatever. But then, that meant...

His mind exploded with sudden realization. He hadn't picked her up and had a fling with her that landed them on the beach last night. He'd engaged in wild bunny sex with

her on the assumption that it was a repeat performance...*but it hadn't been.* He'd just gotten in the panties
of a *client.*

He swore long and hard inside his head.

His life might have gone completely to hell, and he might
have let himself go completely to hell, but that didn't mean
he'd abandoned his professional standards in the rare
moments when he was actually still working. Hell, his standards were all he had left.

Rule one: no drinking and flying.

Despite what Marquez thought, rule two: no drinking and
fighting. He was too lethally trained for that to be fair to the
other guy. And if he were being brutally honest with himself,
he didn't trust his self-control enough not to seriously hurt or
even kill someone if he mixed booze and violence. The only
time he'd gotten in a fight here on Vanua Taru, he'd been
sober. Hungover and grumpy as hell, but sober when a local
kid decided to test him and see what the old man really had.

And last, but not least, rule number three: no messing
around with his female clients. Ever. He cursed violently
under his breath.

Marquez was talking again. "Look, Laruso. I don't like
you. And I expect you don't much like me. But you and I both
know your qualifications for this job, and frankly, they're
better than mine."

Tom was surprised. It took a big man to admit something
like that. Plenty of people wouldn't have been able to make
such an admission. He nodded in silent acknowledgment,
both of the truth of the statement and of the maturity it had
taken to make it.

But to take on another protection job... Creeping dread
climbed his spine one horrified vertebra at a time. He couldn't

do it. He couldn't jump back into the arena. Especially not with another beautiful blond princess's life on the line.

"You got a gun, Laruso?"

He answered the sheriff absently as he fought down his panic attack with only limited success. "Yeah. Several."

"Keep one with you at all times. And keep it loaded, buddy. This Sex on the Beach Killer is a sick bastard...pardon me, ma'am."

Maddie nodded in what looked like abject terror. Tom was certain that wide-eyed shock in her eyes had nothing to do with hearing the word *bastard,* however. Maybe it had more to do with being stuck with a bastard—him—until this killer was caught. Hell, if she knew what was good for her, she'd be terrified at the thought.

In a last, desperate bid to escape this nightmare, Tom admitted the one thing he'd never said aloud before, never even barely allowed himself to think. "I lost the handle, Marquez. I'm afraid. Can't do it anymore. I lost one, and I can't lose another."

"Then catch the killer."

"Dammit!" Tom exploded. "Don't you understand what I'm saying? I've been sitting on my ass for months, drinking myself to sleep at night, not working out. My reflexes are shot, I'm in crappy shape. Hell, I can't even hold my hand steady enough to shoot." As evidence of that last, he held out his right hand, which was, indeed, shaking. With pure, unadulterated terror.

The sheriff slapped him on the shoulder. "Time to crawl out of the bottle and rejoin the living, old man."

"But—"

"The way I hear it, you functioning at fifty percent is better than most lawmen operating at full capacity. You're not wiggling out of this, so get over it and get on with it. Consider this your penance for past sins."

Tom staggered backward. Actually, physically staggered. An image of Arielle's mutilated body flashed into his mind's eye. No amount of penance could make up for that failure. None. He looked over at Maddie in mute appeal. "Don't let him do this to you…"

She frowned. "I don't know what's going on, but I know I want to get off this island. Can you do that for me?"

He latched on to the idea like a drowning man grabbing a life preserver. "That's a great idea! I'll fly you out right away—"

"Sorry," Marquez interrupted. "Aren't you forgetting that your plane is at the bottom of the ocean?"

"I'll borrow someone else's."

"Yeah, right. And one of the other pilots is gonna let you fly their plane in this weather. Seas are running thirty to forty feet above normal and the winds are gusting up to sixty knots. No floatplane can take off or land that. You're not flying anywhere until Kato passes."

Tom closed his eyes against the despair overwhelming him. Damn, damn, damn. "When's the storm gonna be over?"

"The main cyclone should hit tomorrow, late morning. The eye is forecast to pass over late afternoonish. Then the back side of the storm. Two, maybe three days, all told."

Tom swore under his breath. Three days to guard a principal around the clock by himself? Even when he was in top form, that would have been a bitch of an assignment.

The sheriff said grimly, "Precisely because of your past history, you'll protect her better than anyone else on the island could." A pause. And then Marquez added quietly, "Including me."

The two of them had been butting heads for months. It couldn't have been easy for Marquez to ask him for help. No easier than it was for him to admit that Marquez was right.

He exhaled heavily. "What can you tell me about this Sex on the Beach Killer?" If he was going to have to protect Maddie from the bastard, he might as well learn everything he could about the guy. Knowledge was perhaps the most crucial ingredient in keeping a subject safe, particularly knowledge of any threats to the subject.

Marquez surprised him by slapping a nearly six-inch-tall pile of folders down on the desk. "Here's everything I've got."

Tom eyed the stack. Then he eyed Madeline, who shifted impatiently even as he glanced at her. It would take him hours to even skim through the files, let alone study them thoroughly. She wasn't going to like sitting on the bench in the corner and cooling her heels while he combed through this monster pile of paperwork.

"Can I take this home to read?" Tom asked in deep resignation.

"Yeah, sure. I've been through it so many times I've about got it memorized." Marquez laughed shortly. "Besides, it ain't like I'm gonna have time to look at it in the next few days."

"Herman, could you or one of your boys escort Madeline down to Trudi's place? She lost her luggage in the crash last night. She might like to do a little shopping while I take a preliminary glance at this stuff. And I don't want her alone."

The sheriff sighed. "I don't have time for it, but I'll run her down. I suppose I owe you that. The summary file's on top. Take a look at that first."

Tom nodded tersely while Madeline, who'd perked up considerably at the mention of shopping, wasted no time heading for the door.

Before the sheriff followed Maddie out the door, Tom

pulled out his still damp wallet, which had somehow managed to stay tucked in his back pocket all through last night's ordeal. He passed Marquez a credit card to cover Maddie's purchases. After all, she'd saved his life. It was the least he could do to say thank-you. And, if it kept her out of his hair and from turning into a "I-have-nothing-to-wear" harpy, he was all for financing a shopping trip. He didn't think he'd ever seen Arielle wear the same outfit twice. And she'd been worse than a harpy when she didn't get her shopping on.

The sheriff paused in the doorway. "Find this guy, Laruso. Capture him or ki—" Marquez broke off. "*Whatever* it takes. Just stop him. You get my meaning?"

Tom heard the guy loud and clear. He was green-lighted to kill this psycho if need be and no questions would be asked about the circumstances of the takedown. He nodded grimly, his gut in a hopeless twist. "I hear ya. Loud and clear."

"Thanks, Tom."

"Yeah, sure. And Marquez?"

"Yeah?"

"You're a sonofabitch."

Laughing heartily, the sheriff slapped his tan cowboy hat on his head and walked out of the building, leaving Tom alone to ponder the dossier of the man he was supposed to hunt down and kill.

Maddie stepped into the boutique, housed in yet another wood and thatch structure and gasped in delight. It might not be Rodeo Drive, but it was crammed wall-to-wall with a selection and quality of goods that rivaled anything Beverly Hills had to offer. Trudi turned out to be a German expatriate who'd moved to Vanua Taru some twenty years previously and had opened this shop to cater to the resort crowd. And, oh, how she catered. After Trudi agreed to close the shop and lock the doors behind him, Sheriff Marquez left to tend to other things and the two women dived into power shopping with gusto.

Maddie picked out beach casual wear, a little, black Versace cocktail dress from the recent Milan collection and a barely there bikini that made her think of Tom. She added lingerie, designer cosmetics and hair-care products and even several pairs of crashingly expensive shoes to the growing pile. She figured she deserved a treat after yesterday's ordeal and having to be seen in public in nothing more than a man's T-shirt. Her one consolation was that Tom's shirt didn't have a beer logo on it.

Trudi served her a light lunch of fresh tuna fillets, a pine-apple and coconut salad to die for and mango white-wine spritzers. Trudi even offered to give her a quick manicure. By the time the German woman was done pampering her, Maddie felt almost fully human. She made a mental note to mention Trudi's shop in her review.

She asked her hostess, "Can I buy a cell phone on this island? I lost mine yesterday." Some octopus was probably having a great time running up text-messaging charges with it at this very moment.

"Not here. Besides, once Kato hits, the phone tower will go down."

"You mean it'll lose power?"

"No," the woman said and laughed. "I mean it'll blow over. Fall down."

Maddie lurched in alarm. "Just how bad is this storm supposed to be?"

Trudi shrugged. "Depends on how direct a hit we take and which side of the eye we end up on."

"What are the weather reports saying?"

Trudi replied, "We're hoping the worst of it slides north of the island. But we are expecting close to a direct hit."

And there was a killer running around on the loose. Who Tom was apparently going to try to catch. "Trudi, what's the latest on the Sex on the Beach Killer?"

"They haven't caught him. It has been two weeks since he killed anyone. Folks are saying it's about time for him to strike again."

Maddie closed her eyes for a pained moment. She didn't care what the sheriff and Tom said. She was warning this kind woman. "I was just over at the sheriff's office, and he has reason to believe the killer might be here on Vanua Taru. Be careful, will you, Trudi?"

The woman laughed off the warning. "It's not like I'm planning on going down to the beach and making whoopee at my age. I never could stand to get sand down my knickers, anyway. I'll be safe enough, don't you worry, now. Besides, after that last murder got so much publicity, I don't think anybody's going to be fooling around on beaches anywhere in the South Pacific until this weirdo's caught, sweetie."

Trudi cleared away their lunch plates and moved over to the cash register. She started ringing up the purchases as it dawned on Maddie that, along with her cell phone, her purse and its entire contents were also sitting on the bottom of the ocean right about now.

"Oh, no!" she exclaimed. "I don't have any way to pay for all this. I know my credit-card number, though. Could we call my company and verify my card or something?"

The German woman waved a breezy hand. "Not to worry. Tom Laruso is picking up the tab."

Maddie stared. Felt her face go red hot. Tom was paying

for all her new clothes? It felt suspiciously like payment for services rendered last night. And she didn't like the feeling one bit. Give a guy sex and get a lavish shopping spree, huh?

Something cynical in the back of her head muttered, *And that's not what you'll be doing when you marry for money? Keep the rich husband happy and in return, help yourself to his wealth and security?* A bitter taste accumulated on her tongue.

Trudi startled her by laughing knowingly and announcing, "The local girls will be plenty disappointed that you've landed Vanua Taru's most eligible bachelor. They've been eyeing him for months. Heck, if I thought he'd pay attention to a woman ten years older than him for more than a second, I'd be after him myself. That boy's hot. Even if he does drink a little too much now and then. But that's nothing a good woman couldn't cure him of quick enough. I figure he's just lonely."

Maddie closed her eyes, mortified. As soon as word got out that he'd paid for this elaborate shopping spree—and she knew without a shadow of a doubt that it would—her reputation would be in shreds. Except ultimately, who would know? This was a dinky little island in the middle of nowhere. She could stand the leers of the locals for a day or two until she could get off this godforsaken rock.

"How long will it be until transportation off the island is restored?" Maddie asked in resignation.

Trudi shrugged. "A week. Maybe two. Depends on the damage and how fast the storm passes. The worse the damage is, the faster we'll get relief flights and boats."

Great. Either pray for a natural disaster and a quick escape or put up with a killer stalking her—and the bodyguard that came with the killer.

Please, Lord, wipe this island out!

Chapter 6

"Feeling better?"

A thrill raced through Maddie at the sound of Tom's rich voice behind her. She turned around, modeling a flirty silk camisole and miniskirt ensemble for him. It floated around her, whispery light. One of the spaghetti straps slipped off her shoulder, and she ran a freshly manicured fingernail underneath it to slide it back up. She noticed Tom's hungry gaze on the movement, and she couldn't resist making a slow tease of it.

What *was* it about this guy? She never threw herself at men. She was the ice queen, the unassailable goddess that men panted over and chased down. At least that was the idea. Every how-to book she'd ever read on landing the perfect husband was clear on that point. Make the guy come to you. Never, ever, be the one doing the chasing.

Of course, the good news was that Tom Laruso was emphatically not marriage material. He definitely fell into the category of fun for the moment, but don't brag about him to your friends.

"This your haul?" he asked casually, gesturing at the row of glossy shopping bags lined up by the counter.

She glanced down at the bags in chagrin. Maybe she'd gone a little overboard on his credit card. "As soon as I get new credit cards and checks issued to me, I'll pay you back."

He waved a negligent hand. "Don't worry about it. You've more than earned it, sweetheart."

Trudi's carefully plucked eyebrows shot practically past her perfectly highlighted hairline. Maddie's cheeks burst into flame—that was how they felt at any rate. She peeked over at Tom to see if he was even vaguely aware of what he'd just insinuated.

The cad was smirking.

Fat cat swallowed the canary, knew damn well what he'd just implied, *smirking*.

Her gaze narrowed. Two could play that game. She purred, "Baby cakes, you really shouldn't have. I'm sure you'll be able to..." she paused for dramatic effect "...perform...next time. You didn't have to buy me all this stuff to apologize."

She wasn't sure whose jaw dropped farther, Tom's or Trudi's. Time to go for the kill. "After all," she continued, waving a negligent hand in blithe dismissal, "a man your age...these things are bound to happen. Fortunately, I hear that some of the new medications for it are working wonders."

Hoo baby. Good thing she wasn't planning on spending any more time with this guy after he delivered her to Paradise Cove. He looked about ready to do her serious bodily harm. Thankfully, he was going to be busy running around the island chasing after the Sex on the Beach nutcase while she did a quickie site survey of the resort before Kato arrived.

While she vacillated between unholy amusement and alarm at what she'd just done, Tom did the weirdest thing. He shut down. She couldn't think of any other way to describe it. His face went completely blank and all expression whatsoever drained from his eyes. It was as if the man just went away, leaving a cold, hard automaton standing in his place. She expected him to break out any second with a deadpan, "Just the facts, ma'am."

Instead, he scooped up all the bags with smooth efficiency and coolly said, "I'll be outside whenever you're ready to go."

Even Trudi looked perplexed at his sudden personality shutdown. "You take care of yourself, Madeline. You'll be nice and safe over at the resort. My husband worked on it when it was built, God rest his soul, and they constructed it to withstand bigger storms than this."

Maddie nodded, bemused, and took the receipt for her purchases. She winced at the total. Her current bank-account balance wouldn't cover it, but she could pay Tom with a credit card and then chip away at the debt for the next few months. Of course, she'd have to severely curtail her incidental expenses for some weeks to come.

It was a painful reminder of why she'd embarked on the whole Madeline C. project in the first place. She was determined not to live out her life in the backbreaking, spiritbreaking, relentless financial uncertainty in which she'd grown up. She told herself fiercely that she wasn't so coldhearted as to plan to marry purely for money. But if she did eventually fall in love and marry, why not do it with a rich guy?

This chance to hang out at high-dollar resorts was perfect

for meeting the right kind of man. She'd be a fool to blow such a golden opportunity by getting hung up on a fling with Tom Laruso, when Mr. Right might be here at this very moment, waiting for her.

She stepped outside, and the afternoon's muggy heat hit her like a brick wall. Even in the uncertain sunshine the humidity made breathing difficult. In a matter of seconds, she felt her carefully applied makeup making like a goose and migrating south toward her chin. *There's nothing like the feel of your face melting to know it's hot outside.*

The latest band of thunderstorms had spun past, leaving the island in a gap before the next spiral band of bad weather moved in. Tom lounged in the driver's seat of a covered golf cart, her bags already stashed behind him.

"Are we going golfing?" she asked in surprise.

"Small island. Gasoline has to be shipped in and gets pricey. Solar cells recharge electric carts for free."

She climbed in the seat beside him. Crud. He was back to his irascible, untalkative self of the day before. Her and her big mouth. She'd liked him a lot better when he was relaxed and open with her, before she'd made the wisecrack impugning his sexual performance.

"Look, Tom. I'm sorry about what I said. I was just joking around. Really, I didn't mean anything by it. It's just that, in the circles I run in, you either go on the offensive or expect to be the brunt of the jokes."

He spared her only the briefest of glances. "Maybe you need to get new friends."

She smiled ruefully. "Those are the new friends."

He made no comment. She noticed his gaze scanning all around continuously as he drove down an asphalt strip barely wide enough to qualify as a road. As they left the village, the jungle pressed in around them and over them, creating a living tunnel of green. She expected Tom to relax once they were under the cover of the foliage, but if anything, he waxed even more tense.

"Everything okay?" she asked cautiously.

"Just doing my job."

"Staring at the trees?"

He grunted. "The good news is this guy's partial to knives."

"And that's good news, why?"

"He's less likely to shoot us."

"Shoot us?" she exclaimed. "What for?"

He glanced over at her long enough to frown. "You heard the sheriff. The Sex on the Beach Killer thinks we saw him. He has to kill us now."

"Well, yeah. But if we stay off the beach and don't mess around in a public place, everything will be okay, won't it?"

"What the sheriff meant was, if necessary, this guy will depart from his usual mode of killing to silence us. What *I* meant was that I doubt he brought a gun with him to the island, and I also doubt he's had time to secure himself one since last night. But, don't kid yourself. He *will* try to kill us. And *that's* why I'm watching the trees."

Funny, but she suddenly developed a burning need to watch trees, too. Or rather the spaces between them. The jungle's underbrush wasn't nearly as dense as she'd pictured it. Ferns and flowering bushes carpeted the jungle floor, and a surprisingly wide variety of trees created a lush canopy overhead. She became aware of the smell of the place, fresh and alive, with a faint overlay of exotic spices.

The cart rounded a bend and she gasped in delight. A magnificent water garden unfolded before her, with flowing waterfalls and dancing fountains creating rainbow sprays across the interlinking pools. Red, oriental temple-shaped towers rose out of the pools, and quaint pavilions dotted small islands among the ponds. To say it was magnificent didn't even begin to do the expansive garden justice.

"Wow," she breathed.

Tom commented, "Take a good look now. The cyclone will wipe it out. They'll have to rebuild this more or less from scratch."

She looked more closely and spied a pair of gardeners tipping over one of the temple statues and passing it to more workers on shore. She heartily hoped they could save most of the major garden elements before the storm.

Tom followed the driveway around the garden to a spacious hotel lobby built in the open-air Balinese style. Impressed, she stepped out of the cart and walked into the spacious atrium, admiring the intricate carvings covering the giant logs overhead that made up the structure's framework. Cool air blew down on her from somewhere, driving back the muggy afternoon heat and giant pots of greenery and tropical foliage gave the place a comfortable, welcoming feel.

A man in white linen pants and a turquoise polo shirt greeted them and Tom made the introductions. Maddie recognized the name Nigel Cumberland. He was the resort's general manager. "Miss Crummby, welcome to Paradise Cove," Nigel said in a British-accented voice.

He was around six feet tall, trim and handsome. Made a good first impression for the resort.

"I'm afraid you haven't caught us at our best, Miss Crummby. Unfortunately, I fear you won't get to fully enjoy our amenities."

She smiled warmly. "I'm just glad to have gotten here before the storm, even if I can only see this place at its best for one day. I heard it was gorgeous, and that's very true."

Nigel smiled warmly. "We'll do our best to make you comfortable in what little time there is before the cyclone hits. And I assure you, our storm shelter is second to none. You'll be perfectly safe with us."

He actually sounded calm about the approaching cyclone. Score one for Nigel and company.

"If you'll step into my office for a moment, Miss Crummby, I have a bit of paperwork for you. Sheriff Marquez rang me up a little while ago and filled me in on your mishap last night."

Frowning, she followed him. This was not a typical hotel check-in—and she should know. She'd done dozens of them in the past year. Nigel sat down at his desk and gestured for her to have a seat across from him. He passed a thin file over to her.

"Am I correct in guessing that you've lost all of your identification, money and credit cards?"

She nodded.

He continued, "I took the liberty of contacting your bank, and they've wired you emergency funds—which you'll find in the white envelope—traveler's checks in the amount of two thousand U.S. dollars. Also, they faxed me a document…" He leaned across to fish out a printed form and pointed for her to see. "If you'll sign here, I've filled out a travel insurance claim on your behalf and only need your signature to complete it. I'll fax it back to your carrier in a moment."

Stunned at his efficiency, Maddie nodded and signed where he pointed.

Nigel continued, "Within the week, ten thousand dollars of travel insurance monies will be deposited in your checking account by your credit card company. If you have any other personal travel insurance, you will need to file that claim yourself when you return home. The American Embassy in

Suva is working up a temporary passport for you. It will be ready in three days. Best I could do with a cyclone coming. But, they agreed to courier it over to Nadi and have it waiting for you at the International Airport. Oh, and your airline tickets have been replaced and will also be waiting for you in Nadi when you're ready to fly home to Chicago."

Numb with shock, Maddie signed the remaining papers he placed before her. She looked up at the British man. "Where can I get one of you to take home with me?"

He smiled, a dashing grin that all but rolled her socks down. "In my experience, the character of a person—or an institution—is most evident in times of crisis. It is our pleasure here at the Cove to help you."

If his observation was true, then what did jumping Tom's bones last night say about her character? She was afraid to look over at him with that thought foremost in her mind.

Nigel got up from his desk and poured them all glasses of ice water. As he handed a crystal tumbler to Tom, he commented, "You're looking good, mate."

"You mean I'm looking sober?"

Maddie looked back and forth between them as the two men traded grins. Obviously buddies. Hard to picture the suave Brit and the scruffy American having anything in common.

Nigel said, "Don't be a stranger around here, Tom. I said you're welcome at the Cove as my guest anytime, and I meant it."

Tom replied with what sounded like genuine regret, "I didn't want to bring down your property values. You never know when there's a resort reviewer lurking nearby."

She glared at Tom, and he grinned back unrepentantly. He turned back to Nigel. "Marquez is forcing me to clean up my act whether I want to or not."

"Blighter!" Nigel exclaimed.

"Bastard," Tom agreed fervently.

Maddie rolled her eyes. No matter what the nationality or culture, male bonding was the same the world over.

"If you'll follow me, Miss Crummby, we've left your villa open. The cyclone shouldn't arrive until tomorrow, so you can spend at least one day in paradise."

The walk to the villa was nearly as magnificent as the water gardens, with an artfully naturalized tropical garden on her left and the ocean below on her right. Nigel pointed out various native plants and birds along the way.

They arrived at a spacious *bure* not unlike Tom's. As Nigel unlocked the door, he apologized, "I'd put you in a villa down on the beach, but the main storm surge is due in late tonight. I didn't want to take a chance on you getting flooded out."

Maddie laughed. "Gee, thanks. I've had enough unplanned dips in the ocean for one lifetime already on this trip."

She noted Tom's momentary frown. It looked as if he'd just remembered something. Maybe a snippet of that god-awful swim for shore had come back to him.

"Stay here with Nigel," Tom bit out. He disappeared inside the *bure* while the Brit slipped behind her, placing himself squarely between her and the jungle.

"Let me guess. You're some sort of fancy bodyguard, too."

"Ex-bobby, miss."

"Ex-what?"

"British police. Scotland Yard. I don't have anywhere near the personal security expertise that your man does, but I picked up a bit here and there."

"Tom's that good?" she asked in surprise.

"He was. Until Arielle."

She opened her mouth to ask more, but Tom appeared in the doorway behind her. "All clear."

"In you go, then," Nigel said cheerfully. "Tea's at four. Dinner at seven. I'm afraid the menu will be somewhat limited tonight. The kitchen staff has been a wee bit occupied preparing and storing nonperishable food for the next week."

Tom spoke up. "Anything I can do to help you around here?"

The Brit shook his head. "We've got things well in hand. All my disaster-preparedness training finally came in handy after all."

With a pleasant nod, he strode off down the path, leaving Tom and Maddie alone on the porch.

"Let's get you under cover," Tom murmured.

She frowned and stepped into the villa. It was lovely, but lacked the character of Tom's place. "Aren't you supposed to be running around the island looking for the Sex on the Beach Killer?"

He shrugged. "No need to run around."

Foreboding flooded her. "Why not?"

"He'll come to me."

"He will?" Alarm—and something else dangerous and breathless that she didn't care to examine too closely—raced through her. "How?"

"He'll come to *us*, actually. Marquez gave me two jobs to do. First, he told me to keep you safe. Second, he told me to catch the killer. The only way to pull off both of those assignments is to stick by you until the killer shows up and then grab him."

The killer...come to them? "You're kidding." Cold terror stole her breath away.

"Do I look like I'm kidding?"

She studied him closely. He looked like he needed a shave.

He looked tired. And he looked distinctly more focused than before their visit to town. A certain grim set about his mouth was new, too. Nope, not kidding. He looked dead serious.

"How close are you planning on sticking to me?" she asked cautiously.

"Like glue."

Glue? A distinctly sexual flutter tickled her innards. She told herself sternly that there would be no repeats of last night. That had been an anomaly, born of nearly dying and the crazy rush of having survived. She was calm now. In control. And so was he. This sticking like glue bit would be all right.

She nodded belatedly. "Okay. Until the killer's caught."

Tom set down her bags, and she hung up her clothes neatly in the closet, lining up each pair of shoes just so under the outfit they went with. As a kid, she'd never owned more than two pairs of shoes at a time—one pair of tennis shoes and one pair of school/church shoes. Of course, she had a clunky pair of rubber boots that came nearly to her knees for when she mucked out the barns, but those hardly counted as shoes. It was no surprise, then, that Madeline C. delighted in frivolous, flirty and downright un-sensible shoes.

When the stilettos, espadrilles and sandals were arranged to her satisfaction, she looked up and asked reflectively, "When you say, 'Like glue,' are we talking at the same resort, or within shouting distance?"

"We're talking within kissing distance," he replied as dry as the desert. In summer. In a drought.

Oh, my.

They both slept through tea. But after the night they'd had last night, it was no surprise to Tom. He allowed himself the nap on the assumption that the killer a) didn't know where they were yet and b) wouldn't have the *cajones* to strike in broad daylight. Besides, he and Maddie both were going to get precious little sleep over the next several days if he didn't miss his guess. Between the killer and the storm, they needed to stock up on all the rest they could get now.

He was just as happy to shack up in the *bure* and order room service, assuming it was still operating. Maddie, however, was having no part of that. For a woman who ate like a rabbit—an anorexic one at that—she was surprisingly adamant when she woke up that she needed a real meal tonight. Thank goodness. He'd seen some pretty whacky diets during his years in the celebrity security business. The whole business of starvation and fad diets had always bugged him.

While Maddie disappeared into the bathroom to dress for supper, he eyed the fully stocked bar in the corner of the living room askance. He wasn't getting the shakes or uncontrollably restless, but he felt a definite craving for a shot of scotch. Rule two, dammit. He was not mixing firearms and alcohol and that's all there was to it.

Not only was Maddie's neck on the line here, but so was his. If the killer had any sense at all, he'd be more interested in killing the big, athletic man who'd seen his face and had been prepared to fight him off than the tiny, weak woman who would be easy prey as soon as her companion was picked off. It was a novel sensation, being the primary target of a stalker for a change. Usually, he was only an annoying obstacle to be gotten around or passed through. That anonymity had helped him do his job, in fact. But now, he felt…exposed.

As recently as two days ago, he'd frankly have shrugged at the prospect of getting killed. Maybe even would've welcomed the idea on some unconscious level.

But now, with a job to do—and face it, with the booze-induced haze of the past few months beginning to lift—he was suddenly much less interested in dying. He wondered sardonically if the great sex with Maddie was the cause of that. He snorted to himself. Better not confess that to her or she'd be insufferable from now till kingdom come.

Maybe it was the challenge of the woman herself that was restoring his will to live. Her quick wit and quicker tongue were certainly keeping him on his toes.

She emerged from the bathroom and he did a sharp double take. The little black dress was simple, but it clung to her in all the right places. Her hair and makeup were perfect. He had to admit, she looked pretty damned good gussied up like that. Had she gone to all that trouble for him? Momentary warmth spread through his gut at the idea. But then reality intruded upon the concept. She was probably only concerned with the resort's dinner dress code. A pang of regret stabbed him. It would have been nice if she'd done it for him, though.

"Still hungry?" he asked. In his experience, women who stood in front of mirrors for too long tended to lose their appetites.

"Starving." Her gaze raked down him as if he was the main course for dinner, shooting an answering shudder of lust through him. "Is that what you're going to wear?" she asked neutrally.

Too neutrally. He glanced down at his black Bermuda shorts and black Hawaiian shirt with its understated royal blue print. For him, this was pretty damned dressed up. As his tan could attest to, he'd barely seen the inside of a shirt since he'd arrived in Fiji. No doubt about it. He'd turned into a bum.

He drawled. "Hello. *Black* shorts and Hawaiian shirt. Evening wear."

She didn't say anything, but her tacit disapproval was evident. Tough. The big city girl could get over her silly ideas on proper clothing and count herself lucky that he was wearing any clothes at all…or that she was still wearing hers, for that matter. That dress was positively calling to him to strip it off her.

As they set out for the main lodge, the foolishness of her clothing rapidly became apparent, her shoes in particular. Her spike heels caught between the path's pavers, and she ended up having to cling to his arm for dear life or else risk breaking an ankle. Not that he was complaining about the clinging part, of course.

After a few minutes of walking with her plastered to him from shoulder to knee, he murmured, "Switch sides, will you?"

"Am I drooling on your shoulder?"

He laughed. "No. I want you on the ocean side where there's less threat, and when we approach the lodge, I want my shooting hand free."

Her face clouded over, but there wasn't anything he could do about it. Fact was, a threat lurked out there somewhere, and they'd be suicidal to ignore it.

In the prematurely gathering dusk of another line of storms, he walked Maddie up to the main facility. Unlike her, he knew what was coming and wasn't taken aback at the formality of the main dining room. He had to give Nigel credit. They were one day from a hurricane, yet the white linen tablecloths were still starched within an inch of their lives, the crystal still spotless and the cuisine as exquisite as ever.

Okay, so he did feel a little weird walking into a four-star gourmet restaurant in shorts. Once upon a time he'd owned a whole closet full of suits, and even a custom-made tuxedo that lay correctly over a concealed shoulder holster. He wouldn't have minded dressing up for Maddie if he'd had any of his old clothes with him. But he hadn't been thinking that far ahead when he'd tossed a few things in an overnight bag, not after the curveball Marquez had lobbed at him this morning. Fortunately, many of the guests tonight were also dressed down as they made their last preparations to ride out Kato.

What did take Tom totally by surprise about the meal was watching Maddie eat. Oh, she consumed her food as politely as the next person, daintily even. But with each bite, she would close her eyes and savor the taste on her tongue for a moment before she swallowed. By the third course, he was about ready to drag her under the table and have his way with her. No way was he making it through four more courses. His shorts felt way too tight, and he was distinctly overheated about the gills before she duly savored and consumed the last bite of her berry-custard flan.

"Let's go for a walk," he growled.

She nodded blissfully and followed him from the restaurant in a practically postcoital fog. Damn. He might have to take up gourmet cooking if great food did this to women!

He guided her down to the beach, and her head swiveled every which way, taking in the terraced gardens dotting the steep hillside leading down to the white sand. Little gasps of delight escaped her lips now and then, and it was all he could do not to ravish her on the spot. High tide was in, and most of the beach was swallowed by pounding waves. The surf wasn't bad, with waves down here on the south shore, out of the brunt of the arriving storm, running between ten and twelve feet. But the waves rolled in heavily and continuously. Definitely some serious energy building up offshore.

He waited while she kicked her shoes off and dangled

them in her fingertips. Then, as they stepped out onto the beach, he draped his arm across her shoulders. Gratifyingly, she reciprocated and readily twined her arm around his waist. The profile on the Sex on the Beach Killer said he was attracted to and repulsed by public displays of affection... probably a result of some sort of childhood trauma involving pornography.

Tom sincerely hoped he and Maddie didn't have to resort to public pornography to draw the guy out, but something along those lines seemed like the most efficient way to get this guy to show himself. He'd really love to nab the bastard before Cyclone Kato got here. That way, he could tuck Maddie into a storm shelter, go back home and retreat into a nice, safe bottle of scotch to ride out the storm.

They strolled along the widest stretch of beach, but no weirdo with a knife leaped out and confronted them. They stopped near the steps leading back up to the lodge. The latest line of thunderstorms had broken and sunset bled across the turbulent ocean, creating a spectacular tableau at their feet.

He couldn't bring himself to ruin the moment by jumping Maddie's bones, so he settled for drawing her back against his chest and propping his chin lightly on the top of her head while they watched the sunset together. With her high heels off, she was a tiny little thing. Made him feel...protective. Must be the old instincts of his job starting to come back.

As the last vestiges of twilight faded from the sky, Maddie looked around nervously. Why he persistently thought of her as Maddie and not Madeline, even as brightly polished as she was now, he couldn't really say. The one name just seemed to fit her and the other seemed wrong, somehow.

"Shouldn't we go inside where the bad guy can't get a clear shot at us?" she asked.

"On the contrary. That's the whole point of being out here. We *want* to attract his attention."

"You don't have any idea where or who he is, though."

He shrugged. "We know he's around six feet tall and Caucasian, which means he won't pass for a native of Vanua Taru. Of the Caucasian transplants to the island, everyone who lives here recognizes each other on sight. So, our killer has to hide among the tourists, or he'll be spotted in a second. And there's only one resort on this little island. Our guy has to be here at Paradise Cove." And as he uttered the words, he knew in his gut they had to be true.

Abruptly, he felt the killer's presence nearby. Another old instinct roaring back to life? Had his famous intuition finally returned? Although in all fairness, it hadn't ever really left him. He'd *told* Arielle not to go out that night. He'd had one of his gut feelings that something very bad was going to happen, and he'd shared it with her. She'd just laughed, and then disobeyed him and snuck out without any guards—and died.

"I don't like it out here," Maddie announced. "I feel… naked."

He bit back a snappy comeback about wishing she was. He was reluctant to go out of his way to make her mad, even if her snarky comment at Trudi's place did deserve a bit of revenge. Amusement rippled through him. Failure to perform…hah! She hadn't had any complaints about his performance last night!

That hadn't been good sex, or even great sex they'd had. It had been epic, mind-blowing, out-of-this-world sex. He could seriously go for more of that— *Hold on, there, big guy.* She was now the client again, thanks to Sheriff Marquez. *Note to self: strangle Marquez the next time I see him.*

Paradise Cove was, indeed, built on a cove, a teardrop-shaped affair rimmed by the whitest, smoothest sand beaches he'd ever seen. They walked all the way to the southeast point of the cove, and Tom helped Maddie climb the boulder-strewn promontory to view the ocean beyond as night fell and stars winked into the sky.

"Wow," she breathed.

From there, they caught glimpses of the pale arc of the island's barrier reef, mostly obscured by the beginnings of Kato's storm surge. Beyond it, the Pacific Ocean heaved, magnificent and endless, stirred by Poseidon's angry hand.

Maddie shivered as the full force of the wind—around forty knots and gusting higher—whipped at her dress, plastering it to her lithe body. She really did have a great figure.

"Cold?" he murmured.

"A little. But I'm glad you brought me up here. This is incredible. There's nothing even remotely like this where I come from."

"I dunno. Lake Michigan is pretty fierce sometimes. They don't call Chicago the *Windy City* for nothing."

"I'm not from Chi—" She broke off, if he wasn't mistaken, in embarrassment.

"Where are you from?" he asked, curious to know why that odd note had entered her voice.

"Manhattan, actually."

Ah. That explained the sharp-tongued humor. But New York City? He'd lived there on and off for years, chasing his clients around in pursuit of exclusive shopping and publicity exposure. Maddie didn't strike him as a Big Apple girl. Something indefinably…New York…was missing in her. He was definitely off his game at people-reading where she was concerned.

She shivered a little more noticeably, and he used it as an excuse to draw her close to his side. She snuggled up against him greedily, trying to absorb even more warmth from him. Perfect. They looked just like a pair of lovers, out enjoying the evening before finding someplace secluded to engage in plenty of hot sex.

Are you looking, you crazy sonofabitch? Do you see us? We're climbing all over each other here. Come out, come out, wherever you are...

The man adjusted his binoculars to bring the couple into sharper focus, crawling all over each other right out in the open for all the world to see. He used the zoom feature to bring the couple's faces into plain view...and stared, stunned. Rage simmered low in his gut, building quickly into a boiling cauldron of molten fury.

Had they learned *nothing* from their lesson last night? They'd been supremely lucky he hadn't sent them both straight to hell!

By his grace, and his grace alone, they'd been given a chance to redeem themselves. To repent of their sinful ways. It had been a novel sensation, knowing he'd given someone forgiveness, had granted them life. But to throw his reprieve in his face like this!

Oh, they would surely die now.

They would bleed until their sins were purged, would bathe in their own blood until they were washed clean. And then they would *die*. Both of them. He'd make sure of it next time.

And now he knew where they were staying. How very convenient that they'd wandered right onto his home turf like this. Hapless little flies. Didn't even know they'd just landed in the spider's web.

Oh, but they would. They would.

Chapter 7

Maddie frowned as they made their way back to the resort proper. She heard the faint, but distinct sounds of Donna Summer's music. What was the classic disco queen doing belting out a tune in a place like this?

Tom's arm tightened across her shoulder. "Everything okay?" he murmured, his head turned toward her, but his eyes roving everywhere but on her.

"Yes. Why do you ask?"

"You frowned."

"How would you know that? You weren't looking at me," she replied.

"I felt it."

"How?"

"I'm psychic."

"Seriously?"

He stopped in the middle of the path. Fully faced her.

"Actually, I kind of am. If you work in a business like mine for long enough, you develop a sixth sense about stuff. Mind you, I don't rely solely on gut feeling to do my job, but I do pay attention to it." He grinned boyishly at her. "Besides, you hunch up your shoulders a little whenever you frown. I felt the hunch."

Okay, he got full points for noticing details. But part of her was disappointed that it wasn't some sort of romantic simpatico between them that made him aware of her frown. "When did Donna Summer fly into Vanua Taru?"

He looked perplexed for a moment, then grinned. "Ah. The music. Paradise Cove has a hot disco. When there's not a cyclone bearing down on the place, people cruise in on yachts from other islands and even fly in for the evening to party there. There are usually live bands. The joint's always crammed. But I expect they're spinning vinyls tonight."

"People still use vinyl records?"

He shrugged. "Nigel says when the only thing you need is loud noise and a beat, a record does the job just as well as modern technology…and they have higher 'cool factor.'"

She smiled. "Well, if Nigel says records are cool, I guess they are."

Tom turned and continued up the path, still holding her hand.

"How long have you been in the bodyguard business, Tom?"

"'Bout eight hours."

She rolled her eyes. "Before you came to Vanua Taru?"

"Nearly twenty years."

"Let's see. That would make you about sixty-eight years old."

"Hey! Enough wisecracks about me being an old man. I'm forty-one."

Dang. He was sure well preserved for forty-one. She'd have placed him in his mid-thirties if she had to guess. His body was lean and hard, his thick, dark hair showing not even a hint of gray. He didn't even have laugh lines at the corner of his eyes to speak of.

"What do you do to stay looking so young?"

He laughed helplessly. "I give up. Pardon me while I kick up my heels and die of old age."

She clarified hastily. "I didn't mean it like that. I meant it as a compliment. You look…great." Her breath hitched a little as she stopped to consider just how great he did look tonight. She didn't even care that he was violently underdressed or that a shadow of danger darkened his eyes. She just wanted to grab his shirt, pull him close and take the kiss she could already taste. The kiss she craved.

He'd shaved before supper and his cheeks were smooth and tanned. Her fingertips itched to caress his face. To drift lower, tracing the muscular column of his neck, the hollow of his collarbone, to his muscle-slabbed ribs, his abdomen, which she knew would go rock hard beneath her touch. She distinctly recalled the thin line of dark hair that led downward from his navel, pointing the way to hidden treasures lower down. Mmm. To trace that path with her lips. To lick him like an ice-cream cone…

"You can stop that now."

His voice rasped harshly against her ears.

She blinked, startled out of her reverie. "Stop what?"

"Looking at me as if I'm an edible treat."

Her lips curved up. She didn't even have to say the words aloud. She just leaned forward slowly. First, her breasts, all but pulsing with need, rubbed against his shirt. She groaned in pleasure.

He groaned in pain.

Then she took a small step closer, and her thigh nestled between his. Her hip felt the hard length of him growing harder by the second. She purred her delight.

He growled his discomfort.

She looped her arms around his neck, toying with the soft hair at the back of his neck. And then she stood on tiptoe and licked his lips. Sipped at him, really, savoring the fullness of his lower lip, the way his mouth opened for her, the smooth slide of her tongue across the edge of his teeth.

It was back. All of it. The thundering lust, the pounding need, the uncontrollable wildness that begged her to rip his shirt off, push him to the ground and make love to him right here on the path. To ride him until he shouted his pleasure into the night.

She begged him to do just that.

He swore violently…and refused.

"I'm working," he explained desperately. "I have to keep my wits about me. Protect you from this bastard. I can't…you're too…dammit, I can't think about anything else when I make love to you!"

She pouted.

He apologized. "Honey, that was a compliment. You blow me away. We're…incredible together…it's a *good* thing that I can't think when you kiss me like that…"

She pouted some more.

"Aww, hell."

He kissed her back.

Tom didn't know how long they stood in the middle of the path and tried to inhale each other's lungs, but he did know his knees had gone weak and most of the blood in his body had pooled far, far away from his brain before he finally tore himself away from her.

Maddie was warm and sinuous in his arms, as sleek as a mink. He reached for the hem of her dress, lifting it so he could grasp her buttocks, firm and juicy in his hand. A low moan slipped from her throat…oh, yeah. Right here. Right now. On the beach.

Wait…Sex on the Beach…Killer…

He came up for air, swearing violently.

She dropped her forehead to his chest, panting. At least he wasn't the only one struggling for control. They staggered up the long flights of steps, lost in the lust clutching them both in its grip. So *this* was how the Sex on the Beach Killer was able to sneak up on his victims and stab them to death. If the guy had been standing behind them a moment ago, he'd have been completely helpless to defend himself or Maddie. Hell, he was barely able to form rational thoughts now.

The disco was loud and crowded when they entered. A hurricane party was in full swing, and most of the Cove's guests were drinking and dancing with abandon. Beside him, Maddie assessed the room with the practiced eye of an experienced party girl. She moved unerringly toward a cluster of "beautiful people" in the far corner. He didn't know the faces she'd targeted, but he definitely knew the type. Rich, debauched and wild.

Yup, she had a good instinct for the money in a room. The young men in the group looked jaded, bored by the cover models draped all over their laps. Although in the guys' defense, the models looked just as bored. He recalled well the vapid expressions, the inability to answer simple questions, to follow basic logic. Whether they just weren't that sharp, or their brains were so fried from the drugs they consumed like candy was hard to tell.

How could Maddie stand to be around people like that? She was so bright and clever, how could she even talk to them? Interested, he tagged along to see how she fared. Soon enough, it became clear. She focused her conversational efforts on those in the group who had a few functional brain cells left and ignored the others, who were well on their way to wasted, their eyes bloodshot, their speech slurred. As a group, they smelled bad, looked sloppy and were completely unattractive in every way.

Good Lord. Had he looked like that when he'd gone on his benders over the past few months? The thought disgusted him. Why had it suddenly occurred to him to wonder about that, of all things? Of course, he only had to look up to see the answer. Maddie's sparkling laughter twinkled right through him, and the intelligence in her gaze was balm to his soul.

As he gazed at her, one of the drunks made a clumsy pass at Maddie. Tom surged forward to swat the guy's paws off her, but before he got there, Maddie smoothly captured the guy's roaming hands and unobtrusively replaced them in the kid's own lap. No fuss, no muss, nobody embarrassed. *Nicely done. Classy.*

Tom subsided as she glanced up, made eye contact with him and smiled self-deprecatingly. Why would a hardcore party girl, like Maddie portrayed herself to be, make the effort to save a drunk she'd likely never see again from a little humiliation? In his experience, the women prowling these clubs were looking for sex, drugs and rich boyfriends. They didn't do things like she just had. Yet again, her outward physical persona jarred with her actions. He frowned, perplexed.

One of the less drunk guys asked Maddie to dance, and she glanced over at Tom for permission. He gestured for her to go ahead. It would give him a chance to scope out the room and see if any six-foot-tall, athletic, Caucasian males showed an unusual interest in her.

A hard-driving dance tune blared from the speakers, and Maddie broke into a well-choreographed series of dance combinations. She looked like a cheerleader for a professional sports team. It was slick, practiced and easy on the eye. But the artifice of it left him cold. He leaned back in the booth and casually checked out the room's occupants. Most everyone was involved in shaking their booty or dumping alcoholic libations down the hatch. Maddie's dancing drew a fair bit of attention, nothing beyond ordinary interest, though.

But then, on the far side of the room, in the deeply shadowed alcove of an employee doorway, a faint movement caught Tom's eye. A tall, trim figure lurked deep in the shadows. The man's gaze methodically swept the room, scoping it out as intently and thoroughly as Tom was doing. The guy's gaze lighted on Maddie, slid on. Stopped. Came back to her. Narrowed.

Tom half rose out of his seat. Bingo.

But then the man moved forward a step. Tom laughed under his breath, and sank back into the seat in relief. Just Nigel. Of course he checked out the room like a pro. He *was* a pro.

The song ended and Maddie came back to the table, collapsing into the booth beside him, laughing. One of the only semidrunk guys made an inane comment about how maybe she could give him a private show later.

Maddie made an appropriately vague reply and slid closer to Tom, smiling up at him flirtatiously. "Did you like my dancing, too?"

He shrugged. "Yeah. Sure. As mating dances go, it wasn't half bad. Most of the men in the room watched you."

"Mating! You didn't like it," she accused.

"You performed just fine. I'm curious, though. Do you ever dance just for the fun of it?"

She turned a perplexed look on him. "I spent a solid year learning how to dance like that." When he cocked a skeptical eyebrow, she added faintly defensively, "Dance class was fun. Really."

He nodded, smiling gently. "Right."

"I suppose you can do better on a dance floor?" she challenged.

He shrugged. "Nah. But I have fun when I do it. Dancing's about feeling the music and the moment. I'm not into pre-fabbed routines designed to attract a rich boyfriend."

She looked distinctly stung, and opened her mouth to retort. He was surprised when she stood up instead. "Fine, twinkletoes. Let's see what you've got."

He grinned and slid out of the booth. They had to walk past the DJ's booth on their way to the floor, and he stopped to murmur in the fellow's ear. Tom had helped the guy, a local, a few months back with a belligerent ex-brother-in-law, and the DJ owed him one. He grinned and nodded at Tom's request.

Tom rested his hand in the small of Maddie's back. Her sharp, indrawn breath stoked the slow burn of desire that seemed to be his constant companion around her. The current song ended, and a new one began.

Her eyebrows shot up, and he grinned at her chagrin. It was a slow, sexy, saxophone piece that wailed as smooth as melted chocolate, seducing couples onto the floor. Tom drew her into his arms. Holding her this way felt like coming home. Funny, how in all the months of binge drinking he'd never truly become addicted to alcohol. But after one day with this woman, she was a fire in his blood that he couldn't possibly get enough of.

She moved faintly awkwardly in his arms, as if she wanted to do something but was holding back.

"Relax," he murmured against her temple. "Feel the music. Just let yourself move to it."

She grumbled, "That's not the problem."

He drew back enough to gaze down at her in the dim light. Her eyelashes were long and dark as she peeked up at him through them. "Okay, I'll bite. What's wrong?"

"I want to crawl inside your shirt and feel your skin. I want to nibble your ear and hear that groan you make in the back of your throat. I want…I want you inside me, moving to the music and filling me up."

"Oh, jeez."

She smiled ruefully. "Yeah. That groan."

"Next time, we'll have music."

"What about the beach? I thought we're supposed to do it in public, or at least pretend to, and try to draw out you-know-who."

"That's business. I'm talking about the next time we're alone. In private. Where we don't have to worry about anything but making love until neither of us can stand."

She laid her head on his shoulder. "Mmm. I like the sound of that."

She was pure heaven in his arms, unabashedly plastered against him from neck to knee, boneless and mellow, swaying easily in his arms. Okay, so she could seriously dance. It made him imagine her melting all over him like this when they were horizontal. Of their bodies fusing into one, formless and weightless, floating along on a river of music, sometimes rushing toward oblivion, sometimes pounding hard on rocks of sound, sometimes gliding along so smooth and easy that flesh could barely feel its caress.

Once the image lodged in his brain, nothing and no one was going to remove it.

Lost in a delicious agony of need, he led her off the floor when the song ended. In unspoken, mutual agreement, they moved toward the exit, their arms entwined around each other's waists. Maddie gazed up at him with naked desire, and he indulged in staring deep into her smoky eyes. It was a rare event when he let his real feelings show, particularly in public. But with Maddie, it was so damned easy. He fell into playing her besotted lover as naturally as breathing.

Except…this was work. He had to maintain—and contain—the driving lust surging through his gut *and* keep his brain engaged. Dammit, didn't Sheriff Marquez understand that men weren't wired that way? There was only blood enough in his body to keep one major organ functioning at full capacity. And at the moment, it damned well wasn't his brain!

The recipe for catching the killer was simple. Use himself and Maddie as bait. Fan the incendiary attraction between them into a public wildfire, then adjourn to the beach to wait for the murderer to strike.

Of course, this whole business of falling for the girl wasn't part of that plan. When they were alone together, he could so easily lose himself in her, go crazy for her and start thinking about things like spending the rest of his life with her. Thankfully the public, Madeline C. persona she showed the world was off-putting enough to him that he was managing to hang on to a thread of sanity…a thin one, but a thread, nonetheless.

Grasping at that fragile thread, he tucked Maddie's hand

under his elbow and headed for the beachside door. It was no
great feat of acting to pass through the crowd as if it weren't
there, so involved were they in one another. He didn't look at
anyone else, didn't block out a path for her, didn't use his
body to protect her from possible sight lines a shooter might
use. It went contrary to everything he'd ever been taught
about protecting a client. But it was the only way to draw the
attention of the Sex on the Beach Killer. The guy was too
smart to fall for a blatant trap. He and Maddie had to, no
kidding, be so wrapped up in one another they couldn't see
straight. Thankfully, that wasn't a stretch for either of them.

The very cursory glance he'd had time to take at the killer's
file indicated that the fellow could sniff two things like a
bloodhound. Cops and sex. Which is probably why Marquez
was so hot and bothered to force a non-cop onto the case. As
a private operator, he might not trigger the killer's cop-
warning system.

Not to mention that the scent of sex hung over him and
Maddie as thickly as the pall of smoke hovering in the club.
All the two of them had to do was be in the same room, and
sexual vibes rippled off them like heat waves in the desert sun.
Without exception, the killer went after couples reported to
have been crawling all over each other and all but having sex
in front of audiences shortly before their murders. When the
lovers eventually adjourned to the beach, the killer moved in
on them.

He held the door for Maddie and she slipped by him, blatantly brushing against him on her way past. Vixen. As if he
wasn't already turned on enough. He smiled down at her,
silently promising sweet revenge.

Her eyes snapped in eager anticipation.

He guided her across the wide porch and down the stairs to

the beach. The spot exactly between his shoulder blades itched ferociously all of a sudden. Excellent. He only got that horrible feeling of having a target on his back when someone was studying him intently. *C'mon, you slimy bastard. Take the bait.*

They hadn't quite dropped out of sight of the disco's picture windows when he paused, pulling Maddie into his arms, attempting to extract her tonsils with his tongue.

Oh, man. She tasted like raspberries and mustard. Rich and creamy. Melting across his tongue and filling his head with her effervescence. With him standing one step below her, it put their bodies into perfect belly-to-belly alignment.

She flung herself against him, groaning her need. "What are you doing to me? I never lust after guys like this."

"Haven't you figured it out yet? I'm not just any guy, honey." He propped one foot on the step she stood on. She rubbed high against his inner thigh, and then higher, drawing a groan of his own out of him.

He speared one hand into her hair, holding her in place so his mouth could plunder hers. He drank deeply of her, his head spinning with the taste and smell of her desire.

She tore her mouth away, gasping. "I'm going to faint if you keep that up."

He laughed low, almost a growl. "Those punks back in the disco are boys. They don't know how to pleasure a woman. They're only thinking about getting their own rocks off. When I'm done with you, fainting will be the least of your worries."

He leaned down enough to hook his fingers around the back of her knee. He drew her thigh up and over his bent one, looping it around his hips. His fingers slid up the back of her sleek leg, approaching her feminine flesh and feeling the heat of her growing and growing.

Her hips rolled forward, seeking his touch, seeking the

release already building within her. He could feel it in the vibrations emanating from low in her belly and radiating outward.

His fingers slid across her bare buttocks. Had she gone commando? The thought of her sitting through that formal dinner in that fancy restaurant wearing no underwear made him want to throw her down right here and pound into her until they both fainted.

She arched her whole body forward now, offering up her breasts to him. Her erect nipples strained against the thin silk. He leaned down and captured one in his mouth through the flimsy fabric. He bit down just hard enough to wring a cry of pleasure-pain from her.

She writhed on his thigh, her nether parts chafing against his in desperate supplication. His fingers slid farther forward and touched her throbbing, wet heat.

A thong. She was wearing a thong. The thought just about sent him over the edge. He slipped the tip of his finger beneath the fabric barrier and just inside her tight opening. She flowed around him, as warm and sweet and pulsing as he remembered. His own flesh throbbed in time with hers, grating against his clothes painfully.

Her fingers slipped between them, measuring the length of him behind his zipper. He was rock hard, and even that fleeting touch was enough to make him exhale hard on an impulse to rip her clothes off.

Nuzzling her chest, he discovered that the soft drape of her neckline had enough slack in it that he could pull it to one side and get his mouth on naked skin. He drew her breast into his mouth and rolled around the cherry of her nipple with his tongue, sucking at it and grazing it with his teeth in chaotic abandon.

His zipper slid down, rattling against his shaft as the teeth vibrated loose one by one. He about jumped out of his skin.

Beach. They had to get down to the beach. He couldn't for the life of him remember why. But he was going to lay her down on the sand, spread her wide open and ride her until she couldn't remember her name.

He took a step back. Another. Whimpering, she followed him, chasing him with hands and mouth and body. How they made it down the long staircase to the beach, he had no real recollection. But somewhere on the way down, she released him from his pants and used his length as a handle, running the pad of her thumb across his slick tip until he nearly exploded.

And then the uneven softness of sand made him stumble. Oh, God. Yes. They'd made it. He grasped her buttocks in both hands and lifted her up. She wrapped her legs and arms around him, devouring his mouth in rhythm to the rocking of her hips against him.

Frantic, he searched around for a spot secluded enough that they wouldn't be interrupted. Where he would see anyone approaching...if he could actually see at all. In another few seconds, his eyeballs were going to explode along with the rest of him. He was a volcano about to blow.

He fell to his knees. Leaned over, dumping Maddie onto her back. He tore off that maddening thong in a single violent movement, flinging it aside.

"Yes. Yes. Now, now," she chanted, breathless.

He rocked back on his knees, burying his face between her legs, inhaling the scent of her, dragging his tongue up the length of her pulsing flesh from her opening to the swollen nub of her desire. Her thighs trembled beneath his hands and she gave a sharp cry. He licked again, and another keening cry tore from her throat. She thrashed beneath him, surging up, reaching for him with both hands.

He pinned her arms against the sand and she fought,

mindless, wild with need. He kneed her thighs open. And slammed home his rock-hard flesh all the way to the hilt. The very center of her pushed against him, and her female muscles convulsed around him, drenching him in liquid heat.

He supported his upper body nearly upright, his knees digging deep into the sand, both to give him the right angle and an unobstructed view of the beach. He partially withdrew and slid home again. Hard. Maddie no longer formed words beneath him, singing her lust in moans and shuddering cries and ragged breaths. She bucked up against his hands again where they held her arms down and a note of surprise crept into her shout of release.

A grin of male satisfaction curved his mouth. And if she thought that was great…

He drove into her over and over, churning with the force of a piston, his entire body vibrating with each stroke as he buried himself to the hilt, stretching her to the very limit to take all of him. The ocean roared behind them, primal. Wild. Violent.

She screamed her pleasure.

"Sing for me, baby," he groaned.

She screamed again. More and even more heat drenched him, scorching him, slick and so wet.

Oh, yeah. He picked up the pace, his buttocks clenching tighter and tighter as his own climax built to towering proportions. His breath hitched. Held. Her entire body quivered around him, poised on the edge of an epic orgasm. And he delivered the coup de grâce—a final stroke that touched her very core. His back arched like a bow, and his entire body clenched. And then the world exploded. Stars burst before his eyes, and his orgasm ripped all the way out to his fingertips and toes. Damned if his hair didn't feel like it had caught on fire.

He'd have collapsed on top of her were his elbows not locked, and some subliminal need to stay marginally upright keeping him from going completely boneless.

Something thudded softly into the sand not far from them. He lurched, startled. Not that being startled in any way equated to his brain commencing normal functioning, however. It was just a rock. Fist-size. Loose scree from the cliff above. Another rock tumbled past, clicking against the cliff face before half burying itself in the sand. Damn. They were bringing the cliff down around them.

He swore under his breath, as much in awe as in shock at what they'd just done. He never was that…raw…with a woman, never gave in to unleashed desire like that. Never gave over every last ounce of his being to another human being.

"Are you okay?" he managed to gasp.

A shaky laugh and another shudder that passed through her entire body was his only answer.

He'd take that as a yes.

Sand showered down from above. A small sliver of sanity returned to him. Enough to take a quick, surreptitious glance around the beach. No one. He glanced up. About forty feet up, it looked like a ledge protruded slightly. From here, he couldn't see the shelf. But anyone peering down over the edge of it would've had an unobstructed view of them. His skin crawled with sudden certainty. The killer had been up there just now. And just as certainly, the falling rocks and sand were the remnants of the guy's departure.

If the killer had been up there, he'd gotten a hell of a show. Surprising that he hadn't struck. Tom studied the cliff more closely. Fortunately, to get down to the beach from that ledge, the guy would've had to climb back up the cliff face and come down the stairs. And those were far too exposed for the guy to have made a stealthy approach to them.

Although, he and Maddie had been so caught up in what they were doing, the killer could have walked up to them and asked the time of day and neither of them would have noticed.

Icy fear raced through him at that realization. They'd been as vulnerable as any of the dead couples. *He'd failed to protect Maddie.* Had the killer struck a few moments ago, the two of them would be *dead*. Self-recrimination shredded his gut to ribbons. He was weak. Washed up. Incapable of doing what Marquez had asked of him. He swore long and violently to himself.

What kind of *moron* had a vicious serial killer chasing him and stopped to have sex in the midst of evading the killer?

Him, apparently. If there were an anatomically possible way to kick himself hard in the butt, he'd do it right now. He'd been dumb, dumb, dumb!

The first order of business was to get Maddie off this beach and park her somewhere safe. Then he had to get in touch with Marquez and let the guy know that alternate protection for her had to be arranged immediately, cyclone or no cyclone.

Maddie moved restlessly beneath him. He helped her sit up and attempted to no avail to brush the sand off her wadded clothes and out of her hair.

She shook her head and sand flew every which way. "I need a shower," she laughed.

"That can be arranged." He helped her to her feet and retrieved her strappy little thong and strappy little shoes for her. They readjusted their clothing and started down the beach. She made a turn for the stairs they'd come down, and Tom restrained her gently.

"Let's take the other set of stairs closer to our villa."

"You don't want to be seen in the disco looking like you just got lucky?" she asked curiously. "Most guys want to flaunt the fact that they just got some."

He wrinkled his nose in distaste. "I'd like to think I have more tact than that. I don't care if anyone knows I got the girl or not. I'd just rather be alone with you. And this ocean is incredible."

She glanced over her shoulder at the massive breakers rolling ashore. He did the same. Wave crests crashed down, demolishing the water beneath and sending up huge spumes of spray. "How much worse will this get?"

"I dunno. I've never seen a major cyclone up close and personal. I hear the storm surge is the most destructive part— more so than the wind."

"How tall are these cliffs, again?" she asked in alarm.

"At least fifty feet. Kato's storm surge is forecasted to be around seventeen feet."

"I like that math," she replied, sounding relieved.

While the giant breakers distracted her, Tom pulled out his cell phone and dialed the sheriff's phone number. A few months back, he'd programmed the phone number of every permanent resident on the island into his cell phone out of sheer boredom during an early attempt to climb out of the bottle.

"Yeah?" Marquez growled after several rings.

"It's Tom Laruso. I can't do it. I can't protect Maddie. You've got to come get her. We're at Paradise Cove."

"What the hell am I supposed to do with her, Laruso? In case you haven't noticed, I've got a cyclone bearing down on my island."

Tom sighed. "I don't care. Keep her with you." At Marquez's snort of not-a-chance-in-hell, Tom added, "Lock her up in jail, then. But I can't do this. I've lost the edge. I'm making basic mistakes."

"Yeah, but at least you know they're basic mistakes. Not one of my guys has any personal-protection training. And I don't have time for her. I haven't slept in two days, and I'm not going to get much more than quick naps for the next week. You're gonna have to handle Miss Crummby yourself."

That was the problem, dammit. He was handling her far too much!

"But—"

"No buts, Laruso. You're the best we've got for the job. Suck it up and deal with it, or else I'll deputize you and order you to do it anyway." Marquez disconnected.

Sonofa— Tom pocketed the phone and swore some more under his breath. He couldn't do this! But it looked as if he had to give it a go, anyway.

Thing was, this wasn't just about him being an idiot and getting distracted by sex. It was about fear. Abject, gut-churning, knee-knocking fear that something bad would happen to Maddie on his watch. He cared about her, dammit! He was way too close to her emotionally to be an effective bodyguard. Maybe he should ask Nigel to take over. Except Nigel didn't have personal-protection training either, and the guy had his hands more than full battening down the hatches to ride out the storm and taking care of several hundred guests of the resort.

He was stuck with the job, no matter how badly he did it. No matter that he wasn't fit to do it. No matter that Maddie's life hung in the balance.

He was going to puke now.

Maddie stopped beside him, and Tom realized they'd arrived at the narrow stone staircase which wound up the cliff not far from their villa. Basic-security technique dictated that he go up first, even though he'd have enjoyed following her and partaking of the view of her pert backside. He had to stop having thoughts like that! Yeah, right. He could stop breathing on command, too.

They arrived at the top of the cliff and he turned right, heading down the path toward their villa. The ocean noise didn't drown out all the jungle sounds up here. Insects buzzed and clicked and chirped. The night air was warmer, too. Sticky on his skin. Heavy and oppressive. Made for sweaty sex and lazy ceiling fans.

The dark bulk of their villa came into view. He fumbled with the plastic key card, and Maddie giggled as she tried to help him jam it in the lock. Between the two of them, they managed to gain entrance to the *bure*.

Just inside the door, she turned into his arms, kissing him with mouth and hands and body, stripping him out of his shirt as they twirled toward the bathroom and a hot, naked shower. Their clothes pinwheeled away from them as they made their way across the living room.

He unzipped her dress and she stepped out of it. It pooled on the floor, and she took a moment to scoop it up, laughing. "This cost you a fortune. I'd hate to ruin it. Let me toss it on a hanger."

He took the opportunity to enjoy the swanlike line of her naked back rising from the sexiest black thong he'd ever seen. They'd been lucky to find it on the beach in the dark after he'd flung it away in such haste. She pulled a hanger out of the closet and he reached for the zipper of his shorts. Damned if he didn't want her again, already.

"My shoes." Something broke in her voice. Dawning realization. *Fear.*

"Your shoes?" Warning alarms exploded in his brain, but he struggled to form logical thought past his raging hormones.

"What's wrong with your shoes?" He stumbled over to the closet and looked over her shoulder. They were lined up neatly in a row. Just like she'd left them, right?

"They've been moved. The espadrilles don't go with that outfit. The cork sandals do. The espadrilles should be lined up under the sundress."

Belatedly, his protective instincts broke through the lust, and he grabbed her, wrapping her in a protective embrace that had nothing to do with sex. Cripes. He hadn't even cleared the place when they came in. He had no idea where to put her that was safe. An intruder could be in the back of the closet, the bathroom. Hell, under the bed. For lack of anyplace else to secure her, he poked his head into the closet fast. It checked out empty, and he shoved her inside. "Stay down," he bit out tersely.

She stared up at him, wide-eyed in terror, as he pulled his gun out of the holster tucked in the back of his shorts and growled, "I'll be back in a minute. Don't move."

She nodded and he leaped away, throwing open the bathroom door and spinning into the space low and fast. *Clear.* Under the bed. *Clear.* Behind the breakfast bar. *Clear.* One by one, he checked every possible hiding space in the villa that could conceal a human being. He pulled down the shades and closed the curtains while he was at it, all the while berating himself. Sloppy, sloppy, sloppy. He clicked off the lights. No need to cast any shadows for the killer to watch from outside the *bure.*

Maddie squeaked when the place went dark.

"It's okay, honey. I turned off the lights. It's all clear. I'm coming to get you." When he slid the door open, she tumbled out of the closet and into his arms, shaking in terror.

"Why is this happening to us?" she quavered against his chest.

"Why does it happen to anyone? We were in the wrong place at the wrong time." Is that what had happened to Arielle? Had she crossed paths with the wrong weirdo at the wrong time? Someone who knew her or knew of her, and took the opportunity to murder a famous pop star and gain immortality?

"What do we do now?" Maddie whispered.

"Now, I make a couple of phone calls, while you stay plastered to my side."

"I like that plan."

He guided her over to the bed and sat on the edge of it. He pulled her down into his lap, reached over for the telephone and punched the button for housekeeping.

"Hi, this is the Clifftop Villa. Did any of your people come out here to straighten up while we were at dinner?"

"No, sir," a polite voice said on the other end of the line.

"No turndown service?"

"No, sir. My records show you having requested that we call you and obtain permission before we send anyone into your villa for any reason. Is that incorrect?"

"No. That's exactly right. I was just checking. Thanks." Tom hung up the phone, thinking fast. He punched another button, this time the hotel operator. "I need you to get Nigel Cumberland on the horn. Now. Yes, it's an emergency. I'll wait."

That appropriately alarmed the operator, and she agreed to track down the manager immediately.

Were it not for Maddie on his lap, he'd be pacing like a caged tiger. Along with feelings of inadequacy as a bodyguard, now guilt roared through him, too. He *knew* better than to fool around on the job. And he sure as *hell* knew not to have sex with the client—on duty or off. The Sex on the Beach Killer was close by, waiting to strike, to *kill* them, for God's sake! He deserved to die for his stupidity. Problem was, if he went, Maddie went, too. And she emphatically didn't deserve to die. He swore violently under his breath. Like it or not, there would be no more fooling around between them until the bastard was caught.

While he waited for the Brit to come to the phone, he ordered Maddie tersely, "Get dressed and pack your things. We're getting out of here."

"Can I turn on a light?"

"You can turn on the bathroom lights. And you can crack the bathroom door open if you need a little light in here to see by. Be quick, sweetheart. Don't worry about being neat."

She dropped a brief kiss on his neck and moved away to do as he instructed. He watched her move around the dark room, reaching into the closet for clothes. She pulled out the white sundress.

"Not white. Wear something dark," he instructed quietly.

She gulped and nodded, and hastily put the sundress back. He watched her pull on dark shorts and a tank top, bending and straightening, sliding fabric up her long, slim legs, smoothing cotton down over her womanly curves. Man, she was a looker.

"Cumberland, here."

Tom replied tightly, "We've had an intruder at our villa. I need a ride out of here. Now."

"How soon can you be ready to go?" Nigel asked.

"Five minutes ago."

"Roger. Two minutes. Shoreside."

"Thanks. And Nigel? Come with your lights off."

"Off?" The former policeman sounded startled for a moment, but then responded calmly. "Got it. Will do."

Tom hung up the phone and pulled his duffel bag out from under the bed. He zipped it quickly. There. Packed. Old habit—never unpack, for just this reason. Two seconds, and he was ready to roll.

"Need any help?" he asked Maddie.

"Almost done," she called from the bathroom.

"You've got a minute and thirty seconds."

She skidded to the front door with her last bag in hand ten seconds before her allotted time ran out.

"Not bad for a woman," he commented, grinning, as he eased the shoreside door open and took a hard look around.

She stuck her tongue out at him. "I've no doubt ruined at least half of my new clothes."

He snorted. "Live through this and I'll buy you more."

Her gaze narrowed. "I'll hold you to that. Great clothes are serious business, I'll have you know."

He opened his mouth to make a droll retort but was drowned out by the crunch of tires on gravel. The quiet rumble of an engine announced that their ride was not one of the ubiquitous golf carts so prevalent on the island. It turned out to be a white pickup truck sporting the Paradise Cove logo on its door.

Tom and Nigel traded nods as the former opened the passenger-side door and deposited Maddie inside, instructing her to lie down across the seat. Tom eased the door shut and leaped lightly into the bed of the pickup truck, crouching with his back against the cab, scanning all around. Damn, it was dark out here. Good weather conditions for an escape. Better conditions for a kill.

He banged the roof of the cab lightly. The vehicle moved out.

Chapter 8

Maddie all but fell to the floor as the truck lurched into motion, her head practically in Nigel's lap. He stiffened instantly.

"Sorry," she mumbled up at him, embarrassed. His jaw clenched rock hard. He glanced down at her and the look in his eye was so intent she'd almost call it ferocious. But then, unaccountably, he grinned. "Having fun yet?"

"I have to admit," she replied ruefully, "this business of being a damsel in distress isn't all it's cracked up to be."

He patted the dashboard. "How do you like my white charger?"

"It's perfect."

"Which is to say it's running?" he retorted dryly.

"Exactly."

As her eyes adjusted to the dark, she frowned at the underside of the dashboard. What was that thing sticking out under there? It didn't look like any truck part she'd ever seen before.

And growing up on a farm, she was plenty familiar with the interiors of pickup trucks. She stared at the protrusion as her night vision continued to come in. Slowly, the hilt of a knife took shape, sticking out of a sheath that was attached to the underside of the dashboard by some invisible means. Apprehension blossomed in her gut. Holy cow. That looked like a big knife—almost machetelike in proportions. Of course, living on a tropical island like this, a sticker like that probably came in handy. Did Tom have a knife like that?

Startled that it had taken this long for it to occur to her, she blurted, "Where's Tom?" She started to sit up to look for him, but Nigel put a big hand on her shoulder and gently kept her down.

"He's in the back with a gun, acting as our spotter."

"I don't know what that is, but it sounds impressive," she replied.

The truck turned off the rough gravel and accelerated down a paved road. After about two minutes, Nigel reached up and slid open the small rear window. "Where to?" he called.

"My place."

Nigel nodded and then murmured, "You can sit up now."

Maddie was happy to comply. She'd been starting to get a little carsick, lying on her side in the dark, staring at Nigel's knife.

She looked around, noting the blackness all around them. "Good grief!" she exclaimed. "How can you see a thing?"

He shrugged. "I have pretty good eyesight." The truck rounded a bend in the sandy track and Tom's *bure* loomed in the darkness. Even over the sound of the engine, she heard surf pounding nearby.

Tom said through the window, "Let me clear the house, first. Then I'll be back for you."

She nodded as he jumped out of the truck and disappeared. Suddenly, she felt very alone in this small space with a man she barely knew. The jungle pressing in around them felt forbidding. Menacing, even. This whole Sex on the Beach Killer thing was really messing with her head. What if Tom didn't come back? Raw panic speared into her at the thought.

But on the heels of her panic came the sure and certain knowledge that Tom would come back to her, hell or high water. He was just that kind of man. He would never abandon her. He had promised to keep her safe and he'd die if necessary to keep that promise. He was the kind of man a girl could trust...forever.

She stared out into the night, stunned at the thought. She was *not* attaching the word forever to anything that had to do with her and Tom Laruso!

Was she?

Madeline C., she thought weakly. Her plan...a rich husband who'd take care of her...

And in that moment, knowing exploded in her consciousness. There were different kinds of security, and money was only one of them. The kind of security Tom offered was another...perhaps even more powerful...kind of security. The kind that never wavered for richer, for poorer, in sickness and in health...

Oh, crap.

She'd done a bad thing. A very, very bad thing. She'd fallen for Tom Laruso.

In a minute or two, Tom materialized out of nowhere by her truck window, and she jumped a mile high. How did he do that? She'd been looking for him and still hadn't seen him coming. He opened the door for her and held out his hand. She laid her icy hand in his warm one and his fingers closed around hers, comfortably. Reassuringly. Yup. The kind of guy a girl could trust with her life. All of it, from now till death did they part.

Shivers tore through her from head to foot.

"Let's go, sweetheart," he murmured. "Once you're safely under cover, I'll come back for your bags."

She glanced back over her shoulder as he whisked her into the night. "Thanks, Nigel."

"No worries," the Brit called back to her.

Tom ushered her into his *bure,* his bulk hovering close enough to chase away the boogeyman. His body warmth reached out to her, almost a caress in the cavernous dark. The night and the villa wrapped around them as thick and heavy as a familiar wool blanket. *Safe.* She let out a long breath of relief.

Tom's disembodied voice floated from nearby. "I'm going to booby-trap the doors and windows. So don't touch any of them, okay?"

"Booby-trap? As in blowing up?"

"Nothing quite that violent. I'm just attaching noisemakers to all of them. If someone tries to break and enter, alarms will go off and make a ton of noise."

"What kind of alarms?"

"I'll attach motion-activated sensors to both doors. And I've got firecrackers I'll rig to trip wires in front of the big windows. The kitchen window will get a high-tech pile of delicately balanced pots and pans."

She grinned her appreciation of that one. Her parents had caught her sneaking in late after missing a curfew one night in high school, using the exact same technique. She knew from experience that it was highly effective.

As a gust howled past the villa, she asked dubiously, "All this wind won't rattle one of your alarms into going off?"

Now that she wasn't living in mortal fear of being shot any second, she registered that the wind was noticeably stronger than it had been even an hour ago.

"By the time the wind's blowing hard enough to set off my alarms, nobody will be out running around, anyway. Even our killer will have to take cover."

"Could you call him something besides 'our killer'? That phrase gives me the willies. It sounds entirely too prophetic for my taste."

Tom laughed. "Sure. How about the resident Vanua Taru sicko?"

"Not much better, but better," she replied wryly. "How much longer until the cyclone gets here, anyway?"

"The outer rain bands have already arrived. From here on out, the weather will just get worse. The eye wall is due to hit around midmorning tomorrow."

"And this thatched roof will be okay in high winds?"

"Yup. I secured boards over it to help hold it down yesterday before I flew over to the big island to pick you up. Woven thatch is pretty durable stuff, according to the locals. As long as the wind doesn't lift it up and peel it back—hence the boards—it'll stand up to anything Kato can throw at it. I'm told these cantilevered log structures flex well in the face of a storm and don't tear apart."

"What about your windows?"

"While you were shopping today, I came back here and screwed all of the storm shutters closed."

"Really? Who'd have guessed you were so prepared? You're a regular boy scout!"

He snorted. "You don't have to sound *that* surprised."

"Do we still have water and power?"

"Water, yes. This place has an underground cistern that

collects rainwater. I have a hand pump we can use to draw up water from it. As for electricity, not for much longer, if I had to guess. Sheriff Marquez will shut down the island's main generator as soon as he thinks the power lines are in danger of being blown down. Live wires in the streets are bad things. I wouldn't be surprised if he's already pulled the plug. But I don't want us to turn on any lights, regardless. No candles, either. Nothing to signal to anybody that we're here."

"By anybody, you mean the Sex on the Beach Killer," she retorted.

"Precisely."

She asked lightly, "What *are* we going to do in the dark to pass the time with no power and no lamps or candles?" Anticipation fluttered through her at the thought of taking that shower she'd started with Tom over at the other *bure.*

His regretful sigh floated out of the dark. "We can't."

She didn't even have to ask what he was talking about. Or why. *His job.* He took his bodyguarding duties extremely seriously.

He continued, "I have to stay on top of my game. No distractions."

"You're boring," she teased gently.

"In my world, boring is good. Something's gone very wrong when my work gets exciting."

She could see his point. And she couldn't very well get mad at the guy for wanting to protect her life. Still, she sighed. "I'll make up the sofa while you patrol and stuff, or whatever it is you do."

"You won't be sleeping on the couch tonight."

Her pulse leaped. "Why not?" God, she hoped she didn't sound like an eager puppy who'd just been thrown a bone. One of her favorite Madeline C. mantras rolled through her brain. *Make the guy chase you. Don't seem too eager. And never act desperate.* She made out his black form over by the front door. Even if desperate was exactly what she was.

"The first problem with you sleeping out here," he explained, while fiddling with something attached to the doorknob, "is that the sofa is situated right under a large, plate glass window which happens to face the ocean. Not the safest place in the house to be with a cyclone rolling in. And the second problem is that I need to keep an eye on you while you sleep. The bedroom is more secure and will make that easier to do."

She frowned. "Exactly where will I sleep?"

"In my bed."

"With you?" She couldn't stop the hopeful note from creeping into her voice.

He laughed a touch painfully and replied wryly, "No. I'll be awake, patrolling and stuff."

"Patrolling what?"

"The *bure*. The grounds around it."

Oh. She felt like sticking her tongue out at him. Party pooper. She'd been hoping that, if she could entice him to sleep with her, he might come around and reconsider his no-more-fooling-around-on-the-job edict. For a guy who'd planned to just pretend to have sex with her on the beach to draw out the killer, he'd failed miserably so far in the pretending department. Not that she was complaining, though. Never in her life had she experienced sex even remotely that good. Heck, she could learn to really like making love if it was like that all the time!

If only Tom was marriage material according to her grand plan. Then everything would be perfect. He was so damned attractive. Smart and funny and considerate. And responsible.

An adult. The kind of man who would treat a girl right. Her plan definitely didn't stretch far enough to allow for a recovering drunk-cum-beach bum, though.

Emotional security or financial security? How did a girl choose between the two? Could she give up everything she'd built for herself for a man? Her great job, her great apartment, heck, her great wardrobe, and move to a place like this? Tom's *bure* was basically a two-room cabin, albeit a nice one, in the middle of nowhere. And she'd thought her family's farm had been isolated! This place took isolation to a whole new level.

To be with Tom, she would have to be willing to drop out of society completely. She could do without the loud bars and pretentious, repetitive parties. But to be alone? Really truly alone, with only Tom for companionship? That was a big leap from her life in Chicago. Could he make her happy enough to make up for what she would have to leave behind?

Or was she just seeing Tom through rose-colored and inaccurate glasses, after all? Was he any of the things she thought he was? Did he feel for her the way she thought he did? Or was this all an elaborate act to gain her cooperation so he could collect a fat reward for catching the Sex on the Beach Killer? Sure, she got to have great sex with Tom while acting as bait for a killer. But was the sex worth risking her life for? Did Tom give a damn about her, or was she just a prop in his plan to catch the killer?

Insecurity roared through her. In high school, she had never put on airs—or makeup, for that matter—but at least she'd always known where she stood with people. They took her at face value and either liked her or disliked her as they saw fit. Nowadays, she wasn't so sure. She'd stepped into a world of social climbers where everyone put on a good face and nobody showed their true feelings about anyone or anything. Did she dare trust Tom or not?

Was his infatuation with her real at all? Or was it merely something superficial and temporary for him? After all, the sheriff had threatened Tom with jail if he didn't play along and do his best to catch the Sex on the Beach Killer. Maybe the steamy beach sex was only part and parcel of Tom saving his own hide.

Oh, God. What if he didn't have any feelings for her at all?

Agonizing over whether or not Tom returned any of her feelings, she perched on the edge of the couch and did her darnedest not to puke. This was exactly why she'd sworn off real emotions when she embarked on the Madeline C. project. They made a person's palms sweat and threw their stomach into turmoil. She had to be cool, calm and collected at all times, in control of herself and every situation around her to pull off her grand plan.

But she wasn't the slightest bit in control of Tom. If anything, he was the one pulling her strings. All he had to do was snap his fingers—or kiss her—and, oh, how she danced for him. The abandon of their earlier sex on the beach made her blush just to think about it. But she couldn't find it in herself to be ashamed. It had been glorious. And he'd been as blown away by it as she had, or she knew absolutely nothing about men.

Maybe Tom cared for her a little, after all.

Gradually, her panic attack passed as he prowled around the house, setting traps in front of all the windows and doors. Outside, the wind growled and the ocean roared, sounding like lions sent from heaven to rend all that stood before them. It felt like the storm had reached right into her gut and scrambled her innards, tossing her thoughts and feelings into complete chaos.

Here it came. A major Category Three tropical cyclone. Like it or not, she was about to experience her first really big storm. Up close and personal.

The man stared at the *bure* through the thick undergrowth, fingering the razor-sharp hunting knife dangling at his side. How convenient of his victims to lead him straight to this, their secret hideout. As if they could actually escape him on this tiny little rock of an island.

He still had a while before the storm would get bad enough to drive him inside. Plenty of time to wait out his prey. To choose his moment and strike.

Soon, now. He would let them fall sleep, secure in the knowledge that the storm would keep them safe. And then he would unleash the hounds of hell upon them, and let them reap the bitter fruit of their sinful ways. Compliments of the cyclone, it would be days before anyone found their bodies way out here in this isolated cabin. And after the close call of his last kill, he'd learned to be more mindful of his escape from the scene of the crime.

So many islands. So many tropical beaches. So many debased sinners having sex on those beaches. Really, why would men and women do something so foul—in public, no less—unless they actually *wanted* him to find them and punish them for their debauchery? He was happy to oblige them. After all, he was the chosen instrument of vengeance against the damned. And the next two sinners to join the others of their kind in hell soon were going to be Tom Laruso and Madeline Crummby.

Very soon, indeed.

Chapter 9

Tom sat by the bed in a comfortable wicker armchair he'd dragged in from the living room. An oil lamp burned at his elbow on the nightstand, giving off a small but bright light. Enough to comfortably read the tall stack of manila folders that constituted the police reports to date on the Sex on the Beach Killer. He propped his feet up on the edge of the bed, and the results of yet another homicide investigation spilled across his lap, complete with gory photos and grisly crime-scene details.

Maddie slept peacefully on the far side of the bed, curled into a little ball facing him, her fists tucked under her chin, child-like. For as flamboyant a woman as she portrayed herself to be, she slept in a much less outgoing fashion. In his experience with jet-set party girls, they slept as aggressively and selfishly as they lived, sprawled across the whole bed and irritable—even dead asleep—if anyone dared encroach upon their space.

A study in contrasts, she was. She seemed fixated on the idea of landing a rich guy, which seemed so much shallower than the woman herself. In the midst of all her impractical shoes and expensive makeup and slick dancing, he kept catching what seemed like glimpses of a real woman beneath the façade. A woman who fascinated him and appealed to him like no other woman he could ever recall meeting. A woman he had to stay far, far away from if he was going to do his job and protect her life. As much as he'd love to peel back the layers of this complex woman and find her true core, he didn't dare. Not now. Not while a killer was running around trying to kill them both.

The words on the page blurred before him as his thoughts strayed back to Maddie. Why was she so hell-bent on maintaining her uptown, elite socialite image? Apparently, that was the sort of woman who attracted the sort of man she was after. Unfortunately, that sort of man wasn't him. He'd worked for and dodged fake and conniving, marriage-minded women for too long. He had no use for them. He wanted someone real. Someone who'd love him for himself, not his bank account. Someone who enjoyed a great sunset or a walk on a beach, or just sitting quietly, sometimes. Someone who didn't judge people solely by their clothes or their house or their car. He wanted a woman of more depth of character than that.

Hell, at the rate he was going, he wasn't ever going to have to worry about a woman in his life. A bottle of whiskey was likely to end up being his girlfriend, wife and mistress.

He shook himself out of his dismal thoughts and looked down at the file in his lap once more. The couple in this picture had been beautiful. Both of the victims blond and tanned, in great physical shape. A killer would have to be fast and strong to take out a pair like this. Of course, a well-placed knife to the brain stem, wherein most vital life functions resided, would pretty much take out anyone.

A cold chill chattered down his spine. How close had he come tonight to the same fate? He'd been completely oblivious to anything or anyone around them while he and Maddie had made love on the beach. If the killer had wished it, they'd be as dead as the couple in the picture right now.

Tom flipped to the next photo, of the female victim of the latest killing. Pretty girl. Expensive-looking, beneath the crusted blood and pale mask of death. Definite boob job. Even in death, her breasts stood up proud and resilient above her slender rib cage.

The working theory was that the killer stabbed the men first, killing them instantly with a knife to the back of the head. Then, he used the men's dead weight on top of the women to restrain the female victims long enough to slit their throats—a single knife blow down the chin line and then across the jugular and windpipe. Efficient bastard.

He noticed the female victim's hand, flung out as if in supplication. Nice manicure. He liked women's fingernails natural, himself. The whole lacquered, square-tipped claw bit did nothing for him. They seemed so…plastic. Maddie's nails were buffed, but at least they were real. Yet another inconsistency in the whole package.

He'd hate to think that the hottest woman he'd ever bedded was purely artifice. Surely the sex wouldn't be that fantastic if she was a total fake. Could women put on highfalutin airs while screaming their way through multiple orgasms? There wasn't the slightest doubt in his mind she had been faking those, at any rate. He'd felt her body convulse around him, felt the hot gush of her release bathing him.

He stirred in the chair, growing uncomfortable. He had to stop thinking about sex! Although with Maddie sleeping in his bed, her light, sweet scent wafting to his nostrils, it was damned hard not to.

He forced his gaze back to the file. He finished reading the crime-scene report. Pretty much like the others so far. He picked up the next file. The cases were stacked in random order. Next up was the first murder attributed to the Sex on the Beach Killer, a little over four months ago. He flipped open the manila folder and froze at the first picture that greeted him. A red-haired young woman sprawled on her side, naked and dead in all her glory. Beside her lay an equally dead young man. Both of them looked to be in their mid- to late-twenties. But what riveted his attention was the way the dead woman's back arched unnaturally. He'd seen a pose like that before. Exactly like that. *Arielle.*

He turned quickly to the autopsy report on the female victim and skimmed through the details. Ah, here was the bit he sought.

…victim shows extreme rictus of the spinal column, most likely an autonomic nervous system response to a single knife wound to the base of the skull…

The medical examiner in Arielle's case had told him off the record that Arielle probably had arched backward in extreme pain. The cops assumed that her stalker was torturing her when she died, hence the pose in death. No one had ever said anything to him about a knife wound as the cause of death. Particularly not one to the base of her skull. But Lord knew, her body had been all but unrecognizable as human, let alone female by the time the killer had finished slicing her up. The Malaysian authorities had told him by way of comfort that most or all of the mutilation appeared to have been performed postmortem.

He went back to the photos in the front of the file. In this case, the guy's throat gaped open from a horizontal gash, the ends of his esophagus and trachea protruding from the black wound like gray sausage casings. Why the change in M.O.? In all the other killings, the guy had gotten it to the back of the head and the girl had gotten the slit throat. Why the reversal in this case? And then the obvious answer hit him. The girl had been on top when this couple had been having sex.

Arielle used to brag about liking to be on top when she had sex. She said she liked the power of it. The control. He'd overheard occasional complaints from her boy toys about how rough she was in the sack with them.

Maddie stirred, and Tom looked up. Her eyes flickered open briefly. He nodded at her, and she smiled back, as sleepy and content as a kitten. Her eyes drifted closed once more. A smiled spread across his face. She'd just been checking to make sure he was still there, still looking out for her. Something warm and protective washed over him. *Sweet dreams, little Maddie mine.*

His gaze returned to the pictures of the dead woman. Her hand was frozen in a claw by her ear, reaching backward awkwardly as if to grasp the blade in her neck and pull it out.

Dear God. *Just like Arielle.*

Was this how Arielle had died? From a swift blade to the back of her head?

If she hadn't been by herself when she'd died, had been having sex with someone at the time, on a beach, he'd wonder if the Sex on the Beach Killer had murdered her. But then, Arielle had been alone...*as far as he knew.*

She hadn't died on a beach, either, and the Sex on the Beach Killer had done his work strictly on beaches. Arielle's body had been found onstage at the giant soccer stadium where she'd been scheduled to perform the next night. No one could figure out why she'd gone there—it was completely out of character for her to indulge in anything faintly resembling rehearsal more than four hours before a show.

There had been a beach nearby, though. How near? Near enough for the killer to have stretched his rules? The stage certainly had qualified as a public, exposed place. Tom sorted urgently through his memory. The stadium sat maybe two blocks away from the Pacific Ocean. Close enough to a beach to send warnings humming low in his gut.

Arielle had succeeded at sneaking out on her guards twice before the night she'd died. Both times she'd gone to the wildest disco in town and partied her fanny off. The hangovers both times had taken her days to sleep off.

So why the inexplicable trip to the venue that last night? Right from the beginning, the question had stuck in his craw. But for the past six months he'd been too drunk to give it serious consideration. Now that he was sober again, the old questions crowded forward, demanding attention.

Arielle had been a wild child, but she'd always taken her career seriously. She never got wasted the night before a performance. Especially not a big one. The show scheduled for the night after she died had been the kickoff to the Asian leg of her world tour. It was a full house with sixty thousand tickets sold and scores of journalists scheduled to cover it. If she'd stayed true to form, she wouldn't have gotten passed-out drunk that last night. But she might have picked up some random guy and taken him down to the stadium to show him the elaborate show set…maybe to prove she was really Arielle…maybe to hump him on stage for kicks…

He hadn't been privy to the majority of the police investigation. He'd briefly been a suspect himself; hence he hadn't been allowed access to the details of the case. By the time his alibi was established—he'd been off duty that night, having dinner and trading war stories with a buddy from his days in the Secret Service—a court order had been issued sealing all details of the case to everyone but the investigators working directly on it. The press coverage of the murder had been beyond sensational, and he couldn't blame the family or the publicist from Arielle's record label for their request of the judge. But, it had meant he never got the lowdown on what had really happened.

His mouth turned down cynically. Apparently, it had been more vital not to negatively impact the surge of sympathy sales of her records than it had been to let trained security operatives, who knew the victim extremely well, help the police with their investigation. Nope, mustn't deprive Arielle's parents and producer of the last few millions they could wring from the teen cash cow before she dried up once and for all. Sad, really. Maybe the ongoing feeding frenzy by her family and supposed friends upon her success helped explain why the rock star had snuck out and helped along her self-destruction.

The folder slipped out of his lap and hit the floor sharply enough to make him jump. He bent down thoughtfully to pick it up. What if Arielle wasn't alone that night at the stadium? What if she'd gone there to have sex with some guy she'd picked up?

What if the Sex on the Beach Killer had stumbled across them? Arielle would've undoubtedly picked up a random boy toy in some public place, likely a disco or a bar. The killer could've spotted them there, maybe followed them to the stadium. Had the cops canvassed all the clubs on the beach strip to see if Arielle had been in one of them?

The club owners wouldn't necessarily be forthcoming

about Arielle picking up her killer in their club. Bad for business. If the police hadn't pushed that angle hard, odds were they hadn't gotten even part of the truth, let alone the full story.

The enormous set of light and sound special effects had already been erected for the concert, the raised platforms wired and ready for the sound equipment to come in the next afternoon. A soccer stadium was just as public, if not more so, than a beach. The murder site had been a *stage,* after all. What better place to symbolically murder a pair of sinners?

Tom lurched up out of the chair, swearing, heedlessly dumping the files onto the floor. He rushed into the living room, yanking out his cell phone as he went. He had to call the Malaysian police! Find out if Arielle had been stabbed in the brain stem. If she'd been at a club earlier that night. If there was any evidence she hadn't been alone. If she'd had sex…

The police prefecture in Kuala Lumpur was still on his speed dial list. He punched in the number. His phone beeped to indicate that the call had failed to go through. He swore under his breath. When a dozen more tries failed to produce a connection, he reluctantly gave up. The island's cell phone tower must already be down.

He eased back into the bedroom and quietly picked up and restacked the files. He blew out the lamp, plunging the room into darkness. Too restless to sleep, he slipped outside into the stormy night. To say it was raining didn't capture the ferocity of the deluge pouring down from the heavens. Hello, Kato. The wind gusted strong enough to knock him off balance and he hugged the building, using it for protection from the brunt of the storm.

He did a quick circuit around the *bure.* Nothing out of place. Man, the rain was really coming down. He'd never seen anything like it. In under a minute, his T-shirt was plastered to his skin and he hadn't even stepped away from the relative shelter of the *bure*. Bending low, he ran for the jungle, palm trees flailing wildly overhead. A massive sheet of rain blew in, slamming into his back and driving him into the fringe of trees. A large, dark shape appeared to duck and turn ahead of him, driven inland before the storm just as Tom was being shoved shoreward.

Startled, he squinted into the darkness, trying to make out what he'd just seen. Was that only a shadow, a trick of the night? Or had there been someone there? The rain eased for a moment, and he peered into the gloom. No one there, now. Was his mind playing paranoid tricks on him? He crept forward until he found a stump to crouch behind. He eased down onto his belly in a prone, shooting position and went perfectly still, watching. The storm roared all around him, and the ocean sounded like it was trying to claw its way up the cliff to the *bure*.

Exhilaration filled him. The night's wildness was contagious, calling to something primal buried deep within him. The rain and wind flowed over him and through him, and he became part of the storm. It was a heady thing.

And then a voice intruded on the night. High, scared and calling his name. He leaped to his feet, swearing violently, and sprinted for the *bure*.

He burst around the corner, and Maddie stood in the doorway, her white nightshirt stark against the blackness whipping around her. In one movement he swept her into his arms, lifted her off her feet and carried her inside. The wind slammed the door behind them. The relative silence inside the house was a shock to his senses.

"Intruder?" he bit out.

"I don't know," she answered breathlessly. "Do you think there is one?"

He let out his breath in a huff of irritation. "No. Why did you yell for me?"

"I woke up and you weren't here. I got scared."

"So you went outside in bright-white clothing that makes a perfect target of you, and shouted at the top of your lungs, so anyone within shooting range of you would know of your presence and exact location?" His voice rose with each word until he was nearly shouting. Panic squeezed his chest until he could hardly breathe. Not again! He couldn't let another young woman die on his watch! He was still too raw from looking at the crime-scene pictures earlier to contemplate losing Maddie without freaking out.

She replied altogether too reasonably, "But he kills people on beaches. Pairs of lovers. I wasn't on a beach and I was alone."

"He thinks we've seen him. That changes everything. He'll kill you and me both whenever and wherever he gets an opportunity. He'll gladly change up his M.O. to nail us. A killer's a killer, no matter how he does it."

Her eyes went big and round and black. He made an exasperated sound and stepped forward, sweeping Maddie into his soaking wet embrace. "You scared the living daylights out of me. Don't leave the house by yourself again. And don't shout like that unless you're actually in mortal danger, okay? My heart can't take it."

She sighed against his chest. "I've heard that's what happens when you get old. The heart goes first."

Equal parts surprised and irritated, he laughed. "I'm not old, dammit." But then an alarming thought occurred to him. Maybe that wasn't how she'd meant that comment about hearts going. Had she been talking about love?

Him? Losing his heart to a woman? Particularly a high-maintenance fashionista like her? Nah. Not possible.

Reluctantly, he turned her loose. "I'm getting you all wet. And you've already had a shower tonight. I wouldn't want a fragile young thing like you to catch a chill. It might turn into whooping cough or some other horrible childhood ailment."

"Childhood? You think I'm a child?" she exclaimed.

"If the shoes fits…"

She headed for the bathroom, muttering under breath and casually—definitely deliberately—stripping off her night-shirt as she went. The tease. He shouldn't watch. He didn't need the temptation. But as the fabric gave way to soft, satiny flesh, he devoured each and every tantalizing inch of it. Lightning flashed through the cracks in the boarded-up shutters, revealing her sassy, skimpy, bikini panties with a red heart embroidered on the right rear cheek.

He watched that sexy little heart twitch all the way to the bathroom, completely unable to tear his eyes away from it. *You are in trouble, old man. Serious, serious trouble.*

Dry once more and sporting her only remaining night wear—a sexy little black teddy—Maddie was roundly disappointed when Tom merely tucked her into bed with a chaste kiss on her forehead and then backed away from her. It was sweet, but she'd been hoping for more from him. She was wearing black satin with peekaboo lace in all the right places, for heaven's sake. But, no. The guy wasn't interested. Wash her up on a beach half dead, wearing shredded clothes and no makeup, her hair plastered to her head with salt water and seaweed, though, and the guy was all over her. What was up with that?

That man was really starting to get on her nerves. Of course, he was also really starting to get under her skin. No matter how much of him she got, she still wanted more. And that was totally unlike her. She'd been highly selective in the men she went to bed with in Chicago. After all, a girl couldn't afford to get the wrong kind of reputation and still expect to land a perfect husband. She'd carefully picked lovers she thought could give her the kind of sophisticated sexual experience a rich husband would expect from a wife. And although their technique had been acceptable, the few men she'd been with had left her feeling cold.

Not so, Tom Laruso. Oh, no. He'd curled her toes and all but set her hair on fire. And he was by far the most unsuitable man she'd ever met, let alone had sex with. Temporary insanity. That was it. It had to be a result of her near-death experience. Waterlogged brain. Post-traumatic shock. *Something* diagnosable.

Except, a tiny voice tucked in the farthest corner of her mind whispered that perhaps she was entirely sane to have fallen for him. For the first time in a long time.

Deeply disturbed by the thought, she pretended to go to sleep and watched from behind slitted eyelids as he relit the oil lamp, sat down beside it and picked up the thick pile of folders he'd been reading earlier. His concentration was intense enough that she was able to open her eyes fully and watch him as he studied the Sex on the Beach Killer's files without him noticing her scrutiny. He radiated intelligence. Competence.

Since when? He was the unshaven reprobate who only sobered up long enough to fly a floatplane between islands now and then to make enough money to buy booze. The man beginning to emerge from his enforced sobriety stood in stark contrast to the beach bum she'd first met. Which version was the real man? If she asked him, he'd no doubt make some off-handed comment that neatly avoided answering the question.

Regardless of which version of Tom Laruso was the real deal, she had to wonder how in the world a man like him had ended up out here on the edge of nowhere, doing his damnedest to drink himself into oblivion.

He shut a file and closed his eyes, pinching the bridge of his nose.

She spoke quietly. "Why don't you come to bed? You look tired."

Proof of the depth of his fatigue was the fact that he didn't jump when she spoke to him. Instead, he sighed and murmured, "It's got to be here somewhere. I just have to find it."

"Find what?"

"I don't know. Something. A clue. Some little thing that will give me an edge over this guy."

"The way I hear it, you already have a big edge on him in training and experience."

He glanced up at her for a moment. It was the barest instant, but it was enough to bring her straight upright in bed. The misery and self-recrimination swimming in his black gaze were horrible to look at. She blurted, "What's wrong?"

"I beg your pardon?" he replied cautiously.

She climbed to her knees and asked urgently, "You heard me. What put that look in your eyes? That blackness? What drove you to this island? To the whiskey bottle in that cabinet over there?"

"Sorry. That topic's off-limits. Next subject?"

She crawled on her hands and knees across the mattress. An alarmed look on his face, Tom kicked his legs to the floor. His chair thumped forward onto all four legs.

"What? Are you going to run away from me, Tom? You can't. You promised Sheriff Marquez you'd look after me. Keep me safe. It's what you do. It's who you are!"

"Not anymore!" he retorted.

"Why the heck not?"

He surged up out of the armchair as if he might, indeed, bolt from the room.

She forcibly calmed herself, breathing deeply until her voice came out reasonable and comforting, the same way she did back home on the farm when an animal was hurt or scared. "What are you afraid of?"

"I already told you. I don't want to talk about it."

"It looks to me like it's high time you talked to someone about it. Why not me? When the cyclone is over and this killer is caught, you don't ever have to see me again if you don't want to."

"You don't know what you're asking."

"And I won't until you tell me. I'm game if you are."

"No."

She shrugged. "It's your call. You and I are going to be cooped up in this house together for a very long time with very little to do except make love until neither of us can stand up...oh, wait...and talk. If I needle you about what you're brooding over nonstop for the next week you'll break eventually. I'm patient. I can wait you out."

He scowled, spun away from her, and without further ado, stormed out of the room.

She sighed. That hadn't gone well. But she was right. He did need to talk about whatever was eating at him. Too wound up to sleep, she plopped down in the middle of the bed, sitting cross-legged. Idly, she picked up the folder off the top of the pile on the nightstand and opened it.

Oh. My. God. Two naked people sprawled all over an eight-by-eleven glossy photo before her. Two *dead* naked people. With blood all over them. She slammed the folder shut, breathing hard. That was the most horrific thing she'd ever seen. She squeezed her eyes tightly shut, but the image burned behind her eyelids, as bright as day. Damn. It was indelibly printed on her memory now. She might as well look at the stupid thing again. Reluctantly, she reopened the file. Pointedly ignoring the grisly pictures on the left side of the folder, she started to read the notes and reports carefully collated on the right.

As long as she didn't think about the victims as actual living, breathing people, she was able to read the police report with a certain amount of detached interest. Particularly fascinating was the FBI profiler's report on the Sex on the Beach Killer. The murderer sounded like a real sicko. How could someone as twisted as this guy not be completely obvious to anyone who met him on the street? It made her wonder if she'd ever innocently bumped into or chatted with someone whose inner life was this turbulent and violent. *How creepy was that?*

The FBI profiler believed that the killer spent time watching his victims prior to closing in for the kill. He might even watch them have sex before he killed. Okay, now that really creeped her out. The idea of this guy watching her and Tom make love positively made her skin crawl. No wonder Sheriff Marquez was so hot and bothered to get this guy off the beaches, dead or alive, as soon as possible.

The police reports didn't inspire her, in the slightest, to run down to the beach and act as bait to draw this guy out. In fact, now that she really knew what he was and what he did, the very idea scared her half to death. But, if Tom needed her assistance to nab this guy, how could she not help him?

Tom bumped into something in the outer room and his quiet oath drifted into the bedroom. The sound comforted her. She wasn't alone in facing the Sex on the Beach Killer.

Wearily, she gathered up the scattered files and piled them in Tom's armchair. She shimmied down under the covers and listened to the storm rage outside. The thatched roof and heavy cinder block and stucco walls muffled Kato's fury. But a certain shiver in the walls announced that the storm's intensity was building. It was more than a little unnerving.

Eventually, she slept, albeit restlessly, her dreams beset by bloody images of dead people making love. Sometime in the wee hours of the night, she roused enough to be aware of a big, warm, comforting body crawling into bed beside her and drawing her close. She snuggled against Tom with a sigh of contentment and went back to sleep, more calmly this time.

Sometime before dawn, two things happened simultaneously. A tremendous racket of noise exploded, like a car alarm on steroids. The high-pitched electronic tone screamed deafeningly. The second thing that happened was Tom flew out of the bed, ripping his arms from around her and disappearing so fast she barely knew what had happened.

"Stay put," he barked over his shoulder. And then he was gone, slipping through the door into the living room, the blocky shadow of a gun clutched in his fist.

She cowered under the covers, waiting in an agony of suspense as each minute took an hour to tick past. Why hadn't he called an all-clear yet? It only took a few seconds to check out every nook and cranny of the whole house. Had he gone outside again? Great. Here she was, scared silly and all alone, and he was God-knew-where crawling around the jungle, playing G.I. Joe.

The window shutters rattled. Rattled again. And then a scratching noise issued from the vicinity of the bedroom-shutter latches. Oh, God. Was that someone trying to get in through the window?

She gazed fearfully at the black rectangle in the wall. It was plenty big enough for a grown man to climb through and only about waist-high. If that was the killer out there, he'd have no trouble coming in to get her! One of the shutters groaned open a few inches, the nails holding it shut squealing their protest as wet wood released them reluctantly.

Ohgodohgodohgod. She rolled away from the window, out of bed and onto the cold, hardwood floor, continuing her motion until she was wedged underneath Tom's king-size bed. Wasn't this the first place a bad guy would look for her? Of course, if the bad guy had gotten past Tom, hiding in an obvious place wouldn't be the worst of her problems.

Was Tom out there somewhere, lying cold and wet and hurt? *Dead?* What was happening? Silent screams echoed in her head. Tom had to be okay! She *needed* him!

The shutter creaked again, the nails stubbornly fighting to hang on to the window frame. The wind howled and rain hammered against the house, and her heart all but burst out of her chest with terror.

An eternity passed. She strained to hear something, anything to let her know what was going on. Her knees and elbows started to hurt, and she wriggled cautiously into a more comfortable position—comfort being a relative thing while crammed into a virtual pancake. Her hand bumped against something cold and smooth.

An acrid, familiar odor filled her nostrils. Whiskey. She groped in the dark and her fingers closed around the neck of a bottle. She grasped it in the darkness. It was a sharp reminder that her life rested in the hands of potentially unreliable man. Reversing her hold on the bottle, she clutched its neck like a cudgel. It wasn't much as weapons went, but it was better than nothing.

Something moved past her hiding place. A man's bare foot. Oh, God. Was that the killer? She shook from head to foot.

"You can come out now," a familiar male voice bit out. Tom sounded as tense as he had moments before the plane had crashed.

"Are you sure?" she croaked. She babbled as she wormed out from under the bed. "The window…someone tried to rip the shutter open…or maybe it was just the wind…but I didn't scream…"

"This time you should've screamed."

She gazed up at him from her belly on the floor. "There *was* someone out there?"

"Yeah."

"You're sure?"

"Yes, I'm sure. I made out some footprints before the rain erased them."

Maddie froze in the act of crawling to her hands and knees. "Is he still out there?"

"You think I'd be in here now if he was?"

"I dunno how you bodyguard types work. Maybe you'd rather stick close to me. You know. Just throw yourself on me and take the bullet." She lifted the empty whiskey bottle. "It'd be faster and less painful than dying inside this."

He scowled darkly. "I haven't had a drink since I met you. Since about twelve hours before I met you, in fact, because I had to fly that day."

"Where's our favorite murderer now?"

"No idea. Took off into the jungle. I couldn't leave you alone and follow him. I didn't want to take a chance of him circling back before I caught up with him and him killing you."

"Will he be back?"

Tom snorted. "Of course he'll be back."

Maddie glanced wildly at the window.

"But he won't be back for a few hours. The storm's really picking up. Hell, to get across the last bit of lawn, I had to crawl on my hands and knees. Couldn't stand up in the wind. It knocked me right over. He'll have to take cover until the worst of this blows past. We're safe for a little while. And we'll be ready for him when he comes back."

Maddie sat down on the edge of the bed. "Wanna talk yet?"

"Nope."

She swung her feet up onto the mattress. "Join me?"

"Soon."

Riigghhtt. She heard the lie in his voice loud and clear. And fear speared through her. He was clearly planning on staying awake and on watch. Which meant he wasn't one hundred percent sure the killer wouldn't be back tonight.

Yikes.

"Get some sleep," he ordered.

As if! With a killer human and a killer storm on the loose just outside? Hah!

She pulled the covers up to her chin, cold to the bone all of a sudden. "Let me guess," she forced out between her chattering teeth. "Next time he won't bother trying to approach by stealth. He'll just come in guns blazing and blow us away."

"Something like that."

Oh, jeez. Tom didn't even *try* to deny it.

She groused, "You could've told me everything was fine, you know. That it was just the wind banging that shutter around and there's nothing to worry about." Gathering a head of steam, she continued, "But, no: You had to be honest and admit that we're about to be massacred like lambs for the slaughter. Like I'm ever going to sleep now!"

"Sorry. I'm in the habit of being honest with my clients. They figure out a little sooner than they otherwise might that I'm an S.O.B., but it makes for fewer hassles in the long run."

"An interesting business philosophy. Piss off everyone up front and don't postpone the inevitable. How's that working out for you, anyway?" she asked with light sarcasm.

He shrugged. "No complaints. Everyone's leaving me alone. And that's what I want."

What was she? Chopped liver? The two of them had been extremely not alone—several times—over the past day. "Are you naturally this big a jerk, or do you have to work at it?"

"Comes with the territory, babe."

Ah. She knew that devil-may-care tone of voice. She spent most of her time these days with people trying to put on grand acts. Heck, she was a master of the art. His flippant comment had been purely calculated to tick her off. Her anger dissipated as quickly as dandelion fluff in the face of the cyclone raging outside.

Calmly, pleasantly even, she asked, "Why are you trying to make me mad? So I'll back off from you? What are you afraid I'll learn about you? Is this professional or personal?"

He made an inarticulate sound that could have been anger or perhaps sheer male exasperation. She knew that sound, too. The macho man retreating deep within his cave to avoid the all too insightful woman who wanted to engage in that most heinous of acts—talking about feelings.

She changed the subject to something less threatening to the big bad scaredy-cat. "How soon do you expect the killer back?" she asked with gentle persistence. She might let him off the hook—for now—from talking about his feelings, but she *was* going to make him talk to her.

Tom gave in with surprising grace, even if she did detect a hint of a huff and a certain slump of the shoulders. "The killer will have to think about the fact that our doors were booby-trapped. That'll worry him. Now he doesn't know what he's up against. He probably figured he'd waltz in here, knife us in our sleep and slip away before the cyclone gets too bad. Then our bodies would rot out here for a week or so before anyone bothers to swing by and see how we're doing. He'll be long gone by then, and no one the wiser that he did us in. He might even have been contemplating getting cute and setting up the scene to look like a murder-suicide."

As shivers of horror crawled up her spine, Maddie tried for a little humor to lighten the moment. "Which one of us would've murdered the other one, I wonder? If I had to bet on it right now, I'd lay odds I'm more likely to murder you than you are me. What do you think?"

A reluctant grin tugged at his shadowed features. "You could try to kill me. But you'd fail."

"Oh, you think you're tough?" she teased.

He snorted. "No, I think you're five foot three and I can break you in half with my bare hands."

And the beauty of it was that she had utter, complete, unswerving faith in the fact that he would never, ever lift a finger to her. He was just that kind of guy. He might happily drink himself to death, but he oozed the kind of integrity and responsibility that laid down certain lines in the sand that were never to be crossed. Violence toward women being one of those.

She thought about the door alarm. Tried to imagine what the killer would make of it. "All our guy really knows is that there was some sort of alarm connected to the front door. Couldn't any reasonably nice home have a security system?" she replied. "And this is definitely a nice place by island standards."

Tom shrugged. "Maybe. But alarms aren't the norm on a tiny little island like this."

"Yeah, but if you have money or jewelry or some other valuable collection, you might have an alarm system in your house."

"He'll have to consider the possibility. Of course, he'll also have to consider the possibility that I'm not some sex-starved rube he can just stroll up behind and kill."

Maddie pouted smilingly. "You mean you're not sex starved? I'm desolate to hear it."

Tom's eyes narrowed. But if she wasn't mistaken, humor glinted in their depths as he ordered, "Go to sleep."

"Not happening."

"Then lie down and cover up that scrap of cloth you call pajamas."

"You don't like this?" She threw back the covers to reveal her entire gleaming body, reclining in his bed and draped only in skimpy lace and satin. "I chose it especially for you."

His jaw clenched, and if she wasn't mistaken, that was a sheen of sweat on his brow.

"Well, actually, I chose it especially for you to take off me. Like this." She pushed one thin strap off her shoulder to drape suggestively down her arm.

He growled and took an aggressive step forward. Stopped. Swore. "Not tonight. But when this is all over, I'm stripping that thing off you. With my teeth."

Chapter 10

Tom started awake as something large and solid slammed into the wall behind his head. Probably a tree branch. Damn, Kato was really howling out there. He tightened his arm reflexively around Maddie's shoulders, drawing her closer to his side. She murmured in her sleep and snuggled a little closer. What time was it anyway? His head felt as if it had rocks in it. Too little sleep, too little booze, too few answers. And too little time until the bastard would be back. He wasn't ready. He wouldn't ever be ready to face another killer.

Last night's near miss with the Sex on the Beach Killer had been enough to send his blood pressure through the roof. The old diastolic and systolic still hadn't come back down if the throbbing pain in his temples with each beat of his heart was any indication.

Dull, gray half-light filtered in between the bedroom

shutters. Kato's eye wall was supposed to hit sometime in the midmorning. He glanced at his watch. Eight o'clock. Holy crap! He'd slept for nearly four hours! Back in the day, he could go for sixty hours on stim pills and caffeine. Ah, well, he wasn't in the biz anymore. No need for marathon stints on guard. Just one more job to get through. And then he was done for good.

Small problem: Maddie was not just a job.

What the hell he was going to do about that, he had not the faintest idea.

He'd been lucky over the years. Never had run into any serious problems with female clients putting the moves on him. Sure, women climbed all over him when he was off duty, but on the job, he'd always managed to maintain an unbreachable professional detachment. And then along came Maddie. Of course, in his own defense, she hadn't been a security job when he met her and first made love to her.

And she *had* saved his life, after all. Little pieces of that night continued to come back to him, but the whole experience of his plane blowing up around him still eluded him.

"That's some frown you're sporting there, champ," Maddie murmured from beside him.

He glanced down at her, gazing up at him sleepily. Trust glistened in her eyes. He could get used to a woman like her looking at him like that. If she knew what a loser he actually was, that look would go away quickly enough, though.

"And the frown just got worse. Is something wrong?" she asked as she pushed up to a sitting position and plumped a pillow behind her back.

"Nah. Just thinking."

"About the killer? Any new insights?"

"Nope."

"Nope you have no new insights, or nope you weren't thinking about the killer?"

"Has anyone ever told you you're a nosy woman?"

She replied lightly, "The being a woman bit pretty much implies the nosy bit, doesn't it?"

He chuckled in spite of himself. She did have a knack for making him smile.

"So what *was* on your mind, then?" she pressed.

"I want this job to be over so I can get back to my life."

"What life? You and Jack Daniels, together forever?"

He scowled. "I don't recall asking for your opinion of my personal life."

That put some starch in her spine. She went rigid against his side and then pulled away slightly. "If making love the way we have—more than once, I might add—doesn't make me part of your personal life, then you're either the world's biggest hypocrite, or you're the world's biggest bastard. Do tell. Which is it?"

He stared at her, frustrated. She was right, dammit. He *had* given her the right to poke into his personal life. Hell, he'd done his damnedest to crawl inside her soul, too. Like it or not, they had...something...between them. He shied away violently from putting a name to it. But named or otherwise, it was there, nonetheless.

"Well?" she challenged.

"I'm not a hypocrite. At least I try not to be."

"But it's okay to be a bastard?"

"Something like that."

Unaccountably, she smiled. "News flash, big guy. It's not in your nature to be a bastard. You try hard to drive everyone away from you, but at heart you're not a bad person. If you'd give folks half a chance, you'd have friends. Real ones. The loyal kind who'd stick by you through whatever you're going through right now."

"I'm not going through anything," he blurted defensively. She kept doing that—putting her finger on nerves and leaning on them. She could stop anytime, now.

"Sure you are. You just won't tell me what it is you're going through…yet. But I have at least half a hurricane left to weasel it out of you."

"Let it rest."

"Let me in."

"You don't want inside my head, darlin'."

"I'm asking."

"No deal."

She smiled calmly. "I'm not going anywhere, and neither are you. I'm patient."

A seed of fear took root in his gut. She might just win this contest of wills between them. For a little slip of a thing, she was plenty stubborn. Was he ready to spill his guts to someone? To let her inside his fortress of pain and self-recrimination? The very thought made his gut twist in fear.

She threw the covers back and swung her feet to the floor. "Breakfast?" she asked cheerfully.

He got up quickly. "I'll cook. I don't need any ground-up grass and caterpillars, or whatever you health freaks are eating nowadays."

She grinned. "I was envisioning cooking up the last of the bacon and eggs before they spoil, if your refrigerator and stove are still working."

"The stove is propane. As long as the tank hasn't blown away, it should work. I think I heard the refrigerator cut off about an hour ago. The island's power supply has probably gone down, now."

"Excellent. One last real meal before we go into survival mode."

She sounded surprisingly optimistic about the prospect of eating out of cans and boxes for the next week or more. He wouldn't have guessed it of her.

"Do you want to fry the bacon or scramble the eggs?" she asked brightly.

Darned if her perkiness wasn't actually a little bit contagious. Or maybe he'd just been seriously depressed without realizing it. Someone of normal cheer came along, and she seemed like a bloody ray of sunshine.

Cooking breakfast was an exercise in torture for him. He and Maddie kept brushing into one another in the compact kitchen, having to reach around each other to get things. If he didn't know better, he'd say she was intentionally getting in his way and engineering the contact.

They sat down to breakfast in the gray gloom of the shuttered-up *bure* with a candle to light their table. A certain damp chill hung in the air, but the hot coffee Maddie had brewed chased away the unseasonable cold.

The storm howled eerily, the wind singing a deep-throated threat as it tore past at well over a hundred miles per hour. The entire house shuddered when a strong gust came through, and Tom swore he felt a faint, misty breeze driving between invisible cracks in the windows. It was hard not to hold his breath in concern that the house was going to fail under the onslaught. Had the locals not assured him repeatedly that this place would stand up to the storm, he'd be getting pretty tense right about now.

Maddie looked that tense across the table.

He sighed. He ought to do something to distract her.

Reassure her. And without power he couldn't think of much to offer her...except talk, of course. Damn.

"How are you doing?" he asked in resignation.

"Okay. The wind is getting a little hairy, but this house seems to be holding up pretty well."

"Yeah, it'll do fine. It's a solid place."

"Solid enough to stop bullets?"

Well, then. He guessed he knew where her thoughts were straying to. He glanced at the nearest wall. "Yeah, we're fine in here. It's cinder block and stucco construction. Pretty heavy-duty stuff. It would take a high-powered rifle to punch through that. Such weapons exist, but I doubt the killer will have been able to lay his hands on one here, particularly at short notice right before a cyclone strikes. Besides, he'd need to have some pretty sophisticated infrared gear to target us through the walls. I *know* he can't get that on this island."

She nodded, but the haunted look about her eyes didn't go away. Damn. The reassurance strategy hadn't worked. He was going to have to pull out the big guns to distract her.

"Tell me about yourself," he said.

Her eyebrows went up, and if he wasn't mistaken, a bolt of alarm shot through her gaze like chain lightning and then disappeared. A smooth mask settled over her face. Odd. He took a sip of coffee and leaned back to see what happened next.

"Not much to tell," she said cautiously. "I grew up in Manhattan. Live in Chicago. Work for the Secret Traveler, which is a high-end travel agency catering to an exclusive clientele. I'm one of their scouts. I go to likely places, take pictures, write up a report and then go back to Chicago and put together travel packages for interested clients."

"What do you do for fun?"

"Take dance classes," she shot back.

"Touché. What *else* do you do for fun?"

She shrugged and seemed at a loss as to how to answer that for a moment. "I, uh, shop. Work out. Go out with friends. Take in a restaurant or show now and then."

"Sounds dull."

"It is...I mean it isn't as bad as it sounds," she corrected hastily. "I have fun meeting new people. Seeing new things."

"Do you read much? Do anything outdoors, like hike or camp or ski?"

She opened her mouth to answer, then checked herself. He got the feeling she'd changed her answer before it came out of her mouth.

"I like to sightsee. I guess that can be an outdoor activity." She laughed a little and added completely insincerely, "Shopping definitely counts as hiking. Especially when you're hauling a bunch of heavy bags around a megamall."

"Doesn't sound like much fun to me. I prefer trees and fresh air and nature sounds," he replied.

"Is that why you live way out here in the middle of nowhere?"

He shrugged. "I already told you. I wanted to be alone."

"Wanted, past tense? Do you still want to hide from the rest of humanity?"

"I'm not hiding," he retorted.

"What would you call it?"

He stared at her intently. She wasn't going to leave it alone. Relentless, she was. He sighed. "I'd call it early retirement."

"And why did you retire? Both Sheriff Marquez and Nigel seem to think you were really good at what you did. So why up and quit?"

The words just came out of him. He didn't plan it. Didn't think about it. He just answered. "I didn't turn out to be as good as they think."

Maddie froze. Took a slow sip of her coffee, never taking her eyes off him. He could all but hear her mental wheels turning, even over the screaming storm.

"Did you lose someone?" she asked.

He closed his eyes. He should've figured she'd know exactly how to interpret what he'd said. She was no dummy. No, indeed.

"Who was it?" she pressed.

I do not want to do this! he shouted inside his head.

"Let me guess. A woman. Young and single. It's why you freaked out so badly when the sheriff ordered you to protect me. Who was she? Was she shot?"

He swore under his breath and took a big slug of coffee, burning his tongue in the process. He sputtered and grabbed for a glass of cool water.

"As soon as I get access to a computer, I'm going to be able to search for your name and find out everything," she commented. "You can't keep anything secret anymore, you know. Not with the Internet out there."

He closed his eyes. She was right. But if she looked it up later, when she was gone from here, he wouldn't have to face her. To face himself.

"Are you really that scared to tell me the truth?" she asked insightfully.

She should really quit reading him like an open book like that. He *was* scared. But not of her. Of himself. Of looking himself in the eye and admitting that he should've known Arielle would pull some sort of a stunt. That she would be willful and foolish and reckless. He should've stuck around the hotel that night even though he was off duty and had personal plans. He should've listened to his gut.

He started when Maddie squeezed his hand supportively. She'd reached across the table without him noticing.

"Start with something simple. What was her name?" Maddie asked quietly.

"You don't have to treat me like a child. I'm perfectly capable of talking about this without you acting as if I'm going to shatter into a million pieces," he snapped.

She raised one eyebrow. "Then you can tell me her name without biting my head off, can't you?"

He subsided, reluctantly amused. "Her name was Arielle."

Maddie gaped. "The singer who was killed last year?"

"That's her."

"What happened? I heard she was murdered onstage right before a show."

"It was the night before a show, actually. In a big, open-air stadium. The place was deserted."

"Was she shot?" Maddie asked.

"Nope. Stabbed. And mutilated."

"I'm sorry." Thankfully, Maddie fell silent. But his reprieve was short-lived. "And where were you when all this was happening?"

"Off duty. Out to dinner with an old friend."

"And you feel guilty for not being there to save her."

He scowled. When she put it like that, his gut-wrenching self-recrimination sounded rather trivial and silly. "I *knew* something bad was going to happen. I warned her. Told her not to go out. But she didn't listen. And I left anyway..."

"Who was responsible for watching her while you were out?"

"Two of my men. She snuck past them and out of the hotel."

Understanding broke across Maddie's mobile features. "And then she was murdered. When she was out and about on her own. If the press coverage on her was accurate, she was quite a party animal, wasn't she?"

Tom nodded curtly. "Whatever the press said of her was an understatement."

"Is that what she was doing the night she was killed? She was out partying?"

"Probably. I don't know for sure. The details of the case have been sealed. But it would've been like her to hit the clubs."

"And she ran into her eventual murderer?"

Another nod.

"How did she end up dead onstage, then? Was she killed there or was her body taken there?"

Startled, he replied, "That's an excellent question." He cast back in his memory for what he could recall of the few crime-scene photos he'd been able to convince a detective to show him on the sly. Now that he thought about it, he didn't remember seeing pools of dried blood under her corpse. Which would indicate she hadn't died onstage. Could she have been killed nearby—say, on a beach—and then dragged to the stage and left there as some sort of statement by the killer?

Damn, he really needed to talk to the Malaysian police! What if another body was found that night? A young man, also stabbed, his throat slit, maybe washed up on a beach or left somewhere else nearby? An urgent need to know the truth made him so jumpy he could hardly stay in his chair. He shouldn't be this desperate. After all, Arielle was long dead. Solving the case now wouldn't change that. But it just might give him the closure that had eluded him up till now. It was worth a shot. Anything to put this behind him and get on with his life. The next time a woman like Maddie walked into his life, he'd like to be in a position to go forward with her into a long-term relationship.

Whoa. Long-term relationship? With a woman like

Maddie? He blinked, stunned. He wasn't looking for a relationship. Never had been. His work forced him to travel at the whim of his clients, and he'd globe-trotted pretty much continuously for the past twenty years. No time for long-term relationships, and certainly no stability to offer a woman, let alone a family.

"What?" Maddie asked, alarmed.

"You brought up an excellent point about Arielle's murder."

"Is that a good thing?" she asked carefully.

"Yeah. It may turn out to be a lead for the Malaysian police."

She smiled and gave his hand another squeeze. They finished their mugs of coffee in silence.

Then Maddie stunned him again by saying, "You know, it's not your fault. She knew better than to sneak out. Speaking as someone who's been under your protection for a little while, it's obvious you're not trying to make my life miserable. You're only looking to do whatever it takes to keep me safe. She should've listened to you."

What was that sharp pain ripping through his gut? Grief? Rage? Why now? After all these months? All of a sudden his legs were shaking, and a need to break something with his bare hands tore through him. That little twit! What the hell had she been thinking to sneak out like that? She knew Kuala Lumpur was a big city with all the dangers of any major metropolis. She *knew* better than to go clubbing alone! He and his guys had never gotten in her way, never pissed in her Wheaties if she wanted to drink or dabble in drugs or have kinky sex in front of them. They'd never judged her, never commented on her antics, never limited her behavior in any way. They'd only intervened when it was absolutely necessary to safeguard her life. But that hadn't been enough. She still had to rebel. Had to escape…just because she could. It was stupid! Childish! Suicidal! And…and…

His brain hitched as realization broke over him. More than realization. Understanding. Gut deep acceptance of the truth.

…and it hadn't been his fault.

The knowing washed over him like cold rain, cleansing but painful.

"What's done is done," Maddie murmured.

How did she do that? It was as if she picked the thoughts right out of his mind.

Maddie continued, "No second-guesses are going to change what happened that night. You acted reasonably—you warned her, you left guys guarding her, you had no reason not to go out to dinner. And she made a colossally immature and selfish decision that ultimately cost her life. I'd say she's paid plenty for her stupidity. There's no reason for you to keep on paying for it, too."

He shrugged carefully, like his newfound understanding might shatter if he rattled it too hard.

"Thanks for saying that," he mumbled.

He almost missed Maddie's blush as she ducked her head and her hair swung forward to mostly cover her face. She mumbled back, "I hate to see you suffer. It hurts me, too."

It hurt her—huh?

He studied her intently. "What are you trying to say?" he asked bluntly.

She looked up at him briefly and then her gaze skittered away. "I know we haven't known each other for very long. But…"

"But what?"

She took a deep breath and tried again. "But, I've developed strong feelings for you. I don't want you to be in pain. I want you to be happy. I want…us…to be happy."

Us? Oh, crap.

Chapter 11

Almost sick with anxiety, Maddie risked another glance at Tom. He looked nothing shy of dumbfounded. What? Did he think they could share the kind of lovemaking between them that they had without there being any feelings to go along with their incendiary attraction to one another?

"Now would be a good time to say something," she muttered.

"Uh...I don't...I don't know what to...uh...say."

"Not the most encouraging comeback to a declaration of feelings I've ever heard," she said with patently false casualness.

"Well, uh, of course, I'm complimented..." he stumbled through saying.

Complimented? Ouch. Humiliation started a slow burn low in her stomach and spread upward to encompass her lungs and throat, and finally, her face in fiery heat. She stood up hastily and clumsily picked up the breakfast dishes. She turned to flee for the sink just as he reached out to snag her around the waist. The dishes went flying and shattered with a crash of broken glass and broken dreams on the tile floor.

"Oh, God, I'm so sorry!" she exclaimed, not sure what she was apologizing for.

He started to stand. Opened his mouth to speak, but she cut him off. She couldn't stand to hear him say anything else compassionate and crushing.

"Don't worry about it, Tom. I'll clean up this mess. I've got sandals on. You go put on some shoes and I'll get a broom. I'll have this cleaned up in no time," she babbled.

She rushed for the broom closet and buried her head inside it, rummaging around noisily but not finding a broom. A tanned forearm reached past her head and pulled out the broom leaning in plain sight in the back corner of the closet. She stood up, still staring at the interior of the closet. She looked vacantly at nothing until she realized what she was doing and closed the closet door. She turned reluctantly to face him.

Tom wielded the broom with his back to her, already sweeping up the shards of her heart and the mess she'd made on his kitchen floor. She stood there uselessly, watching him take care of everything with the same silent efficiency he did everything. Like dash her hopes for the two of them in a few simple words.

How could she have been so stupid? He didn't feel anything for her! She was bait to catch a killer. Nothing more. They were supposed to make out. To pretend to have gnarly sex. Who could blame the guy if the game of pretend had gotten a little out of control a time or two? Most men would have a hard time restraining themselves when a naked, horny woman came on to them and crawled all over them looking for sex.

And it wasn't as if she'd been crying foul and calling a halt to the shenanigans between them. She'd been all too eager to help spin things out of control. But it had just been sex after all. Nothing more. Right? And that was why she felt violently ill and was seriously contemplating bolting outside and into the jaws of a major cyclone.

She'd been so stupid!

Her face went hot all over again.

Tom looked over his shoulder dispassionately. He asked flatly, "Could you grab the dustpan? It's on the top shelf in the closet behind you."

Numbly, she found the dustpan and held it for him while he swept bits of ceramic and glass into it. She emptied her dreadful mistake into the trash can and stumbled out of the kitchen, away from the ruins of her heart. How could she have fallen for him? He'd never given her any indication that he was interested in anything more than hot sex.

"Maddie—"

She didn't turn to face him. She couldn't.

She knelt on the sofa and peered through the louvered shutters at the raging ocean vaguely visible below through horizontal sheets of blowing rain. One of the palm trees at the corner of the *bure* had been uprooted and lay on its side, mortally wounded. She knew the feeling.

"Maddie."

She ignored him.

"Look at me."

Frowning, she glanced over her shoulder at him.

He stood in front of the couch, his arms crossed defensively across his chest. "What the hell's going on with you?"

Her eyebrows shot up. "I declare my feelings for you and all you have to say is that you're complimented? That's what the hell's going on with me!" She took a deep breath and continued more calmly, "I get the message loud and clear. I'm sorry you're stuck with me until Kato's blown over. I'll get out of your hair as soon as the storm breaks."

"I didn't say I don't want you around."

"I'm sure you do want me around. What guy wouldn't want freebie hot sex from some groupie chick with a crush on him?"

"That's not how I see you," he protested.

She turned fully to face him, her own arms crossed over her bosom. "How do you see me then?"

He exhaled hard. "I can't see you in any light other than being my client until I catch this Sex on the Beach guy."

Her eyebrows shot straight up. "You sleep with all your clients, then? So you're a full-service bodyguard?"

"No! I never sleep with— Okay, not until you. I've never slept with a client before. And you weren't my client the first time we made love."

"No, that was just a case of 'Hey, we made it, we're alive' sex."

"No, it wasn't. I've had plenty of close calls in my life, and I've never randomly jumped into the sack afterward because I'm so relieved to be alive."

"How would you characterize our relationship, then?" she challenged.

"I...we..." He pivoted and paced the length of the room and back, coming to a halt before her once more. "I'm attracted to you. Really attracted to you. And I shouldn't be. The job...my focus...you're screwing up my concentration something fierce. I'm having lousy luck trying to restrain myself with you. I'm sorry."

"Don't apologize to me! I'm obviously the one who should be apologizing for messing up your work so damned badly."

He scowled. "That's not what I meant."

She huffed and asked with thin patience, "Then what, exactly, did you mean?"

"Maddie, you don't want me. I'm a bum trying to drink myself into an early grave. You deserve better than that. Hell, you *want* better than me."

Her gaze narrowed. "What do you mean by that?"

"Look at you. You're sleek, sophisticated, painfully chic and on the prowl for a man. You and I both know you're hunting for a certain kind of man—rich, successful and interested in being a certain kind of wife."

"And what kind of wife would that be, exactly?"

"A trophy wife. A woman who'll look good at business parties, who'll decorate and maintain a beautiful home, who is a visible demonstration of his success in life."

Her jaw dropped. "You think I'm trophy-wife material?"

He looked flustered. "Well, what would you call it?"

She was so offended she could hardly form words. A trophy? Her? She was bright. Fun. Loving. She was so much more than arm fluff to some guy…wasn't she? Or was that exactly what she'd turned herself into?

"Don't get me wrong, Maddie. You're a great lady. Beautiful, smart, witty. Charming. Uh, well groomed. But you have to admit, you're not my type any more than I'm yours. I mean, you're the ultimate uptown girl. You're from New York City, for crying out loud. You live in Chicago. You turn your nose up at anything to do with the outdoors. You don't like a simple lifestyle. You want bright lights and the big city. Noise and action and chaos. I don't want any of that. I've had my fill of it."

His words were a knife straight to her heart. She loved the outdoors! Loved animals of all kinds, trees and starry skies and the deep silence you could only get way out in an isolated forest on a winter evening. She'd liked living on the farm, for that matter. She just hadn't been able to stand the constant financial uncertainty of the lifestyle. But she'd relished the rest of it.

He spoke again, probably out of nervousness or frustration, trying to fill the void left by her silence.

"I can't figure you out. I keep catching glimpses of a woman I think I could spend the rest of my life with, but then all that city slicker stuff takes over and I think we can't possibly have enough in common to build an entire life on."

But that wasn't true! The uptown girl was an act!

And what would he think of her if she told him so?

Then he could add being a phony and a conniving gold digger to her lengthy list of flaws. She was neatly and completely trapped in her own web of lies. In trying to be someone she wasn't, she'd driven off the one guy who'd have loved her just the way she really was.

The irony was almost more than she could bear. She didn't know whether to laugh or cry. But either way, she felt as if she was going to lose her breakfast.

Tom spoke grimly. "It sounds like the eye wall is about here. As soon as it passes, we'll need to head out. I'd like to make another attempt to draw out the killer, now that I know more about his modus operandi. I'll, uh, be in the bedroom until then…reading the Sex on the Beach files."

Coward. She glared at his back as he beat a hasty retreat for his cave to hide from the inconvenient and unpleasantly emotional female. The storm whipped furiously around the little house, buffeting her even through thick walls of block and concrete. Just listening to the cyclone was exhausting. She felt as if she was trying to walk into the wind and losing the battle.

No, wait. That was just Tom she was trying to walk toward and his walls of emotional resistance blowing her back.

Tom emerged from the bedroom a little before noon, silent and stiff jawed. He was carrying a strange-looking armload of towels and linens and clothes. If she didn't know better, she'd say it looked as if he was about to do a load of laundry.

Tense and unbearably uncomfortable, Maddie found herself developing a fascination with the ceiling beams. Yup, they looked plenty solid, even with Kato's worst winds lashing at them. Although she found it hard to believe, the woven thatch seemed to be holding up to the cyclone's fury just fine. Tom opened and slammed several kitchen drawers in search of something. She flinched at each crash.

He disappeared into the bathroom without speaking to her. Which was just as well. She couldn't imagine him having anything to say right now that she wanted to hear. And frankly, she didn't trust herself not to burst into tears if she tried to talk to him. Actually, she felt pretty darned close to tears right now. She swore under her breath. She didn't need to add being a weepy sissy to her list of flaws.

If only he wasn't right. At least she could be mad at him, then. But as it was, she had only herself to blame for wrecking the best thing she'd ever found. She was honest enough with herself to admit that Tom's observations about the fake person she portrayed to the world were spot-on. And darned if he didn't go even higher in her esteem for having made such an insightful observation of her.

Nope. She couldn't blame him a bit…dammit.

He'd blown anything they might have had between them to bits. But worse, he'd blasted her entire grand plan to smithereens. She'd never thought ahead far enough to ask herself the question of whether she really wanted to spend the rest of her life with someone who could be snowed by her act. Could she love a man who was superficial enough only to care about the outward appearances of a person? Who wanted her for a *trophy wife?* Damn, damn, damn.

Now what was she supposed to do? Faced with the prospect of dropping the Madeline C. persona entirely, panic threatened to overwhelm her. It was as scary as heck to consider putting herself out there for all the world to see as she truly was. To expect an intelligent, successful man who met her high standards in a husband, and who had high standards of his own, to choose her. The real her. The her who knew how to milk a cow and drive a tractor and muck a stall.

She *really* didn't want to go back to the farm. It wasn't a bad life. It just wasn't the life she wanted. A horrible feeling of being trapped closed around her.

But which was she more trapped by? Her rural upbringing, or the fake persona she'd so carefully built for herself? Both of them seemed to have her by the neck, choking the breath out of her. She stared at the raging ocean below. Its Category Three–fury made her feel infinitely small and insignificant.

She started as Tom spoke from practically beside her. "Get dressed. Put on that skimpy bikini I saw in your shopping bags."

Her head pivoted around. She stared up at him coldly. "And why would I parade around in practically nothing for you if I'm such a distraction to you doing your job?"

His jaw rippled as he clenched it. Gradually, his facial muscles relaxed enough for him to reply, "Not for me."

She frowned, not understanding.

"We're going out."

"Where to?"

"North Taru Beach."

The name meant nothing to her. She inferred that it was some sort of beach on the north side of the island, though. He wanted to go to a beach *now?* "In case you haven't noticed, there's a major cyclone blowing outside."

"It'll stop soon."

He was infuriating to converse with when he communicated in nothing but sentences with three words or less! She asked as calmly as she could muster, "And why are we going to this beach?" Maybe a why question would force an entire paragraph out of him.

"We're going fishing."

Fishing? What in the world was he up to? They had plenty of nonperishable supplies in the pantry to see both of them through the next couple of weeks. She frowned. "Let me get this straight. You were just sitting in your bedroom listening to Kato, and you said to yourself, 'Self, I think I'd like to go fishing. Right now. In the middle of a major cyclone.'"

Tom blinked rapidly, apparently startled. But still, he didn't break his silence.

"News flash, big guy," she announced, gathering a head of steam. "Fish may bite when it's raining, but they bloody well don't bite when there's a major storm raging. They go sit at the bottom of the pond, out of the turbulence at the surface and wait it out."

He studied her intently. Finally, he said, "And you know this about fish how?"

Suddenly feeling rather three-word sentence-ish herself, she bit out, "My dad fishes. He taught me."

"Ahh, but can the lady bait her own hook?" Tom mumbled.

Her gaze narrowed. "I may not be able to bait a hook for a damn when it comes to catching men, but I can put a worm on a hook for a stupid fish, thank you very much. For that matter, I can tie my own flies and rig my own fly casting pole."

He opened his mouth to say something but she cut him off. "And, I can take a fish off the hook, even if he swallows it, plus I can clean and gut my own fish. I'll have you know I fry up the meanest pan of brook trout east of the Mississippi River." The glare she shot at him made it clear he'd never get a chance to test her skills as an angler or trout cook firsthand, however.

Tom answered curtly, "Today we're not after trout. We're going fishing for the Sex on the Beach Killer. And you're the bait. So put on your bikini and think tasty thoughts. The eye of the storm will be here soon and we'll need to leave as soon as Kato abates. We'll only have an hour or so."

She was just mad enough to relish the idea of putting on the little red bikini and flaunting what Tom had just dumbassed himself out of having again. She sashayed over to the sideboard where she'd appropriated a drawer last night for her clothes, well aware of exaggerating the twitch of her behind a little for Tom's benefit. *Look all you want, buster. You're not getting any more of this.*

Tom demonstrated remarkable male intelligence and beat a tactical retreat when she turned deliberately to face him and reached for the hem of her shirt. Too bad. She'd have enjoyed doing a wanton striptease for him. It would've served him right.

She was grimly amused when he opened his bedroom door a few minutes later and peered out exceedingly cautiously. She lounged in one of the bar stools, her long legs crossed and prominently on display beneath the T-shirt she'd pulled on over her bikini. Her free foot bobbed up and down in agitation. He eyed it warily and circled well wide of it as he headed for the door.

"The storm's weakening. It's time to go."

She'd been so involved in her private, internal storm that she hadn't noticed the change in the noise outside. But now that he mentioned it, the intensity of the wind was noticeably less. It had gone from screaming to an eerie moan. She almost preferred the former.

Tom opened the door and she gasped as it was all but torn out of his hands. He motioned her to follow him, and with trepidation she stepped outside. Tree branches and palm fronds littered the ground and everything was waterlogged in the extreme. The ground squished beneath her feet as she followed Tom to a shed behind the *bure* that she hadn't noticed before. Several vertical slats of wood siding had been torn off the structure and some roof shingles were missing. Whether Kato's work or just the condition of the structure, she couldn't tell. He wrestled the big doors open and she glimpsed a vehicle inside the garage.

He had a Jeep? Yet he'd made her walk to town the last time they'd gone? The jerk! "Why didn't you drive me to town before?" she demanded.

He glanced up from stowing the pile of clothing and rags she belatedly noticed he'd brought out with him. He shrugged. "You were in such an all-fired hurry to get on with your vacation. I thought you could use a little relaxation. That was before I realized you hate everything to do with nature."

"I don't hate anything to do with nature! Well, okay, I'm not crazy about spiders. But I love the outdoors!"

He swung into the Jeep. Gazed over at her dispassionately. "Could've fooled me."

She swung in beside him with a sigh. She couldn't blame him. "Look. Would you believe me if I told you I'm not always as prissy as I've been coming across?"

He frowned, considering. "I dunno. You seem pretty prissy to me."

She gave him a distinctly unprissy slug in the shoulder with her fist. She commented in an academic tone, "Note the non-girly fist and proper slugging technique."

He winced, rubbing his arm. "Duly noted. Where'd you learn how to do that?"

"I have three brothers. Three big, strapping brothers who like to roughhouse."

Tom's eyebrows shot up. "Remind me never to pick a fight with any of them."

She nodded regally as he eased out of the garage. It took them several minutes to make it down Tom's driveway, such as it was, to the main road. Several times they had to stop, get out and drag debris out of their way. Along the way, he spoke into some kind of walkie-talkie twice. She wondered who he was talking to, but she was still too annoyed to ask.

The sky overhead was clearing rapidly, and patches of bright blue were peeking through the nearly black clouds. How odd was that? They went from a howling nightmare to blue skies and nearly complete calm in a matter of minutes.

Tom seemed to read her thoughts. "If you think this is weird, wait till we go back from blue skies and calm back into the farside eye wall of the storm in a matter of minutes."

She nodded, awed by the towering wall of billowing thunderheads retreating in the distance before them. It truly was a wall of clouds.

Once they hit the main road, it was clear someone had come this way recently. Tom had to weave around downed trees and debris, but they were able to pick their way across the island without having to stop the Jeep.

Her pulse jumped as Tom parked in the lee of a sand dune and got out. She jumped out as well and slogged the last few feet to the top of the dune as he spoke once more into his radio. She gasped as she caught sight of the ocean below. Colossal waves like she'd seen on television in surfing documentaries climbed the shore, clawing at the sand with a ferocity that was breathtaking. And deafeningly loud. She felt Tom's presence beside her. Even though he shouted into her ear from a range of about two feet, she barely heard him say that it was time to get the show on the road.

She slipped and slid down the dune face behind him. What was he doing with that pile of rags under his arm? He stopped at the base of the dune, fell to his knees and commenced shoveling sand for his laundry project. She planted her fists on her hips.

"Are you going to tell me what the heck you're doing with that stuff?" she shouted. The wind ripped her words from her mouth. Tom didn't look up and she wasn't sure he'd heard her. She dropped to her knees beside him.

Without looking up, he called back, "Meet Bob. He'll be your date today."

She stared. "Bob?"

"Yup. Handsome, isn't he?"

"Have you lost your mind?"

Tom grinned at her. "Maybe. C'mon."

Bemused, she followed him the rest of the way down to the beach. A half-dozen surfers bobbed up and down in the swells beyond the breakers, some paddling by hand and others being towed by jet skies farther out into the raging surf.

"Are they crazy?" she shouted.

Tom replied, "Nope. Best surfing on the planet is in the eye of a storm like this one. These guys are big-wave riders. They chase hurricanes and cyclones all over the world in search of extreme waves. Most of them are professionals."

"Professional nutcases!"

Tom grinned. "You don't see me out there messing with Mother Nature."

Maddie shuddered as one of the surfers took a spectacular fall, tumbling down the clifflike face of a wave and disappearing as tons upon tons of white water crashed down on top of him. "Is that guy going to be okay?" she asked in concern.

Tom nodded and fiddled with his armload of clothes. "Yeah, those guys can hold their breath for a couple of minutes and they know not to panic if the ocean pins them on the bottom. He'll pop up once that wave passes. You watch."

She held her breath until, sure enough, the surfer and his neon-yellow board bobbed to the surface. The kid gave a whoop and turned to paddle back out to catch the next wave.

To their left, she became aware of a convoy of golf carts arriving at the beach. She thought she spied the Paradise Cove logo on them, but it was hard to tell at this range.

"What in the world are all those people doing?" she asked as dozens of people piled out onto the sandy beach.

"Same as we are. Wave-watching," Tom replied absently. "Okay. Bob's ready to go. Slip these loops over your ankles and wrists."

Maddie tore her gaze away from the ocean. "What's going on here? What are you up to?"

"I called Nigel and asked him to arrange a field trip over here for his guests to watch the surfers. I'm hoping the Sex on the Beach Killer can't resist the chance to come prowl a beach."

"Are you and I going to give him a show?" Comprehension dawned. "That's why you wanted me to wear this skimpy bikini!"

Tom turned a little red around the gills. "Yeah, but here's the thing. I can't keep my mind on business when you and I together act as bait for the killer. So, I decided to substitute Bob, here, for me."

She frowned. "I don't follow."

"Bob's a life-size dummy made of my clothes. I stuffed him with sand so he's heavy and will move more like a human. I attached an old hairpiece I had left over from an undercover job I was on a few years back. A little of your makeup—I hope you don't mind that I used some of your stuff to draw his face—"

She nodded her okay.

"—but I think the end result isn't half bad. How 'bout you?"

Maddie eyed Bob critically. "He has a bigger beer gut than you."

"Thanks," Tom replied dryly. "But his gut won't show. I need the two of you to lie down by the water and make out. Bob gets to be on top."

"You want me to make out with your laundry?" Maddie asked incredulously.

Tom grinned. "Yup. And you get to act like you're really enjoying it."

Act like—well, heck. She'd been acting like a whole different person for all these months. How hard could it be to act as if she was turned on by Bob?

"What're those loops you want me to put over my wrists and ankles?"

"They're attached to Bob's wrists and ankles. You tie his limbs to yours. Then, when you move, he moves. You put your arm up over your head, he does the same. You put your hand behind your head and it looks as if he's wrapping his arm around your neck."

Maddie laughed at the absurdity of the ploy. "And you really think the Sex on the Beach Killer is going to fall for this?"

Tom nodded grimly. "If he doesn't, you and I have to have sex again for real. And somehow I'm gonna have to see him coming and defend us when I'm totally distracted by you. And I gotta say, babe, so far, keeping my wits about me while you and I are making love hasn't worked out too well."

She couldn't help it. A little part of her was pleased that Tom got so caught up in making love with her that he lost focus on his work.

"I'll be all alone on the beach, then?" she asked in a small voice.

"Well, you'll have Bob. He's not going anywhere."

She scowled.

Tom added, "Never fear, you and I will stay in constant communication. I brought some of the radios and earbuds I used in my protection work. He held up what looked like a pair of cigarette pack–size walkie-talkies. "This is the transmitter base unit. You tuck it in your clothes and use the wireless earbud."

"As small as that is, have you had a look at my bikini? I'm not going to be able to conceal that thing on me!"

Tom grinned. Stepped close. He quickly clipped something small and round onto the top of one of the little triangles covering her chest. And then he reached around behind her, and while his breath teased the short hairs curling at her temple, something cold and hard slipped down the back of her bikini. She lurched forward in surprise, banging into Tom's solid body.

"Easy, darlin'. You'll be lying on your back, remember?

The killer won't see a thing. C'mon. Time's-a-wasting." He glanced to where the guests were starting to fan out from the Paradise Cove carts.

She followed him down the beach a ways to an area with several large rock outcroppings coming almost down to the water's edge. Tom quickly situated her maybe thirty feet away from one of the strings of boulders. He draped Bob over her and adjusted the dummy's limbs. It was uncanny how Bob mimicked her every move. In any other less lethal situation, she'd have found the whole thing hilarious.

"I'll be hiding in the rocks over there," Tom announced. "If you holler, I can be here in three, maybe four, seconds, tops. Okay?"

"Tom, what makes you think this guy will strike in broad daylight on a crowded beach?"

"First, I'm hoping he'll recognize us and desperately want to kill us. Second, I've put you in a secluded spot that can't be seen from the rest of the beach. And last but not least, this guy hasn't killed in a while. I'm hoping his appetite for blood is sharp enough to push him into action."

Tom stepped back, took a critical look at her and nodded tersely.

She nodded back, gulping. And then he was gone. Just like that. She'd had no time to prepare, no time to think about this harebrained scheme. And now, she was lying on cold, wet sand, with a heavy, scratchy dummy draped all over her.

"Radio test. How do you hear me?" Tom said in her ear. She jumped, startled.

"Uh, I hear you fine. Am I supposed to do anything like push a button for you to hear me?"

"Nope. That's a voice-activated microphone I attached to your top. Anytime you talk, I can hear you."

"Great. Now what?"

"Now you make out with Bob."

She writhed experimentally beneath the dummy. "Okay, I feel ridiculous."

"You look ridiculous. Try something simple. Have Bob push the hair out of your eyes."

She reached up and pushed her hair off her forehead.

"That looked great. Bob liked that. So have him wriggle a little."

She wriggled as ordered. "If you giggle at me, Tom, so help me, the Sex on the Beach Killer isn't going to be your biggest problem."

"I don't giggle," he retorted indignantly.

"Fine. No laughing, snorting, guffawing or other expressions of humor out of you. Got it?"

"Yes, ma'am," he replied drolly.

"C'mon, Bob. We're out of here—"

"All right, all right," Tom replied, laughing openly now. "I'll do my best to control myself."

They settled down, with Maddie moving around underneath the dummy just enough to make the thing look alive. Tom, hidden in the rocks, reported in every few minutes from his hidden perch. A few resort guests strolled by in ones and twos. Maddie felt like a total slut, making out for them, even if it was with a dummy. But after she caught a half-dozen people spotting her and averting their gazes quickly, the worst of her humiliation dulled to mere embarrassment. Eventually, even her embarrassment wore off and boredom began to set in. She turned her head to watch the surfers offshore.

Tom's voice brought her sharply back to the moment. "Hey! We're trying to catch a killer here. He only comes out to nail lovers. And I think he only attacks them when they're going at it madly. You've got to put your heart into this."

She sighed. Her heart. Right. That was the problem. Her heart was far too involved with Tom Laruso.

"Bob's crazy for you, Maddie. You're driving him out of his mind with desire. He wants to devour every inch of you and then start all over again."

She blinked. Was that how she'd made Tom feel? The possibility started heat building low in her belly. Tentatively, she pulled the dummy closer and kissed his mouth. Or at least where a mouth would be if he had one. Oh, for crying out loud. She was kissing a pillowcase and probably smearing lipstick all over her face.

Tom's rich, deep voice caressed her ear. "Have Bob trail his fingers down your body. Slower. Yeah, like that.

"He's cupping your breasts—cup your breast, Maddie. You have to move your hand to get him to move his."

She blinked, startled. She reached up tentatively and put her hand over her right breast. New embarrassment flooded her. As if it wasn't bad enough that she was fondling herself in public, Tom was watching her. She didn't know which was worse.

He was talking again. "Bob's kneading until you make that little moan in the back of your throat—knead, Maddie."

She complied. In desperation, to avoid dying of humiliation, she imagined Tom touching her, cupping her trembling flesh, laving it with his tongue, tugging on her nipple with his teeth. Her fingers strayed across her skin, sending tingling sensations shooting low in her abdomen. She moaned faintly.

"Yes. That moan. Now Bob's running his hand down your body. Over your belly. Now lower. Yes, lower."

She followed his instructions, her back arching in spite of herself in reaction to Tom's husky voice.

"Perfect. Uh, now writhe. Think about sex."

"With you?" she asked breathlessly.

He cleared his throat. "Think about the hottest sex you've ever had."

"That would be with you, by a mile."

"Uh, okay then."

She replayed their encounter from last evening on the beach in her head and suddenly didn't have any trouble at all moving restlessly beneath the dummy, casting her limbs wide with abandon, flinging herself into the moment.

She yanked her right wrist free of the elastic loop. Bob's arm flopped to the sand beside her head. She reached up and circled her arm around his neck, pulling him close. She whispered, "This is how you make me feel, Tom." And then she kissed the dummy with all the pent-up passion and loss and frustration inside her.

Chapter 12

Tom gulped as Maddie all but inhaled the dummy. It was just a pile of rags, but the sexual energy pouring off her practically drowned him. It was all he could do not to go tearing down the beach and take Bob's place this second. He wanted her so bad he could barely stand.

He swore under his breath. The idea of removing himself from Maddie like this had been to help him keep his professional and emotional distance from her. And it hadn't helped one damn bit. The mere thought of her was enough to bring him to his knees. That wasn't how this was supposed to go!

He wasn't supposed to be up here sweating bullets, not only because Maddie was doing things that made him so hot for her he couldn't think. He wasn't supposed to have this panicked feeling lurking behind his eyeballs that something bad could happen to her. Wasn't supposed to want to wrap her up in his arms forever and protect her from the entire world

Wasn't supposed to be so desperately in love with her he couldn't do his job!

Whoa. Love?

No way.

Yes way.

He swore long and hard to himself while Maddie panted in his ear, whispering of all the things she loved having him do to her. All the things she wanted to do to him.

It was lust he felt. Just lust. Right?

Wrong.

Lust might be pounding through his body, but that had nothing to do with the jumbled emotions pounding through his head and his heart.

Maddie's sweet voice tickled his ear. "I wish you were here with me, Tom."

"I am with you, baby. Right here."

"No. I mean in my arms. Looking out for me. Making love to me. You make me feel safe—" She broke off, as if the idea of being safe with him was new to her. Didn't she understand?

"You'll always be safe with me, Maddie."

"Really?"

"You have my word on it." And in saying the words, he realized he meant them completely. He wanted to look out for her, to take care of her, always. The insight rocked him violently. He wanted to make all sorts of promises to her. The forever kind.

Shocked to his core, he glanced down the beach absently. Nobody approaching at the moment.

He skimmed the binoculars across the line of rocks opposite his position. He'd chosen this spot because it afforded the killer the kind of cover he seemed to like, and it still had plenty of good hiding spots for Tom to lurk in wait for the killer.

So far, there'd been no sign of the bastard. Tom had been sure the guy would come out and trawl the north beach when so many spectators would be here watching the waves. A faint rumble in the east caught Tom's attention. In the far distance, a line of thunderstorms had appeared on the horizon. The rest of Tropical Cyclone Kato.

They were running out of time.

"Can you make more noise, Maddie? We've got to draw this guy out now."

"Assuming...ohhh, yesss...he's anywhere...right there, yes, yes!...nearby, you mean?"

Tom closed his eyes in actual, physical pain. "Keep that up and I'm going to come down there, beat up Bob and take his place."

She muttered, "I wish you would." Tom jumped as she all but shouted, "Oh, baby!"

She was killing him here.

"Yes! Yes! Yes!" And then, as she and Bob rolled around in the sand, she murmured sotto voce, "I'm channeling *When Harry Met Sally.* How am I doing?"

"Outstanding," Tom groaned.

Maddie rolled over, sat up and straddled Bob. She rocked back and forth fast and hard, looking to any observer as if she was humping the poor guy's brains out. Sweat popped out on Tom's head as vivid recollection of what that felt like rolled over him. He was going to have an orgasm, just sitting here thinking about sex with her! Must. Stay. Focused. He clenched the binoculars painfully tight in his left hand and squeezed the butt of his pistol in the other hand until he thought the grip might bleed.

As Maddie and Bob flailed wildly and Maddie moaned and groaned loudly, a flash of movement from the rocks opposite him caught his eye. Hell.

"Maddie!" he shouted in her ear. "Get on your back! Now!"

Tom leaped up and took off running. Time slowed to an exaggerated crawl, each millisecond registering with frightening clarity in his mind. The sand was deep beneath his feet, swallowing his running steps.

Maddie looked up, surprise etched on her face.

The man running from behind the rocks lifted his right arm. Something flashed, dull and metallic, in his hand.

Maddie's shoulder ducked as she leaned forward to roll over.

Tom staggered forward, his right hand taking forever to lift away from his side. Did he dare take the shot? It would be insanely close to Maddie. A few inches off target and she'd die.

The killer leaped. His knife arced downward, plunging into the dummy, which Maddie had just barely managed to yank across her body in time. The blade slashed into Bob's exposed head, and sand poured out of the gash, a macabre parody of what would have otherwise spilled out had that been his or Maddie's skull.

Tom's index finger clenched, pulling through the trigger in a single smooth movement as he sighted down the short barrel of the weapon. _Caa-rack!_ Just as the pistol fired, the killer dived to the side.

Maddie screamed.

Dear God, was she hit? Had he shot her?

The killer roared in rage, and suddenly time resumed normal speed, accelerating to a frantic scramble of events that Tom reacted to on pure instinct.

The killer pounced on top of Maddie and Bob, and apparently realized the ruse. A scream of fury erupted from the guy's throat as Tom lowered his shoulder and charged. The impact knocked the guy off Maddie, and the momentum sent the two men rolling down the slope of the beach. Tom lost his grip on his pistol and it flew away.

Glaring from a range of about twelve inches, the killer's blue eyes were crazed. Engulfed in rage. Completely insane. And something inside Tom snapped. This son of a bitch had just tried to kill Maddie! As big and strong as the killer was, Tom was just as big and strong. And as crazy as this bastard might be, in that moment, Tom was a little bit crazier.

The two men grappled, their arms straining, hands grasping and punching, knees jerking, elbows flying.

Tom grunted, "Did you…kill Arielle?"

A maniacal grin twisted the killer's face. "That whore… pranced all over stage half naked…incited indecent behavior…lured young boys to pornography…"

The killer grunted as Tom grabbed his thumb and gave it a hard twist. The killer countered with an elbow to Tom's ear.

"Hell, yes, I killed her…sent her and that gigolo of hers… straight to hell."

Tom was so stunned by the admission that, for an instant, he lost focus on the killer. The guy made a fast move and got his hands around Tom's neck. Cruel thumbs dug into his jugular. *Oh, crap.* In a matter of seconds, the blood flow to his brain would be interrupted and he would pass out. Tom thrashed beneath the guy, struggling to throw the madman off him.

A fast-moving object barreled at them from Tom's right. He felt an impact, but no pain. The killer grunted in surprise. Tom gasped for air as the vice around his neck eased. The spots dancing before his eyes subsided.

A meaty thud of knuckles on flesh sounded above Tom, and warm wetness sprayed his face.

A female voice grunted, "Leave. Him. Alone." Two more

juicy punches landed, the second accompanied by a crunching noise like bone breaking. "I love him, you bastard!"

Oh, no. Not Maddie. She hadn't joined the fight, had she? This guy would kill her!

On cue, the killer let go of Tom and twisted to attack this new threat. And therein lay his fatal mistake. Tom let fly with his right fist, putting behind the blow every ounce of his love and panic for Maddie, who'd recklessly dived into this fight to the death. His fist landed on the killer's left temple.

It wasn't a pretty blow, not boxing ring or Hollywood-movie perfect in its target, but it had the intended effect. The killer's eyes rolled up into his head even as he toppled over in the sand and went still.

Maddie flew at their attacker, pummeling him with her distinctly un-girly fists.

Tom shoved the guy's inert weight off him and leaped to his feet. He looked around fast and spotted his pistol half buried in the sand. He pounced on it and scooped it up. Pivoting around, he raised the weapon and aimed it at the prone killer.

He was riveted by the sight that greeted him.

Maddie knelt by the killer with tears streaming down her face. Between blows to the killer's head and body, she sobbed at the assailant's crumpled form, "Don't you get it, you jerk?" *Thwack.* "I love him." *Thwack.* "I'm not a city girl, dammit." *Thwack.* "I was born and raised on a farm! I love nature!" *Thwack.* "I dressed up and moved to the city to marry a—" *thwack* "—rich guy because I was so scared of being poor!" *Thwack.* "But I don't want to be a trophy wife." *Thwack, thwack.*

A smile tickled at the corners of Tom's mouth. He stepped forward. "Honey, I think that's enough punching-bag time for you."

"He tried to—" *thwack* "—kill you!"

Tom said gently, "I'm just fine, Maddie. You can stop hitting the bad man."

"But—"

He reached down and drew her to her feet. She turned and buried her face in his chest, sobbing in earnest, now. "I was so scared."

"You were incredibly brave, darling. When he jumped at you with that knife, I thought my heart would stop."

"That's not what scared me," she sniffled against his chest. "I was scared when you jumped him. I thought you were going to get yourself killed trying to protect me."

He leaned back enough to stare down at her. "What? Didn't you think I could take care of myself? Honey, I'm a black belt in four different martial arts and was a national wrestling champion in college."

"I didn't think. I just saw you in danger and I," she said and sniffed loudly, "sort of flipped out."

"Yeah, I noticed."

"Are you mad at me?" she asked in a small voice.

"That you went ballistic when you thought I was going to die? How can I be mad at you for that? I did the exact same thing."

"Really?" A tentative smile sparked in her watery eyes.

"Yeah, really," he answered gruffly.

"You know what that means, don't you?"

He gazed deep into her eyes, a slow smile spreading outward from his soul to encompass his entire being. "I guess I do. It means I'm plumb-crazy, slam-dunk, head-over-heels in love with you, Maddie Crummby. Fussy makeup and prissy clothes and goofy shoes and all."

"My shoes are *not* goofy!"

"Well, they're damned impractical."

She smiled up at him slyly. "Yeah, but they're sexy, aren't they? You like my toes peeking out at you, don't you? You like my pedicure and the little flowers painted on my toenails. Admit it."

He tucked her under his left arm as they stepped back from the unconscious killer. The commotion of their fight had drawn the attention of people down the beach, and a number of them were coming to investigate. Hopefully, one of them would be Herman Marquez or his deputy.

Silence fell over him and Maddie, punctuated only by the rhythmic crash of the ocean beside them. The wind was starting to pick up again, hinting at the storm to come.

Maddie murmured reflectively, "I thought landing a rich husband was the only way I'd ever be safe. I never realized that having someone care about you enough to die for you is a million times safer than a fat bank account."

Understanding dawned. She wasn't a gold digger after all! She just wanted financial peace of mind. That he could give her. "Honey, I've worked nonstop for the past two decades, all expenses paid and have banked practically my entire salary. And I was damned good at what I did. I didn't make chump change. I've got more money than I know what to do with."

She absorbed that for a moment, then asked, "Do you miss your job?"

"Nope. As of right now, I'm officially retired."

She snuggled against his side, and he savored the warmth of her body nestled trustingly against his. He needed only one protection job, now. This one. In return for keeping his heart safe, he'd joyfully protect and provide for her for the rest of their days. Something peaceful unfurled inside him. Like a sail catching the wind, it filled taut and stretched, straining at its moorings until he thought it might break free and fly. And then it dawned on him. That sail was his life. And Maddie had filled it to overflowing.

Without looking away from his motionless prisoner, Tom murmured, "Okay, fine. I admit it. I like your toes. I particularly like sucking them and licking between them and hearing that funny little catch in the back of your throat—"

"Tom! Stop that! There are people coming to help us and I'd hate to embarrass them all by having to throw you down right here on the spot, rip off all your clothes and have my way with you in front of all of them."

He grinned and gave her an affectionate squeeze. "I'd like to see you try."

"Later," she murmured under her breath as the first people caught sight of Tom's weapon and pulled up short.

"It's okay, folks," he called. "Show's over."

"For now," Maddie murmured under her breath.

"We just caught the Sex on the Beach Killer," he called. "The situation's under control."

"Until I get you alone," she added sotto voce.

"Could someone go find Sheriff Marquez or one of his guys, and maybe a length of rope while you're at it?"

"Ooh. Rope. Gonna get kinky on me, are you? Gonna tie me up? Whatever will you do with me, then?" Maddie murmured.

A visual image of that roared through his brain, erasing all rational thought and sending blood pounding through regions of him that didn't need any more pounding blood just now. "Stop that," he laughed under his breath.

"Stop what?" She batted her eyes up at him, in all-sweet innocence.

"You really are a vixen."

She smiled widely and opened her mouth to reply when a

blur of movement startled her. The killer at their feet surged up off the sand, unbelievably fast. Triumph glittered in the bastard's eyes as his knife—forgotten in the sand—glittered in his hand. In an instant, Tom realized he was out of position to defend Maddie against the blow, and there was no time to aim his pistol and fire.

He did the only thing any bodyguard worth his salt could do. In one fluid movement, he shoved Maddie aside and stepped forward into the blow, giving his body to the killer's knife to save Maddie.

An explosion of noise accompanied the killer's body, slamming into him and knocking them both to the ground. Tom felt no pain, just a hot gush of blood across his gut and down his left side. Someone was screaming his name over and over.

Time froze.

He'd done it. He'd saved his charge this time. He'd gotten it right. Peace flowed over him, along with that pulsing stream of blood. All the guilt and recriminations of the past six months washed away. And in that suspended instant of time, he felt gratitude to the killer sprawled on top of him for giving him the redemption that he'd craved. Tom's gaze met the killer's.

The man's pale blue eyes widened in surprise. And then, ever so slowly, they went blank. Dead.

Huh?

Tom moved experimentally. If he'd been stabbed, he sure wasn't feeling it.

A British-accented voice barked, "Everyone stay back!" The screaming stopped.

Tom looked up. Nigel Cumberland was advancing cautiously, a still-smoking pistol held in a shooter's grip in both hands in front of him. The Brit shoved the killer with his foot. The heavy weight rolled off Tom.

"You all right?" Nigel asked tersely.

Tom took stock. "I guess so." He sat up—and was promptly knocked over again by Maddie. Frantic hands ran over his body, and then she collapsed, sobbing, against his chest.

Nigel pressed a hand to the killer's throat. "Dead," he announced.

Tom looked down at himself as he carefully pressed Maddie slightly away from him. He was covered in blood from where the killer had bled out on him.

"I must've hit his aorta," Nigel commented. "Lucky shot."

Maddie piped up, still a little quavery. "I thought you English police don't carry guns."

Nigel laughed. "I'm not a bobby now, am I?"

"Thank God for that," Tom replied. The two men grinned at each other.

Nigel said, "When you radioed me and asked me to arrange this little field trip to the beach, I figured you were trying to smoke out the killer. I grabbed my Beretta just in case." He patted the weapon, now safely holstered at his side.

A new voice rang out from the back of the crowd. "What's going on here?"

Tom closed his eyes in relief. Herman Marquez. He was more than ready to hand this whole mess over to the sheriff and be done with it, once and for all. "Looks like Nigel, Maddie and I bagged a serial killer, Marquez. You don't happen to have a spare body bag on you, do you?"

The sheriff and Nigel took over shooing away the crowd from the corpse.

A gust of wind lifted Maddie's blond hair, tussling it around her face and transforming her into the fresh, natural, breathtakingly beautiful woman he'd woken up to on a beach a lifetime ago. Was it only two days? It didn't seem possible.

Marquez ordered, "Time to head back home, folks. Kato's still got a little blowing to do. Tom, Miss Crummby, I'll need you to come down to the station and make statements as soon as the storm blows over."

Tom nodded. "No problem."

Marquez looked from the killer's battered face to Tom. "Looks like you worked him over pretty good, Laruso. I gather he didn't go down without a fight?"

Tom grinned. "Maddie's the one who beat him to a pulp."

Marquez looked over at her in surprise and back down at the killer. "A tiny little thing like you did all that?"

Maddie shrugged. "My brothers taught me how to fight like a proper country girl. They said it might come in handy someday."

Marquez grinned. "I should say it did." He looked back and forth between them, his knowing gaze dancing with humor. "Congratulations, ma'am. It looks like you bagged your man."

"What are you talking about?" Tom asked in quick suspicion.

Maddie looped her arm around his waist. "Why don't you come back to the *bure* and I'll explain it to you, darling."

A female voice called out from the grinning crowd. "I've got the bridal issue of *Vogue* at the shop. As soon as the storm's over, I'll bring it over to you."

Maddie called back airily, "That would be perfect, Trudi."

He and Maddie trudged up the dune toward his Jeep. "What's this about *Vogue?* The bridal issue?"

Maddie stopped. Turned to face him and looped her arms around his neck. "Breathe, Tom. It'll be okay. I promise not to plan too big a wedding."

A wedding? A moment's panic gave way to a burst of joy

so intense it nearly brought him to his knees. "Really? You'd actually consider marrying a bum like me?"

"You're a lot of things, Tom Laruso, but a bum is *not* one of them. And I assure you, I'm going to do a whole lot more than consider marrying you. I'm going to make you the happiest man on earth for a very, very long time to come."

Wonderment filled him. How on God's green earth had he landed a woman like Maddie? Out here at the end of the world, lost in a bottle of whiskey and looking to die young? Would miracles never cease?

"You have no idea the roller coaster your life's about to turn into, Tom Laruso. Take my advice, big guy—just sit back and enjoy the ride."

"I plan to, Maddie. I plan to."

Epilogue

FBI Headquarters, Washington, D.C., six months later

Maddie walked into the institutionally plain conference room and wrinkled her travel reviewer's nose critically at the décor. But then she caught sight of a pair of familiar, smiling faces and squealed in delight. "Zoë! Alicia!"

She rushed forward and the three women traded hugs all around while Sean "Breeze" Guthrie, Griffin Malone and Tom looked on indulgently.

"So tell me! What have you two been up to these past few months?" But then she glanced at the wedding band nestled beside Zoë's magnificent diamond engagement ring and her gently expanding waistline. "I can see what you've been up to, girlfriend. Just tell me you got that man to marry you *before* he got you in a family way."

"Absolutely. We tied the knot as soon as we got back from doing those last two resort reviews for the Secret Traveler." Zoë smiled affectionately at her husband, who smiled back at her. The sparks flying between them all but set the room's carpet on fire.

"Did Mr. Cameron finally wise up and put you on the Secret Traveler's A-Team?" she asked Zoë.

Her friend nodded, smiling self-deprecatingly. "He said my reviews have a sexy and romantic flair that will really appeal to his customers."

Alicia teased, "It must be all that detailed and meticulous research you and Breeze did to find the most romantic spots at the resorts."

Maddie and Alicia laughed as Zoë blushed fiercely.

In a transparent ploy to distract them, Zoë asked, "How 'bout you, Alicia? How are you settling into life as a stepmother?"

Their friend's eyes lit up with love and contentment. "Wanna see some pictures of Griffin's—our—daughter? She's a real charmer."

Maddie would never have pegged Alicia as the maternal type, but she'd never seen anyone look happier. Alicia glowed from the inside out. Maddie asked, "Have you two set a date yet?"

"For Christmas vacation this year, the three of us are planning to fly to Fiji. We thought we'd have a small ceremony there. Just family and a few friends. Any chance you and Tom can make it?"

Zoë piped up. "They're having the wedding at our resort. It's only about an hour's flight from Vanua Taru."

Maddie hugged Alicia. "Tom and I wouldn't miss it for the world."

"What about you, Maddie? How are you two getting along?" Zoë asked.

"We're doing great. Better than great. He's taken a job as the chief of security at Paradise Cove, and he's building another room onto his place for me."

Alicia asked playfully, "What's it gonna be? A walk-in closet for all your shoes?"

Maddie laughed. "Actually, we're hoping it'll be a nursery before too long."

Zoë gasped. "Are you—"

"Not yet. We thought we'd get married first. The sheriff on Vanua Taru—he's a friend of ours—has agreed to marry us as soon as we get back to the island. We flew to Chicago last week to pack up the last of my things and sell my condo. Good-bye to bitter Midwest winters!"

"Amen to that." Zoë laughed.

Alicia glanced over at Griffin and the pair's gazes met with an obvious and sexy promise. She commented, "Virginia Beach is close enough to the ocean that the winters aren't supposed to be rough. And I have to confess, I like my four seasons."

Maddie teased, "And those seasons would be hot-and-naked, wet-and-naked, cuddly-and-naked and sweaty-and-naked?"

The three women laughed. "Exactly!" Alicia replied.

Griffin Malone spoke up from across the room. "If you three are done catching up, I'm ready to start the briefing."

Maddie and the others moved over to the conference table. She was glad when Tom sat down beside her and took her hand, pulling it into his lap. His thumb idly caressed her palm, sending a flood of images—to act upon later—rushing through her brain.

Griffin, looking as handsome as ever in a dark tailored suit, opened a file at the head of the table. "The case on the Sex on the Beach Killer has been officially closed. Because all of you played a part in stopping him, the Bureau has given me permission to share the details of the case with you. You understand, however, that we must ask you not to share this information with the public or the press."

Alicia cut in. "Isn't he cute when he acts all official like that?"

Griffin threw her an affectionate, if mildly exasperated, glance that promised retribution later. He continued, "The killer's name was Bronson Spindler. He was born and raised in Philadelphia, and the FBI's profile on him was substantially correct in all aspects."

Breeze spoke up. "Way to go, Grif. Weren't you the guy who worked up that profile?"

Griffin shrugged, but nodded. "This guy's mother was a bona fide nutcase. She abused Bronson pretty harshly as a kid. She was obsessed with sex being evil and showed Bronson extensive pornography, then beat him for showing any response to it. I won't go into the details, but suffice to say, she was a monster and created a monster in her son."

Maddie shuddered and Tom squeezed her hand in reassurance.

"Spindler started killing in the United States. We believe he's responsible for three murders here—one in Florida, one on Cape Cod and one in California. He probably believed the law was getting too close to him and moved his operation to the South Pacific. That's just my guess, however."

Breeze snorted. "Your guesses about this guy have been spot-on right from the start. I'd say odds are you're right on this one, too."

"Thanks," Griffin replied. The FBI agent looked over at Tom. "The Malaysian authorities have found a nightclub owner who admitted that Arielle Michilano was in his place the night of her murder. As you conjectured, Tom, she picked up a guy there and the two left together. The club owner was able to pick out Mr. Spindler's picture from a mug book and remembers seeing him follow the couple from the club. The owner thought Spindler was Arielle's bodyguard, in fact."

Griffin took a deep breath before continuing. Maddie blinked. Wow. This case must have gotten to him more than she'd realized. But then, the Sex on the Beach Killer had nearly killed the woman he loved.

Tom tensed beside her as if he sensed what Griffin was about to say next.

"As a few of you already know, the Sex on the Beach Killer took buttons from the clothes of his victims as trophies. We found his collection and have accounted for all of them. Tom, we found a button from the blouse Miss Michilano was wearing when she died. Spindler definitely killed her."

Tom's fingers clenched convulsively around Maddie's, but then slowly relaxed.

She murmured to him, "Are you okay?"

He nodded, a sad but peaceful look in his eyes. "She knew better, and I warned her. It was her choice. Her responsibility."

Maddie smiled warmly at him. He'd come a long way since she'd met him six months ago when he was all but drowning in guilt over Arielle's death.

Griffin filled in a few more particulars of the case, but the briefing didn't take much longer. Everyone stood up, sobered by the information they'd just heard. It was no surprise to Maddie that she and both her friends turned to their respective men for long, quiet hugs.

Finally, that whole, ugly chapter of all their lives was closed. And from the looks of it, all of them were about to embark on pretty spectacular new chapters. Zoë and Breeze were headed back to Fiji and his resort to make a home and start a family—and Zoë got to keep doing the reviewing job she loved. Griffin and Alicia had already built a family and were happily nesting here in the States. And she and Tom— they were putting down roots in Vanua Taru, and nothing and nobody was going to budge them or tear them apart. Not a cyclone, not even a serial killer.

They'd all had the last laugh on the Sex on the Beach Killer. His goal had been to drive lovers apart, to frighten and terrorize people away from love. But instead, he'd created not one, but three killer couples, all of them building a love that would last a lifetime and beyond.

If only Spindler had known what Zoë and Breeze, Alicia and Griffin, and she and Tom knew. True love conquers everything in the end.

* * * * *

Mills & Boon® Intrigue
brings you a sneak preview of...
Linda Conrad's The Sheriff's Amnesiac Bride

When a woman on the run shows up in his life, Sheriff
Jericho Yates takes her in. The trouble is – she can't
remember who she is or why someone was shooting
at her! As "Rosie" and Jericho uncover bits about her
past, they must dodge the goons who are after her, all
while trying to ignore their undeniable attraction...

Don't miss this thrilling new story available next
month in Mills & Boon® Intrigue.

The Sheriff's Amnesiac Bride
by
Linda Conrad

Still twisting her hands in the backseat and waiting for a good opportunity, the woman with no past and a questionable future bit her lip and stared out the car's window. There was so much traffic here. Surely one of the people in these other cars would see her predicament and come to her aid.

"Son of a bitch, the traffic's even worse now." The car wound down to a crawl as the driver turned around again to speak to her. "Don't get smart, lady. You call out or make any noises like you need help and we'll shoot you. I don't give a rat's damn if that special item the boss wants is ever found or not. The choice between you giving us the answer and you never being able to answer again ain't nothing to me.

"You got that?"

She nodded, but the movement seared a line of fiery pain down her temple. Another couple of pains like that and she might rather be dead anyway.

"Terrific," the goon sitting shotgun said. "Just look at that, will ya? A local smoky. Out in the middle of the highway, directing traffic. Crap.

"What's going to happen, Arnie?" The man in the passenger seat was beginning to sweat.

"We're not doing anything wrong," Arnie answered with a growl. "We're regular citizens just driving down the road. Nothing to worry about. Stash your gun under the seat until we pass him by."

The driver bent and buried his own gun, then twisted back to her. "Remember, sis. No funny stuff. I swear, if you call out, you're dead."

Shaking badly, she wondered if her voice would work anyway. But right then, the miracle she'd prayed for happened. Their car came to a complete stop, almost directly in front of the church.

She bit her lip and tried to guess whether it would be closer for her to head for the sanctuary of the church or to run for the policeman in the street ten car-lengths away. The truck in front of them inched ahead and she decided to break for the church—it was her only real choice.

For a split second she stopped to wonder if she might be the kind of person who made rash decisions and who would rather fight back than die with a whimper. But then, whether out of fear or out of instinct, she knew it didn't matter.

If she were ever going to find out what had happened to her in the first place, she would have to go. Now.

* * *

Jericho heard a popping sound behind his back. Spinning around, he scanned the area trying to make out where the noise had originated.

"Was that a gunshot?" Fisher asked, as he too checked out the scene in front of the church.

In his peripheral vision, Jericho spotted a woman he'd never seen before. A woman seemingly out of place for a wedding, dressed in fancy jeans and red halter top. And she was racing at top speed across the grass straight in his direction. What the hell?

Another pop and the woman fell on the concrete walkway. From off to his left, someone screamed. Then tires squealed from somewhere down the long line of cars. When he glanced toward the sound, he saw a sedan with two men sitting in front as they roared out of the line and headed down the narrow shoulder of the highway.

Chaos reigned. Car horns honked. People shouted. And the sedan spewed out a huge dust plume as it bumped down the embankment.

Jericho took off at a run. He dropped to one knee beside the woman, checked her pulse and discovered she was breathing but unconscious and bleeding.

"Is she alive?" Deputy Rawlins asked, almost out of breath as he came running up. "I got their plates, Sheriff. But I didn't dare get off a shot with all the civilians in the way. You want me to pursue?"

Son of a gun. It would figure that he didn't have his weapon just when an emergency arose.

"Stay with the woman," Jericho ordered. "You and

Fisher get her to Doc O'Neal's as fast as you can. My rifle's in the truck, and..." He looked over his shoulder toward the church door. "Tell Macy..."

Right then Macy appeared at the top of the church steps and peered down at him. He was about to yell for her to get back out of the line of fire. But within a second, he could see her quickly taking in the whole situation.

"You go do what you need to, Jericho," she called out to him. "Don't worry about us. Just take care of yourself. The wedding's off for today."

INTRIGUE

Coming next month

2-IN-1 ANTHOLOGY

HER BEST FRIEND'S HUSBAND by Justine Davis

Gabriel's wife disappeared eight years ago. Now he's falling for her best friend – yet could his newfound feelings for Cara help him uncover a dark, dramatic truth?

THE BEAST WITHIN by Lisa Renee Jones

Jag was torn from his wife, Caren – and the mortal realm – by the soulless Darkland Beasts. Resurrected, he will stop at nothing to recover the love he lost!

SINGLE TITLE

THE MYSTERY MAN OF WHITEHORSE by BJ Daniels

Laci can't keep her eyes off her new boss, mysterious and brooding Bridger. Yet his timely arrival also provides a clue in the murders that haunt the town of Whitehorse.

SINGLE TITLE

PRIVATE S.W.A.T TAKEOVER by Julie Miller

When Liza witnessed the murder of KCPD's deputy commissioner, top cop Holden was appointed her official protector – but falling for her wasn't part of the bargain!

On sale 4th September 2009

Available at WHSmith, Tesco, ASDA, Eason and all good bookshops.
For full Mills & Boon range including eBooks visit
www.millsandboon.co.uk